Mind Reader

Also by Brian Freemantle
in Large Print:

Bomb Grade
Charlie's Apprentice
No Time for Heroes

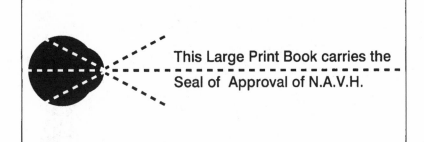

This Large Print Book carries the
Seal of Approval of N.A.V.H.

Mind Reader

Brian Freemantle

Thorndike Press • Thorndike, Maine

Published in 1998 by arrangement with St. Martin's Press, Inc.

Thorndike Large Print ® Cloak & Dagger Series.

The tree indicium is a trademark of Thorndike Press.

The text of this Large Print edition is unabridged.
Other aspects of the book may vary from the original edition.

Set in 16 pt. Plantin.

Printed in the United States on permanent paper.

Library of Congress Cataloging in Publication Data

Freemantle, Brian.
  [Profiler]
  Mind reader / Brian Freemantle.
     p.   cm.
  ISBN 0-7862-1508-9 (lg. print : hc : alk. paper)
  1. Large type books. I. Title.
  [PR6056.R43P76   1998b]
  823'.914—dc21   98-21551

79226

For Norma and John,
with love

AUTHOR'S NOTE

Europol exists.

The idea — and the name — of an FBI for the European Union came from John Alderton, a former Chief Constable of Devon and Cornwall. It was eagerly taken over by Germany which saw itself the motivating and controlling nation of a police organization empowered, like the American Federal Bureau of Investigation upon which it is modelled, to operate across state lines as a supranational force.

The concept of a German-dominated law enforcement agency immediately encountered political resistance from European countries with memories of two world wars. Although Europol was assigned permanent headquarters in The Hague, in Holland — in a building used by the Gestapo during World War II — and staffed by detectives and police personnel from national forces, it was initially confined to being a computerized centre collating drug-trafficking information. The Convention which established Europol's existence extended the remit to include nuclear and conventional arms and explosives trafficking, extortion, blackmail, protection racketeering, investment fraud, aggravated burglary, money laundering and illegal immigration.

The next step must be to expand Europol beyond an information-collecting-and-disseminating agency into a necessary and fully operational investigatory force throughout the European Union.

Mind Reader anticipates that inevitable development.

Preface

The initial horror unfolded in a single week, in early May. No one knew — risked thinking — on that first Monday it was only the beginning.

The severed head of the Asian girl was mounted like a figurehead on the very prow of the *bateau mouche*, one of the glass-topped pleasure boats that ply the Seine. It was only as he finished arranging the outside seating that the deckhand realized the head was human and not an intended decoration he hadn't noticed before.

He vomited, uncontrollably.

It wouldn't have mattered because the vessel had to be taken out of service, but he swabbed up the mess before the police arrived, destroying what forensic evidence there might have been. It was the first of far too many problems and flaws in an investigation hindered and obstructed by increasingly panicked desperation. The name of the boat was *Céleste*. Predictably it was what newspapers christened the unidentified girl in what they labelled 'La Cause Céleste'.

A newly bereaved widow, anxious to be close to the communion rail for Mass, mentally to make her intended recriminations against God and His wisdom, found the hands early on the Tuesday, beside the font of Lyon's Notre-Dame de Fourvière cathedral. Enough of the wrists remained for them to be wired together as if in prayer. The widow wasn't sick, just further confused about God's mysterious ways. She later stopped being such a regular communicant.

The naked torso was propped against the railed prow of a second *bateau mouche,* although far further south than the first, on one of the boats that take tourists through the canal system of medieval Strasbourg. The crewman was stronger-stomached than his Paris colleague. He studied the corpse long and intently enough later to describe to journalists in graphic detail the extent of the obscene sexual mutilation, which fuelled the media frenzy to even greater intensity. Because Strasbourg is one of the alternating capitals of the European Union, with a large concentration of resident foreign journalists, the story was now picked up by newspapers beyond France. It was the Thursday of that initial week and the first time a reference was made to France's own Jack (or Jacques) the Ripper. England's Scotland Yard was later to confirm that the genital disfigurement was, in fact, very similar to the injuries recorded in its Black Museum files on the nineteenth-century Whitechapel killer. The second *bateau mouche* was named the *Hortense* but Céleste remained the newspaper favourite for the girl, whose identity remained unknown despite the widespread, hysterical coverage.

Only one leg was ever recovered. The resident caretaker at Toulouse town hall drowsily answered the repeatedly pressed tradesmen's bell on Friday to confront the right limb, lying across his doorway. He thought it was some macabre joke until he touched human flesh. His bladder collapsed. He lied to the police about not seeing or hearing anything in the street outside, because he'd read all about *La Cause Céleste* and in terror slammed the door without looking or listening for anything, leaving the leg where it lay. It was only when he detected the police sirens that he risked opening the door again and by then there was nothing to see or hear apart from the welcome arrival of the *gendarmerie*. He had, of course, changed into dry trousers and underwear and even managed to shave, in preparation for the interviews and the cameras.

So ended the first week of a continuing terror that was to stupefy France.

Chapter One

Claudine Carter wasn't worried. There was no reason to be. No one else knew about the note. Or ever would. So there was no possibility of embarrassment. Which was all it would have seemed anyway: the thoughtless impulse of someone not supposed to make mistakes — definitely not to be thoughtless — but perfectly understandable in the circumstances.

All right, she was a highly specialized psychologist — the best in her particular discipline, which was why she'd got this new appointment — but that didn't make her Superwoman. She was allowed personal feelings and personal mistakes. What she'd done didn't reflect upon her ability to perform her job. And the job was all that mattered.

The sudden announcement from London of a meeting without any given reason or agenda was intriguing, though. There could be a dozen explanations, none of them connected with Warwick's death. But why was someone coming to her? Why wasn't she being asked to go there? Because, she supposed, she wasn't officially part of an English government department any more. She was working — although working was hardly the description

— for a European organization governed by European directorship, with whatever responsibility she had to London entwined in the upper labyrinths of European Union politics and diplomacy. There was, of course, no reason why she shouldn't ask London what it was all about. Logical that she should, even. But she held back from doing so. Psychologically it was better to leave things as they were, with someone coming to her. It put her in control of the encounter.

Claudine acknowledged that she'd been stupid about the note. She hadn't understood it all — although enough to feel the guilt and the failure — and it had been instinctive to keep something so private to herself. But she shouldn't have done it. Or lied to the police about its existence. But she had and that was that. It was over. Done with. She'd actually put it out of her mind — except perhaps the guilt — until the London message. And there couldn't be any connection, so she had to put it out of her mind again. It was intrusive, confusing, and Claudine didn't professionally like confusion. She liked things logically compartmented. And at the moment there were too many conflicting, overlapping stray ends.

She had a lot to get into proper order. Her whole future, in fact. A new life in a new country, the old one closed for ever: even reverting to her maiden name.

It wouldn't be a problem to be on her own

13

again. It hadn't been before Warwick and it wouldn't be now. Claudine Carter had never felt lonely when she *was* alone: never known the need for anyone else. Of course she'd loved Warwick, if love was deciding to be with someone for the rest of her life and trusting him completely and thinking of him as her best friend and enjoying the sex: she wouldn't have married him if there hadn't been all of those things.

But she'd never surrendered herself absolutely. Maybe not ever, sexually. There'd always been a part Claudine had kept back. Her part, an inner knowledge that despite being joined to someone else she remained an independent person, needing no one else, relying on no one else. She'd actually, positively, thought about it while Warwick was alive: *wanted* to re-assert her personal definition from her own objective self-analysis. The teaching that remained constant in her mind from all the psychology lectures and all the bizarre professional experiences that followed was Plato's creed to know oneself. And there was no one whom Claudine Carter believed she knew more completely and more successfully than herself. Or *had* believed. Now she wanted to regain the belief. To feel absolutely sure of herself again. More than that, even. Become what she'd been before her marriage, a complete, contained, confidently functioning independent person. She wanted to think

— to believe — that she'd never *stopped* being that.

But most of all she was determined to be the supreme professional. That's how — and why — she'd got this appointment. She deserved it and without conceit knew no one could do it better, this job she'd worked so single-mindedly — perhaps too single-mindedly — to achieve. She couldn't allow any personal doubt about that.

She'd been the youngest ever professor — just thirty-three — to get the Chair in forensic and criminal psychology at London University, and the Home Office's first choice after the British government officially acknowledged the science of profiling — identifying a criminal mind before traditional investigators found a face or a name — as a qualified branch of criminal investigation.

And she was here, now, in The Hague, Britain's officially appointed forensic and criminal psychologist to Europol, the European Union's FBI.

About which, Claudine uncomfortably admitted to herself, she was far more uncertain than she was about a sad suicide note safely locked in the safe on the other side of the office in which she now sat. She was a consummate professional but not at this moment, allowing too many competing thoughts at one time.

Europol appeared to have everything. The

nations of the European Union had each seconded their investigators and specialists, creating a crime-fighting capability as extensive
as — maybe even more extensive than — the
copied American Federal Bureau of Investigation. They had state-of-the-art headquarters
here at The Hague, with state-of-the-art forensic and photographic laboratories and un-
rivalled computer facilities: to Claudine's
bemusement there was even, in her own discipline, a visiting American criminal psychologist from the Behavioral Science Unit of the
FBI's violent crime analysis centre at Quan-
tico, Virginia.

What no one had anticipated — or rather,
what everyone refused to anticipate — was the
degree of political and professional opposition
to a pan-European organization legally able to
cross any national border and take over an
investigation from that country's police force.
Opposition which, from what she understood
so far, was total.

Which did nothing to help her personally.
Until there was a complete change in political
will or a crime so awesome it overwhelmed
national capability — and she managed to become involved in it — Claudine felt herself in
limbo, still too occupied by the past. And
Claudine Carter didn't want to live there any
more. It was over, a compartment that had to
be permanently sealed.

Without any conscious thought she got up

16

and made her way across the room towards the safe.

Ironically it was at the end of the week in which the terror began that Claudine Carter moved into her permanent apartment: it was more expensive than she'd budgeted for but there was a distant view of the Vijver lake which the agent had considered a vital selling point.

It might have been wiser if she hadn't carried the new-life philosophy to the extreme of disposing of so much of her life with Warwick. The only thing that could be considered furniture — but wasn't — was the incredible spread of electronic equipment filigreed along one entire wall, which hadn't yet been rigged through the necessary transformer, together with Warwick's even more incredible lifetime collection of jazz memorabilia, records and CDs.

Apart from that there were just personal, intimate things. Their marriage certificate and wedding photograph; his sheaf of academic honours: his proudly smirking graduation pictures; the membership cards to various jazz clubs in London and a lot of tickets to concerts and festivals they'd been to; a pot of keys, few of which she could identify or remember now why she'd kept at all; a broken keyring with the Cambridge motif. Hesitantly she picked out the wedding photograph, setting it up on

17

a shelf close to where she intended the stereo equipment to go. But as she worked, moving back and forth arranging and re-arranging everything, the photograph seemed, irrationally, to dominate the room, her only focus of attention, and towards the end of the Sunday evening she took it down and put it away in a bureau drawer along with all the other hidden things.

An *entirely* new life, she decided. Unless, that is, there was a difficulty she couldn't anticipate from the following day's encounter with the man from London.

Chapter Two

Peter Toomey was the sort of man who sat in the corner seat of the 8.10 every morning, his season ticket in a plastic holder ready for the collector who would know him anyway. He wore a precise grey suit and a precise short haircut and a precise moustache. He hadn't carried one when he entered her office but Claudine was sure he'd have a bowler hat and a tightly furled umbrella to complete his Whitehall uniform. He certainly carried that most essential accoutrement, the government monogrammed briefcase. She guessed at weekends . . . Claudine abruptly stopped herself, irritated. What the hell was she doing! This wasn't profiling. This was caricaturing, making a parody of her art and what she did, an unamusing joke against herself. Worse, she risked underestimating the man, which was stupid until she knew why he'd travelled all the way from London to see her. Unnecessary, even then.

Toomey accepted coffee — tapping in his own sweeteners from a plastic dispenser — and thanked her for seeing him and hoped he wouldn't keep her too long from her other work, which he was sure was very pressing and

Claudine thought she recognized the signs, difficult though it was to imagine. 'I suppose that depends upon what you want to see me about,' she invited. 'Your message didn't say.'

'It didn't,' he agreed. 'It's important, of course.'

Obtuse? Or a trained questioner employing a technique she also thought she recognized? The offered card hadn't designated any department, merely his name and an extension off the main Home Office switchboard. 'You'd have hardly come personally from London if it hadn't been.'

'Quite so.'

A questioning technique, Claudine decided: being attempted by someone who thought he could draw people out. Which was sometimes part of her job. She felt vaguely uneasy.

'I'm afraid it's personal: possibly upsetting.'

About Warwick! That wasn't possible: couldn't be possible. But what else was there, apart from Warwick, that could be personally upsetting? 'Concerning my husband?'

'Perhaps.'

'You're not making sense!' The irritation was positive anger now, at the fatuous word-play in which she didn't intend to take part. The first asthmatic tug snatched at her.

'You know Gerald Lorimer?'

Claudine frowned. 'Of course I know Gerald Lorimer: he was our best man . . . my husband's best man.' Why had she qualified it, as if she might have wanted to distance herself?

'So you're friends?'

'He was more Warwick's friend than mine. They were at Cambridge together.' Qualification again. But it was true: she didn't know Lorimer well.

'I'm sorry,' said the man. 'I should have asked before. Would you mind if I took some notes? A tape recording?'

Very definitely a ploy to disorientate her, Claudine accepted. So what the hell was Toomey's wordgame all about? 'Of course not. But you still haven't told me why you're here.'

Toomey unlocked the monogrammed briefcase with a key attached to a chain looped through his waistcoat. The notebook was new, the sort she'd seen policemen use at the beginning of an investigation, later to be introduced as court evidence. He seemed unsure how to use the recorder. Instead of answering her, the man said: 'When was the last time you saw Gerald Lorimer? Spoke with him?'

'What is this about?' demanded Claudine, intentionally loud-voiced, careless of any rudeness. Whatever it was it had to be something demanding an inquiry. To go on blindly answering questions indicated that she knew something about whatever it was.

'You were aware he worked at the Treasury?'

21

'I asked you what this was about,' repeated Claudine.

'You don't know that he's dead?'

'Dead!' Some coffee spilled in the awkwardness with which she put her cup down. She ignored it. She wanted her inhaler but ignored that, too. 'How? When?'

Toomey stared intently at her. 'Three weeks ago. Suicide. He hanged himself.'

'Oh my God!'

'You sound shocked.'

'Of course I'm shocked! Isn't it obvious that I would be? And why?'

'Why?'

Claudine bit back the immediate response. This didn't have anything to do with her concealing a suicide note. It was obviously something more sinister — something that she *didn't* know anything about — but she had to remain utterly in control to avoid giving the impression that she did have some knowledge. 'That's a crass question! You know damned well my husband committed suicide four months ago. By hanging himself. And you ask me why I'm shocked that his friend — his best friend, his best man! — has done the same. Don't be bloody ridiculous!'

'I'm sorry. It was unthinking of me.' Toomey didn't look embarrassed. Or sorry.

Determinedly, trying to suppress both the anger and the tightening band around her chest, Claudine said: 'Why have you travelled all the way from London to talk to me about a friend of my husband's who's killed himself?'

'It's a strange coincidence, their both committing suicide the same way, don't you think?'

'A distressing one.'

'Quite so.'

'Who are you?' Claudine decided she was being patronized. She didn't like it and certainly didn't intend to endure it.

'You have my card.'

'Which doesn't designate your function.'

'Security.'

'Intelligence?' challenged Claudine.

'Security.'

Claudine looked down at the pasteboard. 'Your card gives the Home Office number and an extension. Gerald Lorimer worked for the Treasury. Which doesn't come within Home Office jurisdiction.'

Toomey smiled bleakly. 'Your appointment here — which *was* made within Home Office jurisdiction — is politically a sensitive one. If you'll excuse the pun, Europol and everyone connected with it is on trial. Your job — the job of every British representative here — will be difficult enough. We're anxious there won't be additional problems.'

Claudine gazed steadily down at her desk for several moments, selecting the words, before looking up at the man. The safe containing the unreported suicide note was directly

23

behind him. Claudine said: 'Mr Toomey, I agreed to this meeting without any idea what it might be about because the message came officially, from my former employers. Who are, incidently, no longer my employers. You have been inconsiderate and deeply offensive. I am not prepared to continue — or to go on being interrogated in the convoluted manner more befitting an out-of-date spy film — without being told what this meeting is all about and why you've come from London to conduct it. Unless I am told, I am terminating it right now. I shall also complain directly to the Home Office and through the administration and personnel mechanisms here. Is that clear?'

'Totally,' said the man quietly, seemingly unimpressed by the tight-lipped threat. During some of her outburst he'd made notes, in his start-of-investigation book, and once checked that his tape was running. Now he sat looking at her.

She was under investigation, Claudine accepted, astonished. She'd been present a hundred times at confrontations like this, watching clever men who worked hard to be underestimated, even dressed for the part as Toomey was dressed, perform with supposed fumbling awkwardness until a suspect made the one, damning incriminating mistake: had even played her part in such a charade. And now it was happening to her. She didn't like it any more than she liked or accepted being patronized. But what was she suspected *of*? Judging from the implication of political sensitivity it might be important enough to affect her appointment. Which made her even more indignant. 'Why am I being interrogated by an intelligence officer?'

Instead of replying Toomey looked briefly into the briefcase, as if searching for something, but put it down beside him again. 'I do not wish to be rude. Or offensive. But really there is no way to avoid offence. So I apologize in advance. If you wish I will suspend this interview and you may accompany me back to London, so that it can be conducted in the presence of your own representatives, although frankly I think that is unnecessary at this stage.'

Claudine's foremost awareness was that the man hadn't denied being an intelligence officer, but other impressions crowded in close behind. It was clearly a threat. She would have to provide an official explanation to the Europol directorate for accompanying Toomey to London and however she phrased it the inference would be that she was being taken back under agreed arrest. 'For Christ's sake, man, tell me why you're here!' She shouldn't lose control. Her anger could be manipulated and turned against her.

'Gerald Lorimer was the deputy in a classified forward planning division within the Treasury. He had access to a large amount of restricted financial information, not just that affecting the United Kingdom but also of World Bank and International Monetary Fund intentions. It was a position which, if wrongly used, could have given unscrupulous people the opportunity to make a great deal of money — millions, in fact — by appearing to speculate in futures on the world's currency markets when they wouldn't have been speculating at all.'

Claudine shook her head, still unsure. 'Insider trading, you mean?'

'That would be a definition,' agreed the man. 'But this would be insider trading of cosmic proportions. It really would involve millions.'

'But what has this got to do with me . . . with Warwick, apart from the coincidence of the two suicides . . . ?'

The smile clicked on and off again. 'I'm not sure it has anything to do with you. That's what I'm here to find out.'

Claudine recognized the qualification. 'With my husband, then?'

This time Toomey did extract something from the briefcase, a single sheet of photocopied paper enclosed in a plastic folder. 'Lorimer left a suicide note,' announced the man. 'It starts: *It's getting too much. He wants too much. I can't do it. So this is the way.*' Toomey looked up at her. 'You're a criminal psychologist, Dr Carter. What would you say that indicates?'

Claudine didn't immediately reply because she couldn't, her mind blocked by the wording of another suicide note, one only she had ever seen. *I wish I could explain, but I can't. There is so much, so very much* . . . Aware of Toomey's quizzical, head-to-one-side attitude, Claudine said at last: 'I don't make assessments on single sentences. It's an impossible question.'

'Your husband didn't leave a note?'

'No,' lied Claudine.

'As a psychologist — particularly one in your very specialized field — didn't you find that surprising?'

'No. Notes are not left in a very large number of cases.'

'At your husband's inquest you said your husband was under great pressure from problems that had arisen in his department?'

So Toomey had studied the transcripts. 'Some of his legal opinions had been rejected.'

'I don't understand.'

Claudine was sure Toomey understood perfectly but wanted to prod the conversation about Warwick in any direction that might produce an opening to whatever it was he wanted to know.

'He specialized in European Union law: was an acknowledged expert. The United Kingdom lost three cases in a row in the European Court, arguing his legal opinions.'

'Losing cases is as much a part of being a lawyer as winning them, surely?'

The patronizing bastard was intentionally goading her. So she — Claudine abruptly stopped the response, more furious at herself for being undermined than at the anything but fumbling questioning. She quietened herself, confronting the challenge. 'My husband was ill. A depression no one recognized. The effect upon him of the legal defeats was not what it would have been upon someone mentally fit.' It wasn't *anyone* who'd failed to recognize it, Claudine thought. It was *me*.

'A similar mental illness to Gerald Lorimer's, in fact?'

'I've no idea what Gerald Lorimer's illness or problems might have been.'

'Can't you form any opinion from what Lorimer wrote?'

Claudine hesitated, wondering whether to refuse. She was breathing more easily and was glad. 'Fairly typical. Overpressured, desperate. That's all, without knowing any more facts.'

'Like your husband . . . although he didn't leave a note?'

Now the bastard was trying to manipulate the answers. With no alternative she said: 'Yes.'

Toomey nodded, going back to the note. *'Why did Warwick have to do it? He knew how* m*uch I needed him. At least our secret is safe but I can never be sure. I can't forgive him. Hate him, in fact.'* He looked up at her again. 'There seems to have been a very close

28

relationship between your husband and Gerald Lorimer?'

This time it took longer for Claudine to respond, another secret passage thrusting itself into her mind. *I wish there was someone to understand, about Gerald. Someone I could talk to.* It took an effort of will for Claudine to say: 'I told you they were best friends. I don't see that what you've just quoted indicates anything more than that. Just part of the desperation . . .' She hesitated, as the professionalism came to her. 'Warwick's suicide would have increased that desperation in Lorimer. Provided the idea how to kill himself, in fact. Maybe even triggered it.' She only vaguely remembered Lorimer at Warwick's funeral: found it difficult — oddly — to remember much about the funeral at all.

Toomey nodded again, as if he were putting ticks in 'yes' or 'no' boxes. 'I have something very personal to ask you. I want to make it clear before I do that it is important. But again, I apologize for any offense.'

'What?'

'Was your sexual relationship with your husband a normal one?' The man coloured, slightly, with the question.

'What?' Claudine couldn't recall ever being so verbally off-balanced: being quite as numbed, unable to form a single, cohesive thought. Not even by the discovery of Warwick's body. Her chest hadn't seized then.

'I'm sure you don't want me to repeat the question.'

Claudine fought for control, determined against losing the duel. 'I most definitely want you to explain it!' Genuine outrage stoked the audible indignation.

Toomey went into his briefcase again. 'I'd rather show you these photographs.'

There were four. Each was differently posed and showed a woman in full evening dress against an indistinguishable background in front of other unidentifiable women. And then Claudine realized the woman was Gerald, made up and bewigged and actually quite attractive. Claudine took her time, needing every second. Toomey was good but not good enough: she could — and would — out-debate him. The priority was breaking his lead in the conversation. 'I asked you to explain a question about the sexual relationship between myself and my late husband. These are photographs of Gerald Lorimer, dressed as a woman.'

'I know they are.'

'*I* know they are,' she echoed. 'That's *all* they are.'

The silence filled the book-lined, new-paint-and-carpet-smelling office with its own personal safe, everything still pristine from lack of activity. Or use. Claudine would have liked finally to mop up her spilled coffee but didn't because that would not have been the act of

30

a person in charge and that's what she was now, back in sufficient control, which was how she always needed to be. She hadn't liked the sensation of being under suspicious investigation for the last thirty minutes. Or of being led instead of leading a nuance-balanced discussion.

Toomey surrendered. 'Could you answer my question, please.'

The 'please' was a mistake, like his blushing. 'What is your question?'

Toomey grew redder. 'Did you suspect your husband was homosexual?'

The response had to be immediate and overwhelming. 'You have no justification — no reason whatsoever — for asking that.' She wouldn't gain anything by exacerbating the man's difficulties but he'd unsettled her — created too many reflections for the future — so there wasn't any reason why she shouldn't hang the bastard out to dry the way he'd tried to hang her out to dry. Now he'd make more mistakes than she would.

'You had a normal sexual relationship with your husband?' persisted her increasingly disconcerted inquisitor.

'If you mean was our relationship totally heterosexual, the answer is yes.' It would be wrong to demand his definition of normal sex. Instead she posed it to herself. Had she held back sexually? Or had Warwick? Claudine refused to consider those ridiculous assessments

31

so beloved in the media about regularity. They'd made love when they'd felt like it, not to a chart or a timetable. And sufficiently, for her needs. What about his? He'd never complained. And she didn't see anything unnatural — anything not normal — in fellatio or cunnilingus or in his anal exploration, which he hadn't practiced a lot anyway.

'Did your husband belong to any clubs?'

Claudine hesitated. 'The Cambridge Union. You mean in London?'

'Yes.'

'Several jazz clubs.'

'What about the Pink Serpent?'

Claudine sniggered. 'What the hell's the Pink Serpent?'

'A predominantly homosexual club in Soho.'

The membership cards of everything to which Warwick had belonged were among the things she'd kept. 'My husband did not belong to the Pink Serpent club,' she said.

'You didn't know about Gerald Lorimer? Your husband never told you?'

'Know *what* about Gerald Lorimer? Told me what?'

'You're not making this easy for me, Dr Carter.'

The capitulation, Claudine realized, her breathing easing. She had to guard against it being another interrogation ploy but she didn't think it was. She judged Toomey to be someone who'd believed he had enough to bring about her collapse, but had faltered at the end of his prepared script when that collapse hadn't occurred. Now was the moment to crush him. 'You're not making it easy for yourself, Mr Toomey. It's fortunate I didn't accept your invitation to return to London. I don't think this in+ rview would have been received particul⌐ .y well before an audience. As it is, your tape recording will probably be embarrassing for you. We've talked for a long time. So far you've told me a few words from a suicide note of an unfortunate friend of my late husband and shown me four completely innocent photographs of the man wearing women's clothes. You've told me nothing to justify any accusation of his being homosexual — or why it would be important if he was — and you've asked me offensive questions about my late husband's sexuality, which I've answered because, distasteful though they were, I saw no reason not to answer . . .' Claudine paused, intentionally raising her voice. 'Throughout it all you still haven't told me why you're here. Do so, right now — or get out of my office!'

Desperately Toomey tried to return to his script. Indicating the photographs he said: 'Wouldn't you say those photographs are incriminating?'

Claudine looked at him in genuine astonishment. 'No.'

33

Toomey blinked. 'What, then?'

'What they obviously — but *only* — are: a man wearing women's clothes.' She hesitated, deciding to chance the question. 'Haven't you ever dressed up for a fancy dress party? And now have photographs that don't look as funny as they did at the time?'

'Not as a woman!'

'What, then?' demanded Claudine, determined to ridicule the idiotic hypothesis. Which had to be idiotic because if he'd had more Toomey would have produced it by now.

'I don't think it's relevant.'

'What, then?' insisted Claudine.

'A Greek warrior,' admitted Toomey.

Claudine came perilously close to laughing outright at the absurdity of the man's admission; that he'd replied at all. 'Greek warriors wore skirts; their ceremonial soldiers still do. And when Greek warriors went to war they took young boys for their brothels because the stamina of young boys — even buggered young boys — was better than women's, on long marches. Which prompts me to ask you a question, Mr Toomey. Are you homosexual?' He'd destroy her contempt if he openly conceded that he was. But Claudine was sure enough, from his attitude so far, not only that he wasn't but that Peter Toomey would regard homosexuality as an aberrant illness that could be cured by cold baths or frontal lobotomies.

'Of course I am not a homosexual!'

'What reason have you got for accusing Gerald Lorimer of being one, apart from four innocuous photographs? Or — worse — asking me the question you have about my late husband?'

'What about Paul Bickerstone?'

Claudine shook her head, refusing the deflecting trick, totally sure of herself now. 'Who's Paul Bickerstone?'

'You don't know him?' There was a tinge of triumph in the question.

'No.' Toomey had got back to his script, Claudine decided. But it was too late.

Another photograph, turning sepia from age or sunlight exposure, was conjured from Toomey's briefcase. 'You're next to him in this group.'

Her first year in London, after moving from France, remembered Claudine: one of the Chelsea Arts Balls, her introduction to a social event everyone else thought wonderful but she'd found disappointing. A total stranger, in a gorilla suit, had his arm round her. Warwick was on her other side, dressed as a bishop. Lorimer, half hidden, was a policeman. Claudine couldn't recall what she was supposed to be, in the flimsy gauze dress bedecked with flowers and with flowers in her hair. Ophelia, maybe. 'I presume the gorilla's Paul Bickerstone?'

'A contemporary at Cambridge of your husband and Lorimer. He now heads a commodity-dealing firm, specializing in currency. Six weeks ago he formed a consortium and bought across the board in London, Hong Kong and Wall Street two hundred million pounds' worth of sterling futures, on fourteen-day spot-price value. A week later the Government announced a six per cent guaranteed bond issue. His profit on the sterling fluctuation was twenty-five million pounds. Gerald Lorimer knew of the intended bond issue.'

Claudine relaxed further back in her chair. 'And in the middle of it all, he hanged himself!'

'Leaving a note that said: *He wants too much. I can't do it.*'

'I think I'm catching up with you at last,' said Claudine, condescending herself now. 'But I don't want to guess: I want you to tell me. Where's the homosexuality come in?'

'Blackmail,' declared Toomey unconvincingly.

Claudine frowned, shaking her head in disbelief. 'You're suggesting that a City financier blackmailed a Treasury official to disclose advance information with the threat of disclosing that he was gay?'

'It's a line of our inquiry,' recited Toomey formally.

'Half Whitehall's gay and the other half doesn't care. Nobody cares. What's wrong with being gay?' Damn, she thought: that final remark sounded as if she might have been condoning Warwick.

Toomey appeared to miss it. 'That might be the private attitude of a lot of people but Lorimer's position would have been untenable.'

'So he made it even more untenable by hanging himself!'

'Men under pressure do strange things.'

'Which is what I've been telling you almost from the moment we began talking: I'm glad you're finally listening.' Claudine gestured to the photographs which Toomey had put on the edge of her desk. 'Is that all you've got to support your hypothesis: just those pictures and the fact that Lorimer and Bickerstone were at university together?'

'I'm not at liberty to discuss that aspect any further.'

'What about my husband?'

Toomey shifted uncomfortably. 'He knew them both.'

'That's all?' Claudine exaggerated the head movement, although her disbelief was genuine. 'That's incredible!'

'Dr Carter, as I've already told you, the reason for my being here is the sensitivity of your position. If there is a trial we need to gauge the extent of any embarrassment if you become involved, through the reference to your husband in Lorimer's note. And your being in the photographs.'

'There is no embarrassment! That photograph was taken very shortly after I arrived in England. I had only just met Warwick. I have no recollection whatsoever of meeting Bickerstone and certainly I don't remember meeting him since. Warwick wasn't gay or a crossdresser. And he didn't know anything was going on between Lorimer and Bickerstone, even if anything *was* going on.' She ended breathless.

'Are you sure you would have known?'

The question stopped Claudine. She wouldn't have known. Not positively. Not if he'd been involved in some ridiculously highflying financial scheme or dressing up in party gowns at somewhere as absurdly named as the Pink Serpent and fucking men and letting himself be fucked by men. She *thought* she knew — thought every suggestion was preposterous — but she didn't *know.* Yes she did! She'd read the note, the apologetic litany of all his imagined failings and his worry about being passed over for promotion within the Home Office legal department and how much he loved her. It had been a confession. A confession she couldn't bear the thought of anyone else seeing but only because it proved how she'd failed him rather than the other way round: because it made her feel guilty. If he'd been gay — been involved in blackmail and financial cheating — he would have confessed that, too. She was a psychologist: knew minds, even though she hadn't recognized Warwick's despair until it was too late. She was positive he would have admitted it, if there had been anything to admit. She was seized by a thought. 'Yes, I would have known! And there's a way you'd know, too. If Warwick had been involved in any financial deceit there'd be a paper trail of the dealings. All you've got to do is get my permission to examine all our bank records. Which I'll happily give you, here and now.'

Toomey coughed. 'We've already examined them, Dr Carter.' Seeing the flare of anger suffuse Claudine's face, he quickly added: 'We are legally able to under the Financial Services Act of 1986 and the Banking Act of 1987.'

Claudine curbed her fury at the intrusion, turning it. 'And?'

'There is no evidence of any financial impropriety whatsoever.'

'You haven't got any evidence of *anything,* Mr Toomey. Certainly not anything improper concerning my husband!'

'I must ask you my final, direct question. If there were to be a trial, involving Bickerstone, and you were called in any capacity whatsoever — either for the prosecution or the defence — is there anything that could be produced that would cause the sort of embarrassment that would make your position here in Europol impossible?'

'No,' insisted Claudine immediately. 'Absolutely nothing.'

After Toomey had left, Claudine stood at her office window long enough to see him emerge from the building and cross the courtyard to his waiting taxi. Then she turned and hurried towards the safe.

From a window two floors above — at the Europol Commission level — there was another observer of Toomey's departure. Henri Sanglier stood much longer at his window, wondering what the meeting had been about. He had enough uncertainty with Françoise. He couldn't risk any more: and this, potentially, could make any problems with his wife pale into insignificance.

That night Claudine picked her way through everything of Warwick's she had kept and brought with her from London. There were, in fact, the about-to-expire cards for four London jazz clubs but none with the ridiculous name of the Pink Serpent.

The horror continued in France, following the same time frame and the same pattern. On the Monday of Claudine's confrontation with the Home Office official a head, again of a teenage Asian girl, was found resting, open-eyed, mouth parted in the near smile of the first victim, on the auctioneer's desk of the Marseille fish market. The hands, familiarly wired together in a praying gesture, awaited the Tuesday dawn duty priest in the confessional at Aix cathedral: he'd just decided five

40

Hail Marys were sufficient penance for a hotel chambermaid's admission of masturbation when he realized the fingers pressed together by the grille were not hers. The priest showed commendable control, letting the girl finish her confession and receive absolution, before running from the booth to raise the alarm. In his hurry he forgot to pray for the soul of whoever the hands had belonged to. The torso, with the legs and arms still attached, sat waiting on a bench for the Wednesday morning cleaner at Paris's Tolbiac métro station. The sexual incisions and removal were even more obvious and described in greater detail than before by the discovering cleaner: it was to take several days for the man to confess to police he'd invented his newspaper account of seeing a black-hatted, black-coated, unusually tall man laughing insanely as he fled the scene.

Chapter Three

A man tensed for any personal setback, Henri Sanglier tried hard to convince himself that Claudine Carter's appointment to Europol was an inconceivable coincidence. It couldn't be anything else. It was official — she was the considered choice of a British government selection board — and she couldn't have influenced such a decision beyond her unquestionable qualifications for the job, every one of which he knew from her personnel record, just as he knew everything about the Carter family. Nor could she have known of his position in Europe's FBI until she'd arrived at The Hague, because his nomination to the controlling Commission had been made after she had joined the behavioural science division.

An amazing fluke then: an accident. But something he didn't want. Was frightened of.

What could he do about it?

Nothing, at this precise moment. Apart from wait. But wait for what? An indication, he supposed: the merest hint. What could he do even then? Still nothing. What if she tried to blackmail him, not openly for money, but by making it clear she expected to be protected by his superior position and influence in the newly born, Europe-spanning organization to which they both belonged? He was a policeman — a good one, deserving every promotion and accolade quite irrespective of the famous family name — and as a policeman he knew that succumbing to it was never the answer to blackmail. Would it really be succumbing to blackmail, to be her protector? Wasn't Europol — wasn't all professional life — a layered structure of people supporting and trusting each other in a basic tribal instinct?

In the solitude of his office, Sanglier positively shook his head against the blackmail speculation. If he acceded just once to pressure it would be he, not Claudine Carter, who would be beholden. And it wasn't Sanglier's style — it wasn't any part of the inherited legend — to be beholden to anyone.

So what, he demanded of himself again, was he going to do? Wait, he decided, just as repetitively. But not wait and do nothing. Wait and anticipate, as best he could. Keep Claudine Carter under a microscope to determine every nuance and innuendo that might give him a clue whether she were a threat.

Which brought him back to the pinstriped man whose name he already knew from the security admission log to be Peter Toomey and whom he'd watched an hour earlier hurry across the courtyard to the waiting airport taxi. A British government official from her old department, according to that same log entry. But what sort of official? And what had brought him from London, instead of summoning her to England? It was exasperating, although proof of how fragile Europol's existence still was, that each country within it occupied its own, closed-off enclave — tribalism again — paying little more than lip service to the much vaunted harmony in which they were all supposed to operate. Peter Toomey's visit had been to a member of the British contingent, not officially to Europol. So there were only two people from whom he could find the reason. One was Toomey himself. The other was Claudine Carter. And there was no official excuse or reason with which he could approach either.

Sanglier felt a wash of helpless impotence and hated it.

Claudine shunned any personal artifice, always observing the 'know thyself' dictum, but the encounter with Toomey had bewildered her and despite the fact that every word of it was burned into her mind she retrieved Warwick's suicide note from the safe before Toomey's taxi had left the Europol compound.

It wasn't, after all, an artificial, unnecessary gesture. It didn't matter how well she knew the words. She had to read every one again, assess every one again, but not as she'd analysed and tortured herself over them before. She had a new context now: possibly a new and even a more understandable explanation for what Warwick had done, devastatingly different from her initial belief and the finding of the coroner that, suffering a recurrence of his teenage manic depression, Warwick had taken his life under the pressure of criticized and sometimes rejected Home Office legal work.

Oddly, considering the bombshell suggestion of ambivalent sexuality, Claudine felt better able now to assess what Warwick had written than she had been at the moment of finding his body and the note, or during the disconnected days that followed. She *had* been disconnected, briefly unable to rationalize despite all her professionalism or rigid self-control. She'd been horrified by his purpled, strangled face, dazed that it should have happened and that she, of all people, hadn't recognized how close to a total and disastrous breakdown Warwick had obviously been.

Today was different: objectively different. Today she felt herself able to look at everything dispassionately, professionally. To study the words and literally how they were written. And what they conveyed, not from Warwick, the man she'd known — or thought she'd known — and loved, but as if from someone else, from a stranger. Which, she supposed, Warwick might have been. The correction came immediately, like a slammed-on brake.

She wasn't being dispassionate, as it was always essential — vital — for her to be. Instead, unobjective and unprofessional, she was allowing herself to be affected by entirely unrelated half-facts and unsupported inferences.

The note then: the note she could quote by heart but maybe hadn't understood at all. Notebook paper. Edges curled. Dirty. Felt-tipped spider words. A man's life — a good, kind, sweet man's life — dismissed on twenty-three lines of ruled paper.

My dear Claudine. Her full name, which he'd rarely used. Usually Claude. Or Clo. Official, then. Like Dear Sir or Madam. Killing yourself was official. End of business. Permanent. Which was what Warwick had been doing, cutting himself off from her for ever. Had that been his warped reasoning at that moment, the awful, irrevocable moment of death, with a mottled face and bulging eyes and an elongated neck where he'd wrongly fixed the noose? Or was it an unthinking admission of belated honesty, having closed himself off a long time before? Assessment on three words. She'd told Toomey the impossibility of that.

I know what I am doing is cowardly. But then you know I am a coward. Tabloid psychology. Suicide, according to some theses, was running away. The ultimate escape, from hurt or responsibility. But not her thesis. To knot a rope — even worse, to knot it wrongly and die in pop-eyed, tongue-protruding agony — and

46

loop it around a beam and kick away a chair wasn't cowardice. Desperation, for whatever reason. But not an act of physical cowardice. What about mental cowardice? A chasm apart. Far more likely to have been what he meant. Or was it? She was intruding her own attitudes, not Warwick's. Not professionally dispassionate. Not professional at all to assess piecemeal. An act was the sum of its contributory parts: not another two-thousand-year-old dictum but a platitude of her Sorbonne tutor. So what made up the rest of the sum?

I am so weak, against your strength. And I cannot go on feeding off that strength. Facile self-pity, on face value of the words, the only criterion she'd applied until today. But still valid, the core to her guilt. The accusation still came like the stinging slap in the face of her first reading. And remained just as hurtful after the innuendo of today's encounter with the man from London. She'd never consciously been aware of overwhelming Warwick during their courtship. Or during their marriage. Only afterwards — after the suicide and her own mental scourging — had Claudine realized how she had dominated their relationship, always the motivating, decisive partner even after the wedding, the date of which she had decided, just as she'd decided the honeymoon and the house — the Kensington cottage she'd bought before ever knowing Warwick — to which they'd returned. What more was there, then, than her first evaluation? Sex, which might or might not be a factor but was the reason for this re-examination. Putting sex into the equation showed Warwick's willingness to be dominated, to acquiesce to any demand of the dominant partner. Surely it hadn't been like that! He'd initiated the lovemaking as often as she had. More so, she imagined, although it was impossible to make a comparison because there'd been no reason until today to produce a tally. No reason, even, to do it at this precise moment. She was isolating a segment again, not judging it as part of a whole.

You have never truly known me, just as I feel I have never truly known you; perhaps if there had been more time, different circumstances . . . People don't know each other. I realize now I never knew someone I thought had no secrets. Easy enough to infer a sexual connotation here. And with Gerald Lorimer. But just as easy not to. They'd only been married for fifteen months. And therefore *hadn't* known each other, not properly. If they'd lived together for every minute of those fifteen months — which they hadn't, because she'd been so determined to prove herself the best practitioner of the new art of forensic and criminal psychology, travelling to any part of Britain to which she was summoned — they still wouldn't have known each other, let alone experienced love: come closer than a million

48

miles to understanding what love was, however it was manifested.

I wish I could explain, but I can't. There is so much, so very much. The passage that had come to her during the confrontation, when Toomey recited Gerald Lorimer's letter. Similar phrasing to Lorimer's but that didn't indicate anything. What did Warwick mean? Possibly something different from her first interpretation, after Toomey's innuendo. But just as possibly the conclusion she'd first reached: a workload with which he could no longer cope; mistakes he was making because of the pressure.

I wish there was someone to understand. That *there was a special friend, other than the one I* *thought I had.* There was. Or had been. She could have understood — should have understood. Become a special friend, for whatever problem or purpose he'd wanted. It was difficult to avoid the unctuous Toomey's interpretation. Thank God she'd kept the note secret!

The following sentence burned into her. *But* *best left unsaid.* What had been best left unsaid? An admission that he was overwhelmed by the demands of the Home Office's legal department? Or the nearest Warwick had been able to come to a personal confession he'd chosen to kill himself rather than make? That would have been Toomey's reading, coupled with Lorimer's letter and some meaningless photographs to stir into the circumstantial stew.

What was hers? Dispassionately professional, she reminded herself. Doubt, Claudine conceded. Circumstantial, unsubstantiated, unrecognized doubt. But doubt, all the same.

I am so very sorry. I have loved you so much. Too much. I know I can never ask you to forgive me. Absolve me. More for Toomey to seize upon, given the opportunity. *Have loved you,* not *do love you.* An experiment in marriage that hadn't worked? I tried, I failed, goodbye. A coward's way out: his own accusation. Supported by what? Ambiguity, emotions badly expressed by a distraught, mentally maladjusted man.

How can you, someone so strong, forgive someone so weak? Understand? The text with which Claudine found the most difficulty. Another reference to her strength, her dominance. Had she dominated — bullied — Warwick when they'd been together, as he'd been dominated and bullied during his every working day? Driven him, perhaps, to someone more sympathetic? The one-word accusation echoed, deafeningly, at her. She hadn't understood whatever it was that had driven Warwick to kill himself. Quickly she corrected herself. Not a failure to understand. A failure to recognize and identify. If she'd done that — shown herself to be the psychologist she was supposed to be — Warwick wouldn't be dead. It was her vocation, her medically taken vow, to understand. Her failure, not Warwick's. Her fault. Her guilt. Claudine positively shook herself against the regression. She'd lapsed into her first time guilt, which wasn't what she was supposed to be examining. So what was new — what changed anything — from what had happened today? Nothing, Claudine determined. She read and judged Warwick's emotions today exactly as she'd read and judged them the first time, wet-eyed then, dry-eyed now. Tight-chested neither time. He'd been asking her to acknowledge psychological not sexual misunderstandings.

But forgive me if you can, for the hurt I am causing. I cannot live up to you. Make myself someone you can be proud of, as you need to be proud of a person you've chosen to be with. Claudine sat back in her chair, for the first time lifting her eyes from the note. Warwick had known her better than she'd known herself. Admitted to herself, at least. She despised weak people — disregarded them — which is why she had despised and disregarded her father. But she hadn't, consciously, considered Warwick weak: certainly hadn't imagined conveying such an impression. Which undoubtedly, from the concluding words in front of her, she had.

I love you, my darling. You will hate me, for what I am doing. And for what I have done, if it ever emerges. I deserve your hate more than I deserved your love. Possible — more than possible — to be construed in the new context.

But again just as possible to remain as she'd first assessed it, a tragic apology from a mentally ill man who'd simply ended the single sheet, torn from an exercise or legal notebook, by writing his name.

Not writing, amended Claudine, professionally. Printing. As if it was important — as if his neck-stretched corpse wasn't sufficient — for her to realize that he and no one else had written the valediction. There was a shake, an unevenness, in the formation of the letters but it was only discernible to her, who knew his handwriting so well. Hardly evidence of someone making their last communication on earth. Jumbled, certainly; agonizingly inconclusive. But with some sort of form. No abrupt erasures or scratching out. As if, even, it was a final copy of an earlier draft. Which was something she hadn't contemplated until this moment. Should she, now? Was she being as dispassionate as her profession dictated? Or was she trying to complete a jigsaw from a new picture, the picture drawn by a man who went to fancy dress parties dressed as a Greek warrior?

Positively, with detached determination, Claudine read the note from beginning to end, refusing any line by line distraction and trying to make a judgement as a whole, without lifting a word or a phrase to support a specific conclusion.

And failed to make that judgement.

It was as easy — as professionally easy, not because she was judging her own husband — to stand by her initial evaluation of it as being written by a mentally flawed man broken by overwork as it was to imagine Warwick torn apart by the shame (what shame, for fuck's sake?) of a sexual preference he had been unable to discuss with her. If that were the case, it was another failing on her part, not his.

Claudine didn't equate sex with love: hardly, even, with a manifestation of it. She believed — or thought she believed — that she could have lived with Warwick's bisexuality, if he were ambivalent. Homosexuality, even, although there would have been an element of rejection that might have been difficult for her to adjust to. But either would have been better — divorce would have been better, as well as more obvious — than his killing himself.

Surely she would have known! Guessed or suspected. Her holding back, which she conceded she might have done, had nothing to do with sexual taboos or inhibitions. Her reluctance had only ever been a reluctance to lose control. She had accepted — initiated — the oral sex. And the anal exploration. Initiated that, too, on occasions. More often, probably, than Warwick. Which would surely have made it easy for him to talk about his sexual preferences. And they *had* discussed sex. Fetishes and fantasies even. She'd talked of imagining being naked, offering herself, in a crowded tube train or a restaurant and being ignored, analysing it for him as a fear of ultimate rejection. And he'd admitted a fascination with being chained and taunted by whores so raddled they had to be diseased but with whom he still wanted sex, although they denied him. Which hadn't been something she had found easy to analyse.

Nor was it easy to re-analyse what lay on the desk before her. Unless Toomey discovered something more — and she'd already decided he'd produced all he possessed, which was totally inconclusive — Claudine realized she would never know the extent of Warwick's friendship with Gerald Lorimer. Not that it was necessary for her to know. It didn't — wouldn't — affect how she'd felt about Warwick. Or mitigate the unalterable, damning fact she had already confronted, that she'd failed him. She was convinced of something else, too, a conviction strong enough for her to consider it another unalterable fact. There might have been things about Warwick of which she wasn't aware or hadn't recognized but Claudine was sure he had not done anything illegal or even questionable. So, logically, there was nothing that could emerge from Toomey's inquiries to disrupt her new life in Holland. That could only be endangered by a professional mistake. And professional mistakes weren't going to happen:

Claudine wasn't going to allow them to happen.

She was actually at the shredder, another so far unused piece of office equipment, when she abruptly changed her mind about destroying Warwick's note. Instead she went further across the office and returned it to the safe.

The horrific killings escalated, sensation feeding sensation throughout Europe with each new discovery over the next month.

The third victim was a teenage Asian boy whose head was displayed to an immediately hysterical American tourist when the elevator doors opened for the first ascent at the Eiffel Tower. The praying hands were close to the shrine at Lourdes. They clutched a severed penis. The seated torso greeted the guard on the early morning Paris to Marseille TGV. One leg was left in Bordeaux, the other on the lawns of the Carlton Hotel at Cannes.

In London the next Asian girl's head was found at the foot of Churchill's statue in Parliament Square. The clasped hands were recovered at a Reading chapel prepared for a wedding which had to be cancelled because the bride collapsed into hysteria. The torso, wrapped like a parcel, revolved into view on the baggage carousel at Heathrow's Terminal Four on the day the Pope arrived on a State visit. A leg was added to the existing two on the statue of Palmerston in the Hampshire town of Romsey, the other placed as an addition to the effigy of Sir Francis Drake in Plymouth.

In Cologne the dismembered and scattered remains of a sexually abused girl — thought to be Turkish because of the large Turkish guest worker population in Germany — were discovered. The butchered girl in Vienna was Chinese. The strongest investigative theory, of monstrously orchestrated and obscene racism, was undermined by the finding in Amsterdam and Brussels of two similarly dismembered and distributed white girls.

Hysteria convulsed the European Union, compounded by the inability of any national or local police to make a single arrest.

There were emergency debates in national parliaments echoing in rhetoric but as silent on practicality as their police departments. For the first time the European assembly in Strasbourg — a victim city — became a centralized, cohesive forum. It was from Strasbourg that the proposal came to post army units at schools and universities. It was adopted in France, Germany, Austria, Spain and Italy. And was expanded in each of those countries with other units guarding and sometimes providing early morning and late night transportation for shift workers. Yet more army units, issued with live ammunition, supplemented police street patrols. Minority group leaders, ignoring the Dutch and Belgian murders, insisted the continent was menaced by a racial pogrom. Among the wilder theories were suggestions of witchcraft and Satanic sacrifices.

Inevitably, in London, there were Jack the Ripper analogies that had begun much earlier with the French killing. Vigilante squads were formed among Asian and immigrant groups in several European capitals and in two weeks four people died and countless others were injured in panicked shootings, fights and disturbances. Immigrant hostels in Germany, Austria and Holland were firebombed and two Turks were shot dead in a reciprocal arson attempt on the Reichstag in Berlin. Immigrant groups were also blamed for the explosion that badly damaged two of the public rooms of the Hofburg royal palace in Vienna. Predictably, synagogues and Jewish cemeteries were vandalized, mostly in Germany, Austria and France.

The German-initiated resolution in the European Parliament that the serial killings were a logical investigation for the newly operational Europol was hailed throughout the Union as one of the few positive suggestions to emerge since the horrors began, even supposedly by jealous national police forces apparently prepared to abandon previous resistant hostility in their eagerness to transfer responsibility for their own shortcomings.

Henri Sanglier immediately recognized the potential benefit of involvement. Utilized properly, it could sensationally establish the reputation and credibility of any investigating force. Designated officers of that force would, of course, be just as sensationally destroyed by failure.

Either way, Sanglier decided he couldn't personally lose. He looked up as Françoise entered the room.

'How was Paris?'

'Wonderful, as always.'

'You were discreet?'

'Don't be such a fucking bore.'

He'd have to be extremely careful how he timed the divorce. 'Anyone new?'

Françoise looked at him curiously. 'How did you guess?'

'You always smell of sex when you've made a new conquest.'

'Her name is Ginette. She's delightful. Only nineteen.'

'Does she know who you are?'

'Who you are, you mean?'

'Does she?'

'No. Stop pissing your pants.'

Chapter Four

The major difficulty in turning Europol into a properly functioning investigative bureau had been achieving unanimous EU agreement on how operational control should be exercised. The eventual resolve had been to form, from senior police officials from individual member countries, a committee of commissioners, the chair rotating every month. The solution achieved essential continuity at the same time as avoiding the impression of any one country's improperly influencing or manipulating decisions.

When the dismemberment serial murders became Europol's first investigation there were still three weeks to run under the leadership of the Austrian commissioner, Franz Sobell. The timing suited Sanglier perfectly. His chairmanship, with its politically necessary but distracting need to shuttle between the EU capitals of Brussels, Strasbourg and Luxembourg, was still six months away — time enough to put into place all the professional stepping stones he intended using for even greater personal success and honour.

Sanglier arrived intentionally early in the conference suite, anxious to prepare his groundwork and immediately pleased that David Winslow, the UK commissioner, was ahead of him. Sanglier, who believed himself the most adept of them all at balancing allies against enemies, considered Winslow the leader of his resentful detractors. The portly, sleek-haired Englishman was deep in conversation with Italy's Emilio Bellimi in the closed off section of the window terrace. Sanglier shook his head against the offered coffee from the hovering attendant, smiling as the two men turned at his approach. Neither smiled back.

'The moment we've all been waiting for,' said Sanglier enthusiastically.

'Are you sure?' queried Bellimi, serious-faced. He was a short fat man whose pursuit of fashion always made him appear to be wearing a slimmer man's clothes.

Sanglier, who at well over six feet towered over the Italian, was glad at the obvious uncertainty, although hardly surprised after the Europe-wide hysteria of the previous weeks. 'Isn't it exactly the sort of investigation we should be involved in?'

Winslow put his coffee cup on the window ledge. Beyond, the greyness of the day made it impossible to distinguish the faraway shoreline of a slate sea. 'I've just finished reading all the exchange traffic: not one investigation, in any country, has got anywhere. We're getting the responsibility for failure dumped on us. And that could mean the end of Europol

as an investigative agency before it even starts!'
Winslow was four months away from the
Commission chairmanship.

'Then it's important to ensure we don't fail,
isn't it?' said Sanglier, meticulously fuelling
the attitude he wanted to engender. After only
a few months at Europol, Sanglier was familiar
with the suspicion in which he was held by
most of the other commissioners, who dis-
dained his appointment as the nepotism of a
legend. But this was the first time he'd consciously cultivated the feeling.

In exaggerated exasperation Winslow puffed
out cheeks already reddened by blood pressure. 'We can't afford to be that glib. It's been
difficult enough getting this far. We're going
to be on trial.'

Other commissioners were entering the
chamber and gathering in small, intense
groups. The smiles were perfunctory, quickly
gone, and Sanglier's expectation grew. He
said: 'We were always going to be on trial, on
our first investigation. And will be, for a lot to
follow.'

'Would you want to be the case officer on
this?' demanded Bellimi, imagining he was being threatening.

Sanglier thought he'd been astonishingly
lucky, immediately hitting on these two. It
wouldn't be necessary for him to move on,
although they still weren't sufficiently irritated. 'I wouldn't give up before I'd even

started, which is the impression I'm getting from this conversation.'

'Have you read the files?' demanded Winslow, his face growing redder.

'No,' lied Sanglier, who probably knew every case note better than anyone else in the room.

'They're spread over six countries the length and breadth of the continent. The way they're dismembered is the only common link,' pointed out the Englishman. 'There's nowhere to start. No focus.'

'We don't know that, without making our own investigation,' said Sanglier, intentionally going beyond his normal arrogance. 'Surely the dismemberment *is* the focus?'

'It began — and has been concentrated — in France,' said Bellimi, not attempting to hide the annoyance. 'If that's the obvious focus it seems to have eluded your people!'

'Because there's no centralized, overall control,' insisted Sanglier. 'Which is what we were formed to provide. There couldn't be a better case — or cases — to justify our existence. Or our operating Convention.'

'Or a worse one to make us appear an ineffective irrelevance,' said Winslow.

Sanglier's provoking was interrupted by Franz Sobell's striding purposefully to the head of the conference table, beckoning the other commissioners as he went. Each place was designated by a country-identifying nameplate. There were headphones at every position already tuned for simultaneous translation from the multilinguists unseen behind their smoked glass windows overlooking the chamber. There was a separate table for the note-taking and recording secretariat. Sanglier's seat was opposite those of Bellimi and Winslow. He smiled again to both men. Once more neither responded. The uncertainty around the table was palpable.

'I hardly think it is necessary for me to stress the importance of what we have to discuss today,' began the white-haired Austrian chairman. 'Or to say I've never imagined a set of crimes like these.' He spoke in English. Only two commissioners — Spain's Jorge Ortega and Paul Merot from Luxembourg — bothered with their headsets.

'There've been official requests for assistance from every country?' queried Bellimi, as if there might be an escape in discovering proper formalities had not been followed. He unbuttoned his tight jacket, breathing out in relief.

Sobell nodded. 'All personally delivered to me in Brussels yesterday, at an emergency meeting of Justice Ministers.' He paused, looking to where Winslow sat representing the country that had been most resistant to creating a federal police force. 'The United Kingdom was the last.'

'I spoke to London by telephone last night,'

said Winslow, unconcerned at being singled out. 'I've been authorized to guarantee full cooperation.'

'I was given the same assurance from everyone yesterday,' said Sobell.

'To ensure they get rid of the problem as fast as they can,' Bellimi put in.

'We can't pick and choose,' said the Austrian. 'I don't think I'm being over-dramatic when I say the seriousness with which we will be regarded in the future stands or falls by how we handle this case.'

'I don't think any of us needs reminding of that,' said Bellimi.

Sobell looked at Winslow again. 'A point that was made most strongly by the British Home Secretary.'

There was a shift of discomfort around the table and Sanglier decided it could not have been going better for him. Now it was time definitely to steer the discussion. 'I'm sure none of us underestimates the importance to this organization of what we have to achieve. But surely, in view of that, we should be talking far more positively than we are.'

Both Winslow and Bellimi looked sharply at him, imagining personal criticism. Several other commissioners who Sanglier guessed held him in the same disdain frowned, too.

'There's a difference between being negative and being objective,' said Winslow defensively.

'I haven't detected it yet,' said Sanglier. 'Each of us knows why we've at last become involved. And how difficult it's going to be. Our function is to centralize the inquiry. So we should be discussing *how* to centralize it, who should run it and how they should operate.'

Now there were several head movements of agreement from around the table and Jan Villiers, the Belgian commissioner, said: 'I'd like very much for us to look forwards, not backwards over our shoulders as if we were afraid of something.'

'No one's afraid of anything!' said Sobell unconvincingly.

'I am,' said Winslow. 'I'm afraid we won't be able satisfactorily to conclude an investigation, thus proving all the critics, my own country chief among them, right in dismissing Europol as an unworkable organization.'

'That's defeatist,' protested Villiers.

'It's objective common sense,' said Winslow.

Sanglier, who anticipated the benefit of two opposing sides, turned at the Englishman's remark. 'For God's sake let's go on being objective!'

'Which I'm sure you've already given a great deal of thought to!' said Sobell stiffly. It didn't emerge as sarcastically as he'd intended.

'Haven't most of us?' asked Sanglier, wanting the commitment of others before committing himself.

'There are at least a dozen separate crime scenes in six separate countries,' said Paul Merot, abandoning the headset and speaking in English. 'We'll need a huge amount of manpower.'

'A minimum at least of five officers to each task force,' suggested Willi Lenteur, the German commissioner, coming into the debate.

'Would that include technical and scientific personnel?' asked Ortega.

'I would have thought they could be assigned as and when they were required,' said the Dutch commissioner, Hans Maes.

'Shouldn't we create a special supervising committee from members of this Commission?' asked Winslow. Looking pointedly at Sanglier, he said: 'Like it or not, there has to be a political consideration exercised at our level.'

'That would probably be sensible,' agreed Sobell.

Although it perfectly fitted what he hoped to achieve Sanglier felt a surge of irritation at the discernible attitude in the room. Every proposal was tentative, half offered to be quickly withdrawn at the first opposition, no one prepared to go on the record with a positive demand or assessment. 'As I've already been reminded once this morning, France has so far been the worst affected by these atrocities,' he pointed out. 'And none of the police forces, spread throughout the country, have made any practical progress.' He paused, looking in turn to the commissioners from the other involved countries. 'Which is the same everywhere else, isn't it?'

There were reluctant nods from those to whom the question had been addressed. Villiers said: 'I am afraid so.'

'Our function is to bring the investigation of crimes committed hundreds of miles apart under a system of overall control,' continued the Frenchman. 'We won't achieve that by setting up six different task forces, each of at least five investigators calling in technical assistance as and when they feel like it. And we won't just be compounding the confusion by establishing a committee from among ourselves. We'll be adding to it . . .' Sanglier hesitated, trying to gauge the reaction around the table. There was some nodding of heads but he would have liked more. 'It would, in fact, result in what we all agree can't happen — Europol's failing on its first investigatory involvement.'

There was another stir of unease around the table.

Sobell said: 'So you do have a proposal?' He pitched the sarcasm more successfully this time.

'There should, initially, only be one task force,' said Sanglier. 'And that restricted to only two or three people. They should assess the killings not individually, as they are being investigated at the moment, but as connected serial murders committed by the same person or group of persons . . .' He hesitated again, knowing he stood more chance of getting what he wanted by spacing his idea. Predictably David Winslow hurried in to attack.

'Preposterous!' he protested. 'How could two or three people possibly investigate a series of murders spread so far apart?'

It couldn't have been better, thought Sanglier. 'They're already being investigated by the entire murder squads of every city in which there's been a body part found. What we don't know — but what we've got to find out — is where to centre the investigation. That's the time to start talking of larger task forces to work with national police units. When there's a place to concentrate them.'

The gestures of agreement were more positive now, but still only among the people he'd already guessed would support him so he wasn't seeking to persuade.

'We'll lose before we even start,' said Bellimi. 'We'll lay ourselves open to the accusation — which we'll deserve — that we're making a totally insufficient response to the most horrendous crime sequence in Europe of the last hundred years, outside the wars.'

'No,' stated Sanglier, juggling the vehemence as delicately as he'd judged every other remark. He allowed another pause, fixing his attention upon Winslow. 'We won't be giving in to hysteria. Instead we'll be reacting in a sensibly balanced way to an unprecedented series of crimes. Which is precisely how we should proceed. And how we can rebut any criticism.' He sensed the mood moving in his favour.

'There is a logic to the proposal,' conceded Sobell.

'As well as too many shortcomings, the most important of which is an effective political monitor,' persisted Winslow.

Almost there, thought Sanglier. 'A committee of commissioners would at this stage be as premature and ill considered as flooding six European countries with yet more investigators.'

'There needs to be a monitor,' insisted the Englishman doggedly.

'I didn't say there shouldn't be,' lured Sanglier, covering his spike-tipped trap.

'Which would have to be from here,' declared Winslow, impaling himself.

'But again not until the focus of the investigation was established,' agreed Sanglier, in apparent concession.

'We're talking about an intermediary between field officers and ourselves,' came in Maes, whom Sanglier positioned on his side of the fence.

'I suppose we are,' said Sanglier.

Briskly — almost triumphantly — Winslow

said: 'A case officer, in fact.'

'That's essential, in view of the importance of this case to our organization,' said Sobell, safely choosing the obvious upon which to appear authoritative.

'Absolutely essential,' agreed Sanglier. How much further could he go without hanging out a sign?

'There's no precedent for a situation like this,' complained the chairman, seeming to forget there wasn't any operational precedent for any Europol activity.

'Our French colleague has expressed himself very forcefully,' said Bellimi, imagining he was preparing an entrapment.

It was as if he had written a script, thought Sanglier. He remained silent.

'I propose Commissioner Sanglier be appointed,' picked up Winslow.

'Would you be prepared to accept the responsibility?' asked Sobell directly.

Sanglier intruded a hesitation before saying: 'On an undertaking to this Commission that as soon as I considered it necessary I would recommend the establishment of the proposed oversight group.' Which would ultimately either shoulder the responsibility for any failure, absolving him of censure, or provide an opportunity for glory if, from his eyrie, he saw the possibility of a successful conclusion. Like the one he saw now.

'That seems very positive,' said Villiers.

'Are we agreed about limiting the task force as well?' asked Sobell. The man was growing more confident.

The Dutch commissioner said: 'I think there's a strong argument for doing so.'

'So do I,' said Villiers.

'It's a decision that could be revised the day a lead emerges,' said Sanglier. 'We're all here, on immediate call.' Once again he paused, momentarily unsure. Then, determinedly, he said: 'In view of today's decision about my function, perhaps I should select the initial task force. For later confirmation by the full Commission, of course.'

The gestures of agreement were virtually unanimous now, like the general impression of relief. Sobell said: 'I think this has been a very productive meeting.'

'So do I,' agreed Sanglier. Never in his wildest dreams had he imagined it would all be so easy.

'I didn't intend anything personal in what I said in there,' Sanglier said.

Winslow looked surprised at being singled out by the Frenchman as they left the conference room. 'I didn't imagine that you did.'

'It's going to be important picking the right people the first time.'

'Let's hope you make the proper choice,' said Winslow.

'I'm wondering about someone from the

71

English unit. Claudine Carter. Would there be any difficulty there?'

Winslow stopped, turning fully to confront the other man. 'What difficulty could there be? I don't understand the question.'

Sanglier made a dismissive head movement. 'I merely thought I'd mention it, as a matter of courtesy. Obviously I don't know anything about her.'

'She's a very private person,' said Winslow. 'Keeps very much to herself, among the British group.'

'Unsure of herself, perhaps?' suggested Sanglier.

'I hardly know her,' Winslow said. 'I've only met her at social events and she doesn't come to many of those. But I've never received any impression of her being unsure. Do you want me to tell her you're considering her?'

'Better if I handle everything from the outset,' said Sanglier. 'I'm the case officer, after all.'

The Council of Ministers' decision to delegate the combined investigations to Europol had been publicly announced from Brussels and caused as much consternation throughout the lower levels of the organization as it had among the governing Commission.

The commissioners were, in fact, still in session when Scott Burrows cornered Claudine in the staff cafeteria, easing uninvited into the vacant seat at her table. He wasn't smoking one of his perfumed American cigars but he exuded their smell. 'Looks like we got the big one.'

'Very big,' she agreed. She noted the inclusive 'we'. Of all the decisions reflecting the uncertainty of Europol's becoming a functioning police entity, Claudine considered the secondment from the FBI of the fat, crinkle-haired American the most peculiar. Bizarre, even. Like so many establishment actions, it had been political, not just a public reminder that Europol's intended function mirrored the US Bureau's but proof that Washington took the European organization seriously enough to become associated from its outset. She was idly curious what the trade-off had been between Washington and the European Union.

'Not much in the books to fit this scenario,' said the man, crumbling the first of two croissants in his coffee saucer.

Claudine wondered to which of his three much acclaimed standard textbooks the man was referring. She said: 'A lot of situations don't fit textbook formulas,' and then wished she hadn't.

Burrows smiled without humour. 'As you're so fond of telling me and anyone else who'll listen.'

So he had been making a familiar point. 'It won't be easy picking up this late.'

'There'll be more to work back from. This is a well organized group, operating to a plan.' He spoke with his mouth full, spraying crumbs.

'What plan?'

'Five will get you ten it's racist.'

'What about the white girls in Belgium and Holland?'

'Blacks hate whites. It's a two-way street.'

'Wouldn't you have expected some Fascist or neo-Nazi statements, to increase the panic among the minorities?'

'The bastards are doing well enough without needing to make any claims.' The American looked towards the cafeteria shelf, restocked with croissants, imperceptibly shaking his head in a private refusal. 'What's your guess?' he demanded, coming back to her.

'I don't know enough about any of the killings to make one,' said Claudine. 'And I try not to guess.'

'Thought how you'd approach it, if you got assigned?'

'No,' Claudine answered at once, honestly. Had that been a casual, psychologist-to-psychologist question? Or was Burrows carrying out an unofficial ground survey for a commissioner over-impressed by the American's reputation? As the most persistent challenger of the man's reliance on textbook dogma of his own creation she stood as much chance of surviving his elimination process as a virgin in a whorehouse.

'If it happens, go the racism route,' urged the man. He made a sucking noise, drinking his coffee.

'I'll remember that,' said Claudine, not interested in continuing the discussion. Serial killing was a crime upon which criminal psychology was invariably used, she acknowledged. A person's reputation would be permanently established by this case. Providing, that is, there was a successful solution.

Sanglier's summons was waiting for Claudine when she returned to her office from the cafeteria.

Chapter Five

The supposition was obvious. But Claudine refused to invest too much hope. She couldn't, though, prevent the anticipation that went beyond the possibility of any prove-yourself-involvement in the serial killings.

She'd lived most of her life in France — she had only spent five full years in England — and with the exception of Europol's French contingent was probably more familiar than anyone else with the aura surrounding the famous name. So she was intrigued by the prospect of meeting Henri Sanglier for the first time.

She had of course seen him from afar at Europol's formation ceremonies, one of the operation-deciding commissioners whose purpose was to turn the organization from a concept into a reality. But that had been like looking at an art gallery portrait of a minor player in a major historical event. Not that Henri Sanglier had ever been regarded as a minor dynastic figure.

Claudine knew that in the past, during his rise to the top of the French police hierarchy, there had been media-reported insinuations about a son whose success was based upon the legend of his hero father. But such insinuations were jealously inevitable. Having the name of Sanglier, with all its wartime connotations, could not have impaired Henri's career. But neither, in Claudine's opinion, would such unimpeded promotion have been automatically guaranteed unless Henri Sanglier had proved outstanding ability.

Now she was going to meet the man. Which, in the course of time, she would have done anyway. Except this wasn't in the course of time. It was now, within a week of an official announcement that Europol was to investigate an horrendous series of murders. And within an hour — minutes almost — of a conversation with the doyen of American criminal psychologists who had sought her out to discuss how she would professionally approach such an investigation.

The impulse was to believe she had already been chosen, but again Claudine held back from an automatic conclusion. There were five other criminal psychologists, all men, assigned to Europol. She could be — perhaps should be — part of a politically required selection process. In line, at least. But that's as far as she was prepared to consider it, as a selection hurdle. Leaving her to jump what remained and come in ahead of the field. Which she had to do.

Being permanently attached to Europol wasn't enough, essential though that was in getting her away from London and its memories. She had to work. Working in her arcane profession — being able to see and interpret and be proved right more often and more successfully than anyone else — was what motivated Claudine. Which she'd already acknowledged to be a fault, possibly *the* fault that had caused the disaster with Warwick. But that was in the past. Now she looked upon it as her salvation. She would survive by working, whenever and as much as possible; by proving herself to be indispensable, becoming the first choice, someone so constantly employed there would be no time for a private life with private thoughts and private recriminations and, latterly, private doubts.

The forthcoming encounter was therefore absolutely vital. If it were a selection process it would be wrong to appear as eager — desperate almost — as she inwardly was. She had, instead, to be utterly, professionally dispassionate. Which extended to being professionally dispassionate towards Henri Sanglier himself. She'd already decided Sanglier had earned his promotions and accolades through his own merits, and a man who had achieved so much would instantly recognize any undue deference and look upon it as an attempt to be ingratiating, which could easily disqualify her from any contest.

If it were a selection process she might anyway be entering at a disadvantage. She was the only woman among the six criminal psychologists from whom a choice could be made. And despite lofty European declarations and proudly adopted European legislation about sexual equality — formulated by men — Claudine Carter suspected Europol of the instinctive male bias against women that she'd encountered in every law enforcement environment in which she'd ever worked: would not have been surprised, even, if hers was a token appointment to belie the hypocrisy.

And not just an hypocrisy of equality. In the short time she had been at The Hague she'd been conscious — even been a target — of more blatant sexism than she'd previously experienced. She was, Claudine accepted, thinking like an Englishwoman and not like the Frenchwoman she might consider herself, having a French mother whom she'd respected far more than her English father and living most of her life in France. It was, she supposed, unavoidable after so recently losing Warwick: an instinctive, protective reaction rather than one that came naturally to her.

Objectively the easily derided and rejected sexual suggestions should do nothing more than irritate her. Certainly the suspicion of bias didn't frighten her. Rather it strengthened the always present determination to do better than any of the other psychologists: better, even, than any traditional investigator with whom she might work. All she needed was the chance, which she intended to do everything to get, short of accepting one of the sexual invitations.

All the executive offices of the former Gestapo building had been totally redesigned and refurbished — apart from the shell, very little remained of its wartime history — but as she entered Henri Sanglier's suite Claudine wondered how many men and women had, more than fifty years ago, entered this same place believing their future depended upon how they conducted themselves before someone of higher authority, as she was doing now. She became immediately embarrassed, angry at herself. It was absurd — obscene even — to attempt any comparison between what she was about to face and the life-and-death situation with which people half a century earlier might have been confronted in these surroundings. The thought prompted a further reflection. How often and in what circumstances might Sanglier have considered the irony of his now working from such a building after what his father had done?

Claudine consciously began her assessment the moment she crossed the threshold, wanting as much advantage as she could get.

The desk behind which Sanglier remained momentarily sitting was at the furthest point from the door, forcing any visitor to make an intimidating approach. So despite the name and his position, Sanglier worked hard at achieving respect. Balancing that immediate interpretation Claudine conceded the positioning put Sanglier directly in front of the window expanse, a natural location. The desk itself stopped just short of being overpoweringly out of proportion to the office, like Sanglier's button-backed leather chair.

Sanglier, centrepiece of the overall impression of power, politely rose at last, but remained behind the desk while Claudine completed her pilgrimage. Which she did unhurriedly, using all her training to read something of the man before officially greeting him.

Very tall, maybe two metres. Lean-bodied, which she guessed to be from a natural metabolism, not any fixation on diet or exercise. Thick black hair only slightly tinged with grey, experienced wisdom rather than age. A full, tightly clipped moustache beneath a slightly flared nose, which gave an expression of permanent disdain. Lips parted sufficiently to show perfectly even teeth but not enough to form a proper smile. An obviously tailored suit perfectly cut, the tie against the pure white shirt with a motif that could have denoted a club but probably didn't. No immediate gesture or word of welcome, deeply blue eyes — black maybe — studying her as intently as she was examining him.

Outwardly a supremely confident man, Claudine decided. Accustomed to automatic deference but determined not to let anyone forget respect was his by right. A seeker of admiration, perhaps. If he were, then he wasn't as confident as he seemed on the surface. Too early to assess that. Maybe someone with a tendency to bully, if the respect degenerated into awe of his being the carrier of the legend. She'd have to be careful he didn't misconstrue her demeanour. Not a problem. She knew she wasn't someone who invited bullying. Wrong to attempt anything more now: a risk of herself misconstruing if she did.

She was taking her time getting to him, Sanglier accepted. Almost prolonging the approach. Not apprehensive of him, as people often were. He would have liked her to be. Not to be could indicate that she did know something. Too soon to make a guess like that. Absolutely essential he didn't make a mistake, a miscalculation. Elfin, far more French than English, in a simple black dress unadorned by any jewellery but wearing matching gold bracelets on either wrist. Different, in person, from the personnel photographs he'd already pored over. Obviously the features were identical but in the flesh there was an animation, a presence, impossible for a camera to capture. Not a beautiful woman — the nose was too long and the lips too full — but definitely an arresting one. Allowing himself the speculation as a man — not as Claudine Carter's superior with a private worry about what she might know — Sanglier was more intrigued by her than sexually curious, well aware that a lot of men found the sort of ambience Claudine Carter generated a stronger physical attraction than a more obvious promise or expectation. Her face was narrow and open, her eyes — a deeper blue than was obvious in the photographs — only lightly colour-shadowed. The lipgloss was muted, too, and the dark auburn hair was shorter than the file pictures, cut tight into the neck. He thought it made her look imperious. The word stayed with him. There could be an imperiousness in the way her steady gaze matched his. Arrogance could be useful, an attitude to be manipulated, as he'd manipulated the other commissioners to gain the control he had achieved.

He finally allowed the proper smile, gesturing her to one of an already arranged half-circle of chairs. As she sat, Sanglier started the concealed tape. He said: 'It's a pleasure to meet you in person.'

'For me also,' said Claudine. She spoke in French, as Sanglier had.

Behind her Claudine heard the door open. There were two more chairs beside her but only the footsteps of one person. She didn't turn. One of the secretaries from the outer office came into her view, cups and percolator on a tray. The woman poured, unasked, offering coffee to Sanglier first. As she left Sanglier said: 'Smoke, if you wish.'

'I don't.'

'Do you mind if I do?' He'd hoped she would be a smoker but he could still create the imagined situation he wanted.

'Of course not.' She hadn't expected the politeness.

'You will have already guessed why I've called you in.'

'The serial killings, obviously.' He was facially quite different from his father, whose pictures she could clearly remember adorning commemorative posters and prints during Resistance anniversaries. The old man had been much fuller faced, although similarly moustached, but Henri Sanglier was patrician by comparison to his peasant-like father.

'Initially there is to be a very small task force, personally supervised by me.' Having lighted one, Sanglier put the Gauloises packet beside the ashtray.

Claudine waited for the man to continue. When he didn't she inferred she was undergoing a test and said: 'To decide the direction of an investigation?'

'Do you consider that the proper way to begin?'

Claudine was curious at being asked her opinion. All part of the assessment, she supposed. Cautiously she said: 'It's the logical way to begin. The geographical separation will be one of the biggest problems.'

'One of a great many,' encouraged Sanglier.

'To be considered in order of priority and sequence.'

There certainly wasn't any lack of professionalism so far.

'Would you have any fear at being part of the initial task force?'

Claudine frowned at the ill-fitting word in the question. 'I don't go into an investigation fearfully. That would be self-defeating. I recognize the difficulties and mitigate or deal with them. So no, I would not be frightened to be part of the initial task force. I would very much like to be.'

'It's an investigation of the utmost importance to this organization.'

'I know that.' Claudine supposed they had to go through the obvious. He was holding the cigarette in his right hand and she was aware of his constantly fingering the blotter edge with his left, as if he were uncertain.

'I mean politically as well as professionally.'

'I understand that, too.'

'It would not concern you?' He broke the cigarette, stubbing it out and almost immediately lighting another.

Claudine was caught by a conflicting reaction, unsure how to reply. It would be as wrong to appear dismissive of the difficulties as it would be to indicate she was apprehensive. Which in any case she wasn't. 'It would be something of which I would be aware, naturally. But I would not consider it primarily my responsibility. My primary responsibility would be a professional investigatory one, leading to detection and arrests.'

'You believe you could dissociate one requirement from the other?'

What commitment did the bloody man want her to make? 'I think I could successfully balance the two, at the level at which I would be working.'

'Even in its limited initial size, the task force would be multinational.'

'Of course.'

'You don't foresee any difficulty working like that?'

Another ineptly worded question. 'I was appointed after a protracted vetting procedure precisely because I satisfied people I wouldn't have any difficulty working like that. My background is more European than specifically English.'

Sanglier lighted another cigarette. 'Not just a European background, in fact, but a very early association with an organization like ours.'

Claudine was bewildered at the reference to her father. It confused her more than anything else so far, although he would obviously have studied her personnel file and know of her father's attachment to Interpol in Lyon. 'A peripheral association.'

'Weren't you encouraged by the work your

father did when you decided upon your own career?'

What the hell had this to do with judging her suitability as a criminal psychologist involved in a serial murder investigation? She had no intention of talking about a man who'd meant so little to her. Shortly, she said: 'Not at all. There is no operational function at Interpol. Just the assembling and dissemination of criminal intelligence. There was no guidance my father could have provided upon what I chose to do.'

It sounded like disrespect for her father, which Sanglier didn't understand. How could there be disrespect towards someone who, according to Claudine's file, had died ten years earlier and with whom she hadn't permanently lived for four years before that, during her time at the Sorbonne? He crumpled the latest cigarette, half smoked, into the ashtray so that it broke like the other one and said, intentionally dramatic: 'I'm sure you are going to be an extremely effective member of the team.'

For the briefest moment Claudine didn't properly appreciate that it hadn't after all been a contest between herself and the other Europol psychologists and that Sanglier was confirming her place on the task force. Formally, wishing there were better words, she said: 'I will do everything possible to make myself so.'

★ ★ ★

The two men entered together, obviously having been kept waiting outside. Claudine at once recognized René Poulard but not the other man. Poulard gave no indication of recognizing her, which was understandable after their previous encounters. She hadn't consciously connected Poulard with her earlier reflection about predatory sexism but her most boorish experience within Europol had involved the thin-bodied, saturnine Frenchman. Having lived so long in France Claudine was accustomed to the inherent Gallic flattery towards women — before moving to England and marrying Warwick she had accepted it as harmlessly amusing, enjoyable even — but Poulard's went beyond hopeful flirtation to overconfident, virtually arrogant expectation. He'd refused to believe her uninterest, clearly imagining instead she was putting up a sexual challenge. Which he'd met with even more persistent after-work drink and dinner invitations until finally she'd intentionally chosen an audience in Europol's cocktail bar for her public rejection, knowingly — determinedly — humiliating the man.

Which made his inclusion in a tight-knit task force engaged on the organization's first, can't-fail operation possibly the worst Claudine could have imagined.

As the two men finished their long walk to his desk Sanglier, who knew of the confrontation because it was part of knowing everything about Claudine Carter and had picked Poulard because of it, was thinking exactly the same thing. Sanglier didn't stand to greet them and delayed inviting them to sit while he made the formal introductions.

Any reaction Poulard might have given at finding Claudine already waiting in the commissioner's room was initially swamped by his being in Sanglier's presence. Claudine thought his attitude came close to the awe she had determined against. The response from the second man, whom Sanglier introduced as Superintendent Bruno Siemen, seconded from the organized crime bureau of the Bundeskriminalamt, was almost as obsequious and Claudine guessed Poulard had briefed the German while they waited outside. Poulard finally allowed himself a gesture with their required handshake, making a caressing withdrawal which Claudine decided was an attempt at mockery. Siemen's contact was perfunctory and limp.

Sanglier's approach to the two men was quite different from that to her and Claudine divided her concentration between the facts of the briefing, with which she felt sufficiently familiar, and how Sanglier conducted it. There was no invitation to smoke, which he stopped doing after one more cigarette, nor the automatic arrival of fresh coffee. And there was a brusqueness in Sanglier's tone, which made

Claudine think again how deference prompted bullying.

Sanglier put far more stress on political pitfalls, the difficulty of working with national forces and the impossibility of failure than he had to her. But he didn't ask for their personal reaction at being selected or whether they felt able to combine the necessary political awareness with the absolute essential of solving the serial murders. Nor did he seek their views about the investigation's beginning with a concentrated task force, which Claudine imagined was a decision about which they might have had professional, contributing opinions. Sanglier promised every technical and scientific facility available at Europol, in addition to those of national forces. Manpower, too, once the way was decided upon for the investigation to follow. Finding that route — the correct route — was their principal objective. An incident room would obviously be made available within the building and their conferences recorded and case files maintained by support staff. He would resolve any difficulty they experienced with national forces at the highest level. The two essentials were speed and a satisfactory conclusion. Sanglier finished by smiling towards Claudine and saying, in a much less official tone: 'As Dr Carter and I have already decided.' He briefly extended the smile to the two men and added, briskly: 'Now! Questions?'

If it hadn't been inappropriate Claudine's

would have been why he'd concluded the briefing by inexplicably involving her like that. Poulard and Siemen remained silent, each waiting for the other to speak. Sanglier shifted impatiently, looking directly at Poulard. 'Well?'

'You are in charge?' said Poulard, weak-voiced.

Excellent, thought Sanglier. 'Yes.'

'On a daily basis?'

'I don't understand,' protested Sanglier, although he did.

'Are we to work with you on a daily basis?' said the discomfited man, unwilling to ask the direct question.

'I'm not sure that would be practicable — even possible — with the murders spread as they are. I will, of course, be available at all times, day or night.' That would sound impressive on the tape.

'So what is the chain of command at our level?' Poulard was finally forced to ask. He only gestured towards Siemen.

'You have equal rank,' said Sanglier, answering the man literally. 'I hadn't imagined a difficulty.'

'I'm sure there won't be one,' said Siemen. He was a large, blond-haired man who had the walked-over face — flattened nose and puffed cheeks — and muscle-turning-to-fat body of a former sportsman. His French was good, although accented.

Poulard at last indicated Claudine. 'And Dr Carter?'

'You've surely worked with a forensic psychologist in the past?'

'Yes.' The man's face was burning.

Sanglier turned to Claudine. 'How do you see yourself operating, Dr Carter?'

'As a perfectly harmonious team,' said Claudine.

'Which is how I insist you must work,' said Sanglier.

By the time Sanglier had finished the word-for-word examination of the meeting it had long ago grown dark outside his locked office and he'd almost finished the second bottle of mineral water to ease the dryness of his throat after chain-smoking the harsh cigarettes. But that, like everything else, had been worthwhile. Choosing to see her first — and alone — had been the master stroke, buttressed by all the other seemingly inconsequential gestures that hadn't been inconsequential in the least. The full ashtray would have registered with both men, as obvious as the coffee she'd been offered but they hadn't. It had been an equally good idea to keep them waiting for more than half an hour after the time he'd summoned them and it was clear from the stumbling, who's-in-charge questions from Poulard that the resentment had been well and truly created.

Sanglier wished he understood the woman's attitude towards her father. It could simply have been surprise at his reference to the man, although she didn't appear someone easily surprised, but he was sure there had been a dismissiveness.

Sanglier decided he'd speculated enough. He rose at last, carefully storing the tape cassette in his personal safe, identical to that in Claudine's office two floors below. It had, Sanglier decided, been a good beginning: better than he could have hoped for.

And it hadn't finished yet, he reflected, as the tentative tap came at his door. Because it was locked Sanglier had to walk the entire length of the room but he didn't mind. This meeting was going to be entirely different.

'Nothing!' exclaimed Toomey, disappointed.

'Not without her,' said the Serious Fraud Office superintendent. John Walker was a large, square-bodied man so obviously a policeman he rarely had to produce a warrant card for identification.

'I think there's enough for a prosecution,' insisted Toomey.

'Recommend it, then,' said Walker.

'Bickerstone is your investigation: it's for you to suggest it.'

The large man shook his head. 'The bastard's been too bloody clever.'

'She's hiding something,' insisted Toomey.

'You mean she was part of it?'

'I don't know. There's something.'

'Find out what it is and we'll have a case,' said Walker simply.

'I'm going to,' promised Toomey. 'She thought she could dance rings around me. I'm going to prove her wrong.'

Chapter Six

In the solitude of the lake-view apartment, with a Duke Ellington tape in the background, it was instinctive for Claudine to seek shape and pattern from the encounter with Henri Sanglier, as she always looked for shape and pattern in her life, privately as well as professionally. She didn't find any and it disorientated her.

She paraded the inconsistencies in her mind, annoyed at questions without answers. Why the prepared-in-advance coffee, relax-with-a-cigarette greeting? And why not for the men? Why had Sanglier sought her opinion about the size and function of the task force, but not theirs? And the biggest, most personal 'why' of all: why had the man suddenly talked about her father and his possible influence upon her?

There was no logic. Introducing her father made no sense, even for someone whose entire life had been entwined to the point of mummification with a genuine icon of a French resistance movement.

Difficult though it was to accept, the only positive, trained impression that Claudine retained was that Henri Sanglier had been nervous during their one-to-one meeting. Which was as preposterous as too much else. What was there to make Henri Sanglier nervous? But the uncertainty — the plucking of the blotter edge and virtual chain-smoking of cigarettes he'd crushed out to destruction — had definitely registered with her as a personal agitation. Towards Poulard and Siemen his demeanour had been entirely and markedly different, forceful to the point of being overbearing but always supremely professional.

The Ellington recording automatically switched to the reverse tracks and Claudine used the remote control to lower the volume. She hadn't wanted to start work at Europol like this. She hadn't had any preconceptions about the crimes she might be called upon to help solve — a preconception was professionally the very last thing with which to enter an investigation — but she had imagined the beginning of every case upon which the leading policemen of Europe were employed would go according to a smooth running pattern she could recognize from familiar experience. There was nothing smooth running or familiar about what had happened so far. So far she'd undergone an inadequate, confusing briefing from a controller whose attitude she didn't understand and been paired with the very Europol detective with whom it could be the most difficult personally to operate . . . while all the time knowing the stature of a much resented and much opposed European FBI was bound up with her contribution in solving what appeared the most bizarre crime in the history of serial murders, which by their very nature formed a chronicle of the bizarre.

Claudine felt burdened, overwhelmed, and it worried her — further disorientated her — because she'd never before embarked on an investigation feeling that there were too many totally disparate and extraneous distractions to get in the way. She got up abruptly, wanting a change of mood as well as music. Warwick had introduced her to modern jazz at a Stan Getz concert and she chose the original recording of *Getz Meets Mulligan*. As Claudine made her way to the kitchen to prepare her belated supper she remembered the other uncertainties to go with all those that had arisen that day.

There was still Peter Toomey and matching suicides and a man she'd apparently met in a gorilla's suit but couldn't remember who'd made £200,000,000 in what could have been a Stock Market scam.

Suddenly her life had become extremely crowded: cluttered and confused and not at all how she wanted it to be.

Sanglier poured whisky into both their glasses and left the bottle on the table between them with a gesture for Poulard to help himself. Sanglier knew the man wouldn't, uninvited, but the offer was more than just to drink more whisky. This was commitment time — as much commitment as it would be possible for him to make — and he was unsure. Not only unsure. Actually frightened. Enough, but not too far, Sanglier decided: he must never lose total control, total respect.

The furniture at this part of the office, where the windows met at a corner angle with a panoramic view of the city, was deep and enveloping, a place to relax, but Poulard remained perched attentively forward, more bewildered than he had been earlier in the day.

It had to be a fellow Frenchman and Sanglier hoped he'd been lucky with Poulard. Sanglier prided himself as a judge of men and assessed Poulard sufficiently ambitious not to know a scruple if it were the size of the Eiffel Tower and outlined in neon. The sanitized personnel dossier presented to Europol had obviously contained no doubtful ambiguities but the Sûreté file Sanglier had discreetly accessed contained sufficient coded references for Sanglier to suspect that the lack of necessary factual proof had never prevented Poulard gaining a conviction to further his career. Sanglier even suspected that after the three successful conviction appeals which immediately preceded the man's transfer to Europol — none of which featured in the personnel record that had accompanied him — Paris might have considered the appointment a heaven-sent op-

portunity to rid itself of a potential embarrassment.

'I want you to understand I am not singling
you out in any special way, seeing you like
this,' Sanglier began.

'I do understand,' Poulard assured him unconvincingly.

'You are all genuinely to work together as a
team.'

'Of course.'

'But failure is not just unthinkable. It's utterly unacceptable. So there needs to be an
understanding between us; a private understanding.' Come on, you fool; show some
awareness of what I'm saying.

'Yes.'

'As the commissioner with ultimate responsibility I have to take every possible precaution.' How could he make himself understood
by this man?

'Of course.'

'Which is what this meeting is about.'

'I understand.'

The cautious bastard was going to understand everything before this encounter was
over. 'Nothing must go beyond this room.
Ever. This is just between the two of us.' He
gestured towards the whisky bottle.

'I understand,' repeated Poulard. He added
to both their glasses, easing back more comfortably in his chair.

'What's your impression of Bruno Siemen?'

'A sound policeman. A professional.'

'His record supports that. There are eight commendations. He was shot in the leg three years ago, ending a siege after a disrupted bank robbery.'

'I'm sure we will work well together.'

'It's imperative that you do.' He'd chosen Siemen as a possible brake upon Poulard. There were so many checks and balances to be put into place.

'Of course.'

'Don't let escalate any difficulties that might arise. If a problem emerges you consider necessary for me to adjudicate, I have to know at once. At once, you understand. And discreetly, of course.'

'Of course.' Poulard settled back completely, crossing one leg over the other.

The moment to hang the sign round the man's neck, Sanglier thought. 'You have conducted investigations with criminal psychologists in Paris, haven't you?'

'Frequently.'

'Do you find their inclusion valuable?'

'Sometimes. Not always,' said Poulard cautiously.

'I think it's necessary here.'

'Unquestionably,' agreed the other Frenchman, taking the lead at last.

'What's your impression of Dr Carter?'

Poulard hesitated, remembering the obvious indications of a more relaxed meeting between the commissioner and the woman before he and Siemen had been included. And then recalling the humiliation the bitch had subjected him to, in front of a lot of sniggering people. 'Reserved. Possibly aloof. I'm not sure about her being a team player.'

At last! thought Sanglier, relieved. 'I hope you're wrong. There's got to be a team attitude.'

'It's impossible to form a proper opinion, after just one meeting,' qualified Poulard hurriedly. He unfolded his legs.

'If a problem comes up, I expect to hear about it.'

'Of course.'

'It's important you do not misunderstand me. I am in no way suggesting you should be disloyal to colleagues. My only concern — the only concern there can be — is that nothing occurs to endanger this case.'

'That can be the only consideration.'

'What made you apply for the transfer to Europol?'

'I regarded it as a substantial career improvement.'

'A successful investigation could guarantee your career. A failure could end it.'

'I fully recognize that.'

From his knowledge — official and unofficial — of Poulard's history Sanglier thought it more likely the application had been pressed upon the man. 'The media hysteria surrounding these murders is incredible, don't you think?'

'Incredible.'

'This could be your opportunity to become as famous outside the organization as within.'

Poulard allowed himself a fleeting smile. 'I am not interested in personal fame.'

For a professional policeman the man lied badly, Sanglier decided. 'Europol has a long way still to go before it is fully accepted. But once it is, it is going to become important within the European Union. As will the recognized officers in it. I hope I can help advance your career here.'

'I hope so to. And want you to know how much I appreciate what you're saying.'

'It was my personal decision to include you in this initial task force, despite the risk of being accused of nepotism. I think it is important to build up a French influence.'

'I won't fail the trust you have put in me.'

'I'm confident it won't be misplaced. Keep me particularly informed about Dr Carter.'

'I will.'

'I meant what I said about being available, day or night.'

'I'll remember that.'

This time Sanglier refilled their glasses. 'To a satisfactory conclusion,' he toasted.

'To a satisfactory conclusion,' echoed Poulard.

They were, reflected Sanglier, drinking to

quite different outcomes.

There was a two-sentence note from Françoise when Sanglier got home. It said: *Gone fucking. Don't wait up for me.*

Sanglier winced. He'd laid the groundwork for any problems Claudine Carter might present. He wouldn't delay much longer resolving the situation with Françoise, either.

Chapter Seven

It was only on that first operational day, when the task force became a formal entity, that Claudine properly accepted how different her working life was going to be.

Europol's criminal behavioural unit was a division in its own right, with its official title displayed on its own entrance and a pooled secretarial and filing clerk staff. There were separate offices for each psychologist and a communal conference area where Scott Burrows had hosted their argumentative seminars to occupy the empty days. But because those days had been so empty — not one European national force asking for its specialized assistance, the basic function of the unit's existence — Claudine had felt an unreality at being there, like getting a date wrong and arriving a day early for a special event.

Now the event had arrived, far more special than she could have ever contemplated.

The most obvious difference — although one, surprisingly, that she hadn't fully confronted until now — was that she was a permanent part of a permanent police organization. She hadn't been in London. She'd been accredited to the Home Office and because of her dedication spent most of her time actively involved in criminal investigations, but there had been no empty days because of her lecturing and teaching responsibilities as the professor of forensic psychology at an outside university with its outside demands and outside distractions.

The feeling of unreality did not, however, entirely go at the beginning of that first day. The move into their assigned incident quarters was like moving into a new house in a new locality, complete with over-interested neighbours who emerged curiously from corridors to watch the setting up of Europol's first operation. Scott Burrows even wished her good luck as she left their section and said he'd see her later.

Claudine had imagined just one large area where an investigation group could all gather at one time to consider the assembled evidence, the sort of arrangement to which she had been accustomed in England. The Europol facilities were far more elaborate. There was a communal conference area — larger than the one available in her specific unit — and provision for wall displays and exhibits as well as photograph and video projection. Down its centre was a rectangular table with six chairs either side. The table was completely covered to the depth of several inches by files. There was a much smaller, separate table forming a T where the display area was set out. Here there were only four chairs, all confined to one side obviously to be occupied by those controlling a meeting. Filing cabinets were banked along an inner, windowless wall and along a second at right angles to it there were four computer stations, the terminals covered with protective plastic hoods, like sleeping birds. The third wall was formed entirely by undesignated offices.

When Claudine arrived, still ten minutes early, two had been claimed by Poulard and Siemen: the German had already installed a flowerless cactus on top of his individual filing cabinet and established his territory with a paperweight surmounted by the German national flag on an otherwise empty desk. Poulard was at the entrance to his quarters, in conversation with a plump young-faced man whose clothes looked as if they'd been bought for someone even larger and hung from him in disarray. There was more resilience in the flag on Siemen's desk. Quite alone but not ill at ease at the bottom of the larger, cluttered table, as if standing guard, was a petite, pale-faced girl whose attractiveness was heightened by the severe way her black hair was strained directly back into a bun at the nape of her neck and by heavy black-rimmed spectacles. Claudine thought the girl was too heavily busted for the tightly fitted blue wool dress. Presented with the choice, which he obviously had been, Claudine would not have expected

Poulard to talk to a haystack of a man. Claudine smiled and the girl smiled back.

'Good morning,' Claudine said, loudly and to no one in particular.

The girl nodded, the smile expanding, and in French said: 'Hello.' Poulard, who Claudine knew had seen her enter, turned as if aware of her for the first time. So did the man to whom he was talking. Siemen came to the door of his office, as if he were protecting it against invaders.

'Not late, am I?' said Claudine cheerfully. Her first priority, today if possible, was to get rid of any residual difficulty with Poulard. She might have mentally over-reacted the previous day by imagining a personal problem in his appointment. She hoped so.

'We've only just arrived,' said Poulard, making no attempt at introductions.

'Volker,' said the dishevelled man. 'Kurt Volker.' He made a vague wave towards the shrouded machines. 'I work with computers. I've been assigned to you. I hope I can help.'

'I'm sure you'll be able to,' said Claudine. The German accent wasn't as strong as Siemen's but the handshake certainly was.

'Yvette Fey,' said the bespectacled girl. 'I'm to decide the amount of secretarial and support staff you'll need. Working by myself, initially.' She looked pointedly at the files.

French, possibly Parisienne, identified Claudine: certainly a northern accent. So she was outnumbered, two to one, by both nation-alities. But hadn't she described herself as a European to Sanglier? It was, anyway, an in-fantile reflection. She wished it hadn't oc-curred to her.

'We waited for you to decide which of the remaining offices you wanted,' said Yvette.

'I don't really have anything to transfer. Why don't you take your pick of whatever room you want,' shrugged Claudine. *Just* like moving into a new house, she thought. She looked around the room. 'At the moment this looks a little too large for our needs.'

'It won't be soon,' predicted Siemen, emerging further into the room. 'At the mo-ment our first need is to agree upon a working practice.'

'And relationship,' Poulard added.

'Why don't we do just that?' said Claudine, moving to the smaller table. As she did so she moved two chairs to the opposite side, to avoid their sitting in an awkward line. After a mo-mentary hesitation, the two men followed her. Both seated themselves to face her. Yvette went to a corner of the room where Claudine for the first time saw the electronic equipment and remembered Sanglier's insistence upon everything's being recorded. It was obviously essential to maintain continuity, but Claudine wondered if at this stage it would be a restric-tive although silent intrusion.

'Am I needed?' queried Volker. 'I've got

quite a lot of stuff I'd like to move in.'

'I wouldn't have thought so,' Claudine said unthinkingly.

'Neither would I,' said Poulard. 'But it conveniently introduces the first necessity for an effective working practice.'

'What?' asked Claudine, as Volker left.

'Decision-making authority,' said Poulard.

Claudine stopped the sigh. 'I thought that was resolved yesterday with Commissioner Sanglier.'

'Who do you see in charge?' queried Siemen.

'Commissioner Sanglier,' she said at once.

'What about at our level?'

'There are only three of us,' said Claudine, allowing the exasperation. 'Surely we can work amicably together.'

'No, I'm not sure we can,' said Poulard.

He intended a heavy innuendo but Claudine refused it, responding literally. 'Then wait until you are. Over and over yesterday the need was impressed upon us to work fast. We're not going to achieve that — achieve anything — with ridiculous demarcation disputes. You do your job, I'll do mine and policy decisions can be left to the commissioner.' This wasn't how she'd intended to establish herself with them and she recognized the risk of alienating them but she hadn't anticipated its being as ridiculous as this, from the very outset.

'We will not always be in the same place at

the same time, capable of reaching a committee decision,' said Siemen.

'I'm sure we won't,' agreed Claudine.

'You're not professionally qualified to reach a decision or judgement on a specific police question,' challenged Poulard.

'And neither of you is professionally qualified to reach a decision or judgement on a specific psychological question,' Claudine threw back. She gestured towards the recording equipment beside which Yvette Fey still stood, watching them curiously. Claudine went on: 'There's a verbatim record being kept which will be supplemented by written reports of everything that occurs outside this office. If a decision on a specific police question is needed urgently, in your absence, it can be referred to the commissioner . . .' She hesitated, unwilling to widen the rift but wanting to end the time-wasting nonsense. 'Would either of you doubt his ability to handle it?'

Both men shifted awkwardly at being out-argued. Poulard said: 'What about a psychological decision in your absence?'

This conversation was worrying, even allowing for the uncertainty they all felt at what they were being called upon to do. It was far too soon even to speculate about, but Claudine wondered if she might have to complain direct to Sanglier to avoid the investigation's becoming bogged down in bureaucratic stupidity. Consciously — professionally — softening her voice to sound less confrontational Claudine said: 'We're supposed to be a team. That's what we've been put together to become. Everything I do will be a contribution towards the investigation you are conducting. No one's going to be called upon to make a medical or mental diagnosis. There can't be a decision-making emergency in my case.'

All three were aware of Yvette Fey as she returned to a room none of them had been aware she'd left. She carried coffee in the same sort of official-issue crockery as the previous day and Claudine hoped it didn't act as a reminder to the men of their inexplicable exclusion. Claudine was conscious of the over-expansive, eye-holding smile Poulard automatically directed towards the girl. He would approve of the tight dress. Claudine made the conciliatory gesture of pouring. As she did so Volker returned with files loaded up to his chin which he took into the office closest to the computer bank.

Siemen accepted his coffee, smiled and said: 'That seems to have cleared the point up as far as I'm concerned.'

Claudine took another offered chance. 'We are a team. And all three of us have a good idea of the difficulties we face, even though we can't yet guess just how difficult it's going to be. What we do know is that the problems will get worse, not better. So let's not create additional and unnecessary ones for ourselves.

We're not in competition with each other. Just as we don't need reminding of the difficulties, we don't need reminding what this means to us personally. I don't intend to fail. I don't imagine either of you do, either. I'm asking that we cooperate at all times, in everything.' She stopped, looking directly at Poulard. 'I'm suggesting any misunderstandings that might have existed up to now are forgotten. And that we take our relationship — and the job we've been formed to do — forward from this moment.'

'That seems perfect to me,' nodded the broken-faced German.

'And to me,' said Poulard.

Claudine noted, impressed, that it was from Siemen's practical suggestion to check the stacked files that they discovered there was only one copy of each and gave Yvette her first positive job, arranging duplicates for each of them to study independently. Yvette's search uncovered several folders of scene-of-crime photographs, none of which appeared to distress her. She actually asked in which order she should set them out on the display boards, before being instructed to do so. Claudine and Siemen went along with Poulard's idea of keeping the murders and each applicable exhibit in chronological order. Siemen, practical again, insisted Yvette create and personally maintain an evidence log in which everything should be listed. Anything removed from the room should be recorded against their signed authority. He was speaking as Kurt Volker made his third and final return with his personal files and Siemen proposed the log be duplicated on a computer database. Poulard appeared uninterested in the basic, pedantic police procedure. Claudine recognized it as such and decided Siemen was an essential part of their team: initially — and probably for some time afterwards — he was likely to make a bigger contribution than either she or the Frenchman. Siemen liked patterns and order, although in quite a different way from herself.

The various decisions took them up to lunch and there was no discussion or doubt that they would eat together. Their entry into the dining room attracted even more interest than Claudine had been conscious of earlier. Poulard responded, smiling and twice making hand gestures to people who acknowledged him. Siemen seemed oblivious of the attention.

Claudine hadn't expected anything resembling a social situation and hardly thought the meal qualified as one, but it was at least an opportunity to soften the edges of a strictly professional relationship. Poulard created it. He began, perhaps obviously, talking of the personal benefits from his Europol posting. He was happy to leave his stalemated career in Paris, after the divorce from his wife, surrounded by mutual friends having to choose sides. It was better for him to start again, in everything. Eliane had the boy and the Europol salary and allowances would help with the alimony, which was too high considering her independent income as an advocate. When he got settled in Holland, he might appeal: get a better lawyer than he had for the divorce, whom Eliane, representing herself, had chopped up in little pieces. Siemen thought the true victims of divorce were children. He had five and a happy marriage. They liked The Hague — they'd already bought a boat to sail on the Vijver lake — but wanted German education for the children. They had left their eldest two sons at boarding school in Munich. The others would go there when they were old enough. It would be a sacrifice. He and Greta had never intended sending them away: he'd even thought of rejecting the Europol job because of it.

Claudine knew she had to contribute but was reluctant. There seemed to be so little to offer, apart from Warwick, and she certainly didn't intend to talk about him. Poulard recognized the name of her mother's restaurant in Lyon, claiming to have had the best pigeon he'd ever eaten in his life there, and because it was something with which two policemen could associate she talked of her English father's career at Interpol, although not of the prematurely enforced, pastis-soaked retirement. That prompted from Poulard the inevitable question about encouraging her into criminal investigation, which she dismissed as shortly as she had to Henri Sanglier.

'Forensic psychology is surely an odd specialization, particularly for a woman?' pressed Poulard.

'What's gender got to do with it?'

There was the suggestion of a smirk, which she guessed the beginning of an open reference to sex, but then Poulard's face straightened. 'Nothing, of course. I've never known a woman practicing it before, that's all.'

'A friend of my father's at the British Home Office mentioned it as an emerging science, a year before I graduated from the Sorbonne. It coincided with my tutor discussing specialization with me.'

'So your father was an influence?' said Siemen.

Never, about anything, thought Claudine. 'He's been dead for ten years.' It was psychologically predictable — because she was a woman — that they would press her for more than they had volunteered but she wanted it to stop.

'After Paris I find the social scene here non-existent,' complained Poulard. 'Don't you find the same thing, after London . . .' there was the staged pause '. . . particularly someone as attractive as you?'

Claudine stretched the disconcerting silence, holding Poulard's eyes. Then she said: 'My husband died suddenly, five months ago. I have no interest in any social scene. I have no interest in anything except the job I'm here to perform.'

Poulard flushed, discomfited, and Claudine thought she'd probably chipped away a little of the working foundation they'd been establishing. But it ended the private lives discussion so it was a worthwhile loss.

All three were impressed when they got back to their incident room to find that Yvette Fey had organized the duplication of all the files on the French and English killings and had been assured the remainder would be copied before the end of the day. What was already available was waiting for them in three neat stacks. The girl had already begun fixing photographs in their dated order on exhibit boards.

Volker had rearranged the computer station set-up, removing the screens separating the terminals to bring them much closer together, virtually side by side and in a half-circle around him. It reminded Claudine of a treat to which her parents had taken her on her eleventh birthday where a pianist had produced recognizable tunes by playing three pianos at the same time. All Volker's screens were on but full of ASCII symbols, numerals and codes meaningless to everyone except him. The man's lips were moving, although he wasn't making any sound, as he swivelled from display to display.

Each collected their individual pile. Poulard and Siemen went into their offices. Claudine carried hers to the small table at which they had sat that morning.

Very shortly after she began reading Claudine turned to the boards at which Yvette was working, confirming an impression although she didn't ask the girl outright, deciding to wait until she'd read everything, even the files so far unavailable. Even before they arrived, she didn't have any doubt. She'd prepared a lined pad and pencils to make notes but had barely filled one side of paper by the time she completed what files she had, late into the afternoon. Her finishing coincided with the delivery of the remainder.

'Any thoughts?' demanded Poulard, emerging from his room.

'None that's going to lead to a Sherlock Holmes solution at the moment. What about you?'

Poulard shook his head. 'Blank walls.'

Claudine stretched the cramp from her shoulders, indicating the newly arrived folders. 'I'm going to finish those off tonight in my own office. Maybe there'll be something more there.'

'Should their being taken from the room by any one of you three be logged?' asked the dutifully efficient Yvette.

'Yes,' said Siemen, from his office door. 'And signed for.'

His back to Siemen, Poulard made a grimace towards Claudine. She gave no response. When she signed the log Claudine saw hers was the first withdrawal entry and wondered if it would be an omen. She couldn't imagine what, exactly, it might be.

Claudine had worked for an hour, the light already on because of the encroaching darkness outside, when there was a knock on her door, immediately followed by the entry of Scott Burrows.

'Midnight oil time?' he said, advancing into the room. His tie was loosened and his overstrained collar undone, which it often was. Perfumed cigar smoke trailed behind him.

'Good to have something to work on at last,' said Claudine, pushing herself back in her chair.

He slumped, uninvited, in the facing easy chair. It wasn't really big enough for the man. 'How's it going?'

'Too soon to say.' She tapped the folders spread over her desk. 'I haven't finished reading the case notes yet.'

'Mind if I take a look?'

Shit, thought Claudine. 'We've established an authorizing system. Stuff has to be officially logged in and out.'

Burrows made the pretence of pulling back

in his chair, as if he'd been slapped. He was too fat for it to work. 'Hey, remember me? Scott Burrows, FBI. Done a lot of work on criminal profiling.'

Claudine shrugged, conveying an unfelt apology. 'It's my assignment.'

'You think I'm trying to steal your glory?'

'There isn't any glory to steal. And might not be.' There was no official reason why he couldn't see them, but Claudine guessed Sanglier, along with every other Europol psychologist, would hear of her sharing files and of Burrows' opinion within fifteen minutes of her making them available to the American. And if there was any glory — the justification for her new life — she didn't intend sharing it with anyone.

'I'm only offering to help. I've got the experience, you know. That's why I'm seconded here. I'd like to show the experiment was worthwhile, beyond those goddamned seminars.'

'I know. And I appreciate it. But this isn't my first case, either. And it wouldn't be right if I fouled up and you were associated with it, out of an act of kindness.' Burrows' secondment was a political one and she'd been warned about political sensitivity, although not in this precise context. Perhaps she should mention it to Sanglier. But if she did he might think it a good idea and she didn't want the opinions she offered to appear to be shared any more than the official recognition of her ability.

His face had stiffened. 'In other words, fuck off.'

Claudine had never been sure whether his swearing was a natural part of his persona or an affectation for a tough guy image. He'd done it from the beginning. The Austrian psychologist, Otto Lang, thought it was directed personally towards her and indicated latent misogyny. It didn't offend her, as Poulard's attitude had offended her. She didn't often utter obscenities aloud herself — it would have indicated lack of control — but often thought them when venting an opinion or confronting hard-headed stupidity.

She had to stop holding back, so she made the effort. 'I want my chance, Scott. By myself. If I don't make it, then someone else will have to be brought in.'

He nodded slowly. 'There's a difference, I guess, between someone like myself who originally came into the business as a trained FBI agent and someone like you, who came in with all the degrees and qualifications. I'm a team player.'

The fact that Burrows was a layman who had invented a science now practised by professionals was another familiar gambit. It had endeared him to traditional detectives whom she'd seen him address. She'd analysed it as a latent inferiority complex, like his relying on the successful profiles of the past instead of risking mistakes by thinking differently about profile indicators in the present or the future. 'I'm a team player, too. The team's been selected and I'm working with it.'

'I've encountered this sort of attitude from professionals before.'

'For Christ's sake, Scott, I haven't got an attitude!' she erupted in final exasperation. 'I've got a new career that I want to succeed in, on my own merits!'

'Sure.' He had difficulty getting up from the chair. Momentarily he stood in front of it. 'If you change your mind. Need a sounding board.'

'I'll remember. I really will.' There seemed an awful lot to remember and consider. And she hadn't properly started on the job she was supposed to be doing. It was a fucking minefield.

She read steadily for another hour before a second interruption. René Poulard came confidently into the room, smiling, and said: 'I'm calling it a night.'

'Any thoughts so far?' invited Claudine, concealing her annoyance at the distraction.

'Not from the files,' he said pointedly.

Surely the arrogant bastard wasn't going to try another sexual approach! 'What, then?'

'Thought it was important you and I sorted out any personal problems.'

'I wasn't aware there were any.'

'I don't want there to be. That's why I'm here. No hard feelings about what happened before?'

'Not on my part.'

'I didn't mean to offend you.'

'It's forgotten.'

'A new start then?' The smile widened.

'A new *professional* start.'

'I wasn't suggesting anything else.' Poulard offered his hand and Claudine took it, embarrassed at the theatricality. Poulard added: 'Which doesn't mean we couldn't have a drink if you felt like it.'

Persistent shit, Claudine thought. She tapped the dossiers and said: 'Too much to do.'

'Another time.'

'Professional relationship,' she reminded him.

Thirty minutes later Sanglier listened to Poulard's account of the working arrangements they had decided upon and said: 'So everything's amicable?'

'She *is* aloof,' volunteered the detective. 'I've got a feeling about her.'

'What sort of feeling?'

'That she might like women more than men.'

Momentarily Sanglier was speechless, the possibilities jostling in upon him. 'What makes you say that?'

'Instinct.'

'I wouldn't want anything like that to inter-
fere with what you're supposed to be doing.
Watch out for it. Let me know.'

'I will,' Poulard assured him.

Chapter Eight

'Inadequate, to the point of being useless, in every single case,' insisted Claudine.

'I thought it was a comprehensive German summary,' said Siemen defensively.

'I'm not making a country-by-country criticism,' said Claudine. 'A summary, comprehensive or not, is no good to us. We've got to find the linking factor or factors. That's not possible from anything we've got so far, from any country . . .' She paused. 'What we've got here is nothing more — in some cases, I'd guess, a carbon copy — of what has gone to Interpol: a précis for their record systems.'

The discussion had gone on for half an hour around the small table, initiated by Claudine who that second morning had arrived before everyone else specifically to check further the exhibits so far mounted by Yvette. Claudine had expected the two men to be as concerned as she was, although she didn't think either had completed the case files overnight, as she had. They didn't seem to be.

'Inadequate for you? Or us?' asked Poulard.

'Both,' said Claudine. 'And for the reason I've already given. We can't divide our roles until we know which direction we're going in.'

Poulard flashed another open smile when Yvette arrived with coffee and Claudine guessed from the previous day's conversation the man had undergone the sculpted dental work before his expensive marriage break-up. And built up his wardrobe, too. Today's outfit was a mohair check jacket with knife-edged black slacks and Gucci loafers. Idly she wondered if the Frenchman tinted his tightly waved hair: there wasn't a hint of grey in the uniform brownness.

'You really think it's that bad?' questioned Poulard.

'Don't you?'

'I've got a lot of questions,' conceded the Frenchman.

'Look!' urged Claudine, stretching out her arm towards the display boards. 'Count the gaps in the photographic selection alone. Each is an allowance for a photograph that should be there, according to the supplied exhibit list. But isn't.'

'And Commissioner Sanglier told us yesterday that every force had been asked to supply everything they'd assembled,' Siemen said.

'Obstructed before we start?' suggested Poulard.

Even now the man didn't appear as irritated as Claudine would have expected. 'Disregarded, certainly.'

'The commissioner should protest,' declared Siemen at once.

'I'd like to complete what's left over from last night before we make the formal complaint,' said Poulard.

Shuffling responsibility like card sharps, thought Claudine. 'Something that should be possible before the end of the day.'

'It could still take time for every force to comply,' Siemen said.

'Why should it?' demanded Claudine. 'We want it all. Which means exhibit officers simply have to copy everything and ship it to us. We were given more than a dozen summaries, which Yvette got copied in one day.'

The girl, still working at the exhibits, briefly turned and smiled at the praise. Today's blouse and skirt weren't as tight as the dress she'd worn the previous day.

'I *do* want to finish what we've already got,' said Poulard, talking directly to Siemen. Briefly he switched to Claudine. 'Which, of course, I will complete today.' Returning to the German he went on: 'But I don't think we should waste time hanging around to be inundated by irrelevant material. We've all agreed speed is absolutely essential. I think we should start work at once.'

Claudine fought back the urgency to speak, looking towards the German as well.

'Start how?' Siemen frowned.

'I was trained to investigate crime by starting at the beginning.'

'Go to each murder scene?'

'Haven't you ever got your lead from something not in an official report: from a remark or an impression? A detective's intuition? I know I have. We'll stand more chance of getting what we want from talking to colleagues and re-interviewing people on the spot than ploughing through millions of words.'

Claudine didn't think she would be able to hold back much longer.

'Starting in France?' nodded Siemen, more in agreement than questioningly.

'That's where it began,' Poulard said. He came back at last to Claudine. 'How would you feel about that?'

She had to avoid being confrontational, Claudine told herself. Or to stretch longer than necessary the objections almost too obvious to need pointing out. 'Where, exactly, were the murder scenes in France? Or anywhere else? Do you intend going to every city or place where a body part was found? That would take for ever.'

There was no facial reaction from the Frenchman, which Claudine thought was hopeful. Poulard said: 'There is a Europol aircraft available. We would not be restricted by civil airlines. Nor need, necessarily, to go to every location. The French killings, for instance, are being coordinated in Paris.'

Which defeated the whole object of going in the first place, mentally screamed Claudine. 'All the scenes were public places. Which have been re-opened. Whatever might have been overlooked or unrealized at the time will have gone by now. All we would be doing is talking to the people who wrote the reports we're asking to be sent to us.'

'We could re-interview anyone we considered a major witness,' Siemen suggested.

'The only witnesses, in every case, were terrified people who found pieces of bodies and made panicked calls to police.' An isolated fact that had been included in the French account occurred to her. 'The Tolbiac cleaner admitted he'd made up his story of the black-caped phantom figure. By now, without knowing it or intending to mislead, half the witnesses who aren't still in shock will have mentally embellished what happened. Think about it. For every one it's the biggest event of their lives.'

'You're telling us we would be wasting our time,' Siemen said.

'I'm setting out the drawbacks I would personally encounter as part of this team,' Claudine said smoothly. 'Scenes of crimes are vital to me. I get the most important guides to a profile more quickly from them than in any other way. But by being there as quickly as possible after the crime has been committed. I'd gain nothing, this late.'

'So you're refusing to come?' said Poulard.

That question was as ill-phrased as some that Sanglier had posed. 'I'm saying it wouldn't help me in any way: that it would be a waste of my professional time, which would be more usefully spent here.'

'I can see your point.' Siemen was wavering.

'This, surely, is how we are going to have to divide our responsibilities in a lot of things.' Needing to argue her case like this was another fundamental change, Claudine accepted.

'Obviously,' agreed Siemen.

'I've case files to read,' said Poulard abruptly, out-argued again.

Both men were still doing that at midday and Claudine was glad she could eat alone. When she resumed Siemen said: 'You're right. They're quite inadequate.'

Sanglier agreed immediately to see them and just as quickly agreed to protest to every force, both directly and to the individual Europol commissioners. There was a hint of irritation when Poulard began to outline, at too great length, the disagreement about personally visiting the murder scenes, which Sanglier curtly cut off by saying he considered that was an operational decision that could be resolved at their level. Sanglier's attitude answered Claudine's uncertainty about raising with the man the previous night's approach from Scott Burrows. By the end of the day copies of each of Sanglier's cables, as well as his internal memoranda to individual commissioners, arrived at the incident room.

'For someone concerned with the politics of

everything that's pretty impolitic language,' said Poulard, surprised at the strength of Sanglier's complaints.

'We've got a commissioner squarely behind us,' said Siemen.

'It certainly looks like it,' agreed Claudine.

Sanglier was genuinely annoyed at what he considered a puerile attempt by national forces to undermine Europol, particularly as it hadn't been isolated but was evident in every case. He was most forceful of all in his complaints to France, knowing the reaction his name would generate, and in addition to all the memoranda he demanded Franz Sobell convene a full meeting of commissioners. It was a situation that perfectly — and very publicly — illustrated the proper control he was maintaining over the operation.

The most essential part of his control — again quite properly — was reviewing the tapes of the incident room discussions. From which, he conceded, Claudine Carter emerged as a formidable, mentally agile woman. Poulard had been an idiot persisting in his efforts to gain control of the group and deserved to be talked down, as he had been. But Sanglier discerned the effort Claudine was making to create an amicable working relationship. She'd made a convincing, justifiable argument against their visiting the scenes of the crimes and he remained uncertain of the benefits —

professional as well as personal — of the idea, which was why he'd insisted the decision should be theirs, until he was better able to assess advantage against disadvantage of being involved. Of all he'd heard so far Sanglier was most intrigued by the woman's vehemently stated determination not to fail, which fitted like a matching piece of a jigsaw with what Scott Burrows had recounted over lunch that day about Claudine's refusal of any help from the American. Sanglier wished he had more than Burrows' account of the meeting: refusing the advice of such an internationally recognized expert in her art could be a major indictment in any disciplinary hearing that might be orchestrated.

Sanglier's office door was unlocked that night so he didn't have to get up to admit René Poulard but he did pour the whisky. Poulard, ingratiatingly, at once thanked Sanglier for the forcefulness of his protests, adding that he hoped national opposition wouldn't be a continuing interference. Sanglier promised that if what he'd already done didn't eradicate the problem he'd insist the current Commission chairman challenge the obstruction at the next meeting of the EU Justice Ministers, which he'd already decided to demand anyway, anxious as he was to get his already well known name circulating in political circles.

The evidence inadequacy was an obvious delay but otherwise Poulard thought they had

131

begun well. There'd been no opportunity yet to judge Kurt Volker's ability but Yvette Fey had already proved herself an excellent administrative assistant. His initial impression of Bruno Siemen had been confirmed: in every discussion so far the man had shown himself to be a sound, practical policeman. He was afraid Claudine Carter might try to exceed her authority within their group but he did not see that as a problem. He admired the way she was working, so soon after the personal tragedy of losing her husband.

Suicide, remembered Sanglier, from Claudine's personnel file. There'd been no discussion on any tape he'd heard. 'She mentioned it?'

'At lunch. Said he had died suddenly only five months ago.'

'How?'

'She didn't say. An accident, I presumed.'

It was understandable she wouldn't volunteer the circumstances. Could there be any connection between the suicide and the visit of Peter Toomey? The British commissioner would be at the special meeting he'd convened, reflected Sanglier. It might be an opportunity to keep in mind. 'Any indication of the personal preferences you believe she has?'

'Not yet.'

'This obstruction nonsense will be sorted out.'

'I still think we should go to where the murders occurred,' said Poulard.

'I thought we discussed that earlier,' said Sanglier, refusing to make the decision for the man.

'Siemen agrees with me.'

'It's for you to decide.'

'We'll go.'

Scott Burrows fully accepted the irony of his being in The Hague as a result of his own profile, although he didn't use the word. He thought of it as a bastard. He felt the Bureau had over-reacted to the danger — they could have surely looked after one of their own, him more than most — but there was fuck all he could do about it. Except wait. Which was the pisser. He'd never been so bored in his life, stuck in a godforsaken country among more squabbling, back-biting assholes than you could shake a stick at. It would have been all right if he could have become officially involved in the serial killings investigation. He could understand the woman, though, not wanting to share with anyone else. He'd have felt the same way himself, at her age. All he felt now was regret: regret at her refusal and at having to wait for the word from Washington DC that was taking for ever to arrive. That was the real pisser. The waiting.

Chapter Nine

Although Claudine was not completely alone — Yvette Fey was annotating the filing cabinets on a country-by-country basis in readiness for the expected murder dossiers and Kurt Volker was creating individual programs for each victim — there was the impression of having the incident room to herself and she welcomed it. She supposed it had been a reasonably good beginning, with no unpredictable disputes, but she still didn't enjoy being part of a committee, with the constant need to consider everything she said and did from the viewpoint of others. That wasn't Claudine's way. She'd adjust, because she had no alternative, but she intended to take every advantage of times like these, when she could operate entirely by herself without the encumbrance of having to persuade others to her way of thinking if she disagreed with theirs.

So what was her way of thinking?

Despite the obstruction of inadequate case notes there were some conclusions she could reach. With the exception of the two white girls in Amsterdam and Brussels — and the girl, believed to be Turkish, in Cologne — all the victims were Asian. So Burrows' racism theory had some validity, obvious though it might be. The killing of the Turkish girl fitted, too. So, letting the theory run, did the absence of identification, in every instance. It was impossible for that many people to die, in such an appalling way and surrounded by such hysterical publicity, without the family of at least one claiming the dismembered body — unless those families had entered the countries illegally and faced prosecution and deportation if they came forward. Age was another common denominator: maybe, even, the strongest linking factor, negative though it might be at the moment. Because there was no identity there was no specific age known for any of the victims but all were young, medically estimated between fifteen and twenty-two.

Picking up the magnifying glass she'd brought from her own office Claudine rose from the small table, going for the first time to Yvette's carefully created photographic sequences, further impressions at once jostling for attention in her mind. Yvette had not just maintained them in dated sequence but had logically devoted individual boards to the remains of each body. Although there were the omissions Claudine had isolated the previous day there were sufficient from each selection to make some preliminary comparisons, which were intriguing both for the similarities in some cases and for the differences in others.

It was most obvious in the genital disfigurement. Although the autopsy reports were inadequate in every case, it appeared that a knife had been inserted into the pubis of the two girls in France, the teenager in London and the Chinese girl in Vienna and drawn upwards, grotesquely elongating their vaginas. Two parallel slash marks had been made on either side of the main wound. As well as having his penis severed, the Asian boy in France had been anally split in the same way, again with parallel cuts on either side. The wounds on all four were completely clean and visible in obscene detail: there was a pathologist's note on the French killings insisting that it was the condition in which the torsos had been found at the scene, not cleaning that had been carried out by the surgeons prior to examination. The Viennese pathologist had recorded that the body of the Chinese girl had contained less than one pint of blood. The entire pubis of the girl in Cologne had been removed and the scene-of-discovery pictures showed the torso lying in so much blood that it was only after the post mortem cleaning in this case that it was possible to understand how she had been virtually disembowelled. The pubic areas of the white girls in Amsterdam and Brussels were both slashed by a series of criss-cross cuts and again there had been heavy blood loss, although in neither case had an attempt been made to disfigure the vagina. Only in these two cases had the breasts been removed, causing further heavy bleeding.

Claudine went carefully but quickly over each board, examining the coupled hands wired into their cupped, praying position, taking far more time on her second examination. The hands of the washed-clean girls and the boy were in every instance held by wire looped three times round the wrist and finally secured by the two ends bent to form opposing hooks. There was only a single strand around the wrists of the Turkish girl and the wire was twisted secure, although it had failed to keep the two palms together. The wire binding on the girls in Brussels and Amsterdam was twisted closed, too, but in both cases was around the middle fingers of the hands, not around the wrists. And every fingertip had been cut away.

'Is the display not done correctly?'

Claudine turned at Yvette's question, her concentration broken. 'It's very well arranged. Made it easy for me to reach some early conclusions.'

'Only a total maniac could have done things like that to other human beings,' said Yvette.

Claudine was still surprised the girl could remain so controlled in front of such images. She suspected the remark was more what the girl imagined she was expected to say than genuine revulsion. She shook her head. 'Maniacs did not do any of this. All of these murders — these injuries — were done by sane, calculating people.'

'You can't be serious!'

'It might make finding them easier,' said Claudette hopefully. Why had it stopped, she wondered for the first time. She shouldn't overlook the interrupted regularity: nothing for more than a fortnight after a killing every week. She was standing by the first board, which showed photographs of the initial French murder, and bent close to it studying intently through the magnifying glass something she'd missed about the tethered hands. She examined the print of one of the recovered legs for confirmation and realized the task force needed another expert in their support group. She didn't see any need to discuss it with Poulard and Siemen: it was so obvious they should have decided upon it before. They'd gone for an indeterminate time and there was no reason to impose her own delay: she could tell them when they made contact, which they'd undertaken to do. She didn't think she had to clear it with Sanglier, either. It would be sufficient to send him a copy of the request, as a matter of courtesy.

She moved from the display boards at last, making her way towards Volker. She was aware of a photo image on the screen in front of the man as she approached, although she was not immediately able to distinguish what it was. She was almost behind the German before realizing it was a digitalized picture of a completely naked woman reclining on a bed, legs splayed to expose her genitalia. The list of sexual services and the prices were recited in English.

'What the hell are you doing?'

The unkempt German turned to her, smiling. 'It's an Amsterdam whores' directory, on the Internet. I looked yesterday at the photo exhibits you've just studied. And couldn't understand why the two white victims had their fingertips sliced off, unless it was to delay identification from after-death prints. Which would mean a police record. So I thought I'd run through the obvious possibilities.'

Claudine was impressed by the initiative. The same thought had occurred to her. 'And?'

The man shook his head. 'Could be I'm maligning the girls. Or if I'm not they didn't advertise. I guess the majority don't. But I've still got Brussels to go through.'

'How did you know how to find out if they advertised at all?' frowned Claudine.

Volker waved towards his inner office. She saw he'd had floor-to-ceiling racks moved in. Telephone book sized loose leafed binders were already neatly arranged. 'There's over a million entry codes and passwords there, hard copy backup . . .' He patted the side of the screen in front of him, like a proud owner acknowledging a favourite pet. 'I've downloaded my disk copies, too. Indexed, of course . . .' He scrolled to the next advertisement. It was of two black girls offering lesbian shows.

'I'm glad I'm forewarned for when the accounts department query our computer charges for accessing sex lines.'

'It won't show as that,' said Volker easily. 'I've hacked into Amsterdam police central computer: I've lodged a parasite program there they don't know about, with my own access code. I'm in every national police computer in Europe. And Interpol. Amsterdam will get charged for this. And it's not just the cost. I can go in and out whenever I want. Entering a target system piggy-back avoids leaving a computer "fingerprint" traceable back to us: some systems have that as part of their security protection against unauthorized access.'

Claudine laughed openly. 'I thought we were supposed to be upholding the law!'

'We're all on the same side,' said Volker, unabashed. 'This way is quicker than going through the bureaucracy of official requests and delivery. If we get anything at all, that is: I was appointed when Europol was just a distribution centre.' He jerked his hand to where her files lay at the other end of the room. 'You were lucky to get those.'

'You hear us complaining yesterday that material has been withheld?'

'I was in and out all the time, collecting my stuff,' reminded the plump man. 'But I heard enough to understand you'd encountered the usual problem.'

'Which you've found your own way of getting around.'

'It wouldn't have been possible to work if I hadn't.'

'What could you get me from national forces about these murders?'

'Everything that's on their database,' promised Volker at once. 'Do you want me to?'

Claudine paused. 'Not yet. Let's stay with the official system for the moment. But it will be a useful double-check.' She was, she accepted, condoning an illegality. But as the man said, they were all on the same side, even if other forces didn't think so. There was even a certain natural justice in the other forces paying for their usage time. She didn't have any moral difficulty with it. She wondered if Poulard or Siemen would.

Volker reached the end of his prostitute bulletin board. He said: 'I don't think this is going to work.'

'There's something else I'd like you to do for me,' said Claudine. 'I want to establish our initial database from a comparison program listing the similarities and dissimilarities between each killing and dismemberment . . .' She hesitated, as the idea came to her. 'Could you access newspaper libraries to get me printouts of the coverage the French murders got in the other countries where there have been

141

subsequent killings?'

'Easily.'

The first began to arrive within an hour, from Belgium, and visually confirmed what she suspected. So did other reports that arrived during the course of the day, although she asked Volker to set up another positive comparison program. One of the English reports was from the *Daily Telegraph*. On the same condensed page was a three-paragraph story reporting that the City of London regulatory body had asked the Serious Fraud Office to investigate possible financial irregularities involving a well-known City entrepreneur. Paul Bickerstone was not identified by name but Claudine didn't have any doubt he was the man to whom the story referred.

That night her mother telephoned from Lyon.

Sanglier's protests were unarguable and he took them to the limit of his exaggerated outrage, knowing everything he said was being officially noted for the record that would portray him exactly as he wanted to present himself for his intended future career. He used words like 'monstrous' and 'ridiculous' and said that unless they complained as forcefully as he was demanding Europol would remain a denigrated and ignored organization — with them denigrated and ignored with it — and never achieve the function for which it had been designed. He directed every point in turn towards the individual commissioners whose countries had failed to provide the files and said: 'They treated us like fools. Which I personally will not accept. Unless the attitude is rectified — and not repeated — I am seriously considering resigning. And in as public a manner as possible.'

There was a discernible stir around the conference room. Sanglier was virtually the only person to have talked during the thirty minutes the meeting had been in progress.

'I don't think we should over-stress what happened,' ventured David Winslow. 'I would —'

Sanglier cut him off. 'How it is possible to *over*-stress it after agreeing how vitally important this entire investigation is for Europol!'

'Have you personally examined every dossier?' demanded Jan Villiers, towards whom as commissioner for Belgium, one of the culprit countries, Sanglier had directed some of his criticism.

Sanglier had anticipated the question. 'All of those from France, my own country. And you will see how I have reacted to that from your copies of my messages to every guilty force. I have also read those from Belgium and Holland. For the remainder I have taken the word of the coordinating task force. Which I do not doubt.'

'I am not convinced it needs to be specifically raised at the next meeting of European Justice Ministers,' said Franz Sobell, reluctant to be the man who would have to do it.

'It's imperative the correction comes from that level,' insisted Sanglier. 'Anything less and some forces will continue to disregard us.'

'Are you really serious about resigning?' asked Holland's Hans Maes, aware that because of his name Sanglier had the highest profile of any commissioner.

'Totally. I've no intention of remaining part of a useless organization,' declared Sanglier truthfully.

'Such a public demonstration would weaken Europol in the public estimation,' said Luxembourg's Paul Merot.

'And that would put it on a par with how it's clearly regarded by every police body in Europe,' said Sanglier. 'Which is what I am trying to correct — against what appears to be concerted opposition from every other representative on this Commission.'

'I don't think there are any grounds for saying that,' protested Sobell weakly. 'Of course it's a situation that has to be corrected. The discussion is surely about how that's to be achieved.'

'My proposal will properly establish us. Anything less will weaken us,' insisted Sanglier. 'I also propose, as an indication of the commitment to this organization, that the vote upon it is officially recorded.'

It was unanimous.

It was the custom for all the commissioners to have pre-luncheon drinks in their private cocktail bar after their regular meetings. Sanglier was alone when David Winslow approached him.

'You seemed to feel very strongly about how we were treated,' said Winslow.

'And embarrassed, that my own country was one of the guilty ones.'

'I'm going to warn London what's to happen at the Council of Ministers' meeting: let them know the depth of our anger.'

'I've decided to appoint Dr Carter to the task force,' announced Sanglier.

There was an uncertain hesitation before the British commissioner shrugged. 'I'll advise London of that, too.'

'I've studied her file, obviously,' said Sanglier. 'I'm curious about her husband's death.'

'As I told you before, acute depression, from what I gather. A tragedy.'

'I wouldn't like anything emerging to be an added difficulty.'

'Quite,' agreed Winslow at once. From the frown it was obvious the man was trying to work out if there could be any personal difficulty for him.

'According to the log someone came to see her a few weeks ago. A man named Toomey. From your Home Office.'

'Are you asking me to make an official inquiry?'

'Not an official inquiry,' Sanglier said. 'I just want to be sure nothing could arise to cause any more problems.'

'I understand,' said Winslow.

'You sure about this?' demanded Joe Hardy.

'Never been surer of anything in my life,' said Burrows. 'They over-reacted. You know that.' He nodded acceptance of another Scotch.

'It was your profile.' Hardy ordered another whisky for himself, too, feeling sorry for the other American. As the FBI station chief in Holland he had an official position, a function and work to do, although he found it as dull as hell. In limbo, as Scott was, it had to be even worse.

'I'm not changing my mind on that. Just arguing their reaction to it.'

'They don't want to take any chances with you. Don't want to lose you.'

'They've already lost me, putting me here. You know who I feel sorry for now?' demanded Burrows. 'I know most of them are scum, guys cutting deals for themselves to escape the twenty years to life that the people they're giving evidence against are going to get, but I feel sorry for all those poor bastards in the Witnesses' Protection Program. I know now just what it's like. And you know what

146

it's like. It's worse than twenty years to life.'

Hardy looked down at the cable Burrows wanted him to send. 'They'll refuse, you know.'

'I gotta try. Miriam's going crazier than I am.'

'She hasn't said anything to Ann.' Hardy and his wife had become friends since the Burrows' posting.

'She doesn't want to sound disloyal, even to buddies.'

'I'll get it off tonight,' promised Hardy. He hesitated, looking around the embassy mess. 'Thought there might have been something for you at Europol with all these killings.'

'So did I,' said Burrows.

Chapter Ten

It was obviously unthinkable that Claudine would not go and the weekend provided the opportunity, but even then she minimized the interruption as much as she could, using Europol's travel department to arrange her flight from Holland late on the Saturday afternoon — giving her most of the day in the incident room — with a Sunday night return on a Paris-routed connection.

Claudine went directly by taxi from the airport to the rue Grenette and it was only when she automatically looked up to the silhouetted outline on the Fourvière heights that she remembered the praying hands of the first unknown victim had been found in the cathedral and wondered if Poulard and Siemen had been to Lyon. Or even intended to.

Claudine was irritated there had been no contact, even after she'd left messages at the Paris hotel in which they'd based themselves. She'd actually delayed offering her initial profile until she'd discussed it with the two detectives. If she didn't hear by Monday afternoon she'd approach Sanglier alone. There was no reason why she shouldn't already have done so, apart from the need —

even more irritating — to appear part of a team. So much for empty gestures.

Monique Carter was exactly where Claudine had known she would be, like a general commanding a battlefield from its best vantage point just inside the white-curtained inner doors to the restaurant, between the till and the zinc-topped bar, with every table in the restaurant in view. It was from here, too, that she personally welcomed every customer and she turned expectantly at the precise moment of Claudine's entry.

The smile was genuine but quick, like Claudine's in return. Quick, too, were the cheek-to-cheek kisses. Neither woman had ever had the need or the inclination for effusive public displays of affection.

'It wasn't necessary for you to come,' said Monique at once.

'Of course it was.' The way her mother was dressed was as predictable as where she would be standing, the long-skirted black linen uniform of the restaurant supremo. It had always drained the colour from her face, to which she'd never as long as Claudine could remember added make-up, and from which her hair was strained back in the style in which she'd always worn it, netted in a bun. There'd never been any surplus weight — how could someone who each day, before dawn, shopped at the markets for meat and fish and vegetables and remained on her feet for fifteen hours

149

afterwards ever be anything but thin? — and physically her mother seemed the same as she always had been. It would have been fatuous to comment about how she looked.

'It's not a drama.'

'I didn't say it was: don't think it is.' How much psychological as well as medical treatment would her mother need?

'It's nothing.'

'It's not "nothing". Don't lie to yourself: don't lie one way or the other.'

'Am I being counselled professionally?' demanded her mother.

'Yes.' The worst thing imaginable would be for her mother to catch her out in any falsehood or exaggeration.

'Do I need it?'

'Probably. I don't properly know yet. Don't you think you do?'

'Of course not!'

'Good.'

'Have you eaten?' demanded her mother, impatient and professional in her own right.

'Later, maybe. Some soup, when it gets quieter.' Every table was occupied: with so much noise Claudine wondered how her mother had been aware of her entry.

Monique turned away, first to check a bill, then to bid goodnight to the customers who'd incurred it. Several more bills and customers followed in quick succession. Claudine remembered the times — too many times —

she'd sat quietly against the bar, even as a child, witnessing the departure ritual which was as ingrained as the person-to-person greeting, always and unerringly by name to those her mother knew. Which, after twenty-five years, numbered hundreds if not thousands.

'It could take a long time,' warned Monique, returning to her.

'I can wait.' Which she had done, Claudine acknowledged: enjoying being on the stool at the end of the bar with her father until she'd grown old enough to understand and then, when she did understand, invoking every excuse until finally being openly rude and ignoring him, preferring as her special place the small office behind the till. There, unbothered by the clamour and distraction of the restaurant, every night she had completed her homework and read her books and daydreamed about a future that had fluctuated between becoming a model or a writer or even, several times during her classical romantic phase, courtesan to a rich and famous man: an exiled king, maybe. Whatever, she'd been certain the choice would be unusual because she'd always intended to be unusual.

'You could go upstairs.'

'I'll stay down here, at the bar.' Wasn't she dramatically admitting a wish to be as close as possible?

'Your choice.'

Which her mother had always encouraged her — forced her — to make once she'd entered puberty: sometimes, even, before. Always there, for advice and guidance, the one person upon whom she could depend, but her life was her choice, her decision. *Be your own person, right or wrong* had been the creed: the prodded-towards bridge to total self-dependence. She was becoming maudlin, with no reason, Claudine decided. The analysis had to be of her mother, not herself. The stool was at the very end of the bar, the closest possible to the familiar office and to her mother's permanent command post. Which was logically convenient: that it was the furthest from where her father had stationed himself, sandbagged behind the permanent yellow pastis like a scout for an opposing army, had no significance whatsoever. The barman, Pierre, was a permanent fixture, like most of the staff. Her hand was kissed instead of shaken, the palm pressed with an ancient gesture at innocent seductiveness, and they danced around a verbal maypole of flattery very different from that she'd found so annoying in Holland. The old man waited although knowing what she would order and brought the Perrier when she asked for it. For more than an hour — over two more protracted Perriers — she watched her mother, looking for signs and finding none. The greetings and farewells were the same, the abrupt kitchen inspections as well timed, the

152

paused and offered complimentary *digestifs* as frequent.

It was almost midnight before the customer-vacated patron's table, just inside the entrance but to the left and still with a commanding position of the room, began to be specially laid. Claudine waited for her mother's invitation to join her, as she always waited.

'The oysters are very good. And the skate,' suggested the older woman.

'Just soup,' repeated Claudine.

'You should eat more.'

'I'm not hungry. Maybe tomorrow.' Her mother was avoiding the purpose of the visit. And she was contributing to the charade, refusing to eat. But she genuinely wasn't hungry. Determinedly she said: 'So tell me about it.'

Monique watered the burgundy that had been automatically put on to the table, not offering the bottle to Claudine, who poured water for herself. Shrugging, Monique said: 'There is very little to tell. There was a lump. A biopsy. The diagnosis was malignant.'

'When did you first notice it?'

Another shrug. 'Two months ago: six weeks maybe. I'm not sure.'

She would be, to the minute, Claudine knew. 'Why did you wait so long before telling me?'

'There was nothing to tell until the biopsy result.'

'When did you get that?'

'In the last week or so.'

Claudine was engulfed by an unprofessionally involved surge of pity, not at that moment at the enormity of what her mother was telling her but at the effort the woman was making to dismiss its importance. Claudine knew just how great that effort would be. She'd inherited everything from her mother — consciously modelled herself upon her — and knew how she felt about illness, how she felt about any frailty. Illogically — even stupidly — both regarded illness not as something that was usually unavoidable but as a preventable weakness. Claudine accepted that for someone of her training and experience it was an attitude about which she should be ashamed. She still couldn't prevent herself feeling that way. Most illogical and stupid of all for someone of her qualifications was that her first reaction, seeing Warwick's body dangling from the rope, had not been shock or grief — there hadn't even been the snatch of asthma — but simply irritation that he'd given way to weakness. It was arrogance, Claudine abruptly and for the first time realized: a patronizing and astonishing arrogance that while everyone else might fall victim to physical or mental illness she in some divine way was immune from succumbing to it. Confronted by the incongruous self-honesty — the acceptance that after all she had avoided the 'know thyself' dictum — Claudine forced another personal admission. The attitude wasn't an inheritance from her mother. The basic feeling, maybe. But not as far as she had taken it; perfected it. What her mother was showing now was something far more easily understandable. Her mother was frightened. 'You should have told me immediately you knew.'

'What could you have done?'

'Come sooner.'

'What for?'

'To talk, like we're talking now.' And for her mother to have got rid of all the 'Why me?' anger and fear and horror, at having something — something like a rat, which had always been Claudine's imagery — gnawing away at her body from the inside.

The arrival of Monique's oysters coincided with yet another shrug. 'You're here now.'

The dismissiveness had to go! 'Just one? Or both?'

Her mother lowered her head towards her right breast, as if looking at something that was not a part of her, which perhaps now was how she regarded it. 'They say it's possible these days just to take out the growth itself but at my age what's the point? I've said they might as well take the whole thing off.'

Claudine recognized the lie, her mother's effort to prepare her. 'What about the lymph glands?'

'They might take something away, as a precaution.'

'And the other side?' pressed Claudine.

'There's something on the X-ray they want to check, while I am in hospital.'

'When's that going to be?'

'Next week. I didn't want you to call and find where I was without my having told you.'

Independence to the point of hurtfulness, thought Claudine: how much had her unthinking independence — not just her dedication to work — hurt Warwick? She gestured around the near empty room. 'What's going to happen here?'

'Gérard,' said the older woman simply.

As if responding to a summons, Gérard Lanvin emerged from the kitchen immediately behind the waiter carrying skate for her mother and the clear fish soup for Claudine. He still wore his chef's whites but no hat. Lanvin had been her mother's lover long before her father's death. Like a lot of other people, her father had known it and not objected to being cuckolded, which Claudine had added to all the other reasons for despising him. After his death Claudine had expected Lanvin and her mother to marry: certainly for the man to move into the apartment above the restaurant. But neither had happened. If anything they behaved with more decorum now than they had when her father had been alive. Lanvin maintained the attitude that night, restricting himself to a formal handshake without even polite cheek-kissing before sitting down between them. He added to Monique's glass before filling his own, gesturing with the bottle to Claudine, prepared for her refusal. He said: 'This is a bad business.'

As the next of kin — her mother's only family — she should see the surgeon to find out just how serious it actually was, Claudine realized. Which she couldn't if she returned to The Hague the following day. 'It's a successful operation in ninety per cent of cases,' she said, inventing the statistic.

The older woman looked at her quizzically. 'I'd like to believe that.'

Claudine couldn't remember lying to her mother before. 'It's a very common operation.'

Monique pushed her plate away, the food virtually untouched. 'Tell me about the new job.'

Claudine hesitated. Gérard's arrival prevented what she'd wanted to achieve. Now the need was to take their minds from the only thing about which it was at the moment possible for them to think. She told them of her involvement with the Europol investigation, and added that Henri Sanglier was the commissioner in charge.

'You — my daughter — are working with *him?*'

Although she'd known the legend Claudine had underestimated the inherited awe in which the name was held. 'Yes.'

'What sort of man is he?'

'Impressive. Very tall. Quite elegant.' What about the suspected uncertainty, at their first meeting? And a lot of the inexplicable conversation? It wasn't because of Lanvin's presence that Claudine held back from mentioning Sanglier's apparent awareness of her father: she knew her mother would not have been impressed even though the reference had come from Sanglier.

'The man himself came into the restaurant in Paris where I trained,' said Lanvin. 'I saw him. He was quite old, of course. A small man. I remember wondering how a small man could have been so brave . . .' Lanvin paused, clearly recounting one of the highlights of his life. 'He ate steak: told the patron that for three years during the war he'd never had a single piece of meat so he always ate it afterwards. I prepared the potatoes. Lyonnaise.'

'Can we tell people about what you're doing?' asked Monique eagerly.

'I don't think so,' said Claudine.

'Of course not,' agreed Lanvin, a man entrusted with a secret. He actually came closer across the table towards Claudine. 'The fish man knows the widow who found the hands here. There were occult symbols cut into the flesh. Witchcraft signs. The way they were held together and left in a cathedral was obviously a mockery of God.'

The elaboration of which she'd warned Poulard and Siemen, remembered Claudine, knowing there had been no symbols. 'We've only just begun the investigation.'

'So you shouldn't have come here,' suggested Monique.

'I intended going back tomorrow. But I don't think I will. I want to see the surgeon.'

'There's no point. You can't affect anything.'

'It's right that I should,' insisted Claudine.

'Because it's the thing to do!' challenged the older woman. Smiling, to take the sharpness from the remark, she continued: 'I'm having a mastectomy. It's one of the most common operations, successful in ninety per cent of cases.'

'We'll talk about it in the morning,' said Claudine.

'I must be going,' said Lanvin, taking his cue. To Monique he said: 'I'll do the markets in the morning.'

Monique did not argue. 'Yes,' she said simply.

Claudine had never known her mother allow somebody else to do that for her. It was a major surrender: an indication of giving up.

Claudine knew it was psychologically necessary, but she hated herself for forcing her mother to accept the facts: briefly hated, even, the expertise which told her she was doing the right thing.

It was ingrained in Monique to get up before

dawn and it was still only half light when Claudine heard her mother moving around, awake — possibly even dressed — but with nothing to do for hours. Claudine waited until she heard her mother go to the kitchen before she emerged from her room to find the older woman.

The balcony was only just big enough for them to sit outside with their coffee, but there was the view of the sun-silvered Rhône beneath the clifftop edifice and it would have been where Claudine wanted to sit if her mother hadn't led the way, unasked. Claudine looked at the cathedral professionally, realizing how carefully it had been chosen for the hideous demonstration over far more easily accessible but just as public places. The conclusion was obvious, although she hadn't included it in her profile. She made a mental note to check the accessibility of every other location, in every country, in which a body part had been found. It might prove nothing, but it could form an important part of Kurt Volker's comparison program.

Monique asked if Claudine was cold, in just a robe. Claudine said she wasn't. Monique said she wasn't either. Claudine topped up both their cups, agreeing that the balcony view had to be one of the best in Lyon. Monique said she wasn't attaching any hope to the rumour but Gérard had heard an unsuspected *Guide Michelin* inspector had eaten in the restaurant and thought there was the possibility of another rosette. Claudine agreed that would be wonderful, aching for the other woman to unlock the mental door behind which she was cowering.

'Maybe it was fortunate he came before Gérard started buying.'

Damn the restaurant, thought Claudine: she could use the remark to prompt, though. 'You know he can do that well enough.'

'Not as well as me.'

'Don't you intend doing it any more?'

Monique looked at her sharply. 'Of course I do.'

'Then there isn't a problem, is there?' The words, intentionally brutal, sounded uglier than she'd thought they would.

Monique didn't respond immediately. Then she blurted: 'I am not going to die. I'm going to lose my breasts but I'm not going to die.'

At last! thought Claudine, relieved. Even more brutally she said: 'Did the doctor tell you that? Or is that what you're telling yourself?'

It took the older woman a long time to answer. 'It would have been better if I'd gone sooner.'

It was coming now, as it had to. 'What else did he say?'

'That there was a chance: that it wasn't too late.'

'You have to lose both breasts? And some glands?'

'Yes.' All the time Monique was looking out over the city, not at her daughter. 'I don't want Gérard to see me afterwards.'

Claudine sought the best reply. 'Have you talked to Gérard about it?'

'Of course.'

'What did he say?'

'That it wouldn't make any difference. But he had to say that, didn't he?'

'No,' contradicted Claudine. Oddly, she had never wondered about sex between her mother and Gérard. He had to be the younger by at least ten years. And she was only sixty-five.

'Of course he did!'

'He could have said nothing. Don't you love him?' Claudine saw nothing odd in asking the question.

Monique gave one of the shrugs of the previous night but didn't speak.

'You're losing your breasts: the symbol of womanhood. You'd be very silly to lose Gérard as well.' Hypocrite, she thought: how easy it was — clinical it was — to lecture another woman, even her mother, on logic when logic had nothing to do with what they were talking about.

'I don't want to lose him,' Monique admitted.

'Then stop talking as if you're going to. Trust him.' Had she ever trusted Warwick, in anything? Hadn't that been why she'd always insisted on doing everything in their marriage: because she'd always thought she could make better judgements?

'He's asked me to marry him.'

'Are you going to?'

'It's pity.'

Claudine was about to speak but then stopped, changing her mind. 'When did he ask you, before or after the diagnosis?'

'When I found the lump.'

'That wasn't an answer. Before or after the diagnosis?'

'Before.'

'Would you have married him if it had been benign?'

'That's not relevant.'

'It's perfectly relevant.'

'I don't want him to feel that he's trapped.'

'Give him the chance to escape, then,' persisted Claudine remorselessly. 'Tell him you're not holding him to the proposal. Give *him* the choice. Don't make it yourself, as you've made every other choice in your life. Let someone else in, to help.'

'We'll see,' said Monique, seeking an escape.

Which Claudine allowed her. 'I'm glad I came.'

'But I don't want you to stay. I want you to go back, as you arranged. What you're doing — particularly considering the man you're doing it with — is far too important.'

'It would just be one more day. He'd understand.'

'He wouldn't, not set against what you're trying to do. You can't afford another twenty-four hours.'

The forensic pathologist would arrive the following day. And her profile — apart from the new speculation about the siting of the cathedral — was waiting to be delivered. 'I could come immediately after the operation.'

'Come next weekend, if you can. When you can take the time.'

On the flight back to The Hague that night Claudine decided her mother was as good a natural psychologist as she was a professional one: each had given the other the escape.

Peter Toomey hadn't expected the approach from the British commissioner at Europol. Nor welcomed it. He'd behaved quite properly, responding to David Winslow as he had, but he didn't want to fall foul of higher authority, although he wasn't sure how important anyone was considered in Europol, even at commissioner level. The inquiry into Claudine Carter had begun, after all, as a concern about possible embarrassment, not an investigation into her complicity. At least, at the very centre of things as he was, he'd know if Winslow took it any further. If he did, Toomey accepted he'd have no alternative but to comply.

Chapter Eleven

There were no messages on the answering machine and the in-tray was empty so she'd missed nothing by being away. But there was a downside to the relief. It meant there had still been no contact from either Poulard or Siemen. Nor a single response from any force from which the complete murder dossiers had been demanded. Claudine decided against calling the Paris hotel again but to hold to her already determined end-of-day timetable before presenting her preliminary profile. That would, at least, give a few hours for some of the local murder reports to arrive. If they didn't she'd complain to Sanglier in a separate memorandum.

She was at Kurt Volker's shoulder, directly dictating the brief addition that had occurred to her on the Lyon balcony, when a solemn-faced man entered the incident room and hesitated briefly to make a leadership choice from among the people there before saying to Yvette: 'You asked for a forensic pathologist. My name is Hugo Rosetti.'

As she crossed the room to introduce herself Claudine hoped his medical judgement was better: whom would he have selected if Poulard or Siemen had been in the incident room? Rosetti didn't appear disconcerted by his mistake. As she led him towards the photographic display Claudine explained the problem of inadequate evidence, making the autopsy reports virtually useless, and apologized in advance for asking him to give opinions based on other pathologists' photographs. 'I don't like trying to create profiles from other people's material, even when it's complete.'

'I'll try,' promised the man. 'And if I can't reach a conclusion I'll tell you. I won't mislead you by pretending.'

Claudine was impressed. She didn't list any of her own conclusions, wanting a totally independent and unprompted opinion from a qualified medical examiner. She was not uncertain of her assessments, just determined that they should be as complete — and therefore as useful — as possible. Unasked, she offered Rosetti the magnifying glass, at once moving away to give him room to work but at the same time studying the man as he went from frame to frame. He was quite small and slightly built with very black, tightly curled wiry hair and the olive complexion of a southern Italian. Coincidentally his sports jacket and dark grey trousers were very similar to those Poulard had worn the day before going to France. But the effect was totally different. Poulard made a conscious effort at urbane elegance to attract the attention he sought:

Rosetti's ambience was natural and unassuming, the attitude of a man who didn't have — or didn't want — to try to create any impression.

Rosetti worked with such absolute concentration that Claudine was sure the man was oblivious of her or anyone else in the room. Occasionally he grunted and several times uttered aloud words in Italian, in private discussion with himself. There were several sighs, either of impatience or frustration.

It was over an hour before he finally turned back to her, blinking as if he'd forgotten someone else was with him. He said: 'None of it will be scientifically justified, you understand?'

'I understand.'

Rosetti nodded. 'How do you want to work, back and forth exchanges or my impressions, all at once?'

So he'd worked tandem with a profiler before. 'Back and forth. It could give a direction neither of us have thought of following.' She had to lead, Claudine supposed. 'I think sex is a factor but I don't think this is sadism: no one got sexual satisfaction from this torture.'

'I agree,' said Rosetti at once. 'Is there any indication in any of the pathology reports you've got — inadequate though they might be — of rape?'

Claudine frowned, gesturing towards the display of genital mutilations. 'You surely couldn't prove rape?'

'I could,' said Rosetti simply. 'Perhaps not to the satisfaction of a court but accurately enough to contribute to your profile. It's conceivably possible, although I must admit unlikely, that I could get a DNA trace from any semen deposit, too. In which case it could form court evidence.'

There was no apparent resentment that he might be adding to her reputation more than his own. 'You think the genital wounding might be an attempt to conceal rape?'

'No. Part of it: part of the humiliation.'

'Which *would* make it sadistic.'

'Not by additionally removing the limbs and the head,' he argued. 'This is different.'

'Rendering them helpless, defenceless, you mean?' said Claudine.

'Part of it again.'

'So we're talking domination?'

'Let's stick with helplessness. I try to avoid obvious labels as much as possible.'

It fitted the original reason for asking for a medical opinion to support the presentation to Sanglier: she'd delay drawing attention to the body marks, to see if Rosetti had noticed them. 'Why is there no blood on the French bodies? Or the girl in London? Or on the Chinese girl in Vienna? The girl in Vienna had less than a pint of blood in her body when she was examined. Would there be that much loss through dismemberment?'

'Possibly. There are too many factors I'd need to consider before giving a positive opinion on that. The cleanliness intrigues me more. And the sharpness of the lacerations on the French victims.'

'A scalpel?' suggested Claudine.

The man shook his head. 'They aren't medical incisions. There is some expertise but it isn't medical. What about some religious connotations?'

Claudine shook her head in return. 'One of the girls in France was obviously subcontinent Indian, the other possibly from Bangladesh. The features of the girl in London could be from northern Thailand or even Sri Lanka. And the Vienna victim was Chinese.'

'Not *their* religions,' qualified Rosetti. 'Have you considered a religious cult, preying upon them?'

Claudine regarded the man seriously for several moments. 'Human sacrifices? Blood drinking?'

'It's bizarre, I know. And I'm not suggesting it should be put at the top of any list . . .' Now he gestured to the photographs. 'But that *is* bizarre. And whoever did it — certainly in the French cases — tried to make gargoyle faces.'

'Gargoyle faces!'

Rosetti rose from the small table, beckoning Claudine to follow. Offering her the magnifying glass, he said: 'Look at the mouths. They're split, at the corners.'

Claudine examined each agonized, contorted expression. Some of the cuts were impossible to see without the magnification. 'Gags, surely?'

'If something hard had been used as a gag the marks would have been more frontally visible. These are virtually internal. I think the killers imagined they could jam the mouths open, probably when the victims were screaming from the pain of what was being done to them, to get their faces frozen into a hideous smile when rigor set in. Except that rigor isn't permanent: it comes soon after death, then recedes. That's why every expression is lopsided. But there again I can't understand why it's there at all. It shouldn't be.'

Part of what he said supported perhaps the most positive opinion in her intended profile. With that thought came Gérard Lanvin's insistence in Lyon that leaving body parts in cathedrals was a mockery of normal religion. Which possibly linked with Rosetti's cult suggestion. Claudine stopped her mental drift, unhappy with the conjecture, and at last pointed to the wired wrists of the severed hands and then to the ankles of the separated legs. 'How would you define the bruising?' she asked.

'Something I would definitely need to examine personally,' said Rosetti, going to the specific prints. 'From the width of the wrist bruising visible in the pictures I'd say the victims were tied to a frame or a bed in a leg-and arm-spread position and jerked violently against the ropes in their agony. See . . .' He pointed delicately with the tip of a narrow silver pencil he took from his pocket. '. . . here and here the bruising is broken where briefly the rope wasn't pulled violently against the skin . . .'

'Rope?' queried Claudine, who'd already decided the answer to her question but needed medical confirmation. 'Not the wire shown in the photographs?'

'Of course not,' said Rosetti, almost impatiently. 'Most of those amputations were carried out while these people were still alive. They would have contorted against their bindings with unbelievable strength. Wire wouldn't have bruised. It would have cut.'

Claudine became aware of Rosetti's habit of twisting the thick gold wedding band around his finger as he talked. She didn't interpret it as nervousness. 'Helplessness again?'

'But there's a difference here,' said Rosetti, moving on to the photographs of the two white girls and unwittingly confirming another of Claudine's theories. 'There's no ante-death rope-bruising on the arms or legs here. It's post-death lividity caused by the wire being tightened around the wrists, to hold the hands in place, after they died.'

'How?' demanded Claudine.

Rosetti's pencil moved to the mutilated

white torsos. 'The only murders where the breasts were removed. Does what's available from the autopsies talk of stab wounds?'

'No.'

'The fuller reports will, if the examinations were properly carried out,' predicted the Italian. 'I believe they were both stabbed in the heart. Which means they didn't go through the agony the others suffered.'

'How long does it take a dead body to begin decomposing?'

'That depends entirely on the conditions around it. In hot conditions, a day or two. In cold, it varies: refrigerated, soon after death, there isn't any decomposition at all.'

Claudine abruptly realized she needed the expertise of this soft-spoken, undemonstrative man who, from photographs alone, had provided enough to back most of her early impressions. And there had been no objection from Sanglier to her calling in a professional pathologist, Claudine remembered, as the idea hardened in her mind. She said: 'What's your feeling about becoming involved in this?'

Rosetti shrugged. 'Interesting. Although I'd hardly consider myself *involved.*'

Claudine was curious at the qualifying response. She'd been very aware of the attitude towards her since her being part of the task force had become public knowledge throughout the building: universal there-but-for-the-grace-of-God relief at escaping from an impossibly difficult investigation. Until now she hadn't imagined anyone simply calling their participation interesting. 'Would you like to be more deeply involved?'

Rosetti considered the question. 'I'd certainly like to examine the bodies myself.'

'Do you believe there'd be a lot more you could learn?'

'That depends, obviously, on how complete the autopsy reports are when they eventually arrive. But I would hope so, yes.'

'To carry out your own examinations would mean travelling to the countries concerned.'

The man frowned, not appearing to understand the point she was making. 'Obviously.'

'We don't have full reports because Europol's participation is resented.'

Rosetti's face cleared. 'I'm not concerned with politics, inside or out.'

'Others are. Perhaps with you more than anyone else it would be seen as a professional challenge.'

'Second opinions are quite common in medicine; even in pathology.' Rosetti's face relaxed when he said it and Claudine realized it was the first time the man had smiled. He hadn't even given that automatic reaction at their moment of meeting.

She smiled back. 'I'll complete all the necessary bureaucracy today. Welcome to the team.'

'It will be an interesting experience,' he said,

using the word again. The smile had gone.

Claudine dictated and signed the necessary memoranda to the forensic division, with copies to Sanglier, before she revised her profile from what she and Rosetti had discussed. Before she finished, the full police reports began arriving, the first from England. By the middle of the afternoon there had been five separate deliveries, and she decided against complaining to Sanglier about those still missing. Even without studying what had come Claudine recognized that the supplying police forces had gone from one ridiculous extreme to the other: having at first failed to provide enough they'd now tried to overwhelm with everything.

Volker was printing out her revised profile when the internal telephone rang. Sanglier said: 'We're under media attack. Have you seen the newspapers?'

'I saw something on television last night,' said Claudine, guardedly. It had added to her concern about being away until late Sunday night and why she had expected a summons to be waiting for her when she'd arrived that morning.

'I'd expected something from you by now.'

'I'll deliver it now. And personally,' said Claudine, detecting the clearly implied rebuke.

The moment she entered Sanglier's walk-the-gauntlet office she recognized the other

174

man with him. For the benefit of his recording, Sanglier said accusingly: 'Poulard has been on several times from Paris, telling me it's slow progress. And that he hasn't heard from you.'

The bastards were bypassing her, Claudine realized. And trying to undermine her. Sanglier had told her enough for her to know she had more to fight with than they had. 'I've repeatedly called their hotel and left messages for them to call me back. Which they haven't. And "slow progress" means they haven't made any.'

'Have you done any better?' demanded Sanglier, unsettled by the strength of Claudine's response.

'Far better.' Claudine smiled confidently. 'I know, for instance, that we're not dealing with one set of killers. There are several.'

'What's taking them so long!' demanded Miriam Burrows. She'd let herself go since the transfer to The Hague but she was still an attractive woman. All she needed to do was drop one or two kilos.

'You know what the Bureau's like.'

'You are sure it would be safe?'

'Don't you think it would be?' There'd been no other conversation between them for weeks.

'You make it sound like it would.'

He decided against telling her of another idea he'd thought of putting up. 'If I don't

175

hear anything in a couple of days I'll have Joe
send a reminder.'

'You're too important to be buried!' protested the woman.

'That's what they think,' agreed Burrows,
twisting her remark.

Chapter Twelve

Henri Sanglier was tight with fury, at himself, knowing he had misjudged and mishandled everything, and now couldn't totally recover.

The weekend media demands for results had by the Monday developed throughout France, England, Germany and Austria into a concerted attack against Europol on television and in newspapers, a large selection of which — together with transcripts of the television and radio accusations, some by government ministers — were being tidied by the secretary from the more comfortable low-tabled conference area to one side of Sanglier's office when Claudine entered.

It was there for the previous two hours — although at no time relaxed — that Sanglier had gone through all the condemnations with Franz Sobell, arguing against a panicked press announcement which, by its blatantly obvious lack of information, would increase the pressure on them. It had been a bad mistake telephoning Poulard while Sobell had been in the room, to be told he and Siemen hadn't uncovered anything they didn't already know, and an even worse one delaying for so long before contacting

Claudine. He'd done that while Sobell was with him, too, anxious to shuffle failure responsibility downwards. Instead, disastrously, he had become stuck with an independent witness to what she was going to say: when the Austrian had realized Claudine might have something to get them out of their publicity crisis the damned man had insisted on staying for the meeting.

If what she had was worthwhile — which from the confidence in her voice it certainly seemed to be — all credit would go to the woman. And that wasn't the end of the personal disaster. Or the last of his mistakes. He'd kept his tape running throughout and now it would not be possible to edit it, as he'd intended, to Claudine's disadvantage.

Sanglier made the introductions reluctantly, concerned that Claudine might get the impression that he needed the support or authority of another commissioner at the moment of a possible breakthrough. He wasn't helped by the enthusiasm of Sobell's hopeful greeting.

Claudine hadn't imagined Sobell was there for support. She'd only seen the local television criticism the previous night but the pile of newspapers was sufficient for her to guess why the Austrian was present. She did, however, see it as a not-to-be-missed name-enhancing opportunity among the hierarchy, particularly after what Poulard had clearly — but so ineptly — attempted.

178

'You have something positive?' demanded Sanglier, setting out to restore as much as possible a balance in his favour.

'I have some profile suggestions,' qualified Claudine at once, refusing to over-commit herself. 'Some I am quite sure about. Others I put forward as worth consideration . . .'

'We want whatever you've got,' interrupted Sobell, showing the anxiety Claudine had already discerned. From his sharp sideways look she also detected Sanglier's annoyance at the other man's obvious concern.

Not expecting a third person at the meeting Claudine had only brought two copies of her initial assessment, one for Sanglier and the other to prompt her verbal presentation. It would have taken only minutes for Yvette Fey to bring a third copy from the incident room. Instead Claudine hesitated sufficiently to ensure both men realized the shortage and then confidently handed her copy to Sobell. Then, dramatically, she announced: 'We are not dealing with a single killer. Or a single gang. There are three separate groups. One — the most important and most likely to kill again — murdered and dissected the three Asians in France, the girl in London and the girl in Vienna. The two white girls, in Brussels and Amsterdam, are unconnected victims. The Cologne killing is different again.'

Sobell shook his head and said: 'Dear God, what are we dealing with, then?' and Sanglier gave the man another irritated look.

Using the question, Claudine said: 'Messages. And copycat murders. I don't know to whom the messages are addressed or what they're intended to convey, but I believe the first group are warnings. Which — because there haven't been any more killings I identify with those five — I'd say were being read and understood. The others are messages, too. Different messages to different people, using the hysteria of the five I've itemized to achieve whatever their aim is . . .'

Now it was Sanglier who interrupted, eager to isolate any weakness. 'Is that opinion one you are sure about? Or merely advancing as a possibility for consideration?'

'I have no doubt that I am right about the three quite separate groups,' said Claudine, immediately conscious of Sobell's impressed head movement, as if it was his opinion, as well.

Sanglier was aware of it too, as he was aware of Claudine's aggressive self-assurance: she wasn't deferring to him or to Sobell. 'And your certainty is based upon what?'

'There are three quite distinct methods of killing and mutilation. Only in the French, English and Austrian killings — let's use the media word and call them the Céleste group — were the bodies distributed over a wide area throughout the country: the other victims were dismembered but the parts were spread around the comparatively confined area of the cities in which, presumably, they died. And there is the date sequences of the murders. Those of the white girls and the possible Turkish youth followed the other five, date for date. I've had a computer comparison created of the descriptions published in newspapers and on television and radio in each case. Nowhere, because it would have been too disgusting, has the genital disfigurement been described in sufficient detail for it to be repeated absolutely. The fact that the hands were wired together in a praying position *was* published, every time. But not precisely *how*. In each of the copied cases the wire was secured in a different fashion . . .'

'I want to understand better your message theory,' protested Sobell. 'I don't follow your reasoning there.'

'Why don't we still have any names? Why haven't the families of the linked five victims come forward to identify the bodies?' demanded Claudine. 'Because they can't. I'm suggesting . . .' she paused, looking directly to Sanglier '. . . offering for consideration the idea that the victims were illegal immigrants. For any family to come forward would result in their being expelled to the country from which they came, possibly after a court prosecution.' Claudine felt completely sure of herself, her breath coming easily.

'So what's the message?' demanded Sobell.

'I've said I don't know, not yet. To conform, in some way. Maybe to pay money they owe.'

'What about the killings you don't think are connected to the five?' demanded Sanglier.

'Illegals again, I suspect,' said Claudine. 'It's the most logical explanation.'

'Are you suggesting three sets of killings by three separate groups, *all* of illegals: three different conspiracies?' sneered Sanglier, imagining a flaw.

'Only one positive conspiracy; the planning and the slaughter of the widely distributed Céleste five,' said Claudine, recognizing the mockery and unable to understand the reason for it.

Sanglier gave a disparaging head movement. 'It's becoming too confused to have any logic.'

'I think it has every logic,' disputed Claudine. 'The killings will divide exactly as I have indicated. And most of the victims — if not all — will prove to be illegals.'

'Police investigations need facts, not impressions,' said Sanglier, regretting the words as he uttered them.

'My function is to provide impressions that lead towards those facts,' reminded Claudine. It was impossible for her to avoid appearing condescending, which she didn't intend. Sanglier's attitude — particularly after their initial encounter — bewildered her. It was positively antagonistic, which was ridiculous.

'Illegal immigration could be part of the

explanation,' agreed the Austrian.

'It's the most obvious, at this moment,' insisted Claudine. She paused for another question, and when neither man spoke she went on: 'Sex is a factor. But I do not believe these are sex crimes in a sense that any of us would normally understand . . .'

'I certainly don't understand that,' persisted Sanglier, seizing a weakness and twisting Claudine's words against her.

'I don't, either — as I've conceded,' said Claudine. 'These aren't killings for sexual gratification committed by sexual deviants. Maybe someone is trying to make them appear to be such, but I'm fairly sure it isn't the case.'

'Why do it, then?' pressed Sanglier.

'To heighten the horror, perhaps. A very early pathological opinion is that in the Céleste cases the mutilation was carried out while the victims were alive. And that some attempt was made to fix the mouths so they would appear to have been smiling when they were tortured. Possibly the murderers expected that to be made public. Can you imagine a more frightening warning message?'

Sobell visibly shuddered. 'Is there any significance in one of your five being male? Is that still sexual?'

'I don't know. But I think so,' said Claudine.

'Are you sure the boy forms part of your grouping?' said Sanglier.

'Definitely. In every case the age is approximately the same. So are the sexual markings. The hands were fixed in the same way, the boy's body was cleaned like the girls and there was substantial blood loss, more perhaps than would have occurred even with the amputations and disembowelling . . .'

'Can you explain the body cleaning and the blood loss?' demanded Sanglier.

'Not yet,' said Claudine, refusing to concede outright defeat. 'There's something else that links these five. All the body parts — essential for the messages I don't yet understand — were left in public places over the course of a week: places where, because of their use by the public, we know they were deposited during the night of the twenty-four-hour period in which they were found . . .'

'What's your point?' frowned Sanglier, genuinely confused.

'They were left in May and June. Hot months. Over a period of a week. And had been killed and dismembered even before that. A lot of autopsy evidence has to be assessed and possibly re-examined, but at the moment there is no evidence of decomposition, which would normally have begun.'

'Meaning what?' pressed Sobell.

'They were stored — and transported over distances sometimes of six hundred miles — in refrigerated conditions. They would have had to be carried in a way that would not attract any specific interest.'

'Could the blood loss be anything to do with witchcraft practices?' Sobell asked. 'There's been a lot of media speculation about that.'

'I doubt it,' said Claudine. 'There would have been more than just blood loss if they were victims of Satanic rites. And the bodies would not have been distributed as they have been. The dismembered pieces would have all been in one place, arranged in some ritualistic pattern.'

'Wouldn't some parts being found in churches support the witchcraft theory?' demanded the Austrian.

Claudine nodded. 'Again it's possible but again I doubt it. I think the reason is far more practical. Cathedrals are places where discovery was guaranteed.' Remembering her conversation with Rosetti, she added: 'I'm not saying we should rule out occult practices or religious mockery. I just don't think, until we understand the significance better, we should put it high on a priority list.'

'What should be higher?' asked Sanglier.

'The racial aspect,' replied Claudine at once. 'It's another important factor, although here again I'm not entirely comfortable with the idea of all of them being *motivated* by race. The murder of the two white girls is the most obvious argument against that.'

'Racial hatred isn't a one way street,' insisted Sanglier. 'Blacks hate whites as well as the other way round.'

Claudine hesitated, caught by the familiarity of the phrase. 'This isn't a racial reversal.'

'More confusion,' said Sanglier.

'No,' corrected Claudine, quickly again. 'A refusal to *allow* the confusion of an automatic assumption.'

He was losing every exchange, Sanglier realized, agonized. 'What other automatic assumptions are there to be avoided?'

'The most obvious, that they're serial killings,' responded Claudine easily. 'The five, certainly, are a *series*. But it's not serial, not in the way of a normal criminal investigation into multiple homicides.'

There was a frown from Sobell. 'Not a single killer?'

It *was* confusing, Claudine conceded to herself, although she didn't feel it as much as the two men obviously did. Her confusion was concentrated upon Sanglier's attitude, which she found inexplicable. Clearly the criticism was far more widespread than she'd understood and obviously the commissioners would be concerned about it. But she wouldn't have expected Sanglier — Sanglier out of all of them! — to have reacted . . . reacted how? Claudine found it difficult to define in a single word, which further confused her: irritated her professionally, because professionally she was supposed to be able to analyse attitudes and behaviour and give them a name-tag. There was definitely a lot of anger, some clearly directed towards her. She was, Claudine conceded, the only available scapegoat, unfair though it was to single her out for attack. But understandable, perhaps, from a man totally unaccustomed to being blamed for any failing or incompetence, which could be put at his door as the controlling case officer. He hadn't been publicly identified as such, so it was hardly a public humiliation. But there had been those tell-tale signs of internal uncertainty at their previous encounters to account for his over-reaction. Whatever, now was not the time to be sidetracked by the reflection. But if she had been preparing a specific patient psychoanalysis it was certainly an observation she would have included in the case notes.

'No,' she said, finally answering Sobell's question. 'We're not looking for a single homicidal maniac: a psychopath.'

'You're saying sane people did this?' exclaimed Sanglier.

Claudine would have thought Sanglier better able to accept that than the strong-stomached Yvette. She decided against exploring the definition of sanity with the man. 'Totally sane, extremely calculating people.'

'I find that hard to accept,' said Sanglier.

'It would misdirect the inquiry not to accept it,' insisted Claudine.

The bitch was actually lecturing him, Sanglier realized, outraged. 'I would have thought an open mind was a much better approach at this stage.'

'Absolutely,' agreed Claudine. 'But the facts, scarce though they are, contradict a lone, insane killer. No one person, by himself, could by chance choose five anonymous victims in three different countries. And lead other psychopaths to choose other anonymous victims in three more countries. And more than one killer would have been necessary to spread the remains over such a wide area. A group of psychopaths, working as a team, is inconceivable even in a case as bizarre as this.'

Sanglier desperately sought a response. 'What about their being the victims of snuff movies?'

Claudine gave a doubtful gesture of acceptance, remembering Kurt Volker's pornographic hike through cyberspace. 'I agree that sex is a factor — we've even considered the two white victims might be prostitutes — and I think it possible that some of the victims, certainly the five I've isolated, might have been filmed while they were being murdered. But I don't think they were primarily killed for snuff movies. The strongest argument against it is how many killings there have been in such a short period of time. A porn ring would have needed studios with Hollywood facilities in permanent production. And professional snuff movie makers are not sending the sort of messages I'm talking about. Why run the risk of distributing the bodies all over Europe?'

She had an answer — a better answer — to everything, thought Sanglier. Trying to force the objectivity, he acknowledged that was her vocation.

Claudine had the most illogical imagery of a flag of surrender when Sobell lifted the written copy of her profile, vaguely gesturing with it.

'Everything you've told us is here?'

'Yes,' said Claudine. 'Supplemented by what's emerged during our discussion, of course.'

'I'm most impressed,' said the man. 'As I am sure Commissioner Sanglier is: it was an excellent choice appointing you to the task force.'

'Yes,' said Sanglier, with difficulty softening his attitude, which he knew anyway to be wrong, like everything else about this day and this encounter.

'Thank you,' said Claudine, welcoming the public gratitude. She didn't think it would have been forthcoming if Sobell hadn't been present. As the thought came to Claudine the Austrian's demeanour hardened discernibly.

'But couldn't we have had this profile much sooner?'

Fuck both of you, thought Claudine, unaware of any discussion that had preceded her arrival but determined against becoming a player in any pass-the-buck game. Pedantically, spacing her words, she said: 'A very strict record is being kept of every stage of this inquiry. The time and the date of my first profile notes and my initial draft are already in a database. I could have given a broad outline before the weekend.'

Sanglier was so stunned by the chance that briefly the retort blocked in his throat, so that when he did speak there was a rasp he hadn't intended. 'Then why did you waste two days — almost three?'

'Also timed and recorded are my attempts to reach the others in my task force. I wanted to make the profile, preliminary though it is, as complete as possible: they might have had something to prevent a mistake. The mistake was obviously expecting cooperation. But then we've already discovered that, haven't we?' What, Claudine wondered, had she done? What she wouldn't do was become a victim.

At no time during his charmed life — never, once, during his professional career — had Henri Sanglier been so disoriented as he had been by the profile session with Claudine Carter. He was corseted by anger and impotence and frustration, unable for a long time — even when he was supposedly discussing the profile and what to do with it with Sobell — to think as he knew he should be thinking. It was only towards the end of the debate with the Austrian that Sanglier achieved any sort of control, and that nothing like the discipline with which he customarily held himself. His first relieved, coherent thought was that the chairman was completely unaware of his difficulty.

Sanglier's mind worked on two levels after Claudine's departure. Outwardly he conducted a reasoned, logical conversation with the other man, frequently agreeing, emptily, as they examined it point by point that Claudine's was a brilliant assessment with which they could rebut the media onslaught. At the same time but quite separately Sanglier was mentally reviewing every word, nuance, inflexion and response that had passed between the three of them in the previous two hours.

Sanglier's overwhelming impression from the meeting and the way Claudine had conducted herself was that she did know something about his father and believed it provided her with hidden security. He also acknowledged that he'd allowed his fixation about the psychologist to supersede every professional consideration. So a lot of the fault, the reason for personal mistake following personal mistake, was his own. Again he believed Sobell had been oblivious. But he didn't imagine the woman had been. He'd been aware several times of her sharp looks of curiosity and the even sharper responses. But he was sure it was only curiosity, not suspicion that he was directing personal animosity towards her. Rather, from her devastating concluding ac-

191

cusation against Poulard and Siemen, that he had been misled by the two men. So everything was recoverable. He might even be able to turn it to his advantage: make a point of hinting that he had been misguided — as close as he intended to come to making an apology — and invite her confidence to get an indication of what he really wanted to discover. The reassurance was limited. He'd still handled the entire episode extremely badly and had to guard against making anything like the same miscalculation again: avoid making *any* miscalculation again.

'A press release will refute all the criticism,' Sobell was saying. 'Turn things entirely in our favour.'

'Issued in my name?' demanded Sanglier pointedly. When there had been nothing upon which to base a media response Sobell had spoken as if it would automatically be made under Sanglier's identifiable authority.

Sobell appeared nonplussed by the question. 'Is it wise to personalize the situation?'

'It seemed to be before we got the profile.'

Sobell's frown remained. 'I don't remember suggesting that.'

Sanglier stared fixedly at the other man, without speaking, until Sobell turned the beginning of a fidget into a shrug. 'Perhaps we should decide it at a full meeting of the commissioners. Decide, in fact, precisely what we intend saying in the statement. A day's delay won't matter: it'll ridicule the criticism even more, if it continues. Which our public affairs division expects that it will.'

A sacrifice for a greater advantage, judged Sanglier, pleased with the way his mind was finally working. The woman's profile was impressive and in many ways as horrifying as all the details of the crimes that had so sensationally preceded it. So their statement would unquestionably re-ignite the sensationalism not just in the EU but worldwide. And the fame-guaranteeing publicity would be even greater if his already famous name was associated with it, as the man leading the hunt for the killer. But there would be the need for many more press releases and even press conferences, some perhaps to explain failures and misjudgements. Far better, at this early stage, to concede the precedent of anonymity at the commissioners' meeting until there was something more positive with which to put himself in the media spotlight. 'Yes. It should be a Commission decision.'

'I'm concerned that the three of them aren't working properly together.'

'So am I,' said Sanglier. 'I had no intimation of a problem until today. It'll be rectified at once.'

'It doesn't seem to be the fault of Dr Carter.'

'No,' said Sanglier tightly.

'I think we should make a point at tomorrow's meeting of letting everyone know what

193

a contribution she's made,' suggested the Austrian. 'Let's face it: without her we'd have nothing to fight back with. And now we've got more than enough.'

'Yes,' accepted Sanglier, even more tightly. 'That's an excellent idea.'

The final concessions forced upon him made it difficult for Sanglier not to slip back into the morass of impotent frustration after Sobell left to convene the following day's meeting. He took out some of his anger on Poulard, whom he succeeded in reaching first time, making a particular point of Claudine's success and the intended recognition of the full Commission, and demanding they maintain daily contact with the psychologist as well as with him.

He'd just poured himself a brandy, needing it, when the call came from David Winslow, so he added another glass for the English commissioner's arrival. Winslow entered the room looking more flushed than normal, and sipped the offered drink before speaking.

'I must admit I'm embarrassed,' he said finally.

Sanglier felt a flicker of hope. 'What?'

'I kept it general, as we agreed. Not official . . .' He took another swallow of his brandy. 'And got a blank wall. So then I got more forceful: asked to speak to Toomey himself. Said as the British commissioner I expected to be contacted as a matter of courtesy during

194

a visit, which I'd learned about from the visitors' log. He apologized but when I asked him what it had been about he said he wasn't authorized to tell me and suggested I make the inquiry formal, through recognized channels, if I wanted to know. Damned impudence!'

'Nothing more than that?'

'When I said I hoped it wouldn't cause any difficulties here he said he didn't think it would. That it concerned something private, in the past . . .'

'Private and in the past?' broke in Sanglier.

'That's what he said.'

'What's the man's job?'

'I did at least get guidance there. Attached to some special investigation unit.'

Sanglier covered his reaction by draining his brandy goblet and then refilling it, immediately. He'd *known* he'd been right.

Hugo Rosetti had already worked his way through the complete French and Austrian autopsy reports by the time Claudine got back to the incident room. The moment she entered he announced there were unanswered questions in every one and very little to change the opinions he'd already reached. Despite Yvette's efforts to put the newly arrived files into some semblance of order, what had come in by courier and special delivery during Claudine's absence looked mountainous.

Yvette helped her carry them all back to the comfort of her own office where she worked, oblivious of the time, until darkness forced her to put lights on, breaking her concentration.

Claudine had decided to work through until at least midnight — longer if she was not too tired — so she telephoned Lyon from her office. Her mother said she was busy preparing everything for the accountant before going into hospital. She'd spoken to the surgeon that morning, who'd told her she was the first on his operating list. She was pleased about that.

'How are you feeling?' enquired Claudine, hating the banality.

'Fine. There never has been any pain.'

'It'll be good to get it over.' More banality.

'There wasn't any difficulty about your coming here at the weekend?'

'None. What could there have been?'

'A hundred things. I want you to concentrate on what you're doing. Not worry about me.'

'What have you told Gérard?'

'About what?'

'You know what,' insisted Claudine, forcing her mother to talk about it.

'I said I wanted to wait until after the operation before deciding.'

'What did he say?'

'That he understood.' There was a pause. 'He also said it would be important to set things out properly in my will, so that there would be no problem with your inheritance if I do marry him.'

Until that moment the legal significance of her mother's remarrying hadn't occurred to Claudine. Nor had she ever thought about an inheritance: her mother hadn't liked Warwick, dismissing him as weak, as her own husband had been weak, but she had been extremely generous throughout the short marriage and unthinkingly Claudine had imagined she'd received her inheritance during her mother's lifetime. She was momentarily unsure what to say. 'I'm not interested in your will. But I suppose it's very responsible of him: very fair.'

'He's a very responsible man.'

'So you should marry him.'

'I still have a lot of work to do. I should be out in front, greeting customers.'

'I'll come down again this weekend.'

'Don't, if it interferes with anything.'

'It won't.'

It would soon be time to see the woman again, decided Peter Toomey. And it would be very different, with what he had now. He would have to proceed strictly according to the regulations, as he had to the British commissioner's inquiry. He hadn't heard anything more from the man but he'd covered himself by inserting a record of Winslow's call into the already substantial file. She'd get a lawyer, obviously. He hoped whoever she chose wouldn't restrict things quite as tightly as the men who had accompanied Paul Bickerstone.

Chapter Thirteen

Claudine worked long after midnight and allowed herself only three hours' sleep before returning to her office. By the time she ferried everything back to the incident room, still before the arrival of anyone else, she only had the Cologne file to complete. The one outstanding dossier — on the Chinese girl in Vienna — had arrived overnight. She went through that first, having already resolved any uncertainty about three separate groupings but still wanting more evidence if it was available. She was halfway through the Cologne information — adding to the earlier confirmation — when Hugo Rosetti arrived. He was laden with the medical reports he had also worked on overnight.

'I managed about three hours' sleep,' greeted Claudine.

'In the end I didn't bother.'

'Hope you've got an understanding wife.'

It was a casual, throwaway remark but the reaction baffled Claudine. The Italian had drawn level with her, at the small table, on his way to the side office he had appropriated. Abruptly, almost disconcertingly, his body as well as his face stiffened as if he'd suffered an electric shock and he jerked his head sideways, fully to confront her. It could only have been seconds but he seemed to remain frozen for much longer. The relaxation was just as abrupt, although his face scarcely softened. Instead of moving on he put his files down and said briskly, as if to break the mood: 'What more have you got?'

Claudine hesitated. 'Like you, a lot of unanswered questions. And proof of why our involvement is so necessary. The most obvious hindrance in the five murders is that the investigation *hasn't* been centralized, which I'm going to add to the profile. Distributing the bodies wasn't just to convey a message. It was to make the investigation that much more difficult. Which shows just how well organized these killings are: planned, considered, expert . . .'

'Professional, in fact?'

'More professional than I'd allowed for,' she agreed.

'A recognized mafia organization?'

'Which one should we recognize?' Claudine smiled hopefully: there wasn't any tension between them but she still didn't understand his behaviour a few minutes earlier.

Rosetti responded with one of his rare smiles, quickly gone. 'I hadn't defined the distribution like you but it makes sense of my major problem, certainly in the five cases. Every pathologist from every police authority made an examination as a contribution to the full report each assumed someone else was making. And no one did. Everything's disjointed . . .'

'Please,' interrupted Claudine. 'I've got a medical query and this seems the right moment. In one of the English summaries there's reference to an unproductive orthodontic check. But there's no reference in any other file to forensic dentistry. Is there anything in what you've read?'

The man gave an exasperated shrug. 'Only with the girl in Brussels, who appeared to have perfect teeth, so it wasn't taken any further. It sums up my problem — our problem. Even in the cases where the recovery was in the same city, more than one pathologist got involved, contributing to the mess. It's not just the teeth, which is surely the most obvious way to try to identify a nameless victim. There was no reference in the précis reports on the five of bone fractures, apart from where they would obviously occur around the point of amputation. In fact there were rib and arm and leg fractures in every case and each time they've been attributed to attack traumas. But there's insufficient evidence of external bruising. Blood loss is attributed, without any supporting evidence, to the amputations. There's no comparison of incisions and two of the torso examinations completely omit cranial or stomach inquiry. And there isn't a reference anywhere to the internal mouth lesions.'

'So?' queried Claudine expectantly.

'I need to carry out my own autopsies. I want initially to concentrate on the five, then go on to the two white victims. There's nothing, in either of their examinations, about stab wounds but there weren't any bone fractures, apart from the ones to be expected.'

'I think it would be essential for you to go, even if the reports had been more complete,' said Claudine. 'How soon could you leave?'

Rosetti looked at the newly arrived dossier. 'As soon as I've read that last medical report. Later today, in fact.'

Whenever possible Claudine had always attended postmortems, prompting tests and examinations to answer her own special and sometimes peculiar questions, as well as those of the pathologist. She was tempted to accompany Rosetti now, convinced there would be positive results making the journey far more worthwhile than that upon which Poulard and Siemen had embarked, but on balance decided it was more practical for her to remain where she was, at the very hub of the inquiry. She didn't have any doubt of a complete exchange of everything from the Italian. She still risked the reminder. 'What about rape?'

'There's no mention of a specific examination — or of a finding — in anything I've read. It's on my list for reexamination.'

So he'd arrived that morning expecting —

and prepared for — her to authorize his own autopsies. 'What about the apparent body cleansing?'

The pathologist sighed. 'There's no mention anywhere of skin tests for chemicals or soap residue. It might not be possible, after so long, but I'll try to find something, obviously. Certainly check.'

'They might have been cleaned to remove indications of the work they did: clothes factories use strong, traceable dyes, for instance. Food processing, too. Can you test the hands — any part of the body — that might show something?'

'That could produce a worthwhile result,' Rosetti acknowledged immediately, showing no resentment at an encroachment upon his expertise. 'People breathe things in, too. I'll take tissue samples from the trachea and lungs, to look for anything.'

Claudine decided it was becoming, virtually without effort, a good working relationship. Despite that, she said: 'You'll keep in touch?'

'Of course,' frowned Rosetti, as if it were unthinkable that he wouldn't.

'Where are you going first?'

'France. That's the concentration of our five.'

'So you can initiate the forensic dentistry?'

'Personally. And then with a forensic orthodontist,' assured Rosetti.

'I'll initiate the dentistry checks everywhere

else apart from France.'

'It should all have been done in the beginning,' said Rosetti wearily.

Wanting to contribute as much as possible to the exchange Claudine said: 'Your input was a great help yesterday, when I met the commissioners.' She should have said more than she had when she'd got back from the meeting. But she had been too anxious to complete the murder files and too preoccupied by Poulard and Siemen's dealing directly with Sanglier, whose strange attitude had been another distraction. However, there was no justifiable excuse for not according Rosetti the proper recognition. She should, she supposed, tell the two detectives of Rosetti's imminent arrival. Not to do so would be descending to their childish level.

'There'll be more,' Rosetti promised. He extracted his particular sections from the last remaining dossier and continued on towards his chosen office.

Yvette and Volker arrived virtually together, a sartorial clash of French chic and charity shop economy. Claudine warned the computer specialist there was a lot to be done but first dictated the pathologist's assignment memorandum to Sanglier and told the girl to liaise with Rosetti before making the flight arrangements through Europol's travel section.

Claudine had studied the full murder dossiers to a prepared plan. She'd made general notes, as she'd read, and then refined them with specific guidance attached to each from which she wanted Volker to create their match programs. She went quickly through each with the man to ensure he fully understood what her notes meant, agreeing at once to his suggestion of separate master databases for her three groupings, with the new comparison charts and individual murder case notes subprogrammed, compartmenting everything in precise sections with itemized indexed entry codes. The specific five were designated by the word Céleste.

'I'll set up a random search program,' promised the German enthusiastically. 'I can run it through everything and it'll pick up any identical spikes beyond the obvious ones we've already codified.'

Another satisfactory working relationship, thought Claudine. 'Sounds like a lot of work.'

'Not really,' smiled Volker. 'That's what computers were invented for.'

Having so recently discussed dentistry, Claudine became aware for the first time of Volker's perfect teeth, which she was sure were natural and not sculpted like Poulard's. Considering the outward appearance she was surprised, too, at the freshness of the man. Continuing the contrast, she decided she preferred Volker's cologne to the overpowering miasma that permanently enveloped the

French detective. The word association was an unnecessary prompt. 'You told me you could get into most police systems?'

There was another smile. 'More than most.'

'What about Cologne?'

Instead of replying Volker lightly touched three keys on the board directly in front of him. Immediately two parallel passwords appeared on the screen. 'Theirs . . .' said Volker, indicating the identification to the left. He moved the cursor sideways. '. . . and my Trojan horse, already installed for whenever I want to slip through their gate.'

Claudine had intentionally finished her briefing with the file on the murdered Turkish girl uppermost. 'They're still withholding things. And doing it stupidly. I've itemized four references to inquiries among neo-Nazi organizations and political parties — one even indicates they're indexed — but they haven't included any organization or party names or what the results have been. And the index is missing, too.'

'No problem,' assured Volker.

'And anything else that hasn't been included,' encouraged Claudine. 'Any dentistry examination, for instance.'

Rosetti had completed the remaining autopsy report and given Yvette his intended itinerary to arrange by the time Claudine moved away from the computer bank.

'There was a crude swastika cut into the

stomach of the girl in Cologne,' he announced at once. 'It wasn't in the précis.'

'And they kept back the neo-Nazi inquiries from what was supposed to be the full file.'

'Trying to solve it before we do?'

'Probably.'

'Are you going to protest again?'

Claudine shrugged. 'We're not in competition: at least I'm not. If they make a successful arrest it's one less for us to deal with.'

'Providing it's a copy, unconnected with our five,' cautioned Rosetti.

'Don't you think it is a copy?'

'Without a doubt.' As the pathologist accepted his travel pack from Yvette he added: 'I thought it made sense for me to stay in the same hotel in Paris as the others. I'm looking forward to meeting them.'

How much might the encounter with the two detectives affect — hamper even — the developing working relationship between herself and Rosetti? It was a paranoid question but an understandable one in the nonsensical circumstances. Things had to be set straight — confronted and settled in an adult way — to prevent the situation becoming any more ridiculous. As it would be ridiculous — childish, she'd already decided — to hold back from another attempt to reach the two men in Paris who were refusing to contact her. She didn't consider herself in competition with them any more than with a German police force which

207

believed, probably correctly, that their victim was the subject of a Fascist racial attack they didn't need outsiders to resolve. She said: 'I think it makes every sense.'

'Any messages?' enquired Rosetti, unaware of the irony.

Claudine added a copy of her profile to the pathologist's travel documents. 'They might be interested to read that. I'd welcome any contribution they could make to improve it.'

'I'll tell them,' promised Rosetti.

And most probably, although unwittingly, convey the impression she was patronizing them for their lack of progress compared to hers. Claudine added: 'There are quite a few things I'd like to agree with them.' Now she definitely had to speak to one of them before Rosetti arrived. Otherwise it would degenerate into the stupidity of their communicating through intermediaries.

'I'll call you as soon as there is something,' said Rosetti, as he left the room.

Yvette answered the external telephone, at once offering the receiver to Claudine. 'It's for you. Paris.'

It was Siemen. There was no reason why it shouldn't have been but Claudine had expected Poulard. But if it had been Poulard the man would have been accepting their equal status, which he clearly didn't. She didn't want a war with either man but she had no intention of surrendering, either. She saw Yvette at the recording apparatus and wondered if the two detectives remembered its existence.

'I called you, several times,' said Claudine.

'There was a confusion about the messages,' said the German.

'That's unfortunate. But I'd expected you to call me anyway.'

'We've been extremely busy.'

'You've got something new?'

There was a pause. 'Not exactly.'

'What then?'

'There's a lot of material to go through.'

'I know. I've gone through it,' said Claudine relentlessly.

'You've managed to get something, then?'

'A lot.'

'That's good.'

'It is, in view of the media attacks.'

'We've only seen the French television and newspapers.'

'It's come from a lot of other countries, too.'

'What's the reaction been back there?'

'Concern, obviously.'

'What are they going to do about it?'

'I don't know.'

'We're cut off here,' complained Siemen.

By your own choice, thought Claudine. 'How much longer do you intend staying?'

'We thought we'd go to Lyon tomorrow, on our way to Marseille.'

'A pathologist, Hugo Rosetti, is arriving to-night. To carry out our own medical examinations. He's bringing the initial profile with him.'

This time the pause was much longer and Claudine suspected the information was being relayed to Poulard. Siemen said: 'Whose decision was it to involve our own pathologist?'

Dear God! thought Claudine, who had no religion. 'It was obviously necessary. The autopsies were inadequate, like everything else.'

'The commissioner thought so?'

'Yes.'

'But you found enough for a proper profile.'

'An *initial* profile,' said Claudine.

'We would have liked to have known about it,' said Siemen carelessly.

'You would have done, if you'd returned my calls. You'll get a printed copy tonight.'

'Congratulations.'

'What for?'

There was another pause. Stiffly, clearly imagining false modesty, the German said: 'The recognition.'

For a further hour Claudine remained as confused about that concluding remark as she was about so much else. Then the written commendation arrived from the commissioners. Claudine's satisfaction was tempered by the awareness that her two supposed colleagues in Paris were still dealing direct with

Sanglier before her. Their embarrassment, not hers. Still, something that had to be stopped. It was unfortunate, too, that Sanglier had told them of the Commission's accolade ahead of her. Too many things seemed to be happening in Europol that she couldn't properly understand. Worse, that she couldn't properly control. What had happened to the supposedly handshake-sealed understanding with Poulard to work together professionally?

The unprofessionalism continued.

Claudine was appalled at the detail — far too much of what she'd clearly specified to be an initial, preliminary profile — included in Europol's press release, which she'd known nothing about until it was quoted on that night's television. It illustrated the organization's desperation to rebut every criticism of its handling of the investigation. Which, she conceded, it probably did. It also provided a blueprint for every copycat racist, zealot, psychopath and mentally ill or maladjusted unfortunate throughout the entire European continent. She already had three different groups conforming to one or other of those categories and she didn't want any more cluttering the pictures that were starting to emerge. But the damage was done and couldn't be reversed.

The release — and its interpretation by the major newspapers throughout Europe —

formed the basis for yet another of Kurt Volker's comparison programs in anticipation of any other atrocities that did not fit the three groupings she was already profiling. It was only when she had Volker make his computer preparations that Claudine went beyond the newspaper adaptations to read Europol's officially issued statement. It angered more than appalled her. Briefly she actually considered making a protest before realizing she could not prove her suspicions. With the commendation still on her desk, it was necessary, though, that she entered some sort of objection to avoid any later accusation of misinterpretation. She could do that without having to make any accusations herself. And not to Sanglier but to the entire Commission, in whose name the official recognition had been issued. Very conscious she might be edging out on to creaking ice, Claudine spent an entire morning writing and revising her memorandum before sending it.

There was an irony that Volker's raid upon the Cologne police records was completely successful and unsuspected, giving her the names of every neo-Nazi body and party they were targeting, all so far without result. Volker drew from Europol archives the identities of as many other Fascist and nationalistic organizations in Germany and included them as well as those already on Cologne's list when she officially suggested to the German investigators that they purge every one, well knowing they'd already drawn a blank on more than ten of them. Volker also obtained a withheld report disclosing European bridgework to the dead girl's front left incisor and Claudine sent a separate cable advising details of any dental work be circulated to every dentist around the city. Claudine very obviously marked the Cologne messages as having been copied to Sanglier, to give them the commissioner's authority. She did the same with requests to every investigating force for the wire used to secure the praying hands to be sent to The Hague, for examination and testing by Europol's forensic scientists. There were only two mentions in anything she'd read of such tests already having been done, in London and in Brussels. Both dismissed the wire as industrial binding in such common and widespread use throughout England and Belgium that batch or manufacture tracing was impossible.

She maintained nightly telephone contact with her mother, repeating on the eve of the operation the assurance of a weekend visit, and called twice from the incident room on the actual day. On the second occasion Claudine spoke with the surgeon, who said both breasts had been removed as well as a substantial proportion of the lymph glands. They would not know for several weeks if they had got all the malignant tumours but he was hopeful. Her mother was a remarkably fit and determined woman. He expected a quick recovery.

And Rosetti kept his contact promise. He'd found sufficient evidence of internal anal and vaginal bruising to satisfy him that the Asian boy as well as the girls had been raped. He'd also recovered semen deposits from which he hoped to get DNA tracings. He hadn't discovered any soap or cleaning fluid residue on the bodies, nor any dye deposit to provide a clue to any employment. Nor had any of the three Asian teenagers he'd so far examined undergone any dental work that might have been recognized by an orthodontist. There were other examinations and tests he was carrying out before moving on to London. If anything he judged to be vital emerged he'd obviously tell her at once but he'd prefer to complete every test and analysis and then discuss them with her in full rather than keep adding piecemeal to her profile. He said he was glad of her immediate agreement, particularly after the pressure from Poulard and Siemen to give them each finding as he made it.

'How are you getting on with them?' asked Claudine.

'They're very hopeful of a lead from my examinations.'

I bet they are, thought Claudine: from her complete assimilation of the French reports she knew it was their only practical chance of appearing to benefit from going to France in the first place. Dismissing the two detectives from her mind, Claudine said: 'Have you confirmed your belief that the mouths were jammed into a smile?'

'Absolutely. The damage is quite extensive inside, the boy particularly.'

'The faces are still frozen into those grimaces?'

'Of course. They're in refrigeration.'

'Could they be improved? Made less horrible?'

'Their families know they've disappeared, and they haven't come forward,' Rosetti pointed out, understanding the direction of the questioning. 'Why should seeing after-death photographs in newspapers or on posters make them change their minds?'

'Because they *are* after death,' said Claudine brutally. 'The shock might just snap them into doing it. And there'll be others, not just the family, who know them. Even an anonymous call would be enough.'

'They could be made presentable,' conceded Rosetti. 'Do you want me to do it before going on to London?'

Claudine weighed the question. 'Yes, if you've completed everything you want to do. And the others, when you've finished your examination.'

After Siemen's ice-breaking approach the two detectives maintained daily contact, too. Usually it was the German but twice the calls came from Poulard. He never once referred to her profile but conceded they hadn't learned sufficient to justify extending their trip by visiting the various French cities where parts of the bodies had been left.

'There seems to have been some misunderstanding about our liaison,' said Claudine, seeing no reason why she had to wait for their return before confronting the stupidity.

'I thought we had divided our respective responsibilities,' said Poulard.

'Between ourselves,' agreed Claudine easily. 'But I imagined you'd have wanted to be associated with our first presentation to the Commission.' The recording apparatus revolved silently in her line of sight on the far side of the incident room and Claudine realized, surprised, how adept she was becoming at bureaucratic guerrilla warfare, even automatically choosing phrases like 'our first presentation' to make clear the separating awkwardness was theirs, not hers.

'Teething troubles,' said Poulard, too glibly.

And who bit off more than they could chew, thought Claudine, amusing herself with the metaphor. 'I'm glad we seem to have resolved them now. Maybe it's something we should talk through when you get back, to make sure there's no misunderstanding in future.'

'Maybe.'

Having made her point, Claudine didn't raise it again on Poulard's second approach from Paris. Neither did he, talking only of the investigations — arrests even, in Lyon and Marseille — he'd initiated on known National Front cells. She had just replaced the receiver after that conversation, on the Thursday afternoon, when Sanglier said he wanted to see her.

He had to attempt the recovery in the way he'd already decided, after the disastrous session with Sobell, but Sanglier knew it wasn't going to be easy. So much had happened since. Immediately after learning of a British investigation too restricted even for the British commissioner to be told, Sanglier had discovered through the travel division Claudine's less than twenty-four-hour visit to Lyon. Since which time, according to telephone records, she'd several times telephoned her mother's restaurant and a Lyon hospital, both of which he'd identified by dialling and apologizing for reaching the wrong number. The explanation for those to her mother were obvious enough: logically, whatever Claudine Carter knew her mother also knew. The hospital remained a mystery. He could only guess there were people working there who'd been associated with the Resistance half a century before. Or who'd inherited some knowledge, as he was sure Claudine had inherited hers.

Other commissioners had even commented to him about the woman's self-confidence —

admiring it as an attribute, not nervous of it as worrying independence — particularly after criticizing the press release in a memorandum to the entire operational committee. Sanglier didn't accept that her objection had rightly gone to those who'd given her the commendation and in whose name the media statement had been made, which was how those admiring commissioners saw it. The cow should have worked through him and she knew it. So to do what she had was positively denigrating him, which she clearly felt able to do without risk of correction.

The most bitter recognition of all was that, for the moment at least, she was right. Worse, even, was that *he* had virtually to make peace with *her*.

Sanglier was standing away from his desk when Claudine arrived. He forced the few cosmetic steps necessary to appear to greet her, ushering her away from the desk to the more comfortable side area where they'd sat with Sobell.

'It's the wrong time of the day for coffee. Something stronger, perhaps? Wine? Whatever.'

The odd uncertainty was there. 'I don't drink, thank you.'

'Then I won't. It's hardly cocktail hour anyway.'

Where were the Gauloises, wondered Claudine. She remembered, belatedly,

Sanglier hadn't smoked during the meeting with Sobell. She sat quite comfortably, waiting.

'I wanted to tell you how impressed I was with your profile,' said Sanglier, the praise thick in his throat. 'I was glad the rest of the Commission agreed sufficiently with me to make the commendation.'

Why did the man find it necessary to claim credit? 'Thank you.'

'But you disagreed with our assessment of it?' A criticism of the Commission would feature well on his personal recording.

'Not with the assessment. With the emphasis given to some parts to the disadvantage of others . . .' Although she was sure she was right, Claudine decided against an open challenge. Instead, recalling the phrase to which she most objected, she went on: 'I did not, for example, insist that "racism was the underlying connecting link". I specifically avoided that conclusion in my presentation to you and Commissioner Sobell.'

Sanglier was ready. 'I fail to see your argument when you advise Cologne racial hatred is the most likely motivation and attach a list of every neo-Nazi organization that exists in Germany for them to investigate!'

'Because that killing probably is racially motivated. But the others aren't.' There was nothing to be gained by complaining the Germans were still withholding material:

she would anyway have had to disclose how she knew.

Sanglier had hoped for a more exploitable response: one that might, even, show the confidence spilling over into above-her-station arrogance. 'Would you have liked the statement cleared with you first?'

'Consultation might have prevented the wrong stress. And the very real danger.'

Sanglier felt a jump of unease. 'What very real danger?'

'I believed my profile to be an internal document, restricted to Europol and to the investigating forces it might guide in their continuing inquiries. The release contained virtually every opinion I offered . . .' She allowed another break, veering towards the earlier avoided challenge. '. . . some, even, that I *didn't* offer, almost as if there'd been another contribution.'

'I still fail to see —'

'I'd hoped to have made it clear in my memorandum to the Commission. Something I did dwell upon in my profile was copy murders. The way the release was phrased could sound like an invitation to a mentally unstable person.'

Why in God's name hadn't Burrows cautioned him about that when he'd checked the proposed wording with the American, instead of stressing the racial aspect? 'More murders, you mean?'

220

'I sincerely believe it to be a risk. I hope I'm wrong. But then, odd though it may seem, I frequently hope I am wrong about some of the forecasts I make.'

Paradoxically it was the sort of remark he would have welcomed very recently, but it didn't excite him now as it once would have done. Instead he decided he'd have to abandon recording these encounters: destroy the tapes so far collected and get the equipment dismantled. Virtually everything that had so far been gathered provided nothing incriminating or usable for his intended purpose but rather created a perfect defence for the damned woman against any accusation of incompetence or inability. 'It is, of course, only your opinion.'

It was too inviting an opportunity to ignore. 'But one which I was appointed — without any outside interference as far as I am aware — to provide.'

'Quite so,' muttered Sanglier. He did, finally, light one of the pungent cigarettes, needing to bring the conversation to its original purpose. 'How are things with Poulard and Siemen?'

'Settling down,' said Claudine cautiously.

'So there have been problems?' pressed Sanglier.

'The expression that Poulard and I agreed upon was teething troubles.'

Sanglier was rapidly changing his mind

about his choice of René Poulard. It was another frustration, but there was nothing now he could do about it. With the decision already made to destroy the tape, he said openly: 'I believe I was misguided by them, from Paris.'

'In what way?' asked Claudine, even more cautiously. The pendulum appeared to have swung back in the direction of the strained friendliness of their first meeting, just prior to her introduction to the two detectives.

'About the exchange of information between you: from whom I could expect any lead to come.' Forcing the words, which were true but not in the way he had to convey them, Sanglier added: 'I was extremely uncomfortable during our meeting with Commissioner Sobell. I felt quite improperly briefed.'

Would that explain the oddness of the man's behaviour? Perhaps, taking into account her belief of Sanglier's inner uncertainty. Except that the problem then hadn't been improper briefing: they'd learned nothing in Paris to brief the man about. She had nothing to lose from accepting an offered olive branch, to further advantage. 'I'm sure you've corrected that during your daily conversations.'

Sanglier began a sharp look towards her but stopped. 'You're also in touch daily, for the same conversations, aren't you?'

'I don't know,' said Claudine smoothly. 'We talk, certainly. I don't know if I talk with them about the same things as they talk about to you.'

The bitch was playing with him, as she always did: she might be able to keep the smirk off her face but she couldn't keep it out of her voice. 'There seems to have been little point in their going to France at all. Not until Rosetti's arrival, that is. And that's not opening up a positive line of inquiry for them to follow. Are you learning anything from it?'

Claudine didn't answer at once. With the exception of a startling pathological discovery — which she'd known about virtually the moment the Italian made it — there was every practical working reason to wait until the man finished his reexaminations of all the remains before updating her profile rather than add each individual piece of the jigsaw as it emerged. But that's how Poulard and Siemen would be offering it in their desperation to appear to be providing something. So Sanglier would know if she held anything back. 'There are some medical findings that don't take us very far forward but might improve the profile when I've had the chance to consider them in their proper perspective. The most important, from an investigatory point of view, is semen deposits from which it might be possible to extract some DNA to identify the killers when they're arrested. It's being analysed at the moment.'

'We recovered extremely well with the press

release: turned every criticism back on the people making it. It's important we maintain the momentum.'

'I understand that.'

'How much longer before you'll be able to provide an enlarged profile?'

'I don't know.'

'If it becomes a problem, you could provide something?'

'Yes,' said Claudine reluctantly.

'I hope there isn't any misunderstanding between us from the meeting with Sobell?'

'None as far as I am concerned.'

'That's good to hear,' smiled Sanglier. 'If difficulties arise with Poulard or Siemen, you'll let me know, won't you?'

Claudine was curious if the identical question had been put to the two detectives. 'I'm sure none will.'

Claudine made her way back to the lower level trying to decide what Sanglier had meant to achieve by calling their meeting. For her part she hoped he'd understood she knew bloody well that he was getting her opinions checked by Scott Burrows. And that she'd frightened him sufficiently to make him think twice about doing it in future.

Yvette was waiting for her in the incident room with Peter Toomey's request that she return his call as soon as possible. Claudine's breath perceptibly snatched.

★ ★ ★

'Motherfuckers!' erupted Scott Burrows. In his anger it took several attempts to light the cigar.

'I'm sorry,' said Hardy, conscious of the looks from people closest to them in the embassy mess. Scott had been pissing into the wind to imagine Washington would change its mind. 'There was a killing that fitted two weeks ago.'

'Identical?'

'Close enough. Raleigh, North Carolina. Highway patrolman. Had a wife and two kids.'

'I know the fuck where Raleigh is!' said Burrows irritably. 'Maybe if I'd been there it wouldn't have happened.'

'At least it wasn't you.'

'It wouldn't have been.'

'Miriam's going to be upset,' said Hardy.

'I think she might leave me.'

The FBI station chief frowned over his glass. 'You're not serious about that?'

'I am.'

'You going to tell Washington?'

'I think I might tell Washington I quit altogether.'

'That's not going to solve anything.'

'We could go back stateside.'

'What if your profile is accurate?'

'I'd be ready.'

'Would Miriam, when you're not around?'

Burrows didn't reply.

★ ★ ★

'There's no point in this, is there?' said Sanglier.

'No point in what?' Françoise frowned.

At least the thin cheroots she smoked didn't smell like the ones the American smoked, but he wished she wouldn't do it so openly in public. The terrace of the Villa Rosenrust was crowded. 'Going on as we are.'

'What's wrong with it? I don't get in your way, you don't get in mine. It's a perfect situation.'

'I don't have a "way".'

'That, darling Henri, is your problem. Why don't you fuck this woman psychologist you're always on about?'

'You're being fatuous. And life doesn't come down to fucking.'

'It does to me. And I'm being totally practical. I think our situation works perfectly.'

'What if I did find someone? And wanted to marry her?'

'You couldn't,' said Françoise simply. 'You're married to me.'

It was going to be more difficult than he'd imagined.

Chapter Fourteen

A lot had unsettled Claudine during the preceding thirty-six hours, but Toomey's urging that she be accompanied by a lawyer was perhaps the most disturbing. But the delay had given her time to rationalize and she was glad she had imposed it. She was in total control of herself again, mentally assembling her for-and-against patterns, like Kurt Volker's computer comparison graphs. She didn't like personal uncertainty. In the last few months there had been far too much.

Most obviously in her favour was that there could be no shock from this meeting greater than that which Toomey had produced the first time. She hadn't collapsed then. Nor would she now, whatever the new reason for this second encounter, if indeed there was a new reason. Toomey had refused to give one: to tell her anything, apart from making the lawyer suggestion.

Logically it could only be a positive legal development in the investigation into Paul Bickerstone and a £200,000,000 currency trading profit. But how positive for Toomey to agree without argument to a meeting at her weekend convenience, not during normal

227

working time? More questions than proof, she guessed. A double-edged reassurance, Claudine acknowledged. True, if it had been urgent, he could have come to her in The Hague, as he had before. But the fact that he'd accepted a Saturday meeting indicated importance. Had that been the intention, like beginning their conversation with an immediate reference to her need for legal help and asking her to come to London and refusing to be specific about anything, all ploys to trick her into some mistake as he'd tried so hard to do at their initial confrontation?

Pointless speculation, Claudine determined. Any more and she'd be committing the cardinal psychological sin herself, introducing too many alternatives into too small a set of circumstances. And there were other considerations, maybe of equal import. Greater, even.

The job had to come first, as it had come first the previous weekend despite her genuine concern for and necessary duty to her mother. Which she'd had to readjust again. It was only a readjustment, arriving at Lyon in the evening instead of the intended morning. But it was still a change to a promised arrangement — a promise to the only person she loved in the world — and she didn't admire herself for having made it, quite regardless of the older woman's uncomplaining acceptance and even insistence that there was no real need for her to come at all. Claudine didn't believe her. Despite the qualified confidence of the surgeon, Claudine was alarmed at the echoing lassitude in her mother's voice and by Gérard Lanvin's stilted reservation when she'd specifically telephoned him to get honest answers about her mother's recovery.

And then there was the job. Although she hadn't anticipated it when she'd refused Toomey's initial demand that she go to London on the Friday, a practical reason for her remaining at Europol had emerged.

It had been Volker's idea to draw digital maps on the computer screen and superimpose lines connecting each body-part city, visually making obvious — particularly in France — something she should have realized but hadn't until it was literally displayed before her in the sort of picture it was her job to create.

So important did she believe the implication to be that Claudine actually considered alerting Sanglier in advance of any secondary profile. In the end she didn't, expecting to hear from Rosetti immediately after the weekend.

By coincidence, he was also spending it in London, dogged by the two detectives, who intended to return to The Hague after the second English autopsy. For re-evaluation, Poulard had said.

Claudine had ordered things so successfully in her mind by the Saturday morning that she even briefly speculated, on her early morning flight, what the two detectives would do in the totally unlikely event of a chance encounter between them all in London. And failed to guess, apart from estimating the speed with which they would hurry to alert Henri Sanglier. Which returned her mind from idle conjecture to serious reflection again.

Quite obviously it was not a question she could answer until after today's meeting, but how endangered would her position really be at Europol if they learned of Toomey's inquiry? She genuinely didn't know anything, legal or otherwise, about Gerald Lorimer or Paul Bickerstone, or of any involvement, legal or otherwise, that Warwick might have had with them. So where was the embarrassment if it did become public knowledge? She'd done nothing illegal, so it couldn't affect her position at Europol. It couldn't impugn her professional judgement or ability or integrity, either.

She actually looked around for familiar faces as she made her way across the Heathrow concourse before realizing the Europol plane would have used the private section of the airport. She gazed intently from the taxi on her way into London, waiting for the tug of nostalgia. The route took her nowhere near the Kensington house but there was a plunge of sadness when she recognized the slip road that would have taken her to it. Otherwise she felt nothing, not even when they stopped at the Home Office which had been almost more of a home to her than Kensington. There was only a weekend skeleton staff — none of whom she recognized — but even fewer visitors, so she was escorted immediately to Toomey's office. It was on the executive floor with a window view of the lake in St James's Park and Claudine realized she might have underestimated the man's Civil Service grade and importance. She wondered if that had been a factor in his asking her to come to London, bringing her this time on to his impressive territory. If it had been, he'd failed: she was neither impressed nor frightened. But the echelon certainly confirmed political as well as criminal implications: the Home Secretary's suite occupied the same level.

Toomey wore a three-piece weekday suit and another vaguely possible club tie under a hard collar. The precise moustache appeared to bristle. A fresh evidence notebook was already open on the desk, separated from his recorder by his thin silver pencil. His polite standing at her entry was a stretch-and-sit exercise. Her straight-backed chair was already positioned directly opposite him.

'I'm afraid there's no secretarial staff on Saturdays. I could probably get coffee from the canteen.'

'I've had Home Office coffee before.'

'Good coffee is one of the many advantages

231

of living in Europe.' A smile flickered but didn't settle. 'Thank you for coming at a weekend.'

Claudine didn't consider she had anything to thank him for. 'We're both making allowances to get this business resolved: whatever this business is.' Coming to London was the only allowance she'd make. Everything had to come from him.

'Are we to wait for your legal representative?'

'I haven't engaged one.'

Toomey frowned. 'Was that wise?'

'How do I know? You refused to tell me what this meeting was about.'

'I would have thought that was obvious.'

It was easy to imagine a replay of their first interview. 'As I think I told you before, nothing is obvious to me.'

'You've a very retentive memory. That's fortunate.'

Claudine ignored the second half of the remark. 'And I remember that first interview ending without your producing any proof whatsoever to support your innuendoes against my husband.' There wasn't the slightest tightness in her chest.

'The Serious Fraud Office have officially begun an inquiry into Paul Bickerstone.'

Claudine decided against telling the man of her inference from the unnamed *Daily Telegraph* reference. Instead she said: 'You've forgotten to put your tape recorder on.'

Toomey had and momentarily she thought she had disconcerted him as he jabbed it into life. 'Are you, Dr Claudine Carter, prepared for this meeting conducted at the Home Office in London on June twenty-eighth to be recorded?'

He hadn't been disconcerted at all, Claudine accepted: rather the attempt was to disconcert her. 'Yes, I am.'

'You were invited to be accompanied by a lawyer?'

'Yes I was.'

'Which you have declined to do?'

'Yes I have.' So she was definitely suspected of involvement in a huge financial fraud. Toomey had clearly rehearsed everything, but in his position she wouldn't have declared herself so forcefully so soon.

'I said an investigation had officially begun into the trading activities of Paul Bickerstone.'

'I heard you.'

'He admits to knowing Gerald Lorimer. And your husband.'

'Where's the admission in that? He did know them.'

'In a friendship that continued long after university.'

'*You* showed *me* the arts ball photograph, indicating that.'

'Which you couldn't remember attending, despite your retentive memory.'

'That's not correct,' said Claudine. 'I remembered the ball very well. It was Bickerstone himself I couldn't recall.'

'According to Bickerstone, the three of them met regularly. He's named clubs. Social occasions.'

'The Pink Serpent one of them?'

'No,' conceded Toomey. 'As a matter of fact it wasn't one he mentioned.'

'Which then?'

'The Garrick. The Travellers.'

'Warwick wasn't a member of either.'

'We know. We checked.'

'Did you check the visitors' book for Warwick's name?'

Toomey smiled triumphantly. 'Your husband was there three times, in the four months immediately prior to his death.'

Why hadn't Warwick mentioned it to her? She didn't know he'd ever been to either. 'Signed in by Bickerstone?'

'By Gerald Lorimer. Whom Bickerstone proposed for membership of both.'

'Was Bickerstone with them when Warwick was there?'

'Members don't have to sign in and out. You didn't know your husband went to such clubs?'

Instead of answering directly Claudine said: 'When I worked from here I travelled a great deal — was away from London a lot.'

'I know. There's a record of your schedule

in the archives. You were extremely busy.'

Toomey wasn't succeeding in prodding the nerves he wanted — he was very far from doing that — but he was getting to her in another way. Could it be true? Could Warwick have lived his life with her on two levels, one entirely removed and secret from the other? And could she have never once, for the briefest moment, suspected? 'It's a demanding profession.'

Her dismissal appeared to irritate the man. 'Are you asking me to believe that your husband never mentioned he regularly spent time with Lorimer and Bickerstone? Didn't you ever talk about what you'd done while you were away and what he'd done while you were away?'

'What you believe, Mr Toomey, is entirely a matter for yourself. The truth is that no, Warwick never talked about being with either of them. If, indeed, he ever was. If I understand you correctly you've only got Bickerstone's word for the friendship.'

'There are other things.'

'People categorically identifying Warwick with Lorimer and Bickerstone in all these clubs and at all these social occasions? Photographs of them together, like the one from the arts ball?'

'Not yet.'

'What then?'

'Certain facts from what Bickerstone has

told us that corroborate those we've independently uncovered.'

'Proving what?'

'Financial dealings.'

'Financial dealings involving Warwick?'

'That remains to be seen.'

It was do-it-yourself psychology time again. 'It always did remain to be seen. It really might help if I could be told what you're talking about.' Again so similar to the first confrontation: Toomey's repertoire was extremely limited for someone who'd got to the top floor with a view of the park and its lake. But Civil Service promotion — even through whatever arcane division Toomey was attached to — never depended upon ability.

'Bickerstone has given us his account of helping Gerald Lorimer financially.'

'Admitted bribing him, you mean?'

'Given his explanation for the movement of large sums of money.'

'Between Bickerstone and Lorimer?' pressed Claudine. Her mind was ahead of the exchange, anticipating in which direction Toomey was trying to lead her. Lorimer and Warwick were dead, unable to confirm or deny anything: prove or disprove anything. Most important of all, unable to give evidence against Bickerstone, if there was evidence to give. So there was no one, provided Bickerstone kept his nerve. Which was the prerequisite of every commodity dealer in the City of London, for every waking moment of their lives. Unless, of course, she had been involved and could be broken. Toomey clearly believed she had: and could be broken, by him. So there was nothing for her to fear. Nor, for that matter, had Bickerstone anything to fear. As he'd know. *Explanation,* Toomey had said. Not admission or confession. That was what he expected her to make, crushed by his interrogation. Her breathing became slightly more difficult, although too marginally for Toomey to realize.

'Yes,' he said, appearing unconcerned at the admission.

She had to peel away the supposition, layer by layer. 'Nothing about the movement of large sums of money between himself and Warwick?'

'Not yet.'

'Not yet?'

'I wanted to have this conversation with you first. That's why I suggested you be accompanied by a legal representative.'

Again Claudine was ahead of the man. 'You believe I can provide information to extract a confession from Paul Bickerstone?'

'Can you?'

'No.'

'Are you sure about that?'

'Positive.'

'I ask you again: are you sure about that?'

'You're accusing me of lying to you!'

Claudine was still entirely confident but conceded that it might have been better if she'd brought a lawyer with her. Except that a lawyer could — and probably would — have concluded the exchange a long time ago and Claudine didn't want it concluded. She wanted to discover the purpose of this second meeting, reduce it to the meaningless and unsubstantiated imputation that it was on a tape recording being made for some evidential use. And by doing that end the whole stupid, fucking thing so she could get back to the far more essential factors in her life, a sick mother and a criminal investigation to confirm her employment within Europol.

'I'm asking you to be honest with me,' said Toomey.

Claudine had sat through dozens — hundreds — of court hearings where clever barristers and clever criminals tossed verbal sallies at each other until one of them — usually the criminal — fumbled the exchange, an exchange like this, because the barrister had the final destructive shot his opponent didn't suspect. Toomey believed he had something to destroy her. 'Let me see or hear, in its entirety, exactly what Paul Bickerstone has told you about himself and my late husband. And then ask me the questions you want answered. Which I will do, in total and complete honesty . . .' she introduced the lull '. . . either here, in this room and on this tape, or in a court of law.'

She'd expected the challenge to knock the man off his carefully prepared course but it didn't. Instead Toomey opened a drawer to his right and pushed a sheaf of papers towards her. For the benefit of the tape, he said: 'This is Paul Bickerstone's account.'

Wrong, Claudine recognized at once: several times wrong. It was unthinkable, until the required exchanges between lawyers, for a possible co-conspirator in a crime, which the man unquestionably believed her to be, to know of any statement made by the main suspect in that crime. So this wasn't the statement upon which Toomey hoped to rely in court. On the man's own admission, this was Bickerstone's explanation. So it wouldn't contain — hint at even — what Toomey imagined he had to ensnare her. She quickly looked up from the closely typed pages. 'This is a narrative, created from a question-and-answer interview similar to this meeting?'

'Conducted in the presence of Bickerstone's legal representative — two, in fact — and after its transcription signed by him. And endorsed by both those lawyers, as a full and true record.'

An even more positive indication that it contained nothing incriminating. 'I'd prefer to hear the tape than read its transcript.'

'It's legally attested to be accurate. It will take a long time to hear the tape.'

'Are you in a hurry?'

For several moments Toomey sat staring directly at her, saying nothing. Then, still unspeaking, he took a tape from the same drawer as its transcript and exchanged it for that which had been recording their encounter. Wrong yet again, decided Claudine. The immediate acquiescence betrayed the man's desperation.

She was startled by the similarity between Bickerstone's carefully modulated voice and the way she remembered Warwick speaking, disliking the unwelcomed reminder. It was Toomey conducting the interrogation, seemingly as rehearsed for it as he'd tried to be with her. On Bickerstone's tape it was possible to hear the background movement and occasional cough from the man's lawyers. Twice there was a muttered exchange, too muffled to be picked up.

Claudine's concentration was absolute, not just upon every syllable but upon the intonations of every word, the imperceptible pauses and mid-sentence deviations. On five occasions the lawyers interceded — always with demands for greater clarity to a question, never with a challenge of legality or refusal to respond — but throughout Bickerstone remained utterly confident, polite, helpful, even contributing more than was necessary. All of which, judged Claudine, he had every reason to be, confident most of all. She didn't speak when the tape ended but switched her concentration to the man on the other side of the desk.

'Well?' she forced Toomey finally to ask.

'You haven't changed the tapes.' This time she thought the reminder — or rather her unfazed reaction — did disconcert the man, although only slightly. After Toomey made the transfer, she said: 'Or identified on the tape the resumption of our meeting, after my hearing the original question-and-answer interview with Paul Bickerstone.'

Toomey delivered the recitation even more formally, with dates and times, making her formality unnecessary. Then he said again: 'Well?'

'That's not it, is it?' she demanded.

For the first time Toomey was obviously flustered. 'Not what?'

'I asked you to let me see or hear, in its entirety, exactly what Paul Bickerstone told you about himself and my late husband.'

'Yes?'

'But *he* told *you* nothing, did he? You told him . . .' She gestured, disparagingly, to the Bickerstone tape that still lay on the desk. 'That recording doesn't contain one single piece of volunteered information! He's always responding to your questions. And your questions are always phrased — badly — showing him the safest way to respond.'

Toomey visibly flushed. 'That's an absurd

assertion, which I resent.' He looked uncomfortably at the tape.

'It's not and you know it!' Claudine stopped abruptly. The man *did* know it, she guessed. Too late, perhaps, but he knew it. Which was why he'd reversed his approach to her today — even, in his desperation, allowed her to hear the tape which had told her far more than she could ever have learned from the transcript — because her hoped-for admission was his last chance. Quickly, determined to crush the man, Claudine picked up with devastating and complete recall: 'Your question: *You retained a friendship with Gerald Larimer and Warwick Jameson after leaving Cambridge, didn't you?* His reply: *Yes.* Your question: *Did you frequently go out with both of them socially?* His reply: *Yes.* Your question: *To clubs and restaurants? Social functions? Things like that?* His reply: *Yes, to things like that.* Your question: *How often did you see Gerald Lorimer and Warwick Jameson socially: once a week, once a fortnight, every month?* His reply: *There was no fixed arrangement. Once, twice a month maybe.* Your question: *It would certainly have been at least once a month, though?* His reply: *Something like that, I suppose.*'

Toomey stared at her, transfixed by the staggering mental performance. Hoarse-voiced, he said: 'It's an admission of a regular and close friendship between a broker suspected of Stock Exchange fraud and a man in a position to have made such a fraud possible.'

Claudine didn't know which advantage to grab first. 'It's not. It's an interview of a man suspected of Stock Exchange fraud to whom every question was phrased in such a way as to provide the answers you expected. So he gave them to you so vaguely they proved nothing and incriminated him in no way whatsoever.'

'What about when we come to the discussion about the money?' demanded Toomey triumphantly.

'What about it?'

'The admissions would be sufficient for any court.'

'No they wouldn't and you know that, too. So do the lawyers advising you. And if they hadn't advised you it wasn't enough we wouldn't be having this meeting today.' Claudine took a deep breath. 'Your remark: *We know about Luxembourg.* His reply: *I don't understand that.* Your question: *You paid Gerald Lorimer large sums of money for information he gave you to carry out insider dealing, didn't you?* His reply: *I have never in my life conducted insider dealing . . .*' Claudine faltered, unsure how much longer she could sustain the effort: just a little longer.

She took another breath, for the final spurt. 'Your question: *How do you explain sums of money amounting to sixty thousand pounds in a Credit Suisse account in Luxembourg?* His reply:

I can't explain why Gerald had a Luxembourg bank account, although there's no reason why he shouldn't have had one. It's not illegal. What I can say to clear up whatever sort of inquiry you're making is that over the years I have loaned Gerald varying sums of money, most of which will be traceable through bank statements I'd be happy to have my accountants make available to you. He was my friend, as I told you. He frequently complained a*bout being short of money. I'm fortunate in being an extremely wealthy man.'* Claudine stopped the verbatim recitation, not wanting to risk any more. 'You've got nothing!' she insisted. 'You told him in advance of discovering a secret bank account, enabling him to explain his bribes away as loans. I'm sure he has made bank statements available to you to account for most of the money. He'd have been stupid not to give himself an escape route: they always do. If Lorimer hadn't killed himself, you'd have probably had a case. Without him you've got nothing.' She wished she'd accepted the canteen coffee, disgusting though it invariably was. 'And you've certainly got nothing against my late husband. Which you also know. You weren't even able to suggest a bribe —'

'Not then,' snapped Toomey. The man stirred, pushing himself upright like a punished boxer preparing to fight back.

'Or now. Nor at any time in the future.'

244

'Your husband was a frequent visitor to Luxembourg?'

'Not frequent,' Claudine corrected. 'He went there from time to time. It's one of the centres of the European Union. His job was European law.'

'Was he ever there the same time as Gerald Lorimer?'

'Not that I am aware.'

'But then you seem unaware of a lot of your late husband's activities.'

'I don't believe I am,' said Claudine, refusing the anger the man was trying to generate. 'I don't think you should base conclusions upon assertions made by someone during an appallingly badly conducted interview.'

Toomey's colour had been subsiding. Now it flared again. 'We recovered Lorimer's passport from his flat. Would you have any objection to letting us have your late husband's passport?'

'Yes, I think I would.'

'Why?'

'I can't see any reason why I should. And because I believe I have cooperated as fully as necessary with a totally unwarranted and pointless inquiry. What would it prove if they were both in Luxembourg at the same time?'

'It would be interesting,' suggested Toomey.

'I thought you were seeking evidence of a

245

serious crime, not coincidences that were interesting.'

The man's colour had begun to subside again. 'You paid the deposit on your house in Kensington in cash. Something like forty thousand pounds.'

'*My* house, purchased before I married Warwick Jameson.'

'You already knew him, though? And it became your marital home.'

'It suited both of us.'

'Like the Jaguar?'

'Yes.'

'That was paid for in cash too, wasn't it?'

Claudine's feeling wasn't outraged anger, the most understandable response; it was astonishment at the depth of the intrusion into her life, as if she'd caught someone spying upon her when she was naked. 'We were given the cash to purchase it, yes. The different driving requirements, you understand?'

Toomey couldn't keep the satisfaction from his face. 'No, I'm sorry, I don't understand.'

Claudine met the man's attitude with disdain, although her breathing was becoming worryingly more difficult. 'My mother, who lives in France, gave us the money as a wedding present. As she gave me the money for the deposit for my house, which I bought long before there was any thought of my marrying. She also paid for our honeymoon, in Antigua. It rained, twice. Warwick was stung by a jellyfish but it wasn't serious.'

'Your mother is obviously an extremely generous person, like Paul Bickerstone?'

'She is, although I'm not sure I like the comparison with Paul Bickerstone.'

'She'd be able to confirm these cash gifts, if she were asked?'

'I wouldn't allow her to be asked. She underwent an extremely serious cancer operation three days ago. The prognosis is still very uncertain.' She'd have to use her inhaler soon.

'I'm sorry to hear that,' said the man, with no regret in his voice. 'There would be bank records, though?'

'I see no more reason to make those available to you than I do Warwick's passport. I have satisfactorily — and honestly — answered all your questions. At great personal inconvenience — delaying a visit to my mother — I've cooperated by travelling here today. There is absolutely nothing more I can do or say to help you.'

'That could be construed as hostility, Dr Carter.'

'Whatever construction you put upon it, like whatever you choose to believe or disbelieve, is entirely a matter for you, Mr Toomey.' Unable to continue any longer without it Claudine took the Ventalin from her handbag and inhaled deeply.

'Are you all right?'

'I suffer from asthma.'

247

'I didn't know the pollution or pollen counts were particularly high today.'

'You're clearly not a sufferer.' Fuck, thought Claudine. Fuck, fuck, fuck.

'It really would have been better if you'd accepted that a lawyer should be present.'

'Nothing that's happened here today has changed my opinion about that.'

'Neither has our prime consideration changed, about your position and any possible embarrassment within Europol. That's why I refused to discuss anything with them.'

'What?'

'I received a personal telephone call from the British commissioner, Winslow, wanting to know the reason for our first meeting. Said he'd got my name from the visitors' security log. I said it was a confidential internal matter. I thought he might have asked you direct.'

'Yes,' agreed Claudine. 'I would have thought so, too.' She managed to wait until she was outside in the street before having to use the inhaler again.

Her mother no longer looked formidable, in control, as Claudine had always thought of her, and Claudine felt cheated. Frightened, too. Not at the cancer that had visibly gnawed away at the woman, the thought of which repulsed Claudine as much as before: more, even, now that she could see the physical emptiness beneath her mother's nightdress. The fear was at the thought of her mother's not being able to overcome it, as she'd indomitably overcome every other obstacle she'd been confronted with in her life. Claudine had never accepted that her mother was going to die. Not be there. It wasn't the reasoning of someone trained to reason; whose job was to reason. But it was a belief — something she knew which couldn't be dislodged — long before she'd been taught to think sensibly and logically. To be grown up. At the moment of walking into her mother's hospital room Claudine didn't want to be grown up. She didn't want a child's belief taken away from her.

Monique was propped up by a support and over her sagged nightgown wore a knitted bed jacket that Claudine wished she didn't because it was thick wool and ornately patterned and overpowered her, making her look older than she was, old and frail and forlorn. A tube, concealed as much as possible by the coverings, snaked into a receptacle that had also been concealed as much as possible beneath the bed. Claudine guessed it was a catheter and knew her mother would have hated the dependency. Her mother's cheek was damp when Claudine kissed her.

'I haven't got any tits left,' announced Monique.

'You knew you weren't going to have,' said Claudine, refusing any response to the bravado. She refused, also, the pretence of telling her mother how well she looked, because she didn't and would have despised the lie. The cherished belief had gone but the honesty there'd always been between them had to stay.

'I might have to have more treatment. It'll make my hair fall out.'

'There are wigs.'

'It won't be very attractive in the bedroom, will it?'

As considerate as always, Gérard had insisted she see her mother alone, promising to come later. 'Have you decided?'

'No,' said Monique. 'He bought me this jacket.'

'It's very nice.'

Her mother looked at Claudine sharply. 'I'm wearing it because he bought it for me.'

'I asked if you'd decided what to do.'

'It's too soon.'

'Did you give him the choice I suggested?'

Monique nodded.

'What did he say?'

'That he still wanted to marry me.'

'So it's up to you.'

'It always was.'

'So?'

'I'm going to wait to see if I have to have this other treatment.'

'You're just putting it off.'

'Of course I am,' said Monique loudly.

'Leave me some dignity.'

'I'm sorry.'

'I'm seeing the notary, though. As Gérard suggested.'

It was the obvious moment. 'I have something to ask you.'

'The restaurant will be yours, obviously.'

'That's not what I meant,' said Claudine. 'You've been very generous to me. The apartment in Paris, when I was at school. The money for the London house and the wedding present. The honeymoon.'

'What about it?'

'There would be bank records, wouldn't there? Debits showing the gifts?'

Monique frowned. 'Why?'

'There's some irritating income tax inquiry, in England. They've asked me to explain where I got the money,' said Claudine, the lie well prepared.

Monique gave a thin, conspiratorial smile. 'Only fools pay income tax, you know that.'

Tax evasion, the national preoccupation of France, Claudine remembered. 'It was all cash?'

The smile widened. 'I've not only got the best and most expensive restaurant in Lyon. It's got the deepest cash register, too. Just enough for them, more than enough for me.'

'So there are no bank records?'

'Of course not.' The satisfaction went from the older woman's lined face. 'Is that a problem for you, in England?'

'No,' said Claudine.

'Tell them you won the lottery,' suggested Monique brightly.

'Yes,' said Claudine, smiling back. 'That's what I'll do.'

She'd fallen into the trap and she didn't know it, thought Toomey euphorically. It was enough to convince the Serious Fraud Office and possibly for a second interview with Bickerstone, although he would have liked something harder, something unarguably incriminating, to put against the man. So why didn't he find it? There was no hurry, now. He could take his time and review everything he'd assembled, to make sure he had everything.

Maybe he'd officially invite Commissioner Winslow to the next meeting with Dr Claudine Carter. He'd bet a month's salary she'd bring a lawyer with her then.

Chapter Fifteen

In the first few moments Claudine came close to being overwhelmed by what Kurt Volker had created. There was every sort of comparison chart, computer graphic and detailed master and subsidiary file, all unlike anything she had seen before and certainly better and more comprehensive than she'd possibly hoped. The German had gone far beyond matching the similarities which unequivocally proved there were three separate sets of killers, and the graphics were the most sophisticated Claudine had ever had to work from. Most impressive of all was the way Volker had used an optical scanner to pick up the horrifically contorted death grimaces of the Céleste five and, by using the computer equivalent of a paint-kit and airbrush, had restored the features to pictures acceptable for reproduction in newspapers and posters for any public recognition appeal. As soon as she saw them Claudine realized that the facial corrections she'd asked Rosetti to carry out after his autopsies were unnecessary.

'You're an artist!' exclaimed Claudine.

'The computer does the work: I just tell it what to do,' Volker said modestly.

The publicly usable in-life image of the victim dominated the fronting sheet of each of Volker's murder files, with the original death mask alongside. Every physical characteristic so far known was listed, including height, weight and body measurements. Each contained the maps which had been Volker's concept, marking in dated sequence the towns and the routes along which the dismembered bodies had been found where the distribution had been countrywide, and in the same order the locations where the discoveries had been confined within a city. Volker had established the continuity not just by date but by recording the precise discovery times given by the various investigating agencies, which had been on Claudine's list of requests but became unnecessary with the completeness of Volker's assembly.

Claudine said what he'd done was magnificent and that she felt superfluous and in apparent embarrassment at the praise Volker's customary quick blinking became even faster. He collected facts, he pointed out: she had to interpret them and he couldn't do that. Neither could his computers, although they'd probably be able to one day.

'I'm not sure you couldn't do it now,' Claudine said. Among so much she didn't understand — and she wasn't thinking primarily of the investigation — time with Volker was like being protected in an oasis against a sandstorm she couldn't see through. It went beyond her need for orderly patterns from precise electronics. She liked his unprompted initiative and his lateral thinking and his total disregard of propriety: the Trojan horses on which he rode into forbidden places in cyberspace. She even liked the don't-give-a-damn way he dressed. In fact she simply liked Kurt Volker.

'I didn't get anything from the prostitutes' directories in Brussels,' Volker apologized.

'It was worth trying.'

'And going on with. I'm trying something else, going through the centralized records in Holland and Belgium to see if they've digitalized their criminal photographic records. If they have and either of the two women have a record — for anything, not necessarily prostitution — I could identify them, in time . . .' Volker pulled up his image of the Amsterdam victim, enlarging it until it occupied the entire screen. 'It's not just a copy of the death mask, tidied up. Every measurement is absolutely correct, like the bone structure and the lip, nose and earlobe thicknesses and protuberances. If I get a similarity I can overlay my picture with theirs for a definitive match. Hairstyle doesn't matter. It's facial contours and configurations that are important and I've got every one.'

'Hugo says the French teenagers were raped. What about anything pornographic involving them or any of the others? Sado-masochism? Snuff movies even?' She realized as she finished speaking that it had seemed quite natural to think of Rosetti by his given name.

'No problem accessing any Web site for all the sex bulletin boards,' said Volker. 'The difficulty might be the sheer volume, even at the speed with which I could eventually run the checks through. And we'd have to buy the films, of course. They're mostly on video, not computer. I can't get into them unless they're on a base.'

'So it isn't practical?'

'I could establish a poste restante box number address for delivery,' offered Volker. 'And hide each purchase through more than one system in any country or several countries, so we wouldn't be identified or charged. That's easy. But all the time we were buying what's available more material would be being produced and advertised, so we could never stop buying. Even if we set up back-to-back, twenty-four-hour transmission monitored with an automatic search program — which I could technically write — it would still take months. And I didn't think we had months.'

'No,' agreed Claudine. 'We don't. I hope we don't have to resort to it.'

Rosetti made contact during the morning, guessing he'd be back in The Hague by mid-week. On the same call he passed the telephone to Poulard, who said they'd decided to stay with the pathologist: he would be able to travel more quickly in the Europol plane and they could go through everything with the investigating officers in each city while Rosetti carried out his medical examinations. Things were coming together very well. Claudine didn't bother to ask the Frenchman what that meant — knowing it didn't mean anything — but wondered if she'd detected a note of annoyance in Rosetti's voice at the claustrophobia of the detective's presence. She wasn't surprised that Poulard and to a lesser extent Siemen had attached themselves to the Italian; they had some misjudgements to disguise. But there was going to be a hiatus until the man returned before she could improve her own profile with his findings.

There was still sufficient to occupy Claudine until then. All the requested hand-binding wire had arrived and she dictated a detailed request to Europol's forensic division on what she hoped to learn from their tests. With as much if not more concentration than she'd devoted to the original disorganized murder files she studied the minutely categorized guides Volker had built up, not to verify the computer expert's data assembly but to confirm her own.

And there was time to consider her personal difficulties, which in view of David Winslow's apparent awareness — curiosity at least — were hardly personal any more but infringed upon Europol and her position in it. Or did they? The core of her several uncertainties remained whether officially to inform the commissioner, particularly knowing, as she did, that Winslow had made an inquiry to Peter Toomey. But not, it appeared, an official approach. Which didn't help a decision. If the inquiry had been official, then so should the response have been. But not from her: from the British Home Office. And it hadn't reached — or been taken to — that level. *Un*official then. And if it was unofficial, there was no reason to make it otherwise. At once the mental debate during the flight to London came back to her, confused by an additional conundrum. *Why* had the British commissioner approached London but not her when he'd been rebuffed, as Toomey claimed to have rebuffed the man? That didn't make any more sense than a lot of other things, chief among them Winslow's assertion that he'd learned of Toomey's visit to The Hague from the visitors' security log.

The fact remained that she wasn't guilty of anything. So there wasn't any reason *not* to tell Winslow, complicated though an explanation might be. Or was there? Not from the criteria of honesty and fact. But what about in the sort of hard-nosed, court-manipulated reality she knew so well? In that reality she was under what appeared to be the most microscopic of investigations which had uncovered her receipt of large sums of money for which there was officially no satisfactory explanation or provable source. And it was unthinkable to ask someone as sick as her mother to confirm the cash transactions in a court of law. For the older woman to do so — even in a statement prior to any court hearing — would expose her to investigation herself by the French tax authorities. And not just her mother. Although her acceptance of tax evasion money had been quite unwitting Claudine acknowledged that legally she *had* received it. Which either made her an accomplice and therefore liable to French prosecution and demands for repayment or, even more ridiculous, a tax authority witness against her own mother. But still with a tax and repayment liability.

And Toomey wasn't going to conclude his investigation. If anything the London meeting, which objectively hadn't been helped by her aggressive ridicule, had ended with the man being more determined than ever to prove her a knowing part of whatever scam Gerald Lorimer and Paul Bickerstone had been running, for God knows how long.

She didn't know what to do, Claudine recognized, hating the admission of failure even to herself. She'd always known what to do, always been in control, always had the right answer. Suddenly not to know *wasn't* acceptable: not acceptable at all. She definitely needed a lawyer, someone with a different viewpoint and better legal knowledge than she had: someone to tell her what to do. Not tell. Advise. A lawyer wouldn't have advised her to keep Warwick's note. She wouldn't tell him about that. Wouldn't have to. It had no relevance. Did Warwick's passport have the relevance Toomey clearly implied, the passport she'd recovered from among Warwick's personal possessions within an hour of her weekend return to The Hague and was now in the office safe, together with the suicide note?

No, she decided, feeling a physical sink in her stomach. European Union passports weren't stamped on journeys between member countries, not even on re-entry into Britain which retained its border controls. Toomey should have known that. *Would* have known that, just as he would have known he could have got Warwick's travel dates from the Home Office's travel records, from which he'd got the details of her absences from London.

It had been a trick demand and she hadn't realized it. And to have responded as she had would have conveyed the impression she had something to hide, which she didn't. Circumstantial, as so much else was circumstantial. But damning, as so much else was damning. And the bastard *had* tricked her: beaten her.

In the end, still undecided, Claudine did nothing, which was as alien to her as not knowing what to do because she regarded both as weakness.

During the working day she was mostly able to concentrate upon the investigation in which she was a leader, not a suspect. At Claudine's suggestion Rosetti addressed to her the specimen shipments he wanted tested, ensuring detailed records were established by the diligent Yvette from which Claudine was able to pressure Europol forensic scientists to have their results and findings waiting for the pathologist's return. Apart from just one, they all were, together with copies of Kurt Volker's dossiers.

Rosetti entered the incident room flanked by Poulard and Siemen, as if they were guarding an asset.

It only took Rosetti an hour to go through the forensic examinations, after which he announced: 'Right! I'm ready.'

He addressed the remark to Claudine, as the person in authority, and she knew the two detectives would have seen it the same way.

'We are, too,' said Poulard.

For the first time they used the larger conference table, because Claudine included Volker in the presentation. She carefully placed herself with him on one side, while the two detectives sat on the other and Rosetti dominated at the head. Claudine thought that for someone who had carried out so many operations in such a short time Rosetti looked remarkably relaxed and alert. The other two men, by contrast, looked strained and tired. It was the first time she'd seen Poulard in clothes crumpled by uninterrupted wear: oddly, the Frenchman appeared more dishevelled than Volker.

'I've taken the examinations some way beyond what we knew in any of the cases,' began Rosetti. 'It's for you to decide whether it helps strengthen the profile . . .' he went from Claudine to the detectives '. . . or carries the investigation in any forward direction.'

From the way the Italian phrased his opening it appeared to Claudine as if he hadn't yet talked his findings through in any detail with the other men, despite travelling with them. She said: 'If you've discovered more, I'm sure it will.'

Neither detective spoke. Poulard was affecting nonchalance.

Rosetti extended the hesitation. 'I hope you're prepared from the photographs.'

'We've all investigated murders before,' said Poulard impatiently.

'Not murders like these,' said the pathologist.

'Why don't we get on?'

Rosetti refused to react, setting out in readiness before him yet more photographs to illustrate what he intended to recount. There was no possible doubt about three different killers or methods of killing, he began. So he'd divided them into their respective categories.

He set out the first of the photographs as he talked. The genital disfigurement of the five had been carried out with a cutting instrument far sharper than any used on the other two groups. That same instrument had in every case begun the dismemberment with a bone-cut made by a fine-toothed blade. The bones had then been separated neatly, he thought by an electric rather than a hand-held saw. Saws had also been used on the girl in Cologne and the two white girls, in Brussels and Amsterdam. The cutting on the two white girls had again been started by a single knife-like instrument, much blunter than in Céleste's case, causing extensive after-death bruising. There'd been no knife or cutting instrument used before the saw in Cologne, so the flesh had been extensively ripped. The bone damage in these three cases was consistent with the use of a hand-held saw. Only the five in the first group had any bone damage additional to that to be expected where the limbs had been amputated and the head severed. There were fractures to ankles, forearms and in two cases to ribs. It confirmed, in his opinion, that the amputations had been carried out without anaesthetic and while the victims were fully conscious. That would be consistent with the breaks having been caused by the violence of the convulsions with which, in agony difficult to conceive, the victims had strained and thrown themselves against whatever secured them. There was an element of expertise in the dismemberment of the five, although it wasn't medical. There was no expertise in the other cases. All three had been hacked and slashed.

Around the table went more photographs. Able visually to examine and measure every part of every body, Rosetti had discovered that in none of the first, five-body group did the limbs match up as they should have done with the torsos, quite apart from the one leg that had never been recovered. In each case, with each leg, there was about eight centimetres missing. He didn't think, either, that one leg found against the Drake statue in England belonged to the rest of the body that had been recovered in England: he'd taken flesh and hair follicle samples for a DNA match which would take at least another week to confirm: the DNA requests he'd made were the outstanding tests still to be completed by the forensic laboratory. He couldn't explain the blood loss, which was not only the result of the amputations. On the buttocks and backs — or on the front, depending upon how the torsos were left after the dismemberment — there should have been post-death lividity, the appearance of bruising where the blood had puddled within the body. There was no such marking on any torso.

'Which isn't the biggest mystery about these five: or what I believe to have been a factor in all five, although I can't prove it,' apologized Rosetti. 'I can only establish it in three instances and wouldn't have investigated it at all if the English pathologist hadn't insisted he'd discovered it during his original autopsy and included it in his report. The doctor who carried out the examination on the first French victim and the Austrian pathologist in Vienna both admitted leaving out the same findings because there was no logical explanation apart from mortuary error . . .'

'What?' demanded Poulard.

The exasperation was over-stressed and Claudine was sure the Frenchman was paler now than he had been when Rosetti started his presentation.

'There were ice splinters in the blood: blood taken *before* the bodies went into mortuary refrigeration. Body temperatures were taken at the scenes where the torsos were found — that's standard procedure — and *all* the torsos were colder than the medical examiners expected, even in the cases where no ice splintering in the blood was recorded . . .' Yet again Rosetti looked at Claudine. 'I guess that compounds our problems: it's a factor, definitely, in three out of those five murders but I don't know how it's going to help.'

Claudine smiled. 'It helps a great deal.'

'What?' repeated the ashen Poulard, convincing Claudine that the Italian had waited until now to detail his examination.

'They were deep frozen,' said Claudine simply. 'It explains so very much else.'

Rosetti nodded doubtfully. 'It would explain the body cleanliness. Ice would form, externally. And clean the skin when it was sponged off when it melted as the bodies thawed. But blood pooling would have been much more obvious. And I've already told you there isn't any.'

'But there are missing leg parts,' reminded Claudine in her turn, conscious of the bewildered looks between the two detectives and Kurt Volker. Deciding the guess was justified, she said: 'All these five bodies are marked by three parallel lacerations, in the case of the girls down the stomach into the genital area, with the boy down his back towards his anus. Is there anything specific about those incisions?'

Rosetti looked at Claudine with his head to one side, smiling curiously. 'Like what?'

'Uniformity of measurement?'

He shook his head, apologetic again. 'There are variations, in every case.'

'You've got the measurements?'

'Of course,' said the pathologist, turning to his own notes.

'There *are* three downward parallel cuts,' Claudine pointed out, leading everyone around the table to their individual copies of Volker's files and turning to the reprinted photographs. 'But look at them again. They're not the same. The central laceration, in every case, is formed by the genital or anal mutilation: by the knife or whatever sharp cutting instrument was used. Ignore it. Concentrate upon the outer two. And what Kurt's computers prove. In each of the five cases those outer two lines are forty-five centimetres apart and measure *precisely* the same. And look where those lines would continue . . .'

'The legs,' said Rosetti, nodding as he began to understand.

The other three men were blank-faced.

'The legs,' agreed Claudine. 'The very tops of which, where they would join the torso, are missing in every case.'

'Hooks!' declared the pathologist.

'Hooks,' agreed Claudine again. 'The sort used to suspend meat carcases in cold storage. These five were slaughtered, just like animals. Cut up, like animals. And then hung on racks sometime before each was ferried around the country to be displayed. That's how the blood drained from them from the amputations, without leaving any trace of lividity. And why those eight or so centimetres of the legs in which the hooks were embedded were removed, to prevent its being obvious . . .'

Claudine looked around the assembled group. No one spoke. Only Rosetti smiled.

'I had some forensic tests carried out,' admitted Claudine, alert for the sharp look from Poulard at her ignoring the working arrangements they'd reached before the men's departure to France. Going to the report which had arrived for her with Rosetti's tests she said: 'The wire which secured the hands of our five victims is of a malleable type extensively used in the food packaging industry . . .' She looked up. 'Holland is the country of manufacture. Yet it was not the type used to secure the hands of the girls found in Amsterdam and Brussels . . .' They all looked at her expectantly. 'That comes from somewhere in the East: it hasn't yet been possible to specify which country, although the restoration of the iron, steel and metal industries was one of the first efforts to revitalize the economy of East Germany after reunification.'

'What about the wire that secured the girl in Cologne?' demanded Rosetti.

'East German.' Claudine waited for the point about the food industry to be recognized by the two detectives. When it wasn't, she instructed: 'Go to the maps Kurt has marked. And see how he's connected where the parts of these five bodies were found, particularly in France . . .' She waited while they located the section. 'Every line parallels a major highway, an autoroute or a motorway or an autobahn — the main delivery routes in every country. The bodies were moved around each country without the slightest risk of discovery in the refrigerated delivery trucks into which they were transferred from refrigerated storage . . .'

'*Food* delivery lorries?' demanded Siemen, his face twisted in disgust.

'The sort of food delivery lorries that go up and down those roads every hour and every day,' nodded Claudine. 'But more importantly, every hour of every night. Look at the times when the remains were found. *Always* first thing in the morning. They were *delivered*, overnight. Look at another graph comparison: the Céleste parts have always been found in the same sequence — head, hands, torso, legs, always beginning on a Monday and finishing on a Friday. A full delivery week.'

'Good God!' exclaimed Poulard. The disgust had been Siemen's but the revulsion was the Frenchman's. He only just managed to turn the retch into a strangled cough. Quickly recovering, he said: 'A way forward at last for a proper investigation!'

'Two ways forward,' corrected Claudine, spelling out the significance of the wire analysis the detectives had missed. 'It could be a long process of elimination but the manufacturer of the wire could be established by a process of scientific elimination, in Holland and in the East. From manufacturers it could eventually be narrowed down to purchasers.'

'It *does* fit!' said Rosetti enthusiastically. 'All of it fits.'

'Let's see what else fits,' prompted Claudine.

All of the five upon which they were concentrating were well nourished, resumed Rosetti. None showed any sign of organic disease, although the trachea and lungs of one of the French victims contained minute particles of cloth fibre. In two cases the heels of the right hands were substantially calloused. There were also odd callouses to the feet of the boy, between his big and second toe and beneath each heel.

Reading aloud the forensic results on his submitted specimens, the pathologist said that although there was not at that moment a confirmed recovery, the laboratory was confident of extracting DNA strings from the semen deposits from the boy, both girls in France and the Chinese girl in Vienna.

Coming up from the laboratory notes, Rosetti said: 'The semen deposits in each of these cases was considerable, like the internal bruising. There was actually some anal membrane splitting with the boy. And although I recovered no semen from the other girl there was again substantial bruising at the base of the vaginal introitus . . .'

'Gang rape,' anticipated Claudine.

'Unquestionably, in my opinion,' said the pathologist.

'Why remove those parts of the legs showing the bodies had been suspended from meat hooks — a positive, thought-out attempt to defeat an investigation — yet be careless about physical evidence like semen, from which we could get sufficient for an actual conviction?' asked Poulard. He was stronger-voiced, becoming inured to the horror.

'That's a good question,' acknowledged Claudine, not having thought of it herself. She'd allowed herself the cynicism of expecting Poulard to try to embarrass her or Yvette by commenting upon the sexual examinations and was glad he was remaining properly professional.

Rosetti shrugged. 'Men rarely use condoms in rape. I've never come across victim testimony where they've been used at all in a mass assault of the sort I think occurred here. Maybe they didn't think there'd be any evidence left, after the mutilation. Or, again, that with so many attackers it wouldn't be possible to isolate an individual string . . .' The man paused. 'Which still might not be possible.'

Going back to the laboratory report, Rosetti said the boy's stomach contained the undigested remains of rice and durum wheat, and meat traces from three of the girls' digestive tracts had been identified as lamb. There was also lentil.

Continuing to read out the analyses, Rosetti said tests on gum tissue from the mouths of the second French victim and the girls in London and Vienna gave areca catechu extract as the cause of the heightened mouth redness he'd found in each. None of the five had any dental work or unusual mouth or dental for-

271

mation to justify a dental or orthodontic survey, particularly in view of the noticeable deposits of calculus he'd found in all five, indicating a lack of dental care. Embedded in the gum between the left canine and seventh premolar of the London girl he'd found a minute piece of gold, which he'd extracted for analysis. Frowning as he came to the last forensic conclusion, he said the gold segment was Asian in origin, possibly Indian, and too soft to be used in the West for crowns or bridgework. Rosetti smiled up, briefly. He'd positively confirmed from the lacerations inside the mouths that attempts had been made in each of the five cases to fix the death grimaces into grotesque smiles: from the positioning of the cuts he guessed the gags had been rectangular pieces of wood. He'd failed to find any wood splinters in any of the wounds.

The bridgework creating a false second left molar between the third and seventh in the mouth of the Turkish girl in Cologne contained non-Asian gold and in the opinion of the German orthodontist he'd asked to examine it the work was recent, within the preceding nine months, and implanted in Germany.

'What about fillings?' Claudine broke in.

'Two, to the right canine and second premolar.'

'Amalgam or composite?'

'Amalgam,' confirmed Rosetti. 'And incidently, it was the second time the police orthodontist had been called in. He'd already carried out an examination for the Cologne force.'

Claudine didn't answer Volker's look. She said: 'I know.'

Rosetti waited but when she didn't say more continued that the Turkish girl, like all the rest, had been well nourished, with no sign of any organic disease. Because a hand-operated, wide-toothed saw had been the only dismembering instrument the external damage was the most extensive of any of the murders they were investigating. It had not, however, destroyed the evidence of her having been strangled: there was certainly no additional bone damage that might have occurred by her throwing herself against her bindings, which were again different from any of the others, narrower in width and breaking the skin on both ankles. From the thin uniformity of the bruising and the skin laceration he thought the girl had been secured by wire. The strangulation, which had crushed the larynx, had also left a regular unbroken mark around the neck, although wider than the wrist or ankle bruising. He guessed the ligature had been a cord and from the uniformity thought it had probably been fashioned into a garrotte. He'd found no evidence of rape and the vaginal mutilation made it impossible for him to say whether or not she had been a virgin. That mutilation had interfered with the effort to carve the swastika on her stomach, making it the last injury inflicted, possibly as an afterthought. The ears were pierced and there were indentations in the lobes showing permanent studs. None had been in her ears. There was also skin discoloration on two fingers of the left hand indicating the regular wearing of rings, one with a cross-piece that had left a discernible mark. They, too, had been missing. The hands were well kept and manicured, unmarked by any sign of manual employment. In the undigested lamb, rice, lentils and yellow peppers recovered from the girl's stomach there were traceable amounts of cinnamon, cayenne and chilli.

Rosetti stopped talking, betraying the first signs of tiredness by the way he momentarily rested forward with his hands outstretched against the conference table. He quickly shook his head against Claudine's suggestion that they take a break but smiled gratefully to Yvette when she produced Perrier, unasked. Glass in hand, Rosetti said he'd been right — fortunately for them — about the Brussels and Amsterdam murders. Both girls, each at least five years older than all the other victims, had been stabbed — in both cases in the heart — before being dismembered and having their breasts removed. The murder weapon had in both cases been a long-shanked knife, one blade 2.3cm wide, the other thicker and 3.1cm wide. The Brussels victim had an unprofessionally imprinted blue-monochrome tattoo to the left of her pubis so nearly destroyed by the genital cutting that it was impossible to decipher the intended depiction. The Amsterdam girl had undergone an abortion. There were also sufficient puncture marks in her left arm and both ankles to indicate she had been an intravenous drug user, although no narcotic had registered in any blood test. There was, however, damage to the septum of the nose consistent with cocaine use. Both showed evidence of torture other than the amputations, which they knew to have occurred after death. There was pre-death lividity to both their faces and to their backs, in addition to after-death puddling to their backs and buttocks.

Their hands showed no evidence of manual labour but were badly kept and unmanicured. Both were nicotine-stained from extensive cigarette use, the left hand of the girl in Brussels, the right of the other in Amsterdam. The natural hair colouring of both had been auburn but was inexpertly dyed blond, the clearly visible root growth uneven from improper application.

Although there was no outward indication, neither was well nourished. There was neglected tooth decay of the sort associated with improper diet and unreplaced teeth: the Amsterdam victim was missing the upper right lateral, which would have been obvious whenever she opened her mouth, and the girl in

Brussels lacked her entire left range at the rear of her mouth; from the seventh to the third molar. The dietary deficiency was also evident in the stomachs, in neither of which was the residue sufficient to provide a definitive analysis apart from a general finding of unidentifiable meat and corn fibre. The intestine of the Amsterdam girl indicated diverticulitis, despite her young age. The duodenum of the Brussels corpse was already ulcerated.

Rosetti took a final gulp of water, looking around the table before sitting down. As he did so he said: 'That's as much as I could find, although I want to go through my notes again.' Concentrating upon Claudine, he added: 'How much further does that take us?'

'A quantum leap,' she said.

Claudine had jotted her impressions during Rosetti's presentation and decided to elaborate her profile on the spot, with everyone still around the table, for it to be a genuinely agreed combined assessment. To reinforce that intention — and avoid the two detectives imagining a staged performance — she invited immediate disagreement and discussion about any opinion she expressed before beginning the dictation to Yvette.

Nothing, insisted Claudine, substantially altered the points she had stressed in her initial profile. To her conviction that the Céleste five were illegal immigrants of whom an example was being made to convey a message, she added that extortion was a factor, although she wasn't suggesting anything as simple as kidnap in exchange for a ransom. Although there had already been a discussion among them Claudine carefully set out her belief that the five bodies had been kept and then distributed in refrigerated conditions, actually breaking off to establish from Rosetti that she hadn't omitted anything from what he'd discovered or that they'd discussed earlier to support that theory. He assured her she hadn't.

'So the killers of our five have access to one or several food packaging centres with cold storage facilities, and access to a fleet of refrigerated delivery lorries,' declared Claudine. 'I think the expertise in the dismembering is butchery skill, used in preparation and packing. It means there are a lot of people involved but that the killers are sure they're not going to be betrayed . . .'

She gestured for Yvette to stop taking notes. 'There was far too much detail included in the first press release. I think there should be a specific warning against disclosure of so much of our thinking in anything further that's released.'

'I don't think we need to worry about that, do we?' said Poulard, showing no signs now of the distress at Rosetti's presentation.

'I didn't imagine we'd have to worry about it the first time but we did,' Claudine said

sharply. She waited for the Frenchman to continue the argument but he said nothing further.

Gesturing for Yvette to resume the note-
taking, Claudine said that from Rosetti's examination of the bodies she thought the five
had been members of close-knit, caring Asian
families newly arrived in the West and still
living in ghetto-type communities maintaining
the culture and the habits of the countries
from which they'd emigrated. Although it was
predominantly a Malay practice the habit of
chewing betel nuts, which released the red-
dening areca catechu stain, was widespread
throughout the East. So was retaining calculus
or tartar on the teeth, in the belief it prevented
decay. The gold fragment too soft to form part
of any remedial dental work had probably
chipped from the detachable decorative gold
coverings with which a lot of Asian girls
adorned their teeth: it would not have been
lifted from the gum by Western-style brushing
because in the East that was not the way teeth
were cleaned.

The stomach contents also indicated each
victim's being part of a traditional family. The
boy, and one of the girls, in whom no meat
had been found, were conceivably vegetarian
Hindus: the other girls probably Muslim. The
callouses on the girls' hands — and upon the
boy's feet — and the fibre particles in the
trachea and lungs could be the result of their

working in ethnically closed-off clothing or carpet factories, using hand warp or foot pedal operated looms or sewing machines.

While the first group of killings were evidently well planned, that in Cologne showed all the signs of being a hurried, snatched-off-the-street affair. Claudine remained convinced it was a racially orientated, nationalistic attack, even to the aping of the Nazi-favoured garrotte method of strangulation. The stomach contents again indicated the girl was part of a family following cultural tradition and supported the initial assumption by the German police that she was Turkish. If she was an immigrant, then her family was wealthy. The bridgework that had been described was expensive. So were white amalgam fillings which matched the natural whiteness of teeth better than the grey composite repair.

Everything she'd heard from Rosetti endorsed the initial assumption from the removal of the fingertips that the white victims had criminal and even prison records: the sort of monochrome tattoo the examination had discovered was typical of the pin-and-ink designs common in jails. From their physical description and general neglect she thought they had been professional although low-class prostitutes: not trusting that either Poulard or Siemen would accept Volker's hacking as readily as she had, Claudine avoiding looking at the computer wizard when she said some inquiries already made on that assumption hadn't produced any identification. She still could not suggest a reason for these two killings, nor why it had been so important for the killers to conceal the victims' identities.

She did acknowledge the German computer expert when she suggested a media appeal throughout the six countries in which the bodies had been found, after the death-mask pictures Rosetti had obtained were compared with Volker's digitalized images to eradicate any visual inconsistencies. She also recommended that photographic checks against criminal record pictures be extended throughout Holland and Belgium and not confined to the national police archives of Amsterdam and Brussels.

'Anything I've missed or points to make?' Claudine invited at the end.

'Of course there's got to be a comparison but as far as I can see the digitalized pictures don't need any adjustment or improvement from those I brought back,' said Rosetti, without any rancour at the duplication. 'So an appeal makes every sense.'

'It's worth remembering that some EU countries — Britain certainly — have established a DNA databank,' offered Volker. 'It's extended beyond paedophiles to all sex offenders. So if we get anything from the semen tests it's a necessary check to run.'

'It's certainly worth remembering,' agreed

Claudine, conscious of the frown Poulard directed towards the German at what he clearly regarded as an intrusion.

The Frenchman said: 'How do you explain the wire binding of the five being made here in Holland, where none of them have been dumped?'

'I can't,' admitted Claudine.

'France is where the delivery route pattern is most clearly defined. That's where our breakthrough is going to come from: where we should concentrate. As I've said from the beginning.'

Why did she always have to appear to be confronting the man? Claudine said: 'Politics isn't our primary consideration but we've got to keep jurisdiction in mind.' The differences between investigatory processes of the fifteen countries of the European Union — particularly the common law system of the United Kingdom against the Napoleonic law-based concepts varying throughout the rest — still operationally remained an unresolved difficulty for Europol. The begrudgingly adopted British-insisted compromise had been copied from the original English division between MI5, its internal security service, and the police. Europol had the cross-border power to investigate but at the point of arrest and prosecution that investigation had to be handed over to the police or to investigating magistrates of the country involved.

The intervention from Bruno Siemen was abrupt. 'There isn't a breakthrough yet: there isn't any factual evidence to suggest there could be, just an intelligent assessment . . .' The German ran out of impetus, giving him the break to take any offense towards Claudine out of his pragmatism. '. . . more than an intelligent, a *brilliant* assessment. But let's take it further, into on-the-ground practicality. How the hell can the police forces of the countries involved possibly bottleneck their major food delivery routes with spot checks on *every* refrigerated truck — which to be effective they'd have to do, in a lot of cases spoiling the contents as they did so — without it becoming known virtually before it begins?'

Claudine had been waiting for the objection and wished she had an answer to it. What she hadn't anticipated was Bruno Siemen's open praise. 'I agree it'll become public knowledge far too soon. But it's obviously got to be done.'

'It shouldn't hold up our presentation of the profile to the commissioners,' argued Rosetti.

'It won't,' assured Claudine, surprised at the remark. 'There's sufficient at last to mobilize a lot of police forces.'

'Should the wording of our warning against media release details be as strong as suggested?' queried Poulard.

It was Siemen, frowning sideways, who answered. 'Isn't the danger of premature public awareness exactly what we're talking about?'

Poulard flushed. 'No fresh atrocity came from the first release.'

'There isn't a time limit,' reminded Claudine.

Poulard engrossed himself in Volker's dossiers and after that the revised profile in order to remain in the incident room long after everyone else had left, so he could respond at once to Sanglier's anticipated approach. There was no brandy or comfortable sofa this time.

'You understood what I said on the telephone about stupid feuds?' demanded Sanglier, still anxious to do all he could to promote one. The tape was disconnected, although he remained unsure whether he shouldn't have run it for this interview.

'It didn't arise intentionally.'

'If I hadn't protected you — and Siemen — you'd have ended up looking idiotic by not contacting her. It could have been construed as endangering the whole organization.'

'It was a misunderstanding,' persisted Poulard.

'Does she accept that?'

'There hasn't been an opportunity to discuss it since I got back.' He gestured to the second profile obvious on the desk between them. 'We worked all day on that.'

'It's impressive.'

'Yes,' agreed Poulard reluctantly.

'Again the work of Dr Carter.'

'It's a combined assessment: the police organizational suggestions are ours,' lied the detective.

'Does that include the warnings about what should and should not be included in media releases?'

Poulard swallowed. 'I argued against it being worded that way.'

'Dr Carter appears to have gained considerable confidence since her commendation.'

'Everyone was very impressed by her analysis today.'

'She was right, wasn't she, about the pointlessness of your going to France?'

'It became useful, travelling with Dr Rosetti.'

'Whose appointment was also her idea. Like everything else in this investigation so far.'

'We can begin a positive investigation now.'

He could disguise the important question, Sanglier decided. 'How did you get on with Rosetti?'

'Well enough.'

'Did he maintain daily contact with Dr Carter?'

Poulard swallowed again. 'Yes.'

'They have a good working relationship?'

'Very good. As she has with the computer man, Volker. She seems to have put him on an equal footing with the rest of us.'

It hadn't been the direction in which Sanglier set out but he decided to follow it.

'Why's that a problem?'

'It isn't, of course. I just didn't expect it. There doesn't seem to be anything he can't do or find out with a computer.'

The unease twitched through Sanglier. 'Accessing records, you mean?'

'Everything, from the way he's put the murder dossiers together.'

Just the murder dossiers, wondered Sanglier. It would be obvious for her to get the best man possible, to search archives. And from his own well-concealed searches he knew a lot of wartime material had been transferred to computer databases. It led him in the direction he intended. 'Has she talked to you about how good he is?'

'There hasn't been time since I got back.'

'Haven't you got to know each other at all?'

Poulard shrugged. 'Lunch, the first day. I know her husband died but she really didn't tell us much about herself.'

'Did she say anything about me?' demanded Sanglier bluntly.

'You?' said Poulard, confused.

Sanglier made a disparaging gesture. 'I'm aware of gossip here, about my appointment. The family name . . .'

'No,' said Poulard. 'She didn't say anything at all.'

'I don't enjoy gossip,' said Sanglier. 'I'm extremely proud of the family name.'

Poulard blinked, his bewilderment growing.

'Of course. I can understand.'

'I'd like to be told, if you encounter it.'

'Of course.'

Enough, decided Sanglier. 'I would like to see far more practical police initiative in the coming days. Don't forget there could be more killings.'

'I won't,' said Poulard.

He wasn't allowed to. The head of the ninth victim was found the following morning, in Rome. The discovery diminished the impact of the arrest of three neo-Nazis for the Cologne killing.

'I think you're right,' agreed the Serious Fraud Office superintendent, John Walker. 'I think the bugger's frightened. We have to keep him that way.'

'How long can he continue to dodge another interview?' demanded Toomey.

'Not long,' said Walker, standing at his office window with the wide, feet-splayed stance of a street-corner constable. 'I'm happy to let him plead pressure of business for a week or two. All he's doing is putting off the evil moment and he knows it. So he'll be putting pressure upon himself, as well as getting it from us. We'll just keep applying to his lawyers. There's no way of their guessing what you've got, is there?'

'No,' said Toomey confidently.

'And we'll see him in tandem this time.

That'll make him twitch.'

'What about the woman?'

'Afterwards,' decided Walker. 'Play this right and they'll collapse in upon each other. One won't be able to dump the shit on the other fast enough.'

'There's the question of political embarrassment, in her case.'

'We'll get her out of Europol long before there's any risk of that.' The large man smiled. 'We're going to make a reputation out of this. That'll be good, won't it?'

Chapter Sixteen

From the occasional rusted ornamentation elsewhere along the ancient wall of the Borghese Gardens, Claudine guessed the head was impaled on a piece of metal to hold it in position. It was of a black woman whose age Rosetti estimated at between twenty and twenty-five. The lipstick was bright red and smudged from her lower lip over her chin. The kohl around her eyes, which were closed, was smudged, too. There were two decorative tribal scars down either cheek. The hair was short and tightly curled, a cap to her skull. There were gold earrings set with a red stone. The ears were pierced and the lobe of the left was torn, at the point of the piercing. From the length of the neck that remained Claudine thought the woman could have been Nubian, although she wasn't sure if Nubian girls were decorated with tribal scars. Apart from where the neck had been severed there were no wounds or contusions. There was no facial contortion. The tribal scars were not intrusive and Claudine decided in life the woman would have been striking.

The head, hidden now within a forensic tent, had been fixed to face the Vatican and the dome of St Peter's, clearly visible from the hill upon which the gardens had been created by the cardinal nephew of a seventeenth-century Pope.

Only the Rome pathologist was inside the tent with Claudine and Rosetti but the area outside was crowded with what Claudine estimated to be twice as many uniformed and plainclothes *carabinieri* as were conceivably necessary. They milled about aimlessly, mostly looking towards where the media people and their battery of television and still cameras were penned behind rope barriers. There was much serious-faced mobile telephone and radio conversation for a lot of which the policemen seemed to find it necessary to walk about.

The ground and grass were littered with discarded cigarette ends. The grass was flattened and the gravel of the paths churned. The grass within their tent was crushed, too, and thick with butts.

Claudine's only language, apart from English and French, was German, so she was unable to follow the intense discussion between Rosetti and the other Italian. He was ignoring her. The Rome police chief hadn't, when they'd arrived, the open appraisal obvious until Rosetti had said something. Now the man, Giovanni Ponzio, waited just outside the tent. Like everyone else he stood facing the banked cameras. He smiled in her direction whenever she looked out of the canvas screen.

'You OK?' asked Rosetti.

'Of course.' She was actually finding it very hot inside the sterile, evidence-protecting suit she'd already decided to be a wasted gesture in view of the chaotic trampling all around her.

'Anything more you want to see while the head's in situ?'

'I don't think so.'

'We want to take it off now.' Rosetti and the other man looked at her, waiting.

'Why don't you then?'

'You don't want to go outside?'

'Why should I?'

Rosetti shrugged, deferring to the local pathologist. The head came off with the faintest of sucking sounds. The fixing had been a metal spike about twenty-two centimetres long that Claudine guessed had originally supported some statuary, maybe even a bust. It would have been easy to repeat the mistake of the *bateau mouche* in Paris, imagining the head part of an intended decoration.

'Clean cuts, so it was a knife,' said Rosetti, in French for her benefit. 'But there are a lot of them: the head was hacked off, in a series of blows. Frenzied even. Larynx appears intact and there's no external evidence of strangulation.'

'From the repose of the face she was dead before the dismemberment,' suggested Claudine.

'Yes.'

Claudine indicated the metal spike. 'Quite a lot of clotting there but not a lot on the stonework itself.'

'It must have been virtually bloodless,' said Rosetti, agreeing again. He scraped some residue off the spike into a glassine envelope. 'There's nothing significant in the skin temperature, except that it is not particularly cold to the touch. Impossible to estimate a time of death within any practical time period. There's enough blood to test for freezing, though.'

Claudine looked closely at the staining on the spike. 'Embedded about ten centimetres: substantial force?'

'I'll need to measure the precise depth, but that's about right. So yes, substantial.'

'A two-handed, downward movement from a balanced position,' guessed Claudine. 'Do you think there's enough smoothness in the earrings to be useful?'

'It's worth mentioning to Ponzio: there's no powder residue,' said Rosetti, understanding the question. 'And you can see there's no mouth tearing. I'll need to check at the mortuary but it doesn't look as if any attempt was made to impose a smile.'

Claudine pointed to the trailed eye make-up. 'That could have been made by the melting of ice that had formed externally, couldn't it?'

'Possible,' conceded Rosetti. 'I think it's far

291

more likely to be lachrymatory, from the natural collapse of the tear glands.'

'It's too soon, obviously, but I don't think she's part of our primary Céleste group.'

'Creating a fourth of her own?'

'That's my thinking at the moment,' said Claudine.

The Rome pathologist stood with the head in his hands, almost as if he were offering it to Claudine. He said something, looking towards her.

'He wants to know if you're finished,' translated Rosetti. 'We are. Here at least.'

'I've seen all I want,' said Claudine.

There was a burst of camera lights when they emerged from the tent, the local medical examiner carrying the bulged plastic exhibit sack. Instinctively Claudine pulled out of sight around to the far side of the tent, taking Rosetti and the police chief with her. Ponzio stopped so that he was still in camera view.

In word-groping English, he said: 'I have promised a press conference. You will take part?'

'No,' said Claudine at once, gratefully stripping off the overalls. Beside her Rosetti did the same.

The man appeared disappointed. 'I thought you would want to represent your organization?'

There hadn't been any discussion with Sanglier about media exposure before she'd left

The Hague but there was no practical benefit at this stage and Claudine had no interest in personal publicity. The opposite, in fact. She hadn't expected the Italian policeman to be willing to share it. She said: 'Our job is to help in the background,' and decided it was the perfect politically correct response.

'The monsters have got as far as Rome,' declared the police chief portentously. Ponzio appeared to think in newspaper headlines. He was fat, with oiled black hair and rings on either hand. The light grey suit was silk but crumpled, with a shine to it.

'I don't think she is necessarily the victim of the same killers as the others,' warned Claudine.

'You mean there are more than one?'

'I don't think you should link them all together and subsequently be shown to be wrong.'

The man nodded gravely. 'It's surely a madman?'

In this case the police chief was probably right but to generate that sort of hysteria could act as incitement and she didn't want any more incitement than already existed. Instead of replying she said: 'The head would have had to be held tightly on either side, to be fixed as it was on that spike. There could be part of a palm — or fingerprint on the earrings.'

The Italian nodded as if he'd already

thought of it, which Claudine was sure he hadn't. 'I will ask the doctors to take them off at the mortuary so that I can have them tested. Anything else?'

Claudine looked across the city, towards the Vatican. 'In some of the cases the bodies have been spread throughout a city: I think that might happen here. If it does the pieces will be left in public places: tourist places. You should police those particularly. Question people carrying odd packages or bags.'

Ponzio frowned at her. 'Rome has more tourist places than any other city in the world. And everyone carries a bag or a sack of some kind.'

'And one of them might be the person who managed to decapitate someone,' insisted Claudine. 'I'm not suggesting it would be easy, just the sort of check that should be carried out.' She looked again across the city. 'St Peter's, particularly.'

'I'll need to get permission. It's a sovereign state.'

'I think it should be done,' said Claudine.

'You're sure about the press conference?'

'Positive.'

'I intend issuing a warning.'

'To whom, about what?' frowned Claudine.

'Women,' said Ponzio simply. 'To be careful.'

It would probably be pointless, causing nothing but panic, but it just might prompt someone to report people carrying with difficulty a torso-like shape. 'You could also issue a photograph of the woman, when the medical examination is finished at the mortuary.'

'Which I'd like to start as soon as possible,' put in Rosetti. 'You coming with me?'

Claudine shook her head. 'I'd prefer to talk to the person who found it.'

'I'll call ahead, so they are expecting you. There'll be every cooperation,' assured Ponzio.

They hung back while he posed the telephone call for the benefit of the cameras, and then got into the same police car, because the American who had made the macabre discovery was at the police headquarters to which the mortuary was attached. Rosetti and Claudine parted in the vestibule, assigned to their respective escorts.

Morton Stills proclaimed his Berkeley faculty, where he was a second-year engineering student, in foot-high lettering on a sweatshirt he wore over shorts and heavy-soled Reebok training shoes. His thinness was accentuated by his height, which Claudine guessed to be just under two metres. He had a severe crew-cut and bit his fingernails. He was doing it as Claudine entered the interview room where he sat with two men, one of whom introduced himself as Bill Hamilton with a consular position Claudine didn't catch and the other of whom produced a card identifying himself as

Henry Pegley, attached to the US embassy's legal division. Pegley said he'd heard of Europol — knew one of their FBI guys was somehow involved — and was quite happy to help if he could.

'Mort's already made his statement: we're just waiting for copies to be translated and signed. As long as the Italians don't mind I don't see why you shouldn't have a copy,' added Pegley.

'That's kind,' said Claudine. 'But would you mind going through one or two things for me just once more?'

'It is absolutely necessary?' demanded Pegley protectively.

'No,' said Claudine. 'But I'd appreciate it.'

'I've got nothing else to do and there isn't a lot to tell,' said the boy.

He'd left the youth hostel before eight, wanting to get some early morning photographs of Rome — he gestured to an elaborate Mitsubishi camera beside him on the table — and had chosen the Borghese Gardens because of their elevation over the city. After taking some pictures of the Villa Giulia and the Temple of Antoninus he took the walk that would have led him out on to the via Veneto, where he'd arranged to meet for coffee the friends he was travelling with. He'd become aware of the view of the Vatican and decided to use up his film. He hadn't realized it was a human head until he'd started focusing his camera and realized what was in the foreground of his view-finder.

'What was the first thing you did?' asked Claudine.

'Looked, to make sure what I was seeing. Close, not through the camera I mean.' He shuddered at the recollection.

'Then what?'

'Ran to find someone.'

'You didn't touch it?'

'Ma'am!'

'How close did you go?'

Stills shrugged, making an expanding movement with his hands until they ended up about a metre apart. 'Maybe this close.'

'What time was it?' asked Claudine.

'I'm not sure. I didn't think to look. Maybe nine. Early, certainly.'

'Were there a lot of people about at that time of the morning?'

'Some. When I was focusing I had to wait for people to pass.'

'Pass how? Walking? Or running? Jogging perhaps, dressed like you are now?'

'I don't remember any joggers, although I said hello to some American guys near the villa: they were wearing Stanford shirts.'

'What about people — a person — running?'

'No, ma'am.'

'We've gone through all this: it's in the statement,' interrupted Pegley.

'Just a few more questions,' insisted Claudine. To Stills she said: 'What about the wall itself, when you were focusing? Apart from the people passing in front of you was there anyone — more than one person, even — standing in your way at the wall?'

The boy didn't answer at once. Then he said: 'I don't think so.'

'You don't *think* so?'

'I'm not sure,' admitted the American, his fingers moving back to his lips. 'I don't think there was but I'm not sure.'

'You suggesting Mort might have *seen* who put it there?' demanded Hamilton.

'I'm not suggesting anything whatsoever,' insisted Claudine, annoyed at the interruption. 'I'm simply trying to get a picture of what happened.' Going back to the boy she said gently: 'Tell me why you're not sure?'

'I just have a vague recollection of something but I'm not sure if it was a person or one of the statues there . . .'

Pegley moved to speak but Claudine raised her hand in a stopping gesture. 'You waited for people to pass, before you took a photograph?'

'Yes.'

'But the person or the statue whom you might have seen wasn't moving: it was stationary?'

'Yes.'

Hopefully she said: 'So did you take a photograph?'

Stills looked anxiously between the other two Americans. 'I didn't tell the Italian detective about this, did I?'

Anxious the boy should not become nervous of authority, Claudine said before either man could speak: 'That doesn't matter: you're telling us now. Might you have taken a photograph?'

'I might have done,' said Stills miserably. 'I don't know. Like I said, I couldn't believe what I saw, when I saw it. I was frightened.'

'That's all right,' soothed Claudine. 'Anyone would have been frightened. It was horrible . . .' She paused. 'You saw the head through your viewfinder, so you lowered the camera to look closer?'

'Yes,' agreed the boy.

'And when you realized what it was did you just run, to find an official? Or did you shout out?'

'I don't remember that, either. I think I may have shouted something . . . said "Oh my God" or something like that. But I really don't remember . . .' His hands were at his mouth again. 'I really fouled up, didn't I?'

'Of course you didn't foul up,' said Claudine. 'When you shouted — if you shouted — and then started to run, what did other people around you in the park do? Did they seem to notice you were running . . . see

299

what you were running *from* perhaps . . . or didn't they take any notice?'

Stills considered the question. 'When I started running I definitely remember calling, "Help." I don't know why I said it: I couldn't think of anything else to say. I wanted to find an official.'

'So people looked at you?'

'I think so, yes. Then I saw someone in a uniform by the via Veneto gate.'

'You remember people looking at you when you ran?' pressed Claudine. 'What about the figure at the wall, which might or might not have been someone?'

'I told you, I'm not sure it was a figure. It might have been a statue.'

Claudine couldn't remember any statues close to where the head had been. 'What did you do when you got to the man in uniform?'

'Tried to make him understand. He spoke English but he couldn't make out what I was saying, so I made signs that he had to come with me.'

'And he did?'

'Yes.'

'Had anyone else realized it was a human head when you got back?'

'I don't think so.'

'There was no one standing around?'

'The garden official screamed when he saw it. Then a lot of people looked. Some women screamed. I think some fainted.'

Hoping against hope Claudine said: 'Did you take any photographs then?'

'I don't think I did. There were a lot of people shouting. I think the official used a mobile telephone to call other guards. Then the police arrived. I suppose —'

The remark was broken off by a sudden bustle at the door. Giovanni Ponzio came in first, followed by the detective who had interviewed Morton Stills accompanied by his interpreter, a bespectacled, tightly corseted woman. The translator carried sheaves of individually clipped paper. Ponzio offered Claudine the topmost copy and said: 'I had one prepared for you,' and Claudine realized her meeting with the American boy was effectively over. She didn't think there would have been anything more to learn.

To avoid any misunderstanding through Ponzio's limited English Claudine explained through the interpreter why the film in Morton Stills' camera should be developed in the police laboratory, and suggested a public appeal be made for anyone who had been in the Borghese park that morning to come forward. The interrogating detective glared at her and Claudine guessed the man had not extracted in his questioning the possibility of something being recorded on film. Ponzio said he'd already initiated both ideas: he'd actually launched the witness appeal at the on-the-spot Borghese press conference, which had gone remarkably well. He'd scheduled another briefing later that day. Claudine could participate if she wished. She repeated that she didn't. The embassy lawyer thought it better that Morton Stills didn't take part, either, which seemed to disappoint the boy until Pegley pointed out the possibility of his making himself a target. Pegley added that accommodation would be made available for Stills in the embassy compound and that any further interviews could be arranged through him. The film was extracted from the camera with promises of a replacement and Ponzio thanked everyone profusely.

Rosetti was waiting in the police chief's office with the other pathologist when Claudine and Ponzio reached it. The only additional finding from the mortuary examination was that the spike had gone in a virtually direct upward line into the head. There were no fixed-grin mouth lacerations or internal skull bruising to indicate any severe blow to the head, although from the downward direction of the ear split he thought it had been caused by an attempt to snatch the earring off. There was no dental work to the teeth. Neither the Italian pathologist nor Ponzio queried the significance of mouth cuts so Rosetti didn't volunteer it. He didn't say anything about the absence of ice traces in the recovered blood, either, and Claudine delayed the question although guessing the answer.

The scene at the Borghese Gardens was still cordoned off and guarded by *carabinieri*, so Ponzio was able to answer Claudine's query by mobile telephone. There was no life-size statue within a fifteen-metre radius of where the head had been found.

There was time for several espresso and cappuccino coffees before Morton Stills' film came back from the laboratory. It had been printed on 25cm by 20cm paper which was still damp, the individual photographs clipped into a separating frame. Ponzio let the technician display them on a wall-attached bench along one side of his office reserved for newspapers, magazines and an impressively large television set.

The American student had unknowingly exposed three frames showing the severed head. None was properly in focus. In the first there were clearly visible the shadows of two people whom, able to judge east from west from her visit that morning and therefore know the position of the sun around 9 A.M., Claudine guessed to have been passers-by for whom Stills had waited to go further into the park. The second featured just the head and was beginning to go off centre from what must have been the American's horrified, hand-jerking awareness of what he was looking at.

And the third posed more questions than it answered.

It was, illogically, the best focused of them

all. The head was even further off centre, possibly from the boy's action of turning away to run. The dome of St Peter's was in sharp silhouette to the right, bisected by the centuries-old wall. Against which, to the left, was the darkness of a shape too indistinct positively to be identified. While they studied it, already knowing it could not be the mark of a statue, Ponzio contacted his officers by telephone again and eliminated a tree branch or trunk. It could, Claudine supposed, have been an odd cloud formation momentarily obscuring the sun. Or the shape of a human figure standing against the wall so close that it would have been impossible not to have been aware of the head, just centimetres away.

'You think it's the killer, just having put it there?' demanded Ponzio excitedly.

'It needs scientific enhancement and analysis,' said Claudine cautiously.

The Italian pathologist uttered three words, to which Rosetti retorted sharply in one. Claudine said: 'What did he say?'

'That it could be a ghost,' translated Rosetti. 'I called him a fool.'

There was another exchange between Ponzio and the technician before the police chief said in his laboured English: 'They are subjecting the negative to more tests, trying to enlarge and sharpen the image. But it's going to take time.'

'So we'll have to wait,' said Rosetti.

'For what? And for how long?' wondered Claudine aloud.

The arrangement was for them to liaise through Sanglier, which Claudine dutifully did from the office Ponzio made available to her and Rosetti. Sanglier's task force division between the new and the old crimes was precisely that for which Claudine would have argued, if she'd had to. Claudine had no functional interest in crimes that were apparently solved, apart from the satisfaction of knowing her profile had contributed, as it had in Cologne. She hadn't argued, either, against the supposed procedural reasons for Poulard and Siemen's going there, to take part in the interrogation and to decide from the evidence and the hoped-for confessions if there were any links with their other murders, knowing there were not. With her customary, even cynical, objectivity Claudine recognized that the split was not at all for her benefit. After the debacle of their totally wasted time in France, Sanglier had obviously decided it was necessary for the two detectives to appear to be part of a successfully concluded investigation and had chosen them to represent Europol in the public awareness of that success.

None of the three arrested skinheads had made any admission, Sanglier told her, but in the home of one had been found diamond stud earrings Cologne police believed to be those missing from the murdered girl, who remained unidentified. There were witnesses to the three boasting they had rid Germany of another coloured parasite and all three belonged to the *Nationalistische Front* neo-Nazi party banned by the German government after racist outrages in 1993.

Claudine told the French commissioner that although she had insufficient evidence to support the opinion, she didn't think the Rome killing fitted any of their patterns: she stopped short of voicing her suspicion that it might be a copycat prompted by Europol's over-detailed initial press release. She didn't, either, mention the shadowed photograph. Potentially it could be of enormous importance — as well as guaranteeing more sensational headlines — but she wanted the results of the photographic analysis before raising the possibility.

She did, however, suggest to Rosetti that they re-examine the scene after registering at the hotel he proposed in the via Sistina, at the top of the Spanish Steps, within walking distance of the Borghese Gardens.

The area was still sealed and Claudine was impressed that the *carabinieri* officer checked their identities and the passes Ponzio had provided before admitting them, wishing the man had been on duty that morning to hold back the trampling hordes. Before they'd left the police chief had said nothing of any forensic value had been recovered.

Claudine confirmed to her own satisfaction that no nearby statue or overhanging tree or branch could have caused the shadow. There was a pillared gazebo about twenty metres away and she even stood behind that to check its sightline, knowing before she did that it didn't fit the east to west movement of the sun at the time Morton Stills took his picture.

'So it could be significant?' queried the pathologist, briefly cupping her arm to help her through the via Veneto gate and the clogged traffic beyond to the wide pavement on the other side.

'Vital, if it can technically be identified as a human figure and some detail picked out. It would have to be the person who put the head there: it's too close for someone to have been there and not seen it.'

'Yet the boy can't remember seeing anyone.'

'He's nineteen years old and was confronted by a severed head,' said Claudine. 'That's a hell of a shock for anyone.'

'He would have surely seen the action of the head being impaled?'

'Maybe it wasn't done then.'

Rosetti frowned. 'I don't understand.'

Claudine hesitated, aware she was about to quote a dictum enshrined by Scott Burrows but persevering because it was an established modus operandi. 'Serial killers really do return to the scene of their crime.'

'You're talking about one killer, not a group like all the others?'

'Serial killers show a lot of anger. There was a lot of anger in the way the head was severed: actually hacked away from the body. And again by the force with which it was jammed into position for at least ten centimetres. At the mortuary you found the entry path directly upwards. It was held between the hands of one man and thrust down. If it had been more than one person it would have been a crooked entry wound . . .' She was rehearsing her profile, Claudine realized. 'And as well as returning to the scene of their crime serial killers often take souvenirs: they represent a sexual reminder of what they did. I think the injury to the ear was an attempt to take one of her earrings.'

'Do you really think it could be the image of a man? A human figure at all?'

It was easier walking down to the via Sistina than it had been climbing up the hill. 'I don't know that it's anything,' warned Claudine. 'And with Ponzio talking of monsters and the pathologist wondering about ghosts I don't intend speculating until we get a definitive photo-analysis.'

'You're talking about it to me,' Rosetti pointed out.

'You don't believe in ghosts and monsters.'

'How do you know?' demanded Rosetti, with unexpected lightness.

'I'm a psychologist. We can read minds,' retorted Claudine, matching his mood, welcoming it.

Although it was obvious Rosetti's immediate family would be in The Hague Claudine supposed some relatives to be living in Rome and half expected the pathologist to announce a private arrangement that night. But in the foyer Rosetti suggested their eating dinner at the hotel, where Ponzio could instantly reach them if more of the body was found. Claudine agreed at once, as readily as she accepted Rosetti's promise to introduce her to better restaurants when there was less chance of their being needed urgently.

Claudine was encouraged by how much stronger her mother sounded, when she telephoned. There had still been no positive decision about chemotherapy, the older woman said. She'd been overwhelmed by the flowers and gifts and get-well messages from customers: there'd been so many she'd lost count. Gérard wanted to take her somewhere quiet in the south, where she could recuperate after leaving hospital, but she'd dismissed the idea out of hand: both of them couldn't be away from the restaurant at the same time. Claudine was unsure if she could get to Lyon at the weekend and her mother told her not to bother. Claudine promised to try.

She bathed and took her time getting ready, critically examining her reflection in the wardrobe mirror — glad she'd included the black dress when she'd packed — before descending to the bar. Rosetti rose politely to meet her but didn't comment about how she looked. It would have been inappropriate if he had — they were two colleagues on an assignment, not an assignation — but as the thought came to her Claudine realized that equally inappropriate though the circumstances were, she was actually involved in a social outing. She genuinely could not remember the last time. It would, of course, have been with Warwick but that didn't help recollection. She certainly didn't think it had been like this, the two of them at dinner. It was probably an office function — hers or his, something else she couldn't recall — a farewell, perhaps, or an engagement. Rosetti accepted, without comment, her announcement that she didn't drink and she accepted, trustingly, his aperitif recommendation, which turned out to be an orange-based cocktail with a sharp acidic flavour that she liked very much. Rosetti drank campari in the bar and ordered only a half-bottle of white Chianti for himself at dinner. At his suggestion she changed from pasta to antipasto to start and chose veal for the main course, as he did.

'Before we leave Rome I'll take you to Alfredo's: they really did invent fettuccine there.'

They *were* colleagues on an assignment so the investigation — in general and in particular — was initially the obvious topic of conversation. Claudine said she would not have been able to conclude as much as she had without his contribution and he said he'd been amazed by her interpretation. She wasn't flattering him and he knew it, just as she knew he wasn't flattering her. Claudine began to feel comfortable, for once not having to balance every word and place it with tweezers into whatever she said.

'What about Europol itself?' she demanded.

'It'll work, given the chance.' He smiled. 'Maybe more than one chance. It has to work: there's got to be something. After more than sixty years the American FBI is tolerated rather than accepted by local forces. So how can we expect anything quicker or better?'

'Happy to be a part of it?'

'Absolutely. You?'

'It answered a lot of needs, personal as well as professional.' Claudine was shocked at her own candour. She felt warm and hoped she wasn't blushing.

He nodded but didn't speak and to avoid an awkward silence she said: 'I thought you might have relatives to see in Rome,' and wished she hadn't, remembering his strange response in the incident room to her remark about an understanding wife. What the hell's wrong with me, she thought, agonized: I'm risking a pleasant evening by talking like a bloody fool!

Rosetti said: 'I might make time tomorrow,

if nothing comes up. I was here last weekend.'

When he didn't continue Claudine said: 'My mother lives in Lyon. She's not well. I'm trying to get there every weekend now but it's not easy.'

'Do you have to be quite so committed?'

The question was defused by his smile but Claudine immediately guessed at gossip while Poulard and Siemen had been with him during the autopsies. 'You don't need me to tell you how important it all is.'

'More important to whom, Europol or you?'

'Both.'

'You can't have any career worries, after what you've already achieved?'

'There hasn't been an arrest yet. Cologne would have succeeded without our input. It won't be acknowledged even though the organization the three belonged to was on our list, not theirs.'

'I wasn't thinking about external recognition which from the way you refused Ponzio's press conference invitation doesn't seem to interest you. I was thinking how you've established yourself within Europol.'

It was an unwelcome reminder of what she'd briefly succeeded in relegating from her mind. It returned in a rush and more to herself than to the man she said: 'Unless something external intrudes to wreck it all.'

'Like what?' frowned Rosetti.

Claudine began to tell him. It started as an

internal debate with herself, which it always had been, and it was not until she got to Peter Toomey's questioning about a suicide note Warwick might have left, as Gerald Lorimer had, that she abruptly realized she was talking aloud and that Rosetti had pushed his plate aside and was listening with his head cupped between his hands. She halted, horrified, trying to remember what she had said (she'd stopped before disclosing Warwick's note: she knew she had!), completely bewildered by what she'd done.

'You've stopped,' he said.

'I'm sorry . . . I don't know what . . .' she stumbled.

'I haven't understood very much, apart from the fact that your husband's friend committed suicide, as he did. And that there's some official inquiry . . .'

'I spoke without thinking . . .' How could she!

'I can't imagine how, but if I can help . . .' He let the offer trail off, invitingly.

'That's very kind.' Claudine was too confused for a cohesive thought to form. What in the name of Christ had she done! Imagined she was doing! She, Claudine Carter, who never lost control or uttered an ill-judged word! She physically shivered, chilled by what she could only think of as a collapse.

'Are you all right?'

Claudine gave an uncertain head movement. 'I'm embarrassed,' she admitted honestly. 'I don't know what . . .'

Rosetti smiled, gesturing to the hovering waiter to clear the plates. 'I'm not sure what there is to apologize for. Nothing, I think.'

'You're very kind,' she repeated, her mind still not functioning properly.

'It's obviously serious? Or you think it could be?'

'There's a lot you don't know.'

'Which you don't want to tell me?'

'I don't think so.'

'I'm not suggesting that I'm the person to give it but if it's official — legal — shouldn't you get expert advice?'

'That's what Toomey told me to do.'

'Why haven't you?'

'It would look as if Warwick did something wrong . . . something that has to be defended. And he didn't.'

'Forgive me,' apologized Rosetti in advance. 'But are you absolutely sure of that?'

'Of course I'm sure.'

'Can you prove it?'

Claudine swallowed. 'No.'

'Get a lawyer,' insisted the Italian bluntly.

'I don't know,' said Claudine, hating the inadequacy.

'I was surprised how easy you found it to watch my initial examination, at the scene.'

Not suspecting the direction in which Rosetti was guiding the conversation — imagining, in fact, that he was trying to let her escape by changing the subject — Claudine said: 'I don't have a problem with medical examinations: autopsies, in fact. I can learn a lot from them.'

'Just as you're accustomed to courts and criminal investigations?'

'Yes?' said Claudine doubtfully.

'But you wouldn't try your own medical examination? Or believe your lay legal knowledge sufficient to argue a case in court?'

'No,' conceded Claudine, understanding at last.

'You're a trained criminal psychologist, Claudine: a brilliant one, from what I've seen. But I think you need professional help: proper guidance.'

She couldn't recall his having called her by her given name before. 'Point made.'

'Are you going to take it?'

'It's more complicated than you imagine.'

Rosetti sighed, although not with exasperation. 'If you want to talk about it again . . .'

'I didn't mean to talk about it tonight. Talk about it at all!'

'You haven't. Not in any way that makes sense. And just in case it worries you later, I don't discuss what I've heard in confidence. Which is how I regard this conversation.'

'Hardly the way to relax after a hard day's

work,' offered Claudine, desperate to recover, hurrying her best effort at the lightness there'd been earlier.

'Would you believe I've enjoyed it?'

'It would be difficult.'

'I have.'

Even more difficult to believe was that she had, too. Despite her inexplicable collapse or giving way to weakness or mental aberration or whatever it was that had made her say what little she had, Claudine had enjoyed being with the man. Maybe, even, *because* of it. He'd been sympathetic and understanding and kind, accepting what she'd divulged but not pressing her an iota beyond the point at which she'd stopped. Been, in fact, the perfect psychologist. Still striving to lift the mood, she said: 'Would you believe I have, too?'

They had coffee back in the bar and Rosetti tried, too, managing anecdotes about medical examinations and investigations that were not macabre but funny enough to make her laugh, which was something else she couldn't remember doing for a very long time.

In sudden recollection Claudine said: 'Ponzio made a remark when I arrived at the Borghese Gardens but stopped smiling at what you said to him?'

'It was nothing,' said Rosetti. 'Stupid.'

'Tell me.'

'He said if Europol provided travelling com-

316

panions like you, he was going to apply for a transfer.'

Claudine suspected he'd cleaned the remark up. 'What did you say?'

'That he should stop thinking with his trousers and listen to what you said: that you were his best chance of avoiding making himself look a fool, although fool wasn't the word I used.'

'Thanks for making it clear you weren't sharing my bed.'

'Or you mine,' said the Italian, in a qualification Claudine didn't understand.

It was Rosetti who suggested they go upstairs, without any awkwardness or connived double entendre, escorting her to her door with the promise to see her for breakfast and moving on to his own room the moment she turned the key in the lock.

Claudine didn't go to sleep. Instead she lay with the bedside light on, staring unseeingly at the far wall, evaluating and re-evaluating what had happened, every time failing to find an explanation that satisfied her for what she'd done. It had to have been an aberrant mental collapse, a fortunately brief but understandable breakdown after all the catastrophes and pressures of the last few months. She'd been lucky it had happened with Hugo Rosetti, whom she trusted not to tittletattle about the episode to anyone in Europol. Even more inexplicably she actually felt relieved at having shared, however incompletely, a little of her problem with someone else.

Claudine was still awake at 3 A.M. when Giovanni Ponzio telephoned.

'*Announce* you're going back!' exclaimed Hardy. Miriam and Ann were in the kitchen, clearing away. He and Burrows had just opened the brandy.

'Why not?'

'You know damned well why not!'

'It could work.'

'And it could get you dead.'

'Not done properly.'

'They'd never agree. And you'd make yourself look a goddamned fool by suggesting it. This can't go on for ever. You're acting like someone who's stir-crazy.'

'I *am* stir-crazy.'

'You haven't got to stay *here*, for Christ's sake! You're in Europe. Take a vacation. See the sights at their expense.'

'I want to get involved in these European killings. It fascinates the hell out of me.'

'You've no legal right.'

'That could be gotten around.'

'You suggested it?'

'To the gal who's got the job. She gave me the stiff middle finger. I thought Washington was empire-crazy. Europol makes it look like a teddy bears' picnic.'

Hardy looked up as the women re-entered

the room. To Burrows' wife he said: 'I'm trying to persuade Scott to take you on a vacation.'

'I know just where I want to go!' announced Miriam. 'A cabin in Alexandria, overlooking the Potomac.'

Their weekend house.

Chapter Seventeen

From the numerous responses to a photograph shown on late night television there was a name as well as a torso. The dead girl was not Nubian but Ethiopian. Her full name was Elia Duphade but for the modelling career she had just started she had only used her given name.

Ponzio and the Italian pathologist were already at the Coliseum when Claudine and Rosetti arrived. The body was lying in what Ponzio immediately identified as one of the underground cages that two thousand years earlier had held the wild animals — tigers, he thought — in readiness for their fights to the death with gladiators under the Flavian emperors. Claudine, already apprehensive of the newspaper interpretation of Ponzio's press conferences, decided the media weren't going to be disappointed that day, either.

Where the arena floor had once provided a roof, canvas sheeting had already been stretched across the surviving walls and the entire cell was whitened by arc lights rapidly creating a temperature matching that of the previous midday in the Borghese Gardens, although it was still before dawn. As they both climbed reluctantly into the sterile overalls

Rosetti said: 'So much for any feasible body temperature reading.'

'It's academic anyway,' suggested Claudine.

'It's part of a properly conducted medical examination,' corrected Rosetti.

At least, reflected Claudine, there hadn't this early been the build-up of camera-conscious *carabinieri*. Even Ponzio and the Rome examiner appeared to have remained outside the brick-walled enclosure, a rectangle about three metres wide by five metres long, while the overalled forensic technician completed his search: when they arrived the man was photographing indentations in the dirt floor before making his plaster cast. They waited, too, for him to lift his impression, trying to assimilate what they could from the doorway.

The headless torso was naked and lay on its back. At the far end of the cell, close to where the head would have been, was what appeared to be a crumpled bundle of dirty grey paper. As he left the room, displaying through his clear plastic exhibit bag the clear impression of a footprint, the technician indicated the paper bundle and said something in Italian.

'That's how the body was carried in here,' translated Rosetti, as they made their way inside.

The left leg and the right arm remained, although the hand was missing. The body was pitted with blood-clotted stab wounds and there was too much blood for a proper count to be made at the scene of the number of slash wounds to the pubic area. There were deep cuts in what remained of the missing arm and leg and at Rosetti's invitation Claudine crouched close to see there were other injuries apart from the stab wounds to the breasts.

'Bite marks,' identified the pathologist.

'How definitive?'

'Very.'

'Trophy bites?'

'I'd say so, although the left nipple has been bitten off.'

'So I'm probably right,' said Claudine.

'Looks like it, unfortunately.' He supported the weight of the body when the local pathologist turned it. The lividity was discernible on the back and buttocks, despite the natural skin colouring. There were more bite marks on the buttocks.

There was a rapid exchange in Italian and Claudine was aware of the other pathologist and Ponzio gazing curiously at Rosetti. She did the same when he announced he was going to use the arc light generator to power the American-manufactured Luma-Lite, which he could run through a transformer. Claudine had read of the device, which showed up fingerprints, fibre and bodily fluid, particularly semen, but had never seen one in use.

Becoming aware of her look Rosetti grinned and said: 'It's a useful tool. No reason why I shouldn't have something that works, just because it's not generally recognized in Europe,' and Claudine decided Kurt Volker was not the only unconventional member of the team.

The body abruptly became a neon of particles initially invisible to the naked eye but there was no semen register.

As Rosetti picked off the traces and dropped them into individual exhibit bags Claudine said: 'She won't have been raped and there won't be any vaginal deposits. And he won't have masturbated.' She looked for a few moments at the mutilated corpse in front of her. 'He's gone a long way past that: this is a hell of a deterioration. One of the worst I've seen.'

'He might not have dismembered before,' Rosetti reminded her. 'There could have been murders that haven't been linked. Maybe we'll need Kurt.'

'We've got him,' said Claudine, a reminder for her part. 'He's just a computerlink away.'

Rosetti cupped the feet in his hand and said: 'Well pedicured. So the hands will be cared for. The fingernails might produce something.'

'We've got a lot already,' said Claudine.

'And a fourth category.'

'Unquestionably.'

Rosetti continued lifting the foot, testing the rigidity of the limb, trying and failing to bend both legs at the knee. 'Dissipating rigor, additionally affected by this heat. At a rough estimate I'd say she's been dead thirty-six hours:

forty-eight maximum.'

'Which fits,' said Claudine. 'An up and coming model would have a wide circle of friends. There would already have been an alert if she'd been missing any longer.'

Claudine's face twisted at the abrupt snatch of stomach cramp she hadn't expected for at least another two days and Rosetti said: 'What is it?'

'Nothing,' said Claudine. 'Nothing to do with anything here.' The discomfort made her even hotter than she was, encased in her protective suit.

She reached beyond the body, pulling the sack closer to where they were crouched. Lettering became visible as the heavy industrial paper was stretched out and Rosetti said: 'It's a cement bag.'

From the doorway Ponzio said: 'There's some restoration work being carried out at the Arch of Gallienus.'

'The rigor is sufficiently gone to bend the torso but not enough for it to look like a body. It would, in fact, have looked just like a sack of cement.'

The air filter in Claudine's face mask prevented her detecting the odour inside the sack when she opened it. The interior was gouted with blood and Claudine said at once: 'She was put in here very soon after being killed.'

She offered Rosetti the mouth of the sack. Surprised at her intention he took it, hauling against her as she turned the already forensically examined sack completely inside out. The effort strained her aching stomach even further. 'Let's try the Luma-Lite,' she said.

Obediently Rosetti turned on the invisible beam. The cement residue glowed iridescent but nothing else did. They returned the sack to its correct shape, minutely examining the outside. There were varying stains around the base and a concentration along one side.

'Where it was laid, possibly with her inside,' suggested Claudine. Lightly touching the heavier, black marks — several blotched white where forensic samples had been lifted — she said: 'That will be oil.'

'Let's hope they'll narrow the possibilities even further,' said Rosetti, pointing to some lighter discolorations. Continuing the gesture to indicate the body, he said: 'Do you want any special tests carried out here?'

She shook her head. 'Maybe at the full autopsy.'

Her discomfort was settling into a permanent dull ache and she wished she had brought some analgesics with her from the hotel. This looked like being one of the bad months.

It was very narrow in the outer tunnels — they had to retreat into adjoining chambers for the mortuary attendants to get to the body with their collapsible trolley — and Claudine supposed the animals had been herded this way.

Their autopsy clothing was even more elaborate than that for the scene-of-crime examination, an AIDS-preventing, internally air-conditioned space suit totally enclosing the body and face, with microphone communication and air-filtered oxygen packs.

There was a female changing section attached to the mortuary and Claudine was able to get tampons and painkillers from wall dispensing machines before suiting up. She did so in only bra and pants, despite the air conditioning of her suit. The two pathologists were waiting when she entered the examination theatre. Giovanni Ponzio watched expressionlessly from the glassed-off observation room.

The two pathologists shared the autopsy, dictating in Italian as they carried out their routine dissections through a link-up into overhead microphones permanently suspended above the guttered steel examination table. It was the first time she had seen Rosetti work. She was immediately aware of the care — respect even — with which he treated the body. She'd often in the past been offended by the casualness with which post-mortems were conducted, incisions made roughly and sutured even more haphazardly. Rosetti operated with the precision of a plastic surgeon and closed openings with matching neatness: confronted with an example, the Rome pathologist's openings and closings visibly improved as the examination progressed.

Claudine intruded only twice. Once was to discuss with Rosetti the emptiness of the stomach, the little contents of which were digested beyond identification. The second was specifically to establish, when Rosetti took his unproductive semen swabs, that the pubic cutting was external — a total of twenty-seven separate slash wounds — and that there had been no positive vaginal mutilation.

'It's frenzied. Manic,' said Rosetti. 'He stood over her, just stabbing and slashing.'

'I can see,' said Claudine.

Rosetti was scanning the body once more with his imported Luma-Lite when the space-suited forensic orthodontist shuffled awkwardly into the operating theatre. The man was as intrigued by the device as Claudine had been at the Coliseum and there was a brief conversation about it before Rosetti guided him to the bite marks. The dental specialist studied the wounds under magnification before producing a smaller and more refined version of the cast-making equipment with which the forensic technician had worked earlier.

Rosetti pulled away from the table and said: 'He says it will be easy. There's marked protrusion to the right and left centrals.'

With no reason to remain any longer Claudine left the chamber ahead of the men and showered before getting dressed again.

The painkillers appeared to be working and she swallowed two more before rejoining the beaming Giovanni Ponzio in the outer corridor. The man was burdened with newspapers that he immediately offered her. The universal preference had been the photographs of the police chief in the Borghese Gardens rather than at the second press conference. There was a wide selection on all the front and several inside pages of Elia Duphade, who had indeed been a strikingly attractive girl. There was also a wide variety of artists' impressions, most veering towards the ghostly, of the shadow by the wall, upon several of which the artists had reimposed the girl's head. Claudine didn't need to know Italian to understand the frequent reference to monsters. She flicked through each newspaper, glad there was no long-range photograph of her in the Gardens.

Rosetti joined them while Claudine was checking and took the newspapers from her, one by one, briefly reading the sensational coverage. He quickly stopped, smiling wryly at Claudine. 'No woman is safe alone on the streets of Rome,' he summarized.

She looked at him seriously. 'The irony is that it's absolutely true.'

They were on their way in Ponzio's official car to breakfast at the Excelsior when the radio message crackled into the vehicle. At once, at Ponzio's shout, the driver triggered the siren and the lights and swung around in a violent

U-turn to the horn-blasting outrage of other drivers in either direction.

'The hands have been found in St Peter's Basilica,' said Rosetti.

Ponzio twisted from the front passenger seat. 'I applied to the Vatican to post guards: they hadn't replied. Now it's a desecration!'

By the time they reached the Corse Vittorio Emmanuelle they had been joined by two other klaxon-blaring police cars so they arrived at the Piazza Pio XII in cavalcade. Early morning worshippers and tourists were being shepherded out into the huge, saint-statued circular piazza beyond as Ponzio officiously led the way into the basilica.

The hands were in the Crucifix Chapel, which Claudine thought was probably appropriate but didn't say so, on a chair next to the wall and quite close to the Cavallini carving. The same forensic officer as earlier that morning was kneeling before the chair upon which the hands had been placed. Claudine saw, impressed, that he was dusting that chair and several around it on the top and the back, the likeliest places to have been touched by someone moving along the line, although there were no visible smudges. He'd finished taking photographs and was delicately extracting something from between the wire-clenched hands as they approached. It was paper. They watched as he gently spread it out with tweezers on a neighbouring chair and tested it for fingerprints, seeing the disappointed shake of his head. The man glanced up and nodded familiarly when he became aware of their presence.

'There's something written on it,' said Claudine. 'What does it say?'

'It's badly constructed. Badly written, too.'

'Literally,' insisted Claudine. 'Every word as written.'

'I are best than all others,' translated Rosetti.

'What do you mean by badly written?' asked Claudine, imagining she could see for herself but wanting the man's confirmation.

'The individual letters are awkwardly formed, not properly joined in a lot of places.'

'Like a child? Or someone unfamiliar with the language?'

'Yes.'

The technician backed out through an adjoining row for them to get to the hands. The wire that strapped them tightly together was covered with a green plastic and bound in six strands around the wrists, which again were badly hacked. The little finger of each had been removed, leaving bloody stumps. The nails of the remaining fingers were perfectly manicured, painted a deep red which would have matched the previous day's smeared lipstick, and unbroken. Nothing was trapped beneath them.

'A very different pattern,' mused Rosetti.

'One all of its own,' agreed Claudine. 'But

easy enough to read.'

Rosetti looked at her sharply. 'You think so?'

'I wish it weren't.'

'What's that mean?'

'That the headlines fit,' said Claudine. 'He's a monster and he needs to be stopped before he kills again. Which he will, very soon.'

They turned, at noise from the chapel entrance, as the Rome pathologist entered, speaking to Ponzio and Rosetti at the same time.

Rosetti said: 'He was on his way here but diverted to the Pantheon when the other call came in.'

'The missing arm?' anticipated Claudine.

'And the leg,' said Rosetti. 'He's left everything for me to examine. Do you want to come?'

She should, Claudine supposed. But she didn't need anything more for her profile. She was tired and the cramps were nagging and she wanted a relaxing, easing bath.

'I've got enough, although I'd obviously like to know anything that comes from your mortuary examination . . .' To Ponzio she said: 'I'll need until this afternoon to get everything together: hopefully to hear the result of your tests. Then I'll tell you who you're looking for and how to find him.'

The bath had helped and she'd dozed in it

and afterwards slept properly for two hours on her bed. She'd closely studied the photographic selection from a fresh batch of newspapers, finding what she'd wanted, and by the time she returned to the police headquarters the fingerprint tests had been completed and an excited Giovanni Ponzio was able to announce the photo-analysts believed the shadow was of a man: they'd be positive in another twenty-four hours. Twenty people had responded to the witness appeal and two thought they had seen a man by the wall, in the same place as the shadow picked up on Morton Stills' film. Marks on the outside of the sacking in which the girl had been carried into the Coliseum had been identified as engine oil and brake fluid and the small particles picked out by Rosetti's Luma-Lite had mostly been badly dyed cloth fibres. There was a partial fingerprint on the earring in the torn lobe.

Rosetti had found a single, after-death stab wound to each palm, like a crucifixion mark, when the hands had been parted. There were no binding marks on either the wrists or the ankles. The knife that had killed her, with a single thrust to the heart so forceful it had emerged beneath her left shoulder blade, had a curved, double-edged blade that had to be almost sixty centimetres long, virtually a small sword. The preliminary dental cast showed pronounced protrusion of both left and right central and lateral teeth.

Claudine had only prepared notes, waiting for all the additional information, and Ponzio summoned a secretary to take an official record. In addition to Rosetti, the Rome pathologist and the forensic experts whom she recognized, there were six men and two women to whom she was not introduced. They assembled in a conference room adjoining Ponzio's office.

'You're hunting a man totally out of control, someone conforming in every detail to the classical profile of a serial killer,' Claudine announced, concentrating everyone's attention upon her. 'He isn't one, yet. But he'll become one, very soon: a mutilating serial killer whose atrocities are going to get worse every time he kills. There's enough to catch him . . .' she looked directly at Ponzio '. . . but you've got to be very quick.'

The silence in the room was so total it was possible to hear the scratch of the note-taker's pen.

The killer would have a criminal record, Claudine insisted. It would include burglary, possibly escalating to the rape of women he'd found alone in the houses or apartments he'd entered. He would have threatened his victims — controlled them with a curved, sword-like weapon. He would be foreign, with a limited knowledge of Italian and how to write it. When he was arrested, they'd find souvenirs of every robbery — certainly every rape — he'd committed. That's what the fingerprinted earring had been intended to be, a souvenir he'd tried to tear off. And the missing little finger from each hand: she suggested they corroborate it with Elia Duphade's agent or customary photographer but in several newspaper photographs she'd studied the girl had appeared to wear heavily ornamented, perhaps ethnic, rings on each of her smallest fingers. Claudine expected the killer to keep the fingers as well as the rings: possibly the clothes he'd stripped from her, too. They would be his trophies, just as having absolute power over Elia Duphade's dead body had granted him the trophy bites to her breasts and buttocks. Claudine picked up the forensic orthodontist's cast of the protruding teeth, turning again to Ponzio.

'Those teeth will be obvious in any photograph in your criminal archive. Concentrate upon men arrested for burglary, robbery and sexual assault, committed separately or together. Run an unconnected fingerprint check, if that partial print lifted from the earring is sufficient . . .' She stopped at a sudden snatch of discomfort, wishing she could sit down. Staging another dramatic announcement, she said: 'But there might be a quicker way of finding him.'

She thought Elia Duphade might have known her killer. Or trusted him, not from knowing him but because of the job he did.

Her perfectly kept nails had been unbroken, with no skin or debris beneath them to indicate she'd tried to fight her killer off. So she hadn't felt endangered in his presence. Rosetti's estimate of the girl's having been dead for thirty-six hours before her torso was found timed her killing during the evening, which fitted the almost complete emptiness of her stomach. Models ate sparingly, rarely more than one meal a day. Claudine thought Elia Duphade had been on her way to dinner, either in a casually hailed taxi or being driven by someone she recognized from a regular hire company she frequently used. Claudine inclined towards a hire company driver using his own vehicle who did his own servicing. He would be a single man with access to a garage or workshop, where he dismembered the girl after killing her with the single thrust to the heart, and the already available cement sack had been stained with engine oil and brake fluid.

The cement sack was important for several reasons. Claudine suggested questioning every building worker employed on the restoration of the Coliseum's Arch of Gallienus, particularly any who admitted to a friendship or acquaintanceship with a buck-toothed driver familiar with the opening hours of Rome's major tourist sites.

'All of which should remain under surveillance,' Claudine finished.

'Are you telling us he'll not only strike again but again dump his victims at tourist sites?' demanded one of the unidentified men in the conference room.

'I've no doubt whatsoever he'll strike again,' said Claudine. 'And when he does the mutilation will be terrible. He'll choose a beautiful girl and literally deface her as much as possible: he chose Elia Duphade because she represented success and beauty and wealth, none of which he knows. A classic characteristic of serial killers is that they stay within their own culture and colour. The man who killed Elia is probably black. But that isn't my main reason for saying a watch should be kept on the best-known tourist sites, particularly those he's used already. As a car hire driver his job is to ferry tourists to places like that. He knows them all, intimately. Feels comfortable with them. And that isn't the only reason. I told you his profile was classic. It's classic for serial killers to return to the scene, to gloat at police efforts to find them. Power is important to them, in all things. It's something they don't have, in their ordinary lives. Certainly this killer hasn't. So at the places he's already used you should specifically watch for a loitering, frequent visitor whose teeth stick out like this cast.'

'I've studied cases of serial killing,' said one of the unidentified women. 'There is the escalation you're warning about but in everything I've read the escalation has been from the first murder. It hasn't *begun* with mutilation as horrific as this.'

'No,' agreed Claudine. 'I've never encountered it either. That's why I think this man is so dangerous.'

'What made him erupt immediately into this level of violence?' persisted the woman.

Claudine hesitated, knowing only Henri Sanglier and the other commissioners he might have told of her protests would understand the significance of her reply. 'He was able to read and hear on television and radio the details of all the other dismemberment murders we're investigating. His mind's twisted it into a personal challenge, the one chance in his ignored, menial life to achieve more than anyone else has achieved: to become famous. That's the meaning of the message found in the hands today, in the basilica. He's set out to be the best — or worst — serial killer there's ever been.'

Sanglier appeared surprised to hear Claudine intended returning to The Hague. He needed to be persuaded the Rome atrocity, although a pitiful copy, should not become part of the other investigations and that there was nothing more she could contribute towards the Italian investigation. She didn't argue against Poulard and Siemen's flying down from Cologne after that day's press conference

337

to disclose the neo-Nazis' confession of their copycat murder, which was to be coupled with the final identification of their victim. Her name had emerged to be Sulva Atilla. She was the illegal immigrant daughter of a Turkish *Gastarbeiter* whom Cologne police suspected of trafficking heroin from Istanbul. He'd disappeared from Cologne the day after the discovery of his daughter's body and Germany was officially demanding his extradition if he had fled back to Turkey.

In her hotel room Claudine leapfrogged the television channels to pick up the Cologne press conference. Poulard and Siemen were at the further end of a line of self-satisfied German police officials: the German commentary and question-and-answer exchanges were blurred behind the Italian voice-overs and Claudine had to strain to hear the original. She didn't detect any reference to Europol and in the edited clip neither man spoke.

They didn't, either, on the transmission she watched on English language CNN. She was still watching CNN when Rosetti called to say he had family commitments preventing his eating with her that night. Claudine, relieved, said after the interruptions of the previous night she intended eating in her room and going to bed early.

'Poulard and Siemen are arriving tomorrow but I'm going back to Holland after I've seen them. There's nothing to keep me here,' she said.

'I'll stay on for a couple of days, in case he kills again,' said Rosetti.

Claudine didn't see the point but said nothing. She'd have enjoyed travelling back with the Italian, just as she would have enjoyed the restaurant promise for which there hadn't been time.

Sanglier didn't try to suppress the fury. 'Someone named Ginette called.'

'Wonderful!' said Françoise. 'Did she leave a number?'

'She said you had it.'

'I told you about her,' reminded the woman, putting down her packages. 'She's gorgeous.'

'It means she knows this number,' said Sanglier, as evenly as he could.

She frowned at him, from the drinks tray. 'I would have thought that was fairly obvious, if she called it.'

'So she knows me!'

'No she doesn't,' said his wife, exasperated. 'All she has is the number.'

'Why?'

'She's special. I wanted her to keep in touch.'

'How will you explain who I am?'

Françoise walked across the room to sit opposite, grinning broadly. 'Who would you like to be? My guardian? My gruff-voiced lover?

The man who came to fix the drains?'

'I don't want to be anything. Certainly not your husband.'

'Now don't be tiresome, Henri. We've talked all about that. There's nothing more to say. Now I've got to ring Ginette.'

Chapter Eighteen

It hadn't gone — wasn't going — as Henri Sanglier intended. Unwittingly — which made it even worse — Claudine Carter was eclipsing *him*.

Virtually everything Europol appeared to have so far achieved in its first and supremely important operational involvement in European crime had come from her professional expertise. At that day's meeting Franz Sobell had only just stopped short of proposing another commendation for her profile in the Rome investigation, and David Winslow had made a point of stating for the record how accurate her assessment had been in every respect on the Cologne killing. And all he had been able to do was sit and listen and agree, powerless to steer the conversation to her condemnation of their first press release because he would have appeared to be criticizing one of his own task force personnel. And when he'd recounted how he'd personally briefed the French authorities on the delivery route interceptions — as well as pressing each of the five countries still involved to publish the death mask photographs in a national identification appeal — he'd appeared to be following rather than leading the investigation. Which, he conceded, he was. The most un-welcomed admission of all was that at the moment — and for God knows how much longer — he *needed* Claudine Carter.

He had to regain the initiative, Sanglier decided: *any* initiative. Which meant making an objective, dispassionate re-examination of everything, not just about the woman and what danger she might represent to him but going back to the very beginning, to assess what he knew and didn't know — but suspected — about his father. And then, if possible, separating one from the other for a total re-evaluation.

His father first then. And all the publicly accepted parts of the legend that had been glorified in the two films and more soberly established in the books and the rolls of honour and in that most honourable chronicle of all, the French national archives in Paris.

His father, born Marcel Temoine in Grenoble, the only son of a Customs officer and his waitress wife, had been the deputy director of Interpol's secretariat in June 1940 when the Nazis overran France and transferred the entire international police liaison organization and its archival treasure trove from the Paris suburb of St Cloud to Berlin. And transported Sanglier's father with it, forcing the man to maintain Interpol's Nazi-plundered records while he — just two years old — and his mother remained hostage with relatives in Grenoble. It had been almost three years before they'd even known he was alive and had not died in a labour camp.

And it was not until his return to France that they — or anyone else — discovered just how much he'd known about labour camps and extermination centres.

The code-name Sanglier — French for boar — emerged first in captured Gestapo files. They recorded in minute detail the two-year cat-and-mouse SS hunt for the spy whose death warrant was personally approved by Hitler after 'Sanglier' was identified as the man isolating the targets for Allied bombing raids in the Ruhr. Everyone else in the Ruhr cell was uncovered, captured and executed. Sanglier never was. The hunt continued after the war, taken up by historians and film-makers unaware of the extent of the story they were pursuing.

That only emerged after Marcel Temoine was identified as Sanglier — the name he legally adopted like other French resistance heroes — from the genuine Interpol records he'd risked his life to maintain alongside the fabricated version the Nazis created in the last year of the war to obscure and deny their atrocities.

Those genuine files provided a graphic narrative of a man using the Berlin-based Interpol communication system, under the noses of SS men hunting him, to re-route and redirect ordered deportations and even misdirect execution instructions to save the lives of dozens of French and English prisoners and nationals.

Henri could remember now as vividly as he had felt it in those early, reunited years the adulation, almost reverence, in which the renamed Sanglier family was held. And he enjoyed it now as much as he had enjoyed it then; had grown up knowing no other attitude from virtually everyone with whom he came into contact.

It was only much later, when he'd embarked upon his own name-enhanced police career, that he had fully realized that the French adoration of their resistance heroes was a counter-reaction to the deeply rooted national embarrassment at wartime collaboration and the Vichy government.

He could recall just as easily his father's self-effacing modesty and determined refusal to consider himself a hero, the reluctance for several years to cooperate with the most esteemed historians, and the outright dismissal of film-writers and biographers as parasites, trying to make money from the lives of those he'd failed to save.

Which the old man had himself steadfastly refused to do, throughout his lifetime. He'd accepted the National Assembly-voted lifetime pension. And the medals, France's Légion d'Honneur and Britain's George

Cross. But he'd rejected the company-offered sinecures and the invitations to assured political office and most fiercely of all the huge advances offered by publishers for his own account of those years.

And he had refused to tell the story to his own son, even when the events that linked him to the Carter family had made it necessary and despite Henri's insistence that he didn't intend writing a book for general publication but simply wanted to re-establish lost facts and mislaid material. That adamant, totally inexplicable rebuff had shocked — offended — Henri. Remaining dispassionately objective he supposed it had been an over-reaction at the time, hardly sufficient to justify the uncertainty that followed. But it had been difficult for him to understand because it was the first thing — and the most important — his father had ever refused him.

Enough has been written; it's over, in the past. As clearly as he could remember everything else Henri recalled the precise words of his father's rejection. As he could call to mind the other remarks. *The truth is not what it seems.* And *There are many ways to be brave, some which aren't brave at all,* so similar to another remark *To be brave is not to be stupid.*

None, by themselves or even together, anything more than what, as a trained policeman, he would consider circumstantial. Scarcely even that. Which was all, he conceded, other remarks by another dead man could be regarded as.

But the internal Interpol inquiry into the affair of William Carter shouldn't have been circumstantial, although that's how it had largely turned out. Any more than it should have been internal in the first place. It should have been a public inquiry into the crass incompetence of William Carter, Interpol's English archivist entrusted — honoured — with assembling and annotating all the uncollated material about the organization's most famous officer.

Both reasons put forward for the secret inquiry — the national embarrassment a public hearing would create, either at Interpol's inefficiency or at the reminder of the wartime French ignominy — were ludicrous. As the inconclusive verdict — 'a regrettable administrative error' — was ludicrous, as ludicrous as the punishment of William Carter, enforced premature retirement on a reduced pension.

But most inexplicable of all had been his father's reaction to it all, even making allowances for the illness from which the old man died six months later. *It's unimportant,* he'd said: *only the details about me have been lost. The Nazi efforts to escape their guilt are still there.* And then he had uttered the most incomprehensible remark of all. *Better this way: all gone. Ended at last.* Made even more incomprehensible by the abject refusal — tight-lipped, head-shaking, won't-speak refusal — to explain what he'd meant by that or any other enigmatic statement.

The only way the entire episode, the entire story, made any sense was if there was a basis — still-hidden facts that could yet emerge — for Henri Sanglier's doubt about the complete truth of his father's acclaimed heroism. If there were — and the hidden information became public — it would not only expose and disgrace a dead man whom he'd adored and respected whose reputation he would do anything to protect, it would make impossible the career Sanglier intended to pursue after Europol. Which couldn't — wouldn't — be allowed to happen, whatever he had to do to prevent it.

Sanglier had genuinely had no intention of trying to write a book, despite his father's dismissal as exaggerated nonsense — another remark on Henri's circumstantial list — everything that had been published about his exploits, which had surely justified a definitive, correcting biography. Henri had quite simply wanted to complete the gaps which William Carter's blundering — *I can only think I destroyed material before ensuring it was properly copied . . . maybe files were taken and not returned . . . the record system was chaotic* — had created: simply wanted to *know*. He'd read, several times, all the books and every article and seen, several times again, the two films based upon his father's life. And always ended with a trained investigator's dissatisfaction at what was never properly explained, even before the Interpol loss.

Which, after his father's death, he'd set out to correct. It had not been an act of disobedience against his father's wishes but a gesture of love, to ensure his father's reputation endured.

By the time Sanglier had made that decision he'd been a *gendarmerie* commissioner in Paris, able to use all his authority — both official and that inherited with his adopted name — to access the incomplete Gestapo documentation and obtain every transcript of the Interpol inquiry to supplement what remained of the Interpol material, after William Carter's losses, which was now preserved in the vaults commemorating the heroes of France.

And created for himself far more gaps than he succeeded in closing. The Gestapo annals were genuine, captured by advancing American forces and actually produced as court evidence in the Nuremberg war crime trials. At those same trials were also produced — and proved accurate by comparison with other surviving, independent documentary evidence — the secret Interpol files his father risked torture and death to maintain.

The only facts uncorroborated by independent documents or by a surviving resistance worker had been those establishing his father's legend. In most cases there were photographs of the Allied agents with whom his father worked. Street addresses and family details: messages intercepted, between one and another. But never Sanglier, the boar. His father had even drawn attention to it himself, in the account he'd begrudgingly given the official war historian preparing his national archive entry, one of the few occasions he'd cooperated fully to expand the acknowledged facts.

The old man had confided that he'd trusted no one, relaxed with no one, never allowed his whereabouts or even his real name to be known by those to whom he was secretly passing information. Nor had he needed to. For four enforced years he had been at the hub of a communication machine, not just Interpol but units of the Gestapo and the Abwehr: that had been how, using their unchallengeable authority, he had been able to re-route the deportation trains and intercept the execution orders in the chaos of the collapsing Reich. It was from one of those intercepted arrest warrants that he'd been able to pass on his Ruhr targets to the cell subsequently executed. He had always passed on his Ruhr targets by mail, using Berlin's central post office, never once making any personal contact: the routine had been for him to provide the German production locations for the established cell to confirm before alerting London.

The totally unexpected and official approach from London — to him as a private individual, not a police commissioner — had moved Sanglier's half-formed, amorphous doubts into positive fear. It had come from the Scotland Yard unit investigating war criminal residency in Britain after London's highly publicized legal extension of the statute of limitations.

On the face of it, the inquiry was a further acknowledgement of his father's wartime bravery. A Nazi transportation major responsible for sending British prisoners of war to the two labour camps from which the incomplete records showed his father had diverted trains was suspected of living, now in his late seventies, in Wales. Was there any unpublished, family-retained material about the train diversions — the cited heroism for his father's George Medal — that Sanglier could make available in evidence of the major's activities?

It had not, of course, been necessary for Sanglier to go to London but he had, not to offer the requested additional information — there wasn't any — but to learn as much as possible of the British investigation. There was no British doubt about his father's activities in Berlin in the last two years of the war: indeed Sanglier had been received in London with practically the same respect to which he was accustomed in France. The inconsistencies were attributed to the confusion of the war's end and the Nazi success in covering their tracks. And although the British shared his frustration at the totally inadequate Interpol inquiry, they didn't question its being held *in camera* or suggest there might have been some official connivance in the disappearance to disguise the fact that his father might not have done all — or even part — of what seemed to be irrefutably confirmed by what official documentation remained. But Sanglier was made very aware of the war crime unit's determination, spurred by the personal loss of the father and the elder brother in German captivity of the Jewish-born superintendent who headed it.

'I'm in this job until the end of my career,' the man had claimed. 'And at the end of that career there won't be one of the bastards I haven't tracked down or a fact about any of them I haven't uncovered. And I don't care what I've got to do to achieve that.'

It had been two long, worrying years, up until just a few months before his Europol appointment, before Sanglier was freed of his fears that the British would uncover something that might expose his father. Throughout all that time he kept in touch with London on the pretext of offering a few unimportant scraps he knew, from having studied it in the beginning, to be missing from their file. And then, just before the Europol approach, the determined superintendent had told him their

Welsh suspect had died and their investigation with him.

'But there'll be others,' the man had said. 'Maybe you and I will be in touch again.'

Which, until Claudine Carter's arrival at The Hague, Sanglier had dismissed as a casual remark from someone he'd come to know well, albeit at a distance.

Now he wasn't sure any more: wasn't sure about *anything* any more. But had to be. Unless he learned why Claudine Carter had been assigned by Britain to Europol, if indeed there was anything to learn, he'd be back living, as he had been living since her arrival, in those apprehensive months of regular London telephone calls. Except that now there was no one to call.

So what, objectively and dispassionately, did he know about Claudine Carter?

That she was the daughter of the barely disgraced William Carter and a Lyon restaurateur and, according to the much-studied personnel curriculum vitae, had excelled as a criminal and forensic psychologist in London as she was unquestionably excelling at Europol. That she'd suffered a personal tragedy in the death of her husband after just fifteen months of marriage. And that according to the British commissioner, René Poulard and Scott Burrows she showed no interest — a definite rejection, he knew, from witnessing her cocktail party humiliation of René Poulard — in making friends within the organization. Not even, Sanglier reflected, in making a professional effort with him.

None of which, persisting with his objectively dispassionate examination, was in any way sinister. What was, then? Her apparent dismissal of her father, when he'd made an admittedly clumsy effort to initiate a conversation about him, was intriguing, not sinister. And he had not the slightest evidence to imbue her assignment to The Hague with any hidden, personal implications. Yet try as he had, in the failed effort at reassurance, he found it impossible to conceive it as an astonishing coincidence. Just as he found it impossible to believe that Carter had not been able to remember — as he claimed before the Interpol tribunal — some details of the lost documents.

Which was the focus of his every fear: that something — at least what Carter might have told his daughter, at worst an actual surviving document — remained literally to destroy his life.

And that focus led inevitably to the mystery visit of Peter Toomey, the reason for which had been withheld from the British commissioner. And her flight, within a month, to London, which he knew about from Europol's travel division.

It was an effort for Sanglier to remain objective in his conclusion and not build shapes out of shadows. But he did, just. Everything remained, as it always had, circumstantial. But, thinking like a policeman, sufficient for suspicion.

He'd made a lot of mistakes already — panicked, even — but now he'd thought things through, as he should have done in the beginning, he wouldn't make any more.

Perhaps the biggest mistake was betraying any irritation or hostility towards Claudine Carter, which he might have done when she presented her profile to him and Sobell. What he should have done was to appear to make her a friend. And there was still every opportunity for that.

Françoise was emerging as a matching — maybe even greater — immediate problem. Neither had pretended to the other that there'd ever been any love involved in their union, although at first she'd fooled him into believing she was only marginally bisexual. He'd wanted the attribute of a glittering model — in whose circles she still moved to make her conquests — and Françoise, realistically accepting her own career was on the descent, had wanted to exchange it for one of the most famous names in France. He hadn't guessed the strength of her determination any more successfully than he'd gauged her sexuality. It was going to be far more difficult to rid himself of her than he'd imagined.

Claudine was glad to return to The Hague,

although Sanglier had assured her there had been no major developments in their larger investigation. There was no contact from London waiting on her apartment answering machine or channelled through Europol, either, the possibility of which had been another reason for her eagerness to get back.

Police forces in all five countries concerned had accepted the idea of publishing victim photographs in an identification appeal, three of them preferring Kurt Volker's digitalized versions to the actual death mask photographs. Instead of being flattered, Volker protested what he called the illogical limitations the moment Claudine walked into the incident room.

'This is Western Europe. And apart from the Amsterdam and Brussels killings all the victims were Asian. They're far more likely to be known and recognized in the East than anywhere here.'

Claudine regarded the rumpled German quizzically. 'How can we reach Asia, for Christ's sake?'

'By opening our own Web site on the Internet,' announced Volker simply. 'And publishing not just the pictures but a physical description of each victim and the basic details of how they were murdered.'

'It's been difficult enough getting country-by-country police cooperation here,' reminded Claudine, liking the thought but wanting to anticipate the drawbacks. 'And I'm still not totally convinced we're getting it now. How could we begin to organize the authorities in Asia?'

'I don't think we could, not effectively,' conceded Volker. 'But we wouldn't be doing it at street level. It would be on the Net, only accessible to people connected to it. And it would be *our* Web site address. The home page would be right here in this room.'

'Home page?'

Volker gave a slight shift of impatience. 'Where every Internet message would come to.'

'We couldn't go over the heads of national or local forces,' argued Claudine, ever conscious of political sensitivity.

'I'm not proposing that we do,' persisted the German. 'Every country in Asia belongs to Interpol. All we've got to do is advise Lyon and they can disseminate the information as a matter of courtesy. That's their job, international police liaison.'

Interpol, Claudine knew, had been — and still was — one of their strongest opponents. Particularly since Europol had gained its operational function. 'It would cause a hell of a lot of friction.'

'Not our problem,' insisted Volker, smiling his perfect smile. 'Our problem's finding how to solve crimes: helping local forces to solve *their* crimes. Politics is for our lofty commissioners.'

'What about the volume of traffic it might generate? For every genuine response — even if there is one — there could be hundreds of false alarms. It could — and probably would — be used to try to find every missing person in Asia. And I don't think all your computers combined could calculate how many that could be.'

Volker shook his head at the exaggeration. 'I could handle what there would be.'

'It's worth putting forward,' Claudine accepted finally. Which she did, that same morning, in a memorandum to Henri Sanglier in which she tried to counter all the objections that would inevitably be raised.

Claudine was immediately concerned at the obvious drawback in Sanglier's attempt to delay for as long as possible the moment when the mass checks on food delivery lorries became public knowledge. The French commissioner had recommended — insisted in France — that road blocks be diversified as widely as possible throughout the road systems instead of being concentrated in a few bottle-necking locations. In Claudine's opinion what that gained in arguably delaying public — and therefore the murderers' — awareness was more than endangered by the vast amount of gossiping police manpower it was necessary to employ. She immediately sent her second memorandum of the day to Sanglier, suggesting an amendment.

She didn't express her road check reservation when Poulard called. Nor did she tell him of the Internet idea. Poulard said Giovanni Ponzio appeared to be implementing every suggestion she'd put forward and was cooperating with them far more openly than the Cologne police had done. That evening Hugo Rosetti was taking them to eat Alfredo's original fettuccine. Claudine said she hoped they enjoyed it.

She was about to read the updated Cologne file when Scott Burrows shuffled in, engulfed in the smoke and odour of his habitual scented American cigars.

'The glory girl returns from her Italian triumph!'

Claudine couldn't decide if it was an amiable or a mocking greeting. 'It's a case-book serial killer profile,' she said. She nodded to Yvette's raised-eye enquiry about coffee. She didn't want the intrusion, any more than she wanted the smell of the cigar, but there was no cause to be positively rude.

'My case-book,' said the American, predictably. He took the chair directly opposite, enveloping Claudine in his smokescreen.

'And a few others.'

'I was right about Cologne being racist, too.'

'Holy shit, Scott! The kid had a swastika carved on to her stomach!' She was impatient with the man's constant need for recognition. It was weakness.

'I got it right before you knew about the swastika. And racism is the only message in the others, too.'

'You going to argue there's a racist element in Rome, as well?'

'Could easily be.'

'I told you it's a classical serial killer profile. And serial killers always stay within their own culture and colour, like they always stay in an environment in which they feel safe. The Rome killer will be black.'

'Black hates white, white hates black,' parroted Burrows.

Yvette's arrival with the coffee allowed the pause that Claudine wanted anyway, recognizing the sudden reason to concentrate more than she usually did in a conversation with the American. Baiting her trap, Claudine said: 'How do you account for the rapes?'

Burrows shrugged. 'They were going to kill them anyway. Why not get their rocks off every which way?'

'The Turkish girl in Cologne — which *was* racist — wasn't raped.'

'Seven out of eight — three with positive semen traces — ain't bad.' He looked around for an ashtray, shrugged, and dropped his cigar ash in his coffee saucer.

'So it's organized?'

'Seems pretty damned smart to me.'

'One group? Or several, working together?'

'Three will do.'

'What's your feeling about the body part distribution?'

'Clever!' said Burrows enthusiastically. 'It's new: never come across it before. You'll be lucky to get a lead before the interception is blown, though.'

'We're due some luck,' said Claudine, as satisfied at what she'd learned as she was furious with it.

'You a betting girl?'

'No,' said Claudine shortly.

'I'll give you odds I'm right, in every case,' said the American, undeterred.

It was hardly revenge but she'd enjoy it. 'I've just changed my mind. What odds?'

'Choose your own.'

'Ten to one. A thousand francs, at ten to one, says you're not.'

Burrows blinked at the amount. 'Wise money always follows form.'

'Or inside information,' said Claudine, throwing back the metaphor, although with her meaning, not one the man would understand. It had been the black and white, white and black axiom that had registered with her, finally answering the unresolved curiosity she'd felt when Sanglier had paraphrased the same cliché. The bastard was having Burrows check every detail of her profiles, to which only the commissioners and the task force were supposed to have access within Europol. Whose opinion — hers or the American's —

was Sanglier advocating before the Commission? Had Poulard and Siemen been sent to Rome on a counter-argument from Burrows, despite her insistence that it formed no part of the sequences they were investigating? The most important consideration, however, remained, as it had always been, Claudine's readiness to take the responsibility for her own mistakes but refusal to inherit those of someone else.

'You know what they say about two heads being better than one?'

'I didn't think psychologists said it.'

'My offer still stands.'

'So does my reason for wanting to work alone.'

'I'm prepared to take the chance.'

Presented with the opportunity, Claudine said: 'I'm not.'

'This place has got a long way to go before it's like the real FBI. But some things are close enough. It's always useful to have friends.'

Was he trying to give her a clumsy warning? About what? Or whom? Claudine abruptly halted the slide. She was buggered if she was going to jump into Europol's paranoia pit along with everyone else. 'I'll keep that in mind.'

'You do that.' The American lumbered to his feet. 'You keep that very much in mind. Can I give you another piece of advice?'

'What?'

'Go on keeping in the background. Only fools draw attention to themselves at press conferences in our business.'

'Scott, I need more than that. You're talking in riddles.'

'What I've said is good enough.'

'What the fuck are you talking about?'

'You don't need to know,' said Burrows, shuffling out of the room as flat-footed as he'd entered. 'You just need to do as I say. Keep in the background.'

'Bastard!' she called after him, although not angrily.

He didn't reply.

Chapter Nineteen

Claudine's profile trapped the Italian killer, although not before he'd killed again and inflicted even more savage mutilation, which Claudine had also predicted.

An Algerian labourer on the restoration of the Arch of Gallienus remembered an African who'd briefly been employed when the work first began hanging around the Coliseum during the previous month. They'd had a drink together a couple of times. The only name he knew was Ben. The man had said he preferred working as a part-time chauffeur than humping bricks and cement sacks. He'd been intrigued by the African animals the ancient Romans had fought in the arena.

A lot of the labourers at the Coliseum only worked part time and either weren't listed or gave false names on the employment records, to avoid tax or detection as illegal immigrants by the authorities. The only record was an exercise-book log they'd had to sign to acknowledge being paid. Sometimes the acknowledgement was a cross. There was certainly no indication of nationality, which had to be guessed from whatever names had been written. Among the sixty possibilities was a badly scrawled signature that looked like B. Aboku.

All the names were checked against Rome criminal records. A Nigerian named Benjamin Aboku had three convictions for burglary and one for aggravated assault, which fitted Claudine's guidance. A rape victim had failed to identify Aboku in a police line-up and the case had been dropped, but a sexual crime also featured in Claudine's escalation warning. Forensic experts were ninety per cent certain that the partial fingerprint lifted from Elia Duphade's earring matched the right thumb dab on Aboku's crime sheet, which gave an address on the via del Arco Monte.

Giovanni Ponzio included Poulard and Siemen in the police command group that sealed off the entire area and then isolated the fetid foreign worker apartment block. An illegal Tunisian immigrant was in bed with the prostitute for whom he was pimping when police smashed the door down. Aboku had moved out six weeks earlier. There was sufficient cocaine in the apartment for an arrest anyway.

Ponzio cancelled all Rome police leave to swamp taxi and car hire firms in the city. Aboku was identified from police record photographs as one of their night relief drivers by a small car hire firm operating from the via Galla on the day the media finally learned of a manhunt impossible to keep secret because of the number of police involved. Aboku was named on midday radio and television news bulletins. Afternoon newspapers carried his police file photograph.

Ponzio tried his best to stay ahead of the press leaks by keeping in protective custody a co-worker in the via Galla who claimed to know Aboku's new address.

The Italian police chief completely cordoned off the district roughly between the Tiber and the vias Iclid, Circo Massimo and Della Marmorata. The Temple of Diana square was even more tightly encircled, all road junctions blocked by police cars and officers standing shoulder to shoulder. By the time Ponzio gave the order for the special crisis unit to storm the Marcella apartment block with stun and smoke grenades there was a television helicopter fluttering overhead as well as coverage from the ground. The hostage-and-hijack squad, the most appropriately trained and available to Ponzio, wore body armour but the lead officer foolishly did not lower his face visor and was virtually decapitated by the first shotgun blast as he led the charge into Aboku's one-roomed hovel. The following officer was blown off his feet by the discharge from the second barrel but uninjured. At the later shared autopsy, Hugo Rosetti recorded twenty-seven machine-pistol and machine-gun wounds to Aboku's body, seven of them possibly fatal. It was impossible to specify which shot killed the man.

Poulard and Siemen took part in the search of Aboku's apartment, although always deferring to the Italian. They found a wide selection of photographs of Elia Duphade, cut from newspapers: in every one showing the ornate tribal rings her smallest fingers were encircled in red marking ink. The decaying fingers themselves, still with the rings on each, were located in a bedside drawer.

The rented lock-up garage at the rear of the apartment block resembled a charnel house when Ponzio opened it with the key that had been lying next to the severed fingers. The girl's head had already been cut off and lay in the corner of the garage, horrendously disfigured with nose and ears removed and the cheeks slashed: the escalation of which Claudine had warned. The curved tribal knife that had inflicted the thirty-two stab wounds and slashed her pubic region was still impaled where her left breast had been. The floor was thick with blood, some of which was later proved by DNA analysis to be that of Elia Duphade.

The second victim was a twenty-eight-year-old Somali girl named Sami Impete who had worked in Rome for two years as a stripper and who had three convictions for prostitution. Her three-year-old son was suffering from malnutrition and dehydration when police found him in her apartment.

Claudine had a television set moved into the

incident room for Yvette and Volker to watch with her the extended press conference at which Ponzio was flanked on either side by Poulard and Siemen. Behind them was a hugely enlarged print of a man barely identifiable against the Borghese Gardens wall as Benjamin Aboku, captured at the scene by the terrified Morton Stills.

It was Bruno Siemen who spoke first, in halting Italian, on behalf of Europol and he did so extremely well. He described the investigation as a team effort and actually made a reference to Claudine's profiling, without naming her. There was a simultaneous voice-over translation when Poulard said the combined investigation was an example of what the Europe-wide police organization had been created to achieve and Claudine guessed both men had been rehearsed in telephone conversations with Henri Sanglier.

'Another very public success,' suggested Volker.

'Without the slightest breakthrough in our major investigations,' cautioned Claudine. With the case concluded there was nothing to keep Hugo Rosetti in Rome any longer. She refused surprise at the reflection, keeping to her 'know thyself' adage. She didn't want Hugo in Rome. She wanted him back here, in The Hague. And taking far more interest in her than he'd so far done. That self-admission did come close to surprising her. She wasn't sure how she'd react, if he did.

Claudine had expected the checks on the food delivery lorries to be revealed in France, where the concentration was greatest, but it wasn't. The story broke in Austria, with a combined newspaper and television revelation that Vienna was being virtually sealed off between midnight and dawn to incoming heavy lorry traffic. In view of Claudine's suggested improvement to Sanglier's original plan for apparently haphazard road blocks, it was the sort of hoped-for luck that no one could have really expected that fifty kilos of high quality, Turkish-produced heroin was found that same night on one of the intercepted trucks, en route from Istanbul via Romania and Hungary. That fitted perfectly Claudine's suggestion that they use a crack-down on drug-trafficking as an excuse for the checks. The Austrians had ignored Sanglier's guidance but seized the drug interception cover, which the French copied when their night-time, widely spread autoroute closures emerged, within twenty-four hours of the Austrian disclosure, although without being able to produce a convincing drugs haul to support their story.

Which wasn't necessary. The explanation was logical and wasn't challenged by the media, so the hysteria that would have erupted afresh at the idea of dismembered bodies being transported throughout Europe alongside the Union's food supplies was avoided.

Claudine was amused at Poulard's blatant exaggeration of his part in the dramatic conclusion in Rome and guessed from their head-bent, foot-shuffling reaction during the debriefing on the day of their return that Siemen and Rosetti were, too. Claudine couldn't make up her mind whether Siemen was attempting to mock or to dissociate himself when he said, pointedly, that he had been separated from Poulard during the actual assault upon the Marcella apartment and couldn't remember a lot of the detail Poulard recounted.

'Which wasn't part of what we were brought together to investigate,' said Claudine, repeating the reminder she had earlier given Volker.

'Two months now since there's been a killing that could fit any of our categories,' said Rosetti.

'One of which doesn't exist any more, now that Cologne is over,' said Siemen. 'And in which the Céleste killers know their distribution method is cut off, if they've got any sense.'

'I don't believe that would stop them,' said Claudine.

'That's ridiculous!' challenged Poulard. 'Even if they didn't think the road blocks were directed at them they wouldn't take the risk. It would be madness.'

'There's an arrogance about spreading the

bodies around the country,' insisted Claudine. 'It's the arrogance of people believing them-selves beyond the law.'

'So why hasn't there been a killing for two months?' demanded Poulard, still challenging.

'Like I said, there hasn't been the need.'

'So all we can do is sit around and wait until there is. And hope this time there'll be a mis-take we can pick up and move on?' said Sie-men.

'Unless anyone has a more productive idea we can work upon,' said Claudine.

No one did.

Sanglier was pleased at the way his objec-tivity was holding up. Claudine Carter's drug check idea had been a good one and had worked. And there might be a mistake with which he could undermine her — the first he had been positively able to isolate — in setting up an Internet Web at the same time as rele-gating Interpol to its messenger function. San-glier had been particularly careful to associate Claudine by name to the Lyon liaison organi-zation with the Web suggestion.

The newly discovered objectivity was re-flected by his thinking of the woman by name and not mentally trying to demean her as a bitch or a cow, which was juvenile. Sanglier was abruptly caught by the intriguing experi-ment of putting Claudine together with Françoise, to test Poulard's theory about the preference of the psychologist. There'd be the additional irony of a practical use for Françoise, as well.

Sanglier handwrote several drafts of his invitation before formally dictating it. It included Yvette as well as Rosetti and Volker.

'What's there actually to celebrate?' frowned Siemen at the door of his office the following day, when the memoranda were distributed.

'Nothing, I would have thought,' said Claudine.

'He doesn't talk about a celebration,' Rosetti pointed out. 'He calls it an appreciation.'

'With partners!' said Volker, flattered. 'Heidi will want something new.'

Rosetti moved as if to speak but then didn't and Claudine wondered what he'd been about to say. It would mean rearranging yet again her intended weekend visit to Lyon but she decided she had to go. Attending was, she supposed, one of the political necessities about which they were always being lectured.

'The lawyers are still too bloody clever but the bugger's worried,' insisted John Walker. 'I can smell fear and he stank of it today.'

'What do you suggest now?' asked Toomey. 'You sure we're safe?'

'We can put a court order on it, to stop it being opened,' said Toomey.

'We'll do that. And then we'll let Bickerstone sweat. See which way he runs.'

Chapter Twenty

It was an evening of surprise and curiosity for Claudine: she couldn't have anticipated it if she'd tried, which she hadn't.

Sanglier hosted the gathering in a conference room adjoining his office and it was a far larger affair than she had thought it would be. As well as Sanglier, who was accompanied by his wife, Franz Sobell and all the commissioners of the murder-involved countries were there, mostly with their partners. Claudine thought of the wives as a chorus, wondering how many might be high kickers beneath their overly intimidating couture.

Sanglier moved constantly and solicitously around the room, ensuring everyone knew everyone else. Even more solicitously he spent only seconds with her, just sufficient — but no more — to introduce her to his wife who held her hand just a fraction too long, and who said Claudine should call her Françoise, before moving off, although not subserviently, in Sanglier's wake.

Greta, Siemen's wife, was a woman of Wagnerian proportions who even wore her flaxen hair in Brünnhilde-style plaits and whose multi-patterned dress only needed a central pole to be transformed into a tent. She seemed disappointed when Claudine said she didn't have any children. Heidi, the wife of the proudly attentive Volker, was sylph-like by comparison, as slim even as Yvette but appearing far more sophisticated in the straight, dark blue sheath dress with a single diamond pin high on the left shoulder. She wore her black hair long and had clearly practiced rippling it into brief disarray by a sharp head movement before it fell back perfectly into place to her shoulders. She seemed far more comfortable in the exalted surroundings than Volker. Yvette herself had reverted to the sort of overtight and low-cut shift she'd avoided since the earliest days, this one a cream cocktail dress that didn't need the multi-stranded necklace or the long drop earrings. She came with Poulard, which Claudine half expected. She anticipated the immediate interest switch that Poulard showed in Volker's wife, too. Volker beamed, prouder still.

Claudine's first positive surprise was that Hugo Rosetti came alone. Claudine wasn't at first aware that he had because she didn't see him arrive. It was only after she'd assigned partner to partner that it registered. Rosetti smiled to her from across the room but remained where he was, talking to the Siemens. Greta towered over him. Claudine didn't return to the ghetto cluster.

Scott Burrows was the last to arrive, the

half-smoked stogie perfuming his progress across the room towards her. Claudine was surprised a professional psychologist needed such an obvious confidence prop but then remembered his lack of academic qualifications, the most likely cause for his inferiority complex. The tightness in her chest was very vague but she still slightly backed away from the clouded presence.

'We don't get this sort of thing back home,' he said in greeting.

'European sophistication,' Claudine smiled. The lavishness was as much of a surprise as the size of the reception. There were waiters at a hot and cold silver-dished buffet along the entire length of an inner wall, linked at one end to a separate selection of drinks dispensed by more white-coated attendants. Other waiters circulated with a choice of glasses on silver trays. The favourite appeared to be champagne but Burrows was drinking what she guessed to be Scotch. No pastis seemed to be available.

'It'll be dancing girls and a naked broad bursting out of a cake when you solve your serial killings.'

'Let's hope to Christ they're all alive and in one piece,' said Claudine. She hoped he didn't light another cigar when he finished the one he was smoking.

The American grimaced at the professional cynicism. 'You know what they say about all work and no play! Relax, why don't you?'

Claudine had an abrupt and totally illogical flash of recollection, the remark without the speaker first — *You don't like parties, do you? Loosen up, have fun: that's what life's for* — before she remembered who'd made the accusation, which made it even more absurdly confusing. A man in a gorilla suit on one of her first outings with Warwick, the man she'd told Toomey she'd totally forgotten. Why now? And why that aside, rather than anything else? Conscious of Burrows' frowned expectation, she said: 'I'd like there to be a better reason. In fact I don't even know there is one, for all this . . .' Pointedly she threw in: 'Do you?'

Instead of responding to any innuendo Burrows grinned, nodding towards her glass. 'You know what W. C. Fields said about the danger of drinking water?'

'Yes, but this comes guaranteed that fish didn't fuck in it.' Burrows showed no reaction to the obscenity but Claudine mentally threw it back at herself. Wasn't her propensity to swear — more mentally than publicly — nothing more than an inferiority response, the need to become one of a crowd that Burrows betrayed by smoking his peculiar-smelling cigars? The self-question disturbed Claudine, whose personal analysis had always so totally precluded inferiority that until that moment the possibility of her suffering from it had never ever occurred to her. That it had occurred unsettled her, challenging her conviction that she knew everything about herself. Then she rallied. What reason had she to doubt herself in the middle of a reception that wouldn't have been contemplated, let alone held, but for what she had done in the past weeks?

The American exchanged his empty glass for a full one from a passing waiter. 'You don't know what this does to a guy.'

'I do,' said Claudine, serious still. 'Only too well.'

Burrows looked to Claudine to continue but she didn't. They heard the increasing noise of a glass being tapped by a spoon and the room quietened for the current Commission chairman. Sobell disclaimed any intention of making a formal speech, to the usual sniggered disbelief. The organization was being tested by an investigation unique in most people's recollection of crime, anywhere in the world. Europol, by the very nature of its multinational concept, was always going to be an uncertain but necessary crime defeating experiment. They still had a horrendous series of murders to solve — or to assist local forces to solve — but he was confident from knowing in full the contribution they had already made in the Cologne and Rome cases that they would enhance within the European Union the acceptance of Europol that had already been indicated to him by the Justice Ministers of every member country.

Standing where she was, away from most of her group, Claudine wasn't actually included when Sobell looked directly towards them and said he was grateful for all they had so far done.

The gesture increased the nods and mumbles of approval that had throughout accompanied the platitudes from the assembled commissioners. Claudine was conscious of several — David Winslow more obviously than anyone else — looking towards her instead of the main group but didn't respond to their attention.

Sanglier filled the lull the moment the Austrian finished. He thanked Sobell for the confidence that had been expressed and said he was proud of what the task force had achieved and was sure the inevitably successful conclusion would reflect to the further credit of an organization of which all of them were proud to be part.

'Shouldn't there be rousing music with all of us standing wet-eyed to attention?' whispered Burrows, beside her.

'They'd never agree the choice of tune among themselves,' Claudine whispered back and wished she hadn't because the American's snorted laugh was too loud.

Burrows seemed to think so too, wandering off in the direction of the bar immediately after the desultory smatter of applause from people not really sure what they were clapping. Claudine had so determinedly been avoiding any direct attention upon anyone that she was not aware of Sanglier's wife until the woman was beside her.

Françoise Sanglier was an exceptionally tall woman, hardly dwarfed by her husband. She was angular and small-busted, with prominent features accentuated by the style in which she wore her hair, cropped to her neck and with a definitive side-of-the-head parting. Claudine recognized as Versace the green, cerise-slashed dress that did all it could for the woman's figure because she'd seen it in the salon close to the Kloosterkerk. Françoise Sanglier was tall enough to carry it off but Claudine was glad she'd chosen the more subdued black and white Chanel.

'Were you frightened Henri was going to mention you by name?' demanded the woman openly.

Designed immediately to disorientate, gauged Claudine, intrigued. 'It would have been invidious if he had.'

'The fitting modesty of a team player,' Françoise mocked gently.

As close as she was Claudine could very clearly see the faint moustache on the woman's upper lip and wondered why she didn't have it waxed. 'It *is* a team.'

Françoise flipped a dismissive hand-wave.

'Henri admires you very much. Says very little would have been achieved without you.'

What the fuck was this all about? 'That's gratifying to hear.'

This time there was a mocking grimace at the persistent formal modesty. 'Aren't you frightened?'

'By what?' asked Claudine, genuinely disorientated.

'By what you've seen! Henri says you attend medical examinations.'

Sanglier seemed to have an odd choice of dinner table conversation. 'It's an essential part of my job.'

'Looking at women defiled like that! Opened!'

Françoise shook her head at the waiter's approach and Claudine realized Sanglier's wife was empty-handed, not even making the pretence of drinking. It was a fleeting awareness. She'd tried to detect the outrage in the woman's voice but couldn't. 'How can I know people, describe them to those hunting them, unless I see what they're capable of doing? And how they do it?'

'You can come to *know* people, from that?'

'Learn a lot about them.'

'How they feel when they do it? *How* they do it: which they decide to do first?'

'A lot of the time, yes.'

'Fascinating!' Françoise was bright-eyed, intent upon Claudine.

Making a conscious, cocktail party effort to change the subject, Claudine said: 'Do you like living in The Hague?'

The brightness went from the other woman's eyes. 'Not particularly. I'm glad Paris is so near. What about you?'

'I haven't had enough time to judge yet.'

'Henri tells me you've spent more time in France than in England, before you came here?'

'Lyon. My mother still lives there.'

'It's a coincidence that your father worked for Interpol, as Henri's did.'

This was even more bewildering than autopsies in detail. 'I hardly think there's a comparison.'

'He was a very shy man, Henri's father. I could never bring myself to understand how he could have done what he did. As difficult as I find it to understand what you do, I suppose.'

Claudine was unable to decide if this woman was very clever — and if she was, what she was trying to achieve — or only able to appear so for a limited time before the naivety began to show. Or whether she was properly analysing Françoise Sanglier at all. 'I most certainly don't think a comparison's possible there, either.'

'You know about Henri's father, of course?'

'There can't be anyone in France who doesn't.'

'I mean there must have been stories about him, in Interpol?'

'I suppose there must.'

'Didn't your father ever tell you about them?'

'No,' said Claudine.

'Never?'

'He was only in the archive department,' apologized Claudine, badly.

'So was Sanglier.'

'But as I said, two very different people.'

'I'm surprised it was never mentioned.'

The woman wouldn't have been if she'd known her father, Claudine thought: would have found, in fact, the first proper comparison from all her previously failed attempts that evening. She was relieved at the approach of the red-faced British commissioner, who also appeared to be alone. 'Neither of you are drinking! Or eating!' accused David Winslow.

This time it was Claudine who shook her head against the waiter's beckoned approach but she gratefully allowed herself to be steered towards the buffet table. Françoise Sanglier said she wasn't hungry and didn't go with them. Claudine wasn't hungry either but justified her rescue with two pastry boats of caviar. She and Winslow went through the required exchanges of apartment hunting and liking or disliking The Hague and Winslow said, quiet-voiced, that he'd advised London of the full extent of her contribution to the mass murder investigation and Claudine thanked him. It was, she thought, like painting by numbers.

'So everything's OK?'

She immediately recognized the opportunity, ill fitting though the surroundings were, to ask the man why he'd approached Toomey, hesitating for several moments before she said, instead: 'Shouldn't it be?'

'Yes. Of course.'

'It seemed an odd question.'

He was awkward, growing redder. 'Not really . . .' He smiled hopefully. 'Consider myself captain of the English ship here: like to know everyone's happy. No personal problems. Things like that.'

'That's very considerate of you.' She hadn't known what this reception was going to be like but in her wildest dreams she wouldn't have anticipated any of these strange, oddly worded encounters.

'You do understand that, don't you? About the need to keep everything on an even keel?'

From all the boating analogies Winslow had to have a boat on the lake. 'I think so.'

'If anything does arise . . . any problems . . . I'd like to know. I like to do anything I could to help.'

Claudine decided on the spot that if she was going to confide in anyone about the Toomey inquiry it most certainly wouldn't be this blustering, burning-faced man. 'People must be reassured to be told that.'

'They are.'

Knowing that with his back to them Winslow wouldn't detect the lie Claudine excused herself by saying some of her group appeared to want her. As she reached them Poulard was pressing another glass of champagne upon an already flushed Yvette and Greta Siemen was proclaiming to the politely nodding Heidi Volker the joys of motherhood, which was a conversation she'd begun when Claudine drifted away an hour before after admitting she didn't have any children herself. Burrows was just entering that morose stage of drunkenness when it seemed important to examine, without comment, the contents of his glass.

'Quite a party,' said Poulard.

'It certainly has been,' agreed Claudine, to herself more than to the Frenchman.

'It ain't over till the fat lady sings, remember that,' Burrows insisted with inebriated wiseness to anyone who cared to listen. No one did.

'Seems a pity to end it, now we're all together for the first time,' said Poulard. 'We thought we'd all go on to the Chagall, out by the lake.'

'It's very pretty there, among the trees,' Heidi put in, clearly seeking relief from Greta Siemen.

She should make up the party, Claudine knew: to refuse would make her appear aloof to people with whom she had to work, from whom she didn't want to remain aloof and from whose professionalism she most definitely couldn't afford to distance herself. But she didn't *want* to prolong the evening. She didn't enjoy mass social occasions and she'd already endured one which had mostly been bizarre. 'I'm going on a trip tomorrow and I've got to make a very early start. I'd like to, some other time.'

'Maybe after the reception to celebrate our next triumph,' said Poulard heavily.

Claudine ignored the remark, looking around. 'Where's Hugo?'

'He couldn't make it either,' said Greta Siemen. 'He left a long time ago. Didn't he say goodbye?'

'No,' said Claudine.

'She thought I was a total fucking idiot,' protested Françoise Sanglier, naked at the mirror sponging off make-up. 'And I felt like one, too. She was sending out "rescue-me" messages to everyone in the room.'

'Which you recognized.'

'Don't be stupid.'

'Do you believe her father wouldn't have said a single bloody thing?' Sanglier didn't bother to look at his wife as he spoke.

She threw dirty tissues into the bin beside

her. 'I don't give a damn whether he did or he didn't. You shouldn't have asked me to initiate a conversation without telling me what you expected me to find out.'

'I didn't want you to find out anything specifically,' lied Sanglier. 'Her father worked in Interpol, after the war. I was curious if there'd been any anecdotes I hadn't heard about my father, that's all. You know I like to know everything possible about him.'

'If there were any she didn't seem to know them. Or couldn't be bothered to tell me.' She stood up, stretching languorously.

Sanglier got into bed, naked too. 'What did you think of her?'

'Got good dress sense. Nice body. But she holds herself back all the time. I'm fascinated by her watching those examinations!'

'Did you talk to her about that?' frowned Sanglier.

'She said it was essential, for her to do her job.' She got into bed. 'I think it would be exciting to do that.'

'Were you attracted to her?'

'She wasn't interested: there was no response,' insisted Françoise. 'Are you?'

'No. Poulard tried. She humiliated him publicly.' Poulard could have been wrong about Claudine's sexuality as well, but at the moment he was keeping an open and curious mind about that.

'Poulard would risk splinters to fuck a knothole in a tree. He's a joke among the French contingent.'

'You will be careful, won't you?' said Sanglier, increasingly concerned at Françoise's behaviour. 'Don't forget this place is a goldfish bowl.' It was unthinkable that he should still be with her when he switched to politics.

'Haven't I always been discreet?'

'Giving your friends our home phone number wasn't discreet.'

'It was the one and only time, for Christ's sake.'

'Don't let it happen again.'

She didn't bother to reply.

'I thought we might invite Claudine Carter to dinner one night, by herself.'

'Why?'

'Why not?'

Françoise shrugged, beside him. 'Doesn't she have a husband? A partner?'

'Her husband died.'

'If you like.' The woman turned her back on him. 'Goodnight.'

'Goodnight,' he said, turning away from her.

Claudine hadn't been able, either last night back at the apartment or today on her way to Lyon, to find any rational explanation for the behaviour of Françoise Sanglier. The macabre interest in watching bodies dissected did not confuse her, any more than the woman's ob-

386

viously ambivalent sexuality had either confused or offended her, although the combination of both fitted certain and perhaps worrying psychological parameters.

What Claudine failed to understand was the strained effort to introduce into a social conversation France's most famous wartime hero through the tenuous coincidence of her father, a reminder of whom she didn't welcome. Not, of course, that either Françoise or her husband would have known that, nor the reason for her reluctant attitude. That merely concentrated Claudine's mind upon the anomaly more quickly and positively than it might otherwise have done. To no effect.

It didn't make a pattern.

Claudine hadn't promised a time, unsure when she'd postponed the previous day if there would be space on the early morning flight, so her arrival at the rue Grenette was unexpected. It was not, she supposed, possible to be devastated and glad at the same time but she was. Devastated at catching as she did her totally unprepared, disarrayed, vacant-eyed mother, beshawled and bird-limbed: glad at the same time — although for herself, not for her mother — that it was precisely *how* she'd caught her, unwarned and unable to attempt any artifice. Not that any artifice could have disguised the fact that her mother was dying.

Because of which — despite the honesty that was their bond — Claudine cheated, by default. She feigned not to notice the frailty, busily too occupied tidying the apartment to notice the difficulty her mother had reaching the bathroom unaided but as quickly as she could from the specially positioned chair at the window overlooking her beloved Lyon, efficiently rearranging the disordered drug bottles on the bedside cabinet as if she was accustomed to them, guessing from the labels that she would find morphine injections in the kitchen refrigerator. Maybe it would have progressed to pure heroin.

From the transformation when her mother reappeared Claudine recognized determined practice, although the rouge was too hastily applied and too red upon a face that had never known artificial colouring. Oddly it was now, when her mother had made an effort, that Claudine felt the asthma pull, not before when she'd realized how ill the older woman was.

'You shouldn't have done this,' complained her mother openly, returning to her window seat.

'I wasn't sure of the flight.'

'There are airport phones. Don't lie.'

'When do you start the chemotherapy?' asked Claudine.

'I might not.'

'That's stupid.' She'd delay the inhaler for as long as possible.

'It's my choice.'

'I told you to consider others in making it,'

Claudine reminded her, carrying the breakfast coffee to the table beside her mother and pouring it. The older woman didn't attempt to pick up her cup and Claudine said: 'Can I help you?'

Her mother looked at her directly for the first time, without speaking. Claudine replaced the cup in its saucer, picking up her own, saying nothing more.

Monique said: 'It's not going to be immediate, if I accept the treatment. Several months. Even a year. More.'

'Which is why you must have it.' Maybe she was wrong about the morphine and the heroin.

'I can't work in the restaurant any more. And I won't sit there, not like I am now.'

'You could.'

'I don't want to.'

'There is still a lot you can do. You always worked too hard.'

'The restaurant was my life. All I ever wanted to do.'

'Now you can't, not any longer,' said Claudine, refusing the self-pity. 'Accept it.'

'It's difficult.'

'But possible.' Unable to wait any longer Claudine depressed the plunger of the inhaler, sucking in the muscle relaxant.

'It is possible for you to come down during the week?'

'I don't know. Why?'

'I want you to instruct the *notaire*.'

'It's not essential that I'm here. He might not even want me to be.'

'I want you to be.'

'I'll try.'

The older woman at last picked up her coffee with a wavering hand. Some splashed into the saucer and then on to the carpet. 'I've decided to marry Gérard.'

'I'm glad.'

'Not that it will do him any good.'

'You didn't mean that. You shouldn't have said it. It was cruel. You're not cruel.'

'Who knows what anybody is? Do you think you do?'

'I'm supposed to.'

'You don't.'

'Perhaps not,' admitted Claudine, who had no intention of fighting her mother about anything, absolutely wrong though the psychology was. 'When's the wedding?'

'When I'm stronger.' There was a head movement towards the bedside cabinet. 'I've got some pills that will help.'

'I'd like to be there.'

'I want that, too.'

Head sunk forward on her chest, so that it was hard for Claudine to hear, her mother said: 'I'm very proud of you. I always have been. I need to know you understand that.'

'Thank you.'

'Thank *you*. I saw the television, about Rome and Cologne. They talked about Europol. Weren't you involved?'

'Yes.'

'Why weren't you on television then?'

'It's not part of what I do.'

'I'd like to see you on television. For you to be famous: my own *sanglier.*'

'I got a commendation, from the Commission, for what I've done.' It was for her mother's benefit but Claudine wondered about hopefully turning it to her own. 'Sanglier was part of it.'

Monique smiled. 'Can I tell Gérard?'

'Of course.' Claudine made her decision. 'Sanglier's mentioned my father.'

'What?'

'Talked about the coincidence of both of them working in Interpol archives.'

Monique snorted a laugh. 'Imagine, thinking of one with the other!'

'Was it possible they knew each other?'

There was a curt headshake. 'William Carter was posted from England *after* the war: after the transfer here, from St Cloud. Sanglier himself only returned to St Cloud briefly. He only came here for special ceremonies.' There was a smile of nostalgia. 'They were always fabulous occasions . . . bands . . . flags . . .'

It didn't sound unnatural to Claudine for her mother to refer to her father by his full name: she'd begun to do so at the time of the disgrace, as if trying to distance herself from the man. 'So he might have met him, at least?'

There was another headshake. 'I don't think so. On the special occasions here Sanglier was always with the important people. The Director-General himself. Their wives were invited. I never was. I was glad, later.'

'Did he ever talk about Sanglier?'

'William Carter?'

Claudine nodded.

'He may have done, when the visits happened. I can't remember.'

'They were big events? I thought something would have been said.'

Her mother frowned at her. 'Why is it important?'

'It's not. It was just that Henri Sanglier mentioned it. I was curious.'

'William Carter was a failure. A weak man. You know that as well as I do. The two men shouldn't be mentioned in the same breath.'

'I've never been able to understand why he didn't tell you — refused to tell me, when I asked him — why he had to leave Interpol.'

'Shame for whatever he did. Something he was too ashamed to tell *me* about. What else? The same reason he didn't appeal, as he could have done. I *hate* weak men.'

Her mother was flushed, beneath the rouge, and Claudine decided the conversation, pointless anyway, was upsetting the older woman. She was aware her mother had stopped short of including Warwick in her condemnation. She'd only made the accusation once, directly after the suicide which of course she had regarded as a mortal sin. *Both of us were cursed by weak men.* She had stopped short then, too, from saying they were both fortunate to be freed from the burden. 'I have to go out this morning.'

'Why?'

'Things to shop for,' Claudine lied. 'There's no time during the week.'

Her mother's oncologist was named André Foulan and his consulting rooms were on the rue de la Martinière. There was no less traffic in Lyon during weekends than there was during the normal working period but Claudine got there early and Foulan ushered her immediately not into a sterile consulting room but into his comfortable, family-photograph-festooned lounge. It seemed the wrong place for their intended discussion: too personal. Claudine thanked him for making the special appointment and Foulan, a white-haired, professionally sympathetic man, insisted it was not inconvenient.

'It wasn't caught in time, was it?' demanded Claudine bluntly.

'It would have been better if she hadn't delayed.'

'How long?'

'It's impossible to estimate. Your mother is an extremely strong-willed woman when she wants to be. When she's motivated. Which she isn't, at the moment. There's no evidence of secondary tumours.'

'What, then?'

'There's the possibility of a spread to the lymph glands, which you already knew about.'

'Will the chemotherapy help?'

'I hope so. But there are distressing side effects. Hair loss. Diarrhoea. A general weakening.'

'My mother intends getting married again. A longtime friend.'

The specialist pursed his lips. 'That's a good idea. It will give her a focus, to go on fighting. It would be best, for her well-being, for the ceremony to be as soon as possible, before the effects of the treatment.'

'I saw some medication at the apartment this morning.'

'Morphine isn't necessary at this stage. Heroin, either.'

'My mother has accepted she is going to die.'

'I wish she hadn't. She insisted on complete honesty, which is her right.'

'Is there anything I can do?' She was thinking according to her training as a psychologist, not as a daughter.

'Pray,' suggested the man.

'I don't have that option.'

'Make sure she agrees to the chemotherapy. Radiotherapy if necessary. And doesn't abandon it when it becomes unpleasant. Don't let self-pity get a hold.'

'I don't live or work here in Lyon.'

'I know. Arrange the wedding ceremony as soon as possible. And ask the man to come to see me.'

She hadn't arranged her own gynaecological check-up or mammogram, Claudine remembered. She was shocked she had forgotten. She'd do it as soon as she got back to The Hague. 'I'm very grateful.'

'I'll always be available if you want to call.'

'Would it create an ethical problem to ask you to call me, if there's something I should know in a hurry?'

Foulan did not reply immediately. Then he said: 'Probably. But why don't you leave all your contact numbers?'

Back at the rue Grenette Gérard Lanvin abandoned his kitchen and sat nodding over an early cognac to Claudine's account of her meeting. When she finished Gérard said: 'The treatment is precautionary, that's all. It will be much longer than a year.'

'Of course it will,' agreed Claudine, knowing the man's need. 'You'll see Foulan, won't you?'

'This week. As soon as it's convenient for him.'

'I'm glad it's happening. The marriage, I mean.'

'So am I.'

'She didn't think you'd want to.'

'She told me you'd said I should be given

the choice. Thank you.'

'Thank *you*.'

'I'm not doing it out of pity. Or because I feel I should. I'm doing it because I love her.'

Her mother was dozing in her chair when Claudine got back to the upstairs apartment and Claudine dismissed the half-formed idea of suggesting they go for a brief walk, perhaps as far as the river. The older woman managed some soup for lunch, and in the afternoon announced that she intended returning that evening to her restaurant. It took a long time for her to bathe and prepare herself and she didn't make the effort with the unaccustomed rouge this time. It wasn't necessary because the prospect of going downstairs brought some pinkness to her face. The white-bloused and black-skirted uniform did not overwhelm her mother as much as Claudine had feared it might. Throughout the preparation Claudine helped where she could and warned Gérard in advance, so the table at which Monique usually sat at the end of every evening was kept free. Monique didn't question the arrangement, nor insist upon trying to stand at her usual welcoming post, just inside the door.

Instead that night the customers came to her, which they did in continuous homage. Monique ate far more poached sole than Claudine had hoped and Claudine did not have to encourage her mother to go to bed. Monique announced the decision herself, just after nine o'clock. Claudine let her leave the observing restaurant unaided.

Monique went down again the following day, to supervise Sunday lunch, and stayed longer and ate even more fish than she had the previous evening.

Later, upstairs again, she announced triumphantly: 'I can work again! From the table. Everything is going to be almost like it was before,' and Claudine said she'd known it would be all along.

Claudine pressed the wedding discussion to the point of their deciding a provisional date, a Sunday three weekends away to fit Claudine's convenience. Monique promised to start whatever therapy Foulan prescribed immediately afterwards.

Claudine's return flight was uneventful and on time and she made it thinking only of her mother, regretting during part of the reflection that she didn't feel able to pray but encouraged by the enthusiasm that had so abruptly returned to her mother on being in the restaurant again.

The message light illuminated one call on her answering machine when she entered her apartment. She clicked it to replay, her mind so occupied by the weekend that she expected to hear her mother.

Instead it was a man whose modulated tones she'd heard once before on a recording. The voice said: 'Claudine! Long time no see. My fault entirely. I'm sorry . . . sorry that I didn't get to Warwick's funeral, either. Why don't you give me a call on this number? It's Paul Bickerstone, by the way . . .'

Chapter Twenty-One

It was a long night made longer by Claudine's confusion, which was one of the few things she positively recognized and which compounded itself — briefly blanking her mind completely — because one of her few other rational thoughts was that she should have been too well trained, too professional, to give way to the mental and physical numbness that gripped her after listening to a man who absurdly — hysterically, she accepted — always appeared in her mind's eye in a fancy dress gorilla suit. In those first hours the asthma banded vice-like around her chest so that the breath groaned from her and she sat slumped in the chair, gasping the contents of the inhaler into her blocked lungs so often she risked overdosing on salbutamol.

Not even finding Warwick's slowly twisting body at the end of a suicide rope had affected her so badly, robbing her not just of the ability to breathe but of the mental and physical control of which she had always been so confident. It *was* her confidence, the touchstone upon which, until that moment, she had always been able to rely.

It was her anger at that, the feeling of being

robbed, that finally enabled Claudine to start thinking in anything like a rational way, although with gaps in her reasoning. She started breathing more normally, too.

It was her training that made Claudine logically analyse her near collapse — never before needing so much to observe her 'know thyself' precept — and the self-diagnosis satisfied her. Seven months before she *had* found a man she'd believed fulfilled to be her husband dangling from a strangling rope. Then she'd been told he was a suspected homosexual member of an insider trading group at the same time as she herself was assigned to an investigation upon which her entire future depended. And this very day she'd returned, to a message from the man in a gorilla suit at the centre of the £200,000,000 fraud, from having confirmed that a mother who had been the bedrock of her life — the only person *in* her life, now that her husband was dead — was going to die within months.

The surprise was not that for a few brief hours — no more than four, at the most — she had mentally been unable to function and could scarcely breathe. It was that it hadn't been much worse and lasted much longer. That she was, within limitations, functioning normally again proved just how incredibly strong she was, mentally. Most of all it proved she had no cause to doubt herself. It was the most comforting reassurance of all and one she would have clung to if she'd required re-assurance, which she told herself she didn't need but welcomed, snatched at, just the same. *Know thyself* echoed in her mind, mock-ingly.

For the remainder of that night Claudine didn't properly sleep, but in her half-awake, half-somnolent suspension she actually real-ized how the identification appeal could be made successful and became fully conscious thinking more about that than her several-layered personal problems. Which she took as further confirmation that she'd recovered from the totally understandable hiatus and was back in full control of herself again. It didn't solve her overwhelming problem but it wiped away a lot of her subsidiary uncertainties.

Claudine studied herself for a long time in the magnified make-up mirror, resigned that she couldn't do anything about the black hol-lows around her eyes but otherwise satisfied with her appearance, which certainly didn't attract the wrong sort of attention when she arrived at the incident room, or during her presentation of her sleep-suspended idea.

'Amnesty?' demanded Poulard.

'Why not?' said Claudine. 'We've got the facial identification, without the names. So we can't be cheated by any false claims, although inevitably some people will try it. And when they do and are found to be lying they can be prosecuted as illegals and expelled. If we offer the victims' families an amnesty against expulsion, there won't any longer be anything to stop them coming forward. If just one person does . . .' She stalled, briefly, stopping herself from saying 'I'. Instead she continued: '. . . we've got the chance to find out one of the most important — perhaps *the* most important — linking factor in our Céleste killings. We'll get the guide to *why* they were killed. Open everything up.'

'We're assuming that you're right about the families being illegal,' persisted Poulard.

'It doesn't matter if I'm wrong about that,' insisted Claudine, her enthusiasm growing for her idea as they discussed it. 'It's a way of getting the families to make themselves known, which is all that matters. And none of the countries offering it would be making any general concession whatsoever. They'd just be solving crimes terrorizing them.'

'It's inspired!' enthused Siemen, although quietly.

'If it produces something,' qualified Poulard.

'And if it doesn't, nothing's lost,' said Rosetti.

'Exactly,' said Claudine.

It occupied less dictation time and written justification than any suggestion she'd so far put forward, although she obviously presented it as a joint, not a personal, proposal. While Yvette was typing it Claudine went to her own office to arrange her too long delayed appointment with a gynaecologist recommended by Europol's medical unit, enduring the receptionist's silent condemnation at her admission that it had been more than three years since she'd undergone an examination.

With no reason to do so she didn't hurry back to the incident room. Instead, with the visual reminder of the safe and its contents directly in her line of vision on the opposite side of the room, she allowed herself to think clearly about the message that had awaited her the previous night.

She had fully recovered from every reaction to it but was as far away as ever from knowing what to do. Logically — sensibly — she should immediately inform Toomey. To do so would prove to the disbelieving man she knew nothing about any insider trading and had nothing to fear from his investigation. But had she? Toomey's initial inquiry had been — or been phrased, at least — about embarrassment by association for something in which Warwick might have been involved, sexually or criminally or both. Which, inconceivable though she believed either to be, might still exist. So to alert Toomey, who from their last encounter didn't appear to have sufficient to mount a prosecution, could re-ignite an inquiry which for all she knew might have been already abandoned. On the other hand, Paul Bickerstone, who couldn't be bothered to come to

Warwick's funeral, wouldn't have appeared from nowhere if the investigation was over. The fact that he had suddenly materialized had not only to mean that it was still very much alive but that something had emerged to worry him sufficiently to track her down. Into her retentive mind drifted a remark she began by thinking was totally unconnected but then conceded a very real connection. *I can't imagine how but if I can help . . .*

Claudine thrust up, decisively, and made her way quickly back to the incident room, glad that Hugo Rosetti was in the side office he'd taken for himself and that there wasn't going to be a delay during which she might have changed her very uncertain mind. She crossed directly to the Italian's office and when he looked up hurriedly said: 'I'd like to take up the offer you made that night at dinner, in Rome.'

'I'm glad,' said Rosetti.

Her decision had been so impulsive — doubted and regretted within minutes of her blurting out the plea — that Claudine hadn't thought where or when they could talk and was about to refuse the offer of yet another dinner, to suggest instead their meeting at her apartment, when she remembered her limitations as a cook. It might be better, too, to meet on neutral territory. It was not until later that afternoon, still unsure about what she'd done, that Claudine realized Rosetti had made the arrangements at once and for that night, without consulting his family.

Rosetti drove with an Italian disregard for speed limit or right of way. When they entered the park, Claudine realized he had chosen the Chagall, to which they'd both avoided going after the commissioners' reception. There were several boats out on the Vijver lake and Claudine wondered if the nautical-phrased British commissioner was at the helm of one of them.

Remembering she didn't drink he only ordered a half-bottle of wine for himself and insisted she had mussels because they were the Dutch speciality. Claudine accepted the suggestion and the unusual experience of not being the one in control. Which, she supposed, went with her earlier decision to let someone else — a virtual stranger — into her very private and self-enclosed life.

Having made that decision and refused the many second thoughts about it Claudine accepted she had to be completely honest. So she was, aware that she sometimes repeated what she'd already told him in Rome but consciously doing so to fit everything in time and context. Her only hesitation was at the suicide note and then she told him about that, too, alert for any criticism in his face. There was none. Neither did he interrupt at any time while she spoke.

'You've told me the whole story.' It was a statement, not a question.

'Yes?'

'So now you can tell a lawyer.'

'I don't want to put it on an official level.'

'It's already on an official level.'

'Going to a lawyer would be giving in.'

'That doesn't make sense.'

'It does to me.'

'I don't see how your husband could have been involved, directly or indirectly, in any financial crime: he wasn't in a position to help this man Bickerstone.'

'Warwick was a lawyer, a specialist in European Union legislation. He could have guided them on the differences in financial law between the various European countries: the bank secrecy of Luxembourg, for instance.'

'If Bickerstone is a dealer on the scale you say he is, he'd hardly need guidance on that, would he?'

Claudine finished the mussels, glad she'd let Rosetti order for her and wishing for once she'd accepted the wine he'd offered, Frascati, which he'd declared to be excellent. 'I was just putting it forward as a suggestion.'

'We don't know enough,' said Rosetti.

'That's why I've decided what to do,' announced Claudine abruptly. 'I'm going to reply. Meet him.' She uttered the words as they came to her, without thinking what she was saying, as impulsively as she'd thrust into

406

Rosetti's office earlier that day. If there was a difference it was that she didn't regret them as quickly.

For the first time an expression came to Rosetti's face that she could read, a look of total disbelief. 'That's ridiculous! Out of the question.'

'Why?'

'At the moment, suspicious though it looks — awkward though it is — everything is circumstantial. Your only legal difficulty is the cash gifts from your mother.'

'This wouldn't change anything.'

'You'd be willingly consorting with a man under formal investigation for a two hundred million pound fraud!'

'Which doesn't prove I'm part of it. Or that Warwick was.'

'You can't do this by yourself. I've already told you that.'

'I'm a trained psychologist. You even called me brilliant in Rome.'

'What's that got to do with it?'

'If I talked to Bickerstone I could find out the truth. I'd *know*.'

Rosetti shook his head slowly. 'You want some other words, to go with brilliant?'

'Such as?'

'Arrogant, conceited, stupid.'

She wouldn't have accepted them from anyone else. 'I know I could do it!'

'Why?'

'I've nothing to employ a lawyer for.'

'If he's done half of what's alleged against him Bickerstone isn't a small-time crook. He's a very clever man. You said yourself he wouldn't have emerged if he hadn't wanted something.'

'He called me. That isn't clever. He's desperate. I can use that desperation.'

'What if you can't?'

'What will I have lost?'

'We probably won't know — or be able to prevent it — until after you've lost it. And then it will be too late.'

'I'm not frightened.'

'I'm frightened. For you.'

Claudine smiled, enjoying the concern. 'Don't be.'

'How did he find out you were here?' asked Rosetti.

Claudine considered the question. 'I left a forwarding address with the people who bought the house. And at the university. He could have known the Kensington address — and about the university, I suppose — from Warwick.'

'If there was the continuing friendship that Toomey says there was. But you don't believe that.'

'I'll ask him when I see him.'

Rosetti didn't respond to the remark. Instead he said: 'Could Warwick have been gay?'

'Anyone can be gay.'

'That's a psychologist's answer. What's yours?'

'He could have been. Bisexual, possibly. I never had the slightest reason to suspect he was either.'

'Does the possibility upset you?'

'It upsets me that he didn't tell me, if he was.'

'What would you have done, if he had?'

'All I could to help him be happy. Agreed to a divorce, if that's what he wanted. But not stopped loving him, if that's what you mean. It wouldn't have been married love but it would have been love.'

'You really think you could have done that?'

'I know I could. And would have done.'

'What about your own life?'

'We're a long way into speculation,' said Claudine, smiling again, faintly. 'I haven't thought about it.'

'Haven't you thought about getting married again?'

'No,' admitted Claudine. 'I don't think I will but I haven't given it any positive thought. The need hasn't arisen.' Had she been a subject of conversation with Poulard and Siemen, after she'd left Rome? She supposed it was almost inevitable. She didn't think Rosetti completely believed her: probably thought it was the self-protection she was pulling around herself, to keep out the cold guilt of not recognizing Warwick's mental illness.

'You didn't need to talk it through with me . . . tell me everything . . . if you'd already decided to call Bickerstone back.'

'I hadn't decided to, until this moment.'

'Reconsider it. It's madness. You know it is.'

'I have to know what he wants. You said yourself we needed to know more.' The 'we' registered with Claudine. She waited for him to react — protest perhaps — to her so readily considering him a confidant, despite the Rome offer.

Instead he said: 'But not that this was the way to achieve it.'

'I'll be careful.'

'You don't know what to protect yourself against. This is arrogance, Claudine: stupid, unnecessary arrogance. And it could cost you what you're most afraid of losing, your job here at Europol.'

She acknowledged the threat as a genuine one and it pricked her determination. 'I can answer the call, at least.'

'I want you to tell me what happens, when it happens. Whatever the time. At home, if necessary.'

'What about . . .' she started, changing in mid-sentence '. . . bothering your family?'

Rosetti seemed to change his mind from what he was immediately going to say. 'It won't be a bother.'

'Maybe I shouldn't involve you any more.' She wouldn't have done so to this extent if he hadn't instantly responded and she'd had more time to think. Now he knew all about her and she knew virtually nothing about him. Oddly, for someone who'd always had difficulty in sharing her privacy with anyone, even Warwick, Claudine felt no awkwardness. A lot of her attitudes and actions seemed to be changing, very quickly.

'I don't think you can stop now,' he said.

She let him choose the desserts and they took their coffee overlooking the night-shrouded lake and when, belatedly, she wondered if he wasn't anxious to get home he said there wasn't any hurry. He still ignored any speed limit driving back to her apartment.

When he parked she said: 'I really hadn't decided what to do, when I asked you to help. I didn't set out to waste your time.'

'I didn't think you did. Or that it's been wasted.'

For the first time that evening she had a twinge of personal uncertainty with him. Feeling that she had to, she said: 'Would you like to come in for coffee?'

'No,' he said at once. Then: 'I'd still like you to think again, before speaking to him.'

'Maybe I will,' said Claudine, knowing she wouldn't and guessing he knew it, too.

'Why weren't you annoyed when I called you stupid and arrogant?'

She smiled at him across the car. 'Because it's true,' she said.

Sanglier had recognized at once the controversy the amnesty suggestion would create, just as he anticipated the irritation from the Asian countries at having the Internet proposal announced to them, without any consultation. Already there'd been feed-back from France about Interpol's fury at his arbitrary dissemination request with which they'd had to comply. Both fitted perfectly into the presentation he'd carefully prepared for the commissioners' weekly conference.

He knew Françoise had been lying with her glib denial of being attracted to Claudine Carter, because Françoise was attracted to every woman. Could she have been lying, too, about there being no reciprocal attraction? It was an intriguing thought. It would certainly explain the public humiliation of Poulard: even the Carter woman's virtual refusal to involve herself in any social activity, like the quick avoidance of the restaurant visit after the reception, about which Poulard had told him. He would have thought it difficult to conceal in such a gossip-ridden environment as Europol, which was the goldfish bowl he'd described to Françoise. But then she was discreet. Why wouldn't Claudine Carter be? He couldn't think of any way of finding out, apart from using Françoise and that was full of danger.

It certainly justified the idea of a dinner invitation, though.

Chapter Twenty-Two

The fifteen commissioners divided as usual into their several, pre-conference private caucuses. Sanglier didn't bother to join any of them, not believing he had to gain support or manipulate opposition in advance of the actual session: sheep always followed a leader or the barking of a corralling dog and by now he knew how to become either, according to circumstance. He expected the attention he still attracted, however, because his recommendations made up most of the agenda.

Franz Sobell was the last to enter the room, a pretentious custom the man always adopted during his chairmanship. He bustled, too, fussily urging everyone else to the conference table with him: a very small dog with a very small bark, decided Sanglier. He was already seated, ahead of them all. The greetings were perfunctory, unnecessary. Looking directly at Sanglier but addressing them all, Sobell said: 'As you will see from your notes, the first proposal of our French colleague is that we make a complete examination of the progress of the investigation up until now. Any observations on that?'

'I would have thought we were all suffi-

413

ciently familiar — and extremely pleased — with everything that's happened so far,' said Hans Maes, the Dutch representative.

Sometimes, thought Sanglier, there was divine intervention. The barking-dog brusqueness as prepared as everything else, he said: 'If I believed that I wouldn't have asked for it to be put upon the agenda. I think there is very little for us to be extremely pleased about.'

Maes blinked, surprised at the retort, and Sanglier knew he had the attention of everyone. Willi Lenteur, the German commissioner, said with faint mockery: 'Our French colleague clearly has a point to make.'

'A very serious and important one,' insisted Sanglier, quite content for the German to make himself a target. Maes moved to speak again, too, but Sanglier talked over him, the impatience as well feigned as the brusqueness. 'And I hope this will be one of the few meetings during which we can properly fulfil our function.'

There were sideways looks between everyone. Sobell said: 'Is there something we're unaware of?' With only two days to go before the transfer of the chairmanship, there was no concern in the Austrian's voice.

'There shouldn't be but it would seem to be the case. Regrettably,' said Sanglier.

'Riddles,' said Paul Merot. As Luxembourg had been spared the atrocities he felt able to attempt the sarcasm with which Lenteur had failed.

'Only to people too obtuse to recognize the obvious,' said Sanglier, verging upon open rudeness. Without waiting for any formal agreement to his agenda listing, he bulldozed on with his carefully prepared review, isolating every salient point from Claudine's profiles against its relevant factor in each murder and then, talking directly at the discomfited German commissioner, he set out how Cologne's obstruction had failed to prevent Claudine from making a completely accurate analysis. He concluded by recounting the Rome killings, but concentrated upon the cooperation and gratitude publicly expressed by Giovanni Ponzio.

He held the full attention of Lenteur, angered at being so obviously singled out, and of Emilio Bellimi, in contrast pleased at the praise of Italy, but there were varying attitudes of diminishing interest from the others. Spain's Jorge Ortega gazed steadfastly out in the direction of the familiar grey sealine and David Winslow occupied almost the entire reconsideration doodling images of ships.

Maes said: 'I thought the object of the reception was to show our appreciation, particularly of Dr Carter?'

Quickly Lenteur said: 'I was under the impression there was a point to this discussion. So far I've failed to see it.'

'Which is to our disadvantage and it is there-fore fortunate that I have raised it,' said San-glier. 'If it needs to be made even clearer, which it obviously does, then let me spell it out. At the very beginning we each of us ac-cepted the importance to ourselves and to this organization of a successful conclusion. To-wards which we've had the brilliant assess-ments of Dr Carter, assisted to a degree by others of her task force . . .'

'What is your point?' demanded Lenteur, exasperated.

'What has there been in return, from any country those of us here today represent and to each of which our efforts have been passed on, for investigation, according to our Con-vention?' insisted Sanglier formally. He man-aged to stretch the rhetorical silence by looking individually to each of the men grouped around the table, bringing their wavering con-centration back to him. He answered his own question. 'Nothing! None of the local or na-tional police forces, which should be carrying out their investigations based upon our guid-ance, has made any significant contribution . . .' He went quickly to Lenteur, then to Maes. 'The binding wire was manufactured in Holland and somewhere in Eastern Europe, possibly what was East Germany. What prog-ress have your forces made finding every manufacturer and from every manufacturer each purchaser and outlet?'

'Are you serious?' broke in the incredulous Lenteur, to be stopped in turn by Sanglier.

'I couldn't be more serious! It's a logically routine method of continuing a police investigation . . . time-consuming, manpower-intensive, boring but absolutely necessary.' His attention skipped between Sobell and Winslow. 'The trunk road interceptions were covered, just, by their being accepted as drugs operations. Are they still being carried out? I certainly intend asking the most searching questions of the French forces involved, because I don't think they are, any more, I suspect, than they are being conducted with the proper diligence in any other country. I think that because the killings have stopped and the public outcry has begun to diminish all the national forces have relaxed, happy for Europol to be identified in the public mind as the organization responsible for success or failure.'

'I'm still trying hard to follow your argument,' protested Lenteur.

'Europol's working. National forces aren't. The investigations are getting nowhere and Europol is going to be held responsible.'

'You've no evidence whatsoever for that assertion,' defended Jan Villiers. Belgium was taking over the Commission chairmanship from Austria.

'We had, after some difficulty, the initial investigation dossiers forwarded from each

417

country,' Sanglier reminded him. 'I propose today that we demand an update, from every country, of what has positively been achieved since our assistance began.'

'Couldn't that be invidious?' asked Villiers, knowing that for the next month he would be the person dealing with Justice Ministers.

'We know our successes. So, to a lesser extent, do the public. We've got nothing to fear from any comparison.'

'It would be exceeding our remit and our authority,' declared Lenteur.

'It would be doing nothing of the sort,' said Sanglier. 'By a binding decision of European Union Justice Ministers we are the official liaison between the investigating countries. It's our *right* to be kept up to date and it is our *function* to ensure that liaison is as comprehensive as possible. For which we need weekly if not daily intelligence upon which to judge and make further recommendations.'

'Why haven't you insisted upon it before?' asked Lenteur, an almost instinctive responsibility-avoiding question.

'I didn't expect overnight miracles,' retorted Sanglier. 'That would have been ridiculous in view of the circumstances that brought about our involvement in the first place. But no force has made any progress whatsoever. I've waited this long because I am a professional policeman who allowed what I considered a proper period of time for what we provided to be acted upon and to have resulted in some progress.'

'I suppose we've every right to have expected something by now,' allowed Bellimi.

Quickly, not wanting to lose the direction in which he was guiding the discussion, Sanglier said: 'I accept that Dr Carter — everyone in the task force, myself included — has every right to be dissatisfied.'

'Dr Carter has personally protested,' said Winslow, unwittingly on cue.

'Wouldn't you have expected her to, after the contribution she's made?' demanded Sanglier, covering one question with another. Ensuring, too, that the official record would show he had not, in fact, made the categorical claim himself, although from their expressions all of them inferred that he had.

'Isn't Dr Carter exceeding her authority?' demanded Sobell.

Sanglier betrayed no satisfaction. In apparent defence he said: 'Any success Europol has enjoyed has largely been through the professionalism of Dr Carter.'

'Are the next two suggestions you make on today's agenda those of Dr Carter?' asked Lenteur, under pressure.

Again Sanglier hid any reaction not just at the perfect timing but at the phrasing of the question. 'Both are based on sound, practical reasoning,' he said, which again wasn't a confirmation but allowed the inference.

'An amnesty would open the floodgates,' protested Paul Merot.

'It would do nothing of the sort,' said Sanglier, prepared by Claudine's supporting memorandum, which he had not attached to the agenda. 'It would only apply to the families of the victims. You're surely not suggesting illegal immigrants are going to start sacrificing and dismembering their children to gain the right of residency!'

Merot flushed angrily. 'It will be seen as a dangerous precedent.'

'Hardly as dangerous as having teenagers butchered.' Sheep, thought Sanglier: sheep to be shepherded in whichever way he wanted. 'I suggest we announce it at a press conference. The governments will be forced by the strength of public opinion to accept it.'

'What if public opinion is against it?' asked Winslow.

'It won't be, when it's made clear it only extends to the victims' families.'

'I am not sure how it will be accepted in my own country,' said Lenteur reluctantly. 'Incredible though it may seem — embarrassing though it is — there's actually been some support for those arrested for the murder of the Turkish girl. It's a volatile situation.'

'Which is surely a problem — one with which I sympathize — for the German government,' said Sanglier smoothly. 'But not an argument or a reason for not doing something that might bring this investigation to an end.'

'I think it's important to take all aspects of public opinion into account,' persisted Lenteur.

Sanglier quickly seized the opportunity. 'Which is what I am recommending with the Asian appeal on the Internet.'

'That will be resented as much as announcing the amnesty proposal without consultation,' argued Hans Maes.

'We haven't got time to consult.'

'But there is time for a continent-wide search for the source of the baling wire!' said Winslow.

With a pained look at the Englishman, Sanglier said: 'If you wish to propose that this suggestion goes through national channels I will oppose it — and seek a named vote for the record — but will, of course, abide by the majority decision. My reason for opposing it, which I would also insist upon being recorded, would be the risk of more horrific murders being committed in the months it would take to reach a Union-wide decision.'

Winslow backed down at once. 'I was merely making an observation.'

'There's a logical argument for both the amnesty and extending the identification appeal in Asia,' said Jorge Ortega.

'And for the country by country update,' insisted Sanglier, needing every plank of his plan in place.

'That, too,' agreed the Spaniard.

'We risk being accused of exceeding our remit,' warned Merot.

'Which is worse, an accusation of exceeding it or not fulfilling it?' asked Bellimi generally.

Two sheep in the pen, calculated Sanglier: it wouldn't be long now.

'All of us would, of course, be able to advise our various ministries in advance of any announcement or press conference here,' said Winslow.

Sanglier ticked off another entering the fold.

'Do you propose a press statement?' asked Sobell, making the fourth.

'I thought the press conference in Rome had a great impact,' said Sanglier.

'Given by yourself?' queried Lenteur, in a clearly implied sneer.

Sanglier shook his head. 'I think the people doing the actual work should be given the recognition.'

'Would that include Dr Carter, who seems to have formed some very strong views about the progress of the investigation?' persisted Lenteur.

'I would hope so,' said Sanglier.

'Shall we put it to the vote?' suggested Sobell, in one of his last acts as chairman.

The agreement was unanimous.

'Satisfied?' Lenteur asked Sanglier, an edge still in his voice.

'Completely,' said Sanglier. Easily he

added: 'My only interest is in protecting the interests of this organization.'

The radiologist closed the machine too tightly to ensure that her breasts were properly held and it hurt. So did the cervical smear that afterwards caused a small bleed and Claudine didn't enjoy the manual examination of her breasts by the gynaecologist, a white-haired, distracted man named Raufer. He took pedantic case notes and advised that she undergo a yearly examination in future if the current check-up proved to be negative, which he was sure it would be. When she mildly complained of the mammogram discomfort he said it was because she had small breasts, which didn't mean there was any less risk of her developing a cancer. He promised the X-ray and smear results within a week and said she was not to worry. She'd been wise to come.

There was no call from Yvette, with whom she'd left the gynaecologist's number, and Claudine decided to lunch away from the Europol building, wanting time by herself.

She was guilty of every accusation — arrogant, conceited, stupid — that Hugo had made, just as he'd been right about getting a lawyer and telling Toomey of the telephone approach from Paul Bickerstone. And the truest warning of all was that by ignoring everything Hugo said she was risking what was most important to her, whatever future she had at

Europol. Which made the answer easy and obvious, giving her no other choice: don't ignore what he'd said, follow his advice instead and hope everything turned out all right.

But that took control away from her and put it in the hands of others: made her dependent on others. Her scales of reasoning abruptly tilted back into an even balance and then descended in the opposite direction, away from logic. What were the arguments against those of Hugo, valid though she acknowledged his to be? Bickerstone's approach didn't prove anything, against Warwick or herself: at its worst it was nothing more than curious, something capable of a circumstantial interpretation. Peter Toomey would inevitably make one, and if only she could turn it back upon the man it would all be over. All she needed was something positive, one sharp fact to prick the balloon of suspicion and the whole nonsense would end without her having had to rely on someone else, to depend on someone else. Expose herself. But hadn't she exposed herself to Hugo Rosetti? Yes, she admitted uncomfortably. Inexplicably — and now to her burning embarrassment — she had talked more about herself, disclosed more about herself, to the Italian than probably she had to anyone, including even her mother and Warwick. But she hadn't gone as far as to rely or depend on him. Trusted him, certainly. But she was still in control.

Know thyself echoed in her mind. Knowing herself as she did — although unable to understand the aberration with Rosetti — why was she trying to convince herself there was a debate? She knew bloody well what she was going to do, despite all the logical arguments to the contrary. Just as she knew that there wouldn't be any danger in it. Not in simply returning a call. Then was the time to consider telling Toomey or getting a lawyer. But not now. Not yet. The decision made, Claudine abandoned the idea of lunch and hurried back to the Europol building.

There the meeting between Sanglier and Poulard had already been going on for thirty minutes.

'I want to be sure about this,' insisted Sanglier, as if seeking a reminder. 'Rosetti told you she positively avoided any personal publicity?'

'It was only in casual conversation, between Rosetti and myself, just before the Rome press conference,' elaborated Poulard. 'He said Claudine had refused Ponzio's invitation to take part in earlier conferences. And that he agreed with her that personal publicity wouldn't help them. Be a distraction, in fact. That's why he didn't want to get involved. Why it was just Siemen and me.'

Sanglier had allowed Poulard to recount and savour every detail of his Rome experience to get to this point, the most uncertain part of the ensnaring web he was attempting to weave. 'I think she should be invited to participate, though, don't you?'

'Most certainly,' said the French detective. Much of the subservience had gone but he was still properly respectful.

'I won't press her, if she doesn't want to.'

'Of course not.'

'Which would leave it to you and Siemen. Have you any problem with that?'

'None at all.' Poulard only just managed to appear reticent. Yvette wasn't the only one to have opened her legs to him since his Cologne and Rome television appearances: some women didn't object to a fame fuck.

'This is more important than any public appearance you've made before,' cautioned Sanglier. 'I don't want any misunderstanding.'

'I don't think I misunderstand.'

'So what are the points to make?'

'That the amnesty is not an open invitation, but strictly restricted to the victims' families,' recited Poulard. 'And that the Internet appeal is logical in view of the obvious nationality of those killed.'

This man wasn't a sheep, thought Sanglier, exasperated: he was a donkey with a dick to match. 'You must not overlook — although obviously you must not make it obvious — the disappointment of the Commission at the lack of progress anywhere in the Union from the guidance and leads we have provided. National forces should have made more progress by now.'

Poulard stared curiously across the separating desk. 'You've no objection to my talking about our demand for a complete national survey?'

'I think *demand* might unnecessarily antagonize,' suggested Sanglier. '*Invite* would sufficiently convey our dissatisfaction, not just to the police forces but to the general public.'

'Who will be the spokesperson if Dr Carter does agree to appear?'

'I'll decide that after talking to her.' Discerning the man's need and knowing the undertaking could easily be reneged upon, Sanglier said: 'I don't see why her being with you should take the role from you, unless some technical question is raised.'

Poulard smiled, openly and gratefully. 'Talking of technical questions, will Rosetti be with us?'

'No,' said Sanglier bluntly.

There was a moment of satisfied silence. Poulard said: 'What should my response be if I am directly asked if we are dissatisfied with individual national or local forces?'

'That you do not wish to comment upon individual countries or individual investigations.'

'Which could only mean we're dissatisfied with everyone?'

'But which would not be you — or Europol — saying it.' Sanglier decided that it had, after all, been wise — a necessity, in fact — to discontinue taping every conversation.

'The amnesty could be the breakthrough, couldn't it?' said Poulard, his mind more upon the incident room discussion with Claudine herself than with the sometimes ambiguous and convoluted briefing from Sanglier.

'I expect it to be precisely that,' said Sanglier. He added: 'I'm seeing Dr Carter later this afternoon. If she agrees to take part, then of course I'll tell you. But if she doesn't, I think credit should be given to her, if not by name. You'll be presenting Europol to the public. Let them know there's a profiler involved.'

'If you wish,' said Poulard, doubtfully.

'I do.'

For the first time Sanglier initially wondered if he had Claudine's full attention before dismissing the doubt, too professional himself to doubt her professionalism, anxious though he was to find any fault. He realized, instead, that her attitude was entirely understandable. He was obviously setting out to tell her what she expected to hear — which was exactly the impression he wanted to inculcate before arriving at the real purpose of the encounter.

Claudine nodded dutifully but made no comment when he announced that the Commission had accepted both the amnesty and the Internet proposals. And when he pressed for an opinion on the lack of national police progress, Claudine admitted she had hoped for quicker developments in at least one of the murder inquiries, which Sanglier judged sufficient to validate the inference he'd allowed at that morning's conference. Her first full concentration came with the mention of a press conference and his diffident suggestion that she participate. She immediately refused, insisting there would be no professional advantage and adding, because she felt the objection justified, that she did not want the personal publicity. Sanglier was curious at her reluctance and would have liked to explore it further, but having achieved the refusal he sought he didn't want to risk Claudine changing her mind.

'It's not something I shall insist upon.'

'I appreciate that.'

'I'd like one day for you to get your proper, public recognition.'

'I'm content the way things are,' said Claudine.

'Then that's how they'll stay,' smiled Sanglier. He didn't speak for several moments but Claudine guessed he didn't intend concluding the encounter. Then he said: 'I thought it was an excellent reception.'

Where the fuck were they going now! 'I thought so too.'

'Françoise enjoyed meeting you.'

Claudine searched for a proper response. She said: 'I enjoyed meeting her,' knowing as she spoke that wasn't it.

'She wondered — we both wondered — if you'd like to come to dinner. She was fascinated by your work.'

'I would like that,' lied Claudine, with no other choice.

'Why don't you call Françoise at home? Fix a date?'

'I'll do that,' said Claudine, without any intention of doing so.

'We'll both look forward to it.'

She returned early to the apartment with the lake view, refusing to be distracted by yet another peculiar episode with the French commissioner from something more immediate. She wasn't, she knew, allowing a private consideration to supersede a professional demand because there was nothing professional — although there might well be a demand — about a dinner invitation from Françoise Sanglier.

She consciously relegated it in her mind, wanting to prepare herself. She spent some time at Warwick's carefully indexed collection of tapes and CDs before selecting Ella Fitzgerald singing with Billie Holiday at the Newport festival. She remained unmoving for several tracks and then turned down the volume to call Lyon. There was no reply from the upstairs apartment but her mother responded at once on the restaurant extension. She was feeling wonderful and arguing with Foulan about the need for either radio- or chemotherapy. She was spending every evening at her table and hoped in the next few days to get a definite date for a meeting with the *notaire* about the will. Gérard sent his love.

Claudine listened to almost the entire reverse side of the wonderful duet, actually hearing the words although with her eyes on the telephone, before abruptly reaching out to switch the tape, just as quickly lifting the receiver a second time.

She had an inhaler close at hand, expecting a reaction, but her chest remained quite clear as she dialled. There were only two rings before the cultured voice said, without any greeting: 'Paul Bickerstone.'

Chapter Twenty-Three

'Claudine Carter.'

'Claudine! *How* are you?'

'OK. You?'

'Couldn't be better.'

'That's good to hear.'

'I'm so glad you called.'

'I was surprised to hear from you.' Her chest was still free. She was pleased. Curious, too, at the effusiveness and the word stress.

'You've every reason to feel like that.'

'Like what?'

'Annoyed.'

'I'm not annoyed.' He was testing her, as best he could.

'I can't believe that.'

'Why should I be?' Come on, you bastard.

'Warwick.'

'What about Warwick?'

'Not getting to the funeral. Writing even. It's unforgivable.'

'It's all in the past.' She couldn't lose the image of a man in a gorilla suit and wanted to laugh. She swallowed against the urge, concerned at the lapse.

'I'm really very sorry. Bloody work.

Which is no excuse.'

'It's over now.' There was nothing to be gained or earned dancing around the regret maypole.

'It was shocking.'

'Yes.'

'You must be wrecked.'

'I was. Not now.' Had she ever been wrecked? Not really. Offended was the word that came to mind. After the annoyance at herself for not seeing Warwick's need: offended that he should have done it to her. She couldn't remember crying at the funeral. But then she couldn't remember much about the funeral at all.

'Resilient. That's what Warwick always said about you.'

'When?' She kept any eagerness from her voice at the first opening.

'When you first got together.'

'In the early days?' But not latterly, she thought.

'Something like that,' he said dismissively. 'Good idea to get away. New life.'

Another opening was coming. 'We'll see.'

'Not missing England?'

'Hardly.'

'Sorry. That was a stupid question. Of course you wouldn't miss England.'

'That's all right.' Come on! Come on!

'What's The Hague like?'

'Pleasant enough. Small.' She had to do it,

she decided. 'I'm intrigued you were able to track me down.'

'Least I could do, after missing the funeral.'

'How did you find I'd moved?'

'Asked my people. Don't know how they did it. But they did. That's what they're paid for.'

A brick-walled cul-de-sac, Claudine recognized: as she recognized the I-can-do-anything arrogance. The idea of being searched for, presumably by an enquiry agency, was unsettling, although hardly as unsettling as being told by Peter Toomey she was being investigated. 'Why did you want to find me?'

'Guilt, I guess.'

'What have you got to be guilty about?'

'Warwick and I were good friends.'

'So?' She wondered if he would introduce Gerald Lorimer into the conversation.

'Felt I let him down.'

'How?' It was her stomach that knotted, in expectation, not her chest.

'Not doing anything to help when it happened.'

'We didn't see much of you, after the wedding.' Had he even been to the wedding?

'Bloody work. But I felt I owed it to him.'

'Owed him what?'

'To get in touch.' There was a pause. 'Particularly after Gerald.'

'Who?' She could explain it away later as mishearing the name.

434

'Gerald. You know Gerald Lorimer?'

'Of course.' That wasn't a lie: he'd spoken in the present tense.

'Awful.'

'Awful?'

'Killing himself . . . sorry . . . Dying like Warwick . . .'

She couldn't avoid lying. 'When?'

'Just after Warwick. A month or two. You didn't know?'

'I came here almost immediately after Warwick's funeral.'

'It was the same . . . I don't want to upset you . . .'

'You mean he hanged himself?'

'Yes.'

'Why?'

'Gave way under the pressure of work: that was the gist of the inquest.'

'I never quite understood what he did?'

'Treasury. Some high-powered job.'

'There was evidence at Warwick's inquest about overwork.'

'I read it.'

'Poor Gerald. He didn't have a family, did he?'

'No. I thought you might have read about it: there were stories in the newspapers.'

'I don't bother much with English papers. I never did.'

'Not interested in the old country?'

Was she imagining relief in his voice? 'It was

never really my country.' She didn't want the conversation to drift any further. 'It's a dreadful thing to have happened. Awful, like you said.'

'I thought you might have heard officially.'

At last! 'Why should I have heard officially?'

'It was pretty odd . . . two friends . . . the same circumstances . . .'

'No, I wasn't told officially.'

'No reason why you should have been, I suppose.'

'None at all. It could only have been a horrible coincidence.'

'Of course.'

'Did you see Gerald, after Warwick died?'

'He was devastated.'

He'd been well enough controlled at the funeral, Claudine remembered. And only spoken to her once afterwards, although there had been a couple of answering machine messages she hadn't felt like responding to, unlike this one. 'Didn't he give any hint of being pressured at work?'

There was a hesitation. 'Not specifically. Said there was always too much to do, the sort of thing that people always say.'

'You saw him a lot then? More than Warwick?'

'We got together from time to time.'

Not the reply she'd wanted. 'Did you ever get the impression from Warwick that he had trouble at work?'

There was another hesitation. 'Not really.'
Still not right. 'I certainly didn't.'
'I'm sure you don't want to talk about it.'
Better, she thought. 'I do. I want to know.
I still don't understand why.' Which wasn't a
lie.
'He never said anything, the few times we
were together.'
Few times! 'So you don't know, either?'
'I wish I did . . . that I could help you.'
Claudine decided she had to force things
forward again, risky though it might be. 'It was
good of you to call.'
'I've no excuse for not doing so before,' he
said, hurried by the deliberate finality she'd
intruded into her voice.
'You said that already.'
'Say, do you ever get back to England?'
He spoke as if an idea had just occurred to
him.
'I have no need. There was no point in
keeping the Kensington house. Why?'
'I thought we could meet up. Lunch? Dinner maybe?'
'Pity.' For the first time Claudine had to
breathe deeply, against a vague tightness.
'Then it's fortunate you called now! How
far's The Hague from Paris?' He spoke as if
he didn't know.
Her breathing became easier. 'By air, about
an hour. It's Amsterdam and then about
twenty minutes on the train that actually runs

through the airport. Why?'

'I've got some business in Paris that I can fit in, whenever I want. I could come up to see you.'

'I'm sure you're too busy. It would be a chore.'

'Not at all. I've got amends to make.'

Was this how an angler felt, landing a catch? Except this fish wasn't fighting very hard. 'When, exactly, will you be in Paris?'

'I really can make my own time. Fit things to your convenience.'

Claudine hadn't expected it to be this easy. 'I'm involved in something at the moment: things come up unexpectedly. Can I reach you on this number?'

'Involved in what?' he asked, the anxiety echoing in his voice.

Alone in her apartment Claudine smiled openly. 'Work. Which of course I can't tell you about.'

'Of course not. I'm sorry.'

'We were talking about getting back to you,' she prompted.

'On this number, any time. It's my personal mobile. Always in my pocket. Beside my bed.'

'I'll call.'

'Make sure you do. I don't want to lose touch again.'

After replacing the receiver Claudine reached briefly to where the jazz duet had been playing earlier. Her breathing was much more pronounced when she tensed for the reply to her second call, but when it came she recognized Rosetti's voice. There was the distant sound of music, something classical, but not of anyone in the room with him.

'He's desperate,' declared Claudine at once. She didn't have a mental image of a face in a gorilla costume any more.

'You sure?'

'If you don't believe me you can listen to him yourself. I taped the whole thing.'

'Half an hour,' said Rosetti. Her entry bell rang in twenty minutes.

Rosetti wore jeans and loafers and a wool shirt: whatever he'd eaten for dinner had been cooked in a lot of garlic. He looked curiously at the elaborate electrical set-up with all its earphones and remote control and extension recording paraphernalia, along with its racks of discs and tapes. Claudine said: 'It was Warwick's hobby. He was a jazz fanatic. It's the only thing I kept, apart from some personal items.'

'It looks like you could speak to the moon on it.'

'You probably could.'

'And it records?'

'Perfectly. He taught me how. I got the idea from the office. Every discussion we have there is automatically kept, so I thought I'd do it when I spoke to Bickerstone.'

439

'You checked that you got it?'

'I waited for you.'

She had got it. They strained forward, side by side, although it wasn't necessary because the quality was excellent. When it finished Rosetti said: 'You're right. He's anxious about something.'

'Desperate,' insisted Claudine.

'All right, desperate.'

'Is it a conversation between two conspirators?'

'No,' he agreed again. 'But I don't think it's evidence that would be admissible in a court, either.'

'It's going to keep me out of any court.'

'It's not enough, Claudine.'

'It's a bloody sight more than I had two hours ago. And there'll be more.'

'It won't be so easy meeting him face to face.'

'It will be if he comes here, where I can tape him again. And there wouldn't be anything wrong in inviting him. According to him he's a friend, making amends. He might even expect to come here.'

'You any idea the sort of spin Toomey would put on that?'

'Toomey won't know, until I choose to tell him.'

'When — and how — are you going to try to arrange it?'

'I don't know,' she admitted. 'Something

440

could break in the investigation. So it isn't going to be easy.'

'You're not going to listen if I argue against it, are you?'

'I'll listen. But I'm going to meet him. I never guessed he'd be as shaky as this.'

He sat back, looking around the apartment for the first time.

Claudine said: 'I'm afraid I haven't anything to drink.'

He smiled at her. 'Not even coffee? The Italians invented the espresso machine, don't forget.'

'Coffee I have, although not espresso. Filter.'

Rosetti came to the door of the kitchen while she ground the beans. 'Brought up in France and you don't even drink wine?'

Further revelation time, she thought. 'I drank wine, once.'

'But didn't like it?'

'My father drank. All the time when he stopped work. I didn't want to inherit that from him any more than I wanted to inherit anything else.' Trying for the ease they'd briefly shared in Rome and which she would have liked again, she said: 'Time to be fair.'

'Fair?'

'You know practically everything about me there is to know.' She put the coffee on and he backed away from the doorway to allow her from the kitchen. When she reached the room

441

with its distant view of the lake he'd gone back to the music system and was pretending to examine the tape selection. He wasn't doing it very convincingly. Shit! thought Claudine. Shit, shit, shit! 'The coffee won't be long.'

'Good.'

'I'm a rotten cook but you can't really go wrong with coffee, can you?'

'I suppose not.'

'Why don't you choose something? The reproduction is wonderful.'

'I don't know much about jazz. Why don't you choose?'

Because she hadn't replaced it, merely changed it for a blank tape, she put the Ella Fitzgerald-Billie Holiday duet on again. It left her with the recording of her conversation with Bickerstone in her hand. 'I'd better keep this somewhere safe.'

'There's your office safe,' he reminded her.

'That's a good idea.'

'This isn't my sort of music but I like it.'

The perfectly harmonized rendering of 'Lover Come Back' did nothing to fill the silence between them.

Claudine said: 'I'll see if the coffee is ready.'

'Yes.'

It wasn't but she waited. Why had she said it? she demanded of herself angrily. He hadn't asked to become involved. When he had — virtually given no choice — he'd been sympathetic, over-kind maybe with the lakeside dinner and his offer to help. But at no time had they been anything more than work colleagues: she didn't *want* them to be anything more than work colleagues, for Christ's sake! So why had she come on like some gauche virgin wanting his life history? To apologize would just exacerbate his obvious embarrassment. Hers too. She had to get through the next hour — less, if it could be curtailed without even more embarrassment — and not involve him again. Get everything back to how it should be between them, working partners mutually respecting each other's professional ability. She inhaled deeply, although only to prepare herself, before re-entering the main room. He'd abandoned the music exploration and was at the window.

'In the daylight you can see the lake.'

'I'm nearer the centre. No view but it's convenient for the railway station.'

Claudine didn't understand why that was important. 'How do you like your coffee?'

'Just coffee, nothing else.'

The job, decided Claudine: that was the safest subject. The *only* subject. 'Sanglier's planning a press conference. He asked me to take part but I said I didn't want to.'

'What's there to talk about?'

'The amnesty, I suppose.'

'I would have thought a simple announcement would have been sufficient.'

'Sanglier doesn't believe we're getting as

much back-up as we should from national forces. He wants to stage a public protest, I think.'

'I *haven't* been fair,' declared Rosetti abruptly, tired of the charade.

'I'm sorry I said what I did. I'm embarrassed,' admitted Claudine, tired of it too. 'Let's forget it.'

'No,' said Rosetti. 'My wife's name is Flavia. Our daughter was called Sophia. She was three. It was my fault. Flavia's in Rome.'

It was a life story but on a postage stamp, thought Claudine. Which was how it would remain unless he wanted to say more: this much had been visibly hard. Rosetti had put his coffee cup down and was leaning forward with his arms on his knees, not looking at her: not looking at anything.

Haltingly, the words so spaced that sometimes Claudine thought he didn't intend continuing, Rosetti said: 'It had been a party, at Ostia . . . Flavia's parents live there . . . I hadn't drunk anything . . . driving too fast . . . a roadwork lorry had stopped, on a bend . . . I didn't see the other truck . . . Sophia died at once . . . she wasn't in a proper seat . . . Flavia's arms . . . she was asleep . . . never woke up . . .' This time the pause was longer than the rest. Claudine didn't speak. 'The doctor said she wouldn't have felt anything . . . that isn't true, of course . . . trying to help me . . . Flavia's skull was fractured . . . a week before she woke up . . . I told her . . . she could talk that first night . . . said it was her fault for holding her . . . she stayed conscious for two days, that was all . . . she sleeps . . . I mean her eyes close . . . otherwise she just stares . . . sometimes she cries but there isn't any sound . . . the neurologist says it's a form of catatonia . . . she won't recover . . .'

'People do!' Claudine burst in at last, anxious to help but finding her emotions as jumbled as Rosetti's effort to talk about his wife. She pressed on: 'Catatonia is a type of schizophrenia. She wouldn't have been made schizophrenic by the accident. She's in retreat . . .'

Rosetti looked up to her with the startled expression of someone suddenly awoken himself. 'They say she won't. That there's physical wastage, too . . . muscle deterioration . . .' He was talking more coherently, fully aware of Claudine.

'People emerge from comas after years.' She didn't think it was much of a contribution.

Rosetti smiled an empty smile. 'I've burdened you . . . still not being fair . . .'

'You've done nothing of the sort.'

'I love her so much.'

Claudine didn't know if he was referring to his wife or child. 'I didn't want to cause you this much hurt.'

'*You* haven't. I suppose you'd call this an expunging of remorse?'

'I don't think I'd give it a label.'

'I . . .' he began but then stopped.

'What?'

'You're the only one here who knows.'

'Didn't you tell me something in Rome about being able to respect confidences?'

'Thank you.'

'You also said something in Rome about not being sure what *I* was thanking *you* for.'

Claudine had been unaware of the tape reversing itself and she was only vaguely conscious of it finally clicking off. Rosetti heard it, though. He said: 'I'd enjoy introducing you to some of my music.'

'I think I'd enjoy it, too,' said Claudine.

Predictably guarding himself against any unforeseen disasters, Sanglier had Poulard and Siemen extensively rehearsed by Europol's public affairs division, which left Claudine to review what Kurt Volker proposed for the Internet appeal. From its completeness in such a short time — hours from the formal approval — it was obvious the German had worked upon it for several days. When she challenged him outright he offered one of his perfectly formed smiles and said, as always without conceit, that it was such a good idea the Commission couldn't have possibly refused it.

Volker accompanied his visual images of the murder victims with a commentary about bulletin boards and browser programs which

Claudine found much harder to understand than the pictorial display, although she recognized at once how brilliantly Volker had prepared everything. Using the electronic airbrush technique again he'd digitalized the facial appearances and what few details were available about each victim, not just in Roman lettering but in the five most commonly used languages throughout the Asian countries at which the presentation was primarily directed. And that was only the beginning. When she asked about the Cyrillic print Volker reminded her that the binding wire securing the two white girls had been manufactured in Eastern Europe, so as well as including Polish, Czech and Hungarian he'd added Russian.

'People who can access the Internet with a computer are literate?' he demanded.

Claudine frowned. 'Obviously.'

'Just in case someone's looking over their shoulder who isn't . . .' He jabbed a key she didn't see and an audible recital began of the few facts in the various listed languages.

'You want me to tell you I'm impressed?'

'I want you to tell me these are the programs you want put in place.'

'I do. They're incredible.'

Volker regarded her solemn-faced for several moments. 'I think I might have misled you. I'm sorry, if I did. Although no harm's been done.'

'Misled me how?'

'Talking about targeting the Far East.'

Claudine grew more serious. 'What are you telling me?'

'The Internet isn't like a map, with country or continent borders. The Internet hasn't got any borders: it's worldwide because it can't be anything else. Which is why no harm has been done, and why I've included all the languages and the multilingual commentary.'

'You'll have to help me.'

'What we're putting on will be available to *anyone, anywhere* in the world. I didn't realize you all didn't understand until I talked to Poulard, just before he went off to his press briefing. I thought you should know, too.'

'I'm glad you did,' said Claudine. Volker was right. There was no harm done. In fact the total availability could only be to their advantage.

'I thought I'd cheat a little, too.'

'You usually do,' Claudine smiled.

'I've made a bulletin program. I thought I'd access all the sex boards I can find and list our offering, although obviously not as an appeal for help. A lot of people are going to be disappointed but someone just might recognize one of our people.'

'We paying for it?'

'Only for what the Commission approved.'

'How do I know how things get on illegal bulletin boards?' The acceptance was implicit.

For a moment neither of them spoke. Then

Volker said: 'It's going too slowly, isn't it?'

'Far too slowly.'

'What happens if there's another murder that fits our grouping?'

'We're in the shit.' Claudine had no difficulty expressing herself that way.

Volker gave no reaction to her choice of word, instead taking it for himself. 'Not *in* it. Drowned *by* it.'

'She'll break, then him,' predicted the Serious Fraud Office superintendent.

'There was that unofficial approach from the British commissioner,' Toomey reminded him. 'I think I should inform him officially.'

'It's important in the circumstances to do everything according to the book,' agreed Walker. 'We don't want these bastards wriggling off the hook.'

'We could get a court order, to open it up,' suggested Toomey.

Walker shook his head. 'We've already got it sealed. Nothing can happen to it. So let's use the fear factor. Throw it at her. If she doesn't break then — which she will — we can get the order and hit her a second time.'

Chapter Twenty-Four

The worldwide media response to the press conference was completely underestimated by everyone within Europol. So huge was the instant and concerted clamour to attend that the media division initially came close to being overwhelmed. The Commission had less than twenty-four hours to convene a special meeting at which Belgium's newly installed chairman, Jan Villiers, nervous at the prospect of responding to EU Justice Ministers, urged that the whole idea be scrapped. The cancellation argument was lost when Sanglier, caught as much off guard as anyone, pointed out that arbitrarily to abandon it without a satisfactory reason risked the very adverse publicity they were all abruptly concerned about.

It was clearly no longer sufficient for just Poulard and Siemen to appear. Only by agreeing to be on the platform with them was Sanglier able to resist the call that he take over their role as spokesmen. Although once he was identified it was inevitable his name would make him the focus of attention, certainly from French journalists, Sanglier in turn insisted he should be accompanied by the commissioners representing the countries in which the killings had occurred. That proposal was so fervently opposed it had to go, at Sanglier's demand, to a vote which he won, as he cynically guessed he would, with the majority support of those gratefully uninvolved commissioners seizing their chance to evade personal association with any controversy that might arise.

More anxious than ever to have an absent scapegoat for the anger the amnesty and Internet ideas were likely to engender, Sanglier worked hard to prevent any discussion of Claudine Carter's taking part. He failed. Foreseeably it was David Winslow who asked why Claudine wasn't listed to appear and headed the bewildered chorus at her exclusion. None appeared satisfied that it was at her own request or that it was too late for her to be rehearsed for the press briefing. Franz Sobell, to whom Claudine had verbally presented her initial profile, said he couldn't imagine anyone who needed less guidance and Winslow said he was prepared to order her attendance.

Sanglier was forced to improvise, and hated it. He caused more confusion when he said he welcomed Claudine's reluctance to court publicity. None of them needed reminding that hers was far and away the major contribution to everything Europol had achieved, and he did not want their practical policing limitations to become obvious by contrast, particularly when by inference they were criticizing the national forces of the countries involved.

Sanglier tried to listen to himself speak, to avoid any pitfalls, his difficulty made all the more galling by his having to praise the woman he was working to undermine. There was some visible acceptance of his hurriedly created explanation but far too many unreadable or sceptical expressions.

The planning meeting was immediately followed by a session with the head of the Public Affairs Division, a plump and easily perspiring man named Walter Jones, who formed part of the English contingent. Jones was as unnerved as the commissioners by the escalating scale of the press conference. He promised that Poulard and Siemen were fully prepared, and did his best to impress by proposing they maximize the presence of so many international journalists by giving them guided tours of Europol's facilities, followed by a cocktails and snacks reception.

Having had time to recover some of his composure Sanglier pressed for the drinks and food to be offered before the actual conference, to avoid unmonitored lobbying afterwards. Accepting Sanglier's point at once the shiny-faced Jones assured them everything would be recorded from beginning to end on video and sound tape to ensure there was no misquoting or exaggeration. He, of course, would conduct the proceedings.

Sanglier sent a general memorandum to the

incident room, advising that although the conference had escalated to commissioner echelon Poulard and Siemen would remain the task force representatives responsible for answering questions. Siemen said he hadn't realized the conference was going to be this big and wondered why Sanglier wasn't going to take over. Poulard, alert to the personal recognition he was going to get not just from being associated with atrocities terrorizing the Union but by being on the same platform as one of the most famous names in France, said the size didn't affect anything and there was no reason to be overawed. Claudine believed she perfectly understood Poulard's eagerness and tried to help Siemen, who said he couldn't understand either why she didn't want to take part, by saying they knew as much as she did and were much better able to answer questions about EU police investigations, having taken part in two. Poulard said he thought she was right. The German looked unconvinced.

Sanglier's memo also warned of the intended tour of Europol's facilities. Despite the guarantee that no media people would be allowed inside the incident room Claudine left it for her own office long before the scheduled press arrival. She waited, too, until thirty minutes after it began before going to the reception, curious to know what it would be like but anxious to slip in unseen.

There were far more people than she expected, even after Sanglier's note. Beyond a large pile of television equipment and cameras directly inside the door the room was crowded, reverberating with the babble of too many people talking too loudly all at the same time. It was already thick with smoke and briefly her breath caught, before clearing. The Evian water she collected from a passing waiter helped, like the reassuring presence of the inhaler in her pocket. All the commissioners were gathered close to the table upon which the food was laid. Sanglier had already been identified and was in the centre of a group of reporters: as she watched he forcefully shook his head against a photograph separate from the other commissioners. A cigar-waving Scott Burrows was in intensive discussion with two men whom from their clothes Claudine guessed to be American. Poulard and Siemen were by themselves, although Poulard was smiling frequently at the group around Sanglier. Siemen was frowning, anxiously taking a glass of red wine from a waiter the moment he finished the one in his hand. Claudine looked hopefully around the room for Rosetti but couldn't see him. She couldn't see Volker, either. She was aware of David Winslow detaching himself from the group near the table to thread his way across the room towards her, and at once moved away from several people she suspected were close enough to overhear any conversation between them.

'Hell of a turn-out,' the flushed man said by way of greeting.

'It certainly is.'

'Still think it's a mistake you're not taking part, despite what Sanglier says. You're Britain's representative, after all.'

'What does Sanglier say?' Claudine asked curiously.

'Risk of it becoming too obvious that you've done all the work,' said Winslow, in his clipped voice. 'Invidious, he says. Rubbish I say.'

Claudine wasn't sure whether to take Sanglier's reported remark as praise or criticism. 'My taking part would have served no useful purpose.'

'It would have let the people in Britain know we're in the vanguard.'

Caught again by the navalese, Claudine said: 'Do you have a boat on the lake?'

'Thirty-five-footer, gaff-rigged,' beamed the man. 'You sail?'

Claudine was sorry she'd begun the pointless conversation. 'No time. But I was out there recently. Saw quite a lot of boats and wondered if you were among them.'

'Why me?'

'Must have heard something from somebody. Can't remember who.'

'Fancy a trip one weekend, you let me know.'

'I will,' promised Claudine emptily. 'Looking forward to the conference?'

'Hope it goes all right,' confided the man. 'You know how bloody sensitive people are. They could get upset about amnesties and having stuff thrown at them on a computer screen.'

Claudine frowned. 'Both can be justified.'

'How?' demanded Winslow, frowning back at her.

Patiently Claudine explained, unable to believe Sanglier had not included her arguments in his presentation. When she finished Winslow looked towards Poulard and Siemen and said: 'Hope they don't forget to make that clear.'

'So do I,' said Claudine. Following the general direction in which the British commissioner was looking Claudine saw the group surrounding Sanglier had grown. The noise around her seemed to be growing, too.

It registered with Winslow as well. 'Wise move, getting them all mellow like this.'

In her preoccupation with the mass murders Claudine had forgotten the birth-pang uncertainty in which Europol existed. 'Providing there's not an outbreak of food poisoning.'

For several moments Winslow looked at her in concern, relaxing only slightly when she smiled to show she was joking. Claudine wondered how hard it had been for London to find someone like Winslow to illustrate their utter contempt for a European federal police organization. With David Winslow she would have believed they'd carried out a lobotomy to make their point.

Still not totally sure Claudine hadn't meant the remark, the man said: 'Let's hope there's not.'

Claudine was saved by Walter Jones hammering on the food table with a spoon to announce, in English, that there were guides to take everyone to where the conference was to be held. She pushed herself back against the wall for the gradual exodus to pass. Siemen smiled, briefly, but Poulard gave no acknowledgement as he went by. Neither did Sanglier. Burrows detoured on impulse, taking another Scotch from a tray.

'Guys I knew in Washington from *Newsweek* recognized me. Wanted to do a piece. Just spent the entire fucking lunchtime trying to persuade them not to.'

'What sort of piece?' She was grateful he'd finished the cigar.

'The FBI's contribution to its European counterpart . . . that sort of crap.'

'Did they ask if you were involved in this investigation?'

'Of course they did,' said the American, answering her look.

'What did you say?'

He didn't respond at once or look away. Then he said: 'That I wasn't, of course.'

457

'Did they ask if there was a profiler involved?'

'Of course,' said Burrows again.

Claudine didn't ask and the American made her wait, taking several long sips of his drink. 'I know you think I'm an out-of-date asshole and I know why you don't want to share. Understand the last part. But I'm not a jerk. And I don't shit on colleagues, even those who despise me and don't want to be *my* colleague.'

Claudine felt herself flush, confused by the man's anger. 'I think I've been corrected.'

'And you've got a long way still to go, lady.'

Claudine was still discomfited by the encounter when she got to the conference chamber. Burrows was at the very back of the room, to the left. She went to the right. Jan Villiers, bracketed by Sanglier and Winslow, was at the centre of the assembled commissioners ranged along a table that filled the width of the dais. Poulard and Siemen were at a smaller table close to the audience. Walter Jones sat between them. As Claudine entered, press journalists, bent double against photographers' protests, were scurrying back and forth creating a tiny wall of tape recorders on the detectives' table. Sound and television journalists were doing the same with microphones, trailing the leads back to the tripod-mounted cameras banked at either side of the room. There was a brief lighting effect when floodlights were tested. From the body of the hall, where each chair was equipped with an earpiece for simultaneous translation, the hubbub was only slightly less than at the reception.

The echoing sound of Jones tapping his microphone to test its sound level partially silenced the noise, which grew even quieter when he began reading from a prepared statement. The room abruptly whitened under the glare of camera lights. The media director welcomed them to the first press conference of the first investigation in which Europol had become involved. Europol believed it had already made important and useful contributions to its initial assignment and was confident it would make more. With the expectation that this would initiate a continuing and fruitful relationship between Europol and the media, he introduced Poulard and Siemen as 'the two senior officers in charge of the combined investigation'.

Poulard took the microphone, obviously by prearrangement against which Claudine was sure Siemen hadn't argued. The Frenchman began confidently, obviously well prepared, informative-sounding words not immediately obvious as generalities. Their overview of the crimes spread throughout the EU had enabled them to suggest valuable lines of inquiry. They expected early identification of the tragic victims if the countries involved accepted their amnesty suggestion. Establishing a Europol Web site on the Internet was an innovation in criminal investigation they expected to make full use of not just in this case but in other inquiries and to be copied beyond the European Union to become standard police procedure worldwide.

In front of her Claudine was aware of shifts of impatience throughout the room. The press officer on the stage was fidgeting too. She was ready for the challenge when it came, within seconds of the conference's being opened for questions, from a swarthy, dark-haired Frenchman who wanted to know precisely what progress had been made towards solving the murders in his country. Claudine only just prevented herself from wincing when Poulard repeated his valuable lines of inquiry assurance.

'What are they?' demanded the questioner.

'Obviously I don't want to endanger inquiries being conducted by national forces by disclosing operational details,' tried Poulard.

'Are you satisfied with the progress of inquiries conducted by national forces?' called another Frenchman close to the first speaker.

Poulard's hesitation was sufficient answer, before his attempted evasion. 'These are not easy investigations.'

'Is it not a fact that Europol is trying to force its amnesty proposal upon the countries in which killings have occurred?' asked a third.

'No, that is not the case,' intruded Walter

Jones, with attempted forcefulness.

'So the idea was put to each country prior to this conference?' demanded the first man.

Again it was the press officer who replied, grabbing an imagined escape. 'Each country was advised by its respective Europol commissioner.'

'When?' The demand came in a chorus from at least four different parts of the room.

The fat man blinked, trapped. 'I don't know, precisely.'

'Isn't it a fact that no approach was made until yesterday: in some cases as late as last night!'

All the questioners were French, Claudine realized: she recognized two from among the group clustered around Sanglier earlier, which she found curious. Even more curious was why he — or any of the other commissioners — wasn't breaking in to block the attack with the obvious justification for an amnesty.

Jones was saying, 'The question was whether countries were informed before this conference. They were.'

'Would you accept that cooperation between Europol and national forces is bad and that the investigation is being hampered because of it?' demanded the swarthy man.

'No,' replied Poulard. 'Any difficulties there might have been in the beginning were totally understandable. Europol was a new organiza-

461

tion. A working system of liaison didn't exist until these cases.'

'Now it does?' demanded someone quite close to where Claudine sat.

'Yes,' said Poulard shortly.

'Europol's contribution was totally unnecessary in solving the Cologne murder, wasn't it?' The question came, in German, from a bald man near the front.

Both Jones and Poulard looked to Siemen, glad of the respite. Siemen said: 'We suggested a line of inquiry upon which Cologne were already working: our guidance speeded up their case.'

'That's not what Cologne says,' insisted the man.

'I was not aware of any disagreement when I was there for the arrests and arraignment.'

'Did Cologne *tell* you of their line of inquiry, before you suggested it?' asked another German.

'There was no confusion to cause any delay in the arrests,' tried Siemen.

'So they didn't!' said the questioner.

'It was not a problem, merely a difficulty of establishing a system to which my colleague has already referred.'

The stone-faced commissioners on the dais reminded Claudine of funfair targets, waiting to be shot down. This was degenerating into the last thing they must have wanted or expected and they only had themselves to blame.

Poulard and Siemen couldn't be coached in an hour or two to confront trained questioners who had been much more thoroughly briefed by irritated or even hostile sources. Or had the sources been irritated and hostile? she wondered, remembering again the group around Sanglier. Was it conceivable that what she was uncomfortably witnessing had been initiated far closer to home, in this very building? It was the sort of paranoid question she despised from others within Europol but it fitted quite a few other inexplicable things that seemed to happen around Henri Sanglier. Impatiently she thrust it aside but not out of mind.

In front of her an Indian journalist was on his feet and Claudine began concentrating upon the questioning again as the man demanded: 'Why was it not thought necessary to advise my government before creating this Internet Web site of which Europol appear so proud?'

Claudine didn't expect Siemen to take the question but was glad that he did. The German said: 'Our role — Europol's role — is to do all we can to help local police forces solve a dreadful spate of crimes. We are not treating any country with disrespect. We are trying to work as quickly and as effectively as possible. The quickest and most effective way of alerting the Asian countries from which the victims came of the Net appeal was through the well established and accepted information system provided by Interpol.'

For a few brief moments the attack was stemmed. Then, quite unnecessarily, Poulard added: 'From the lines of inquiry I have already spoken about, from the amnesty proposal and the Internet Web, we have every reason to expect an early breakthrough.'

Briefly Claudine closed her eyes in despair and thought *Jesus fucking Christ!* When she opened them four journalists were on their feet, vying for Walter Jones' eye. Before he nominated a questioner the first French journalist in the front shouted over the noise: 'How early? Hours, days, weeks?'

'I don't want to be specific,' said the panicked detective.

'But there's going to be an arrest?' shouted someone else.

'A development,' said Poulard.

'Which country?' yelled the bald-headed German.

'We can't disclose that,' said Siemen, trying to help.

It had to stop, thought Claudine desperately. Why didn't the bloody press director step in and do something? As the thought came to her she saw Sanglier lean forward to attract the attention of the fat man, who stretched backwards for the whispered exchange. Over the hubbub, the man came back against the smaller table and said: 'I am asked by Commissioner Sanglier, who is in overall

464

charge of the Europol task force, to assure you that the moment the breakthrough occurs it will be announced by the country and the force concerned.'

Claudine wasn't sure if it had been Sanglier's intention to be identified as the unit controller but the intervention was brilliant: the man's name immediately drew the pack away from the beleaguered detectives.

The uproar of questions increased and Walter Jones had actually to stand, waving his arms for attention and shouting that he would cancel the conference unless some order was restored. Before that happened there was a flurry of movement among the commissioners and Claudine saw Sanglier moving his chair forward to the front table.

When they settled again Sanglier simply held up an autocratic hand and the hall fell into virtual silence. It would, he knew, look perfect on television but beneath the outward calm he bubbled with several furies, predominantly at Poulard for his inept promise of a breakthrough but also at himself, the rest of the commissioners and the media division for not anticipating the press hysteria, which they should have done since that very hysteria had brought them into the investigation in the first place. He was also annoyed at being identified as the head of the task force before there was an absolutely safe headline-grabbing development for which he could take the unreserved credit.

The questioning was still dominated by the French press but with much greater respect than had been shown to the two detectives. Knowing that it was ridiculous to attempt it — deciding instead to turn the accusations back upon Europol's accusers — Sanglier didn't deny the existence of ill feeling from national forces. Instead he said it was entirely an attitude directed towards Europol, which those within the organization greatly regretted and did not in any way reciprocate. Conscious of the uncomfortable shifting of the commissioners behind him, Sanglier added that he and his colleagues hoped the current investigation would lead to the early disappearance of such attitudes. Europol did not consider itself in competition with any national force. It was an organization with every modern policing technique and technology, as they had been shown that morning. Indeed, Europol's major contribution in these cases had been its accurate profiles. Here he hesitated, turning from the questioner who'd prompted his response to the bald-headed German in the front to suggest, if there was any doubt about the help Europol had given in the German case, that he directly challenge the Cologne police to produce Europol's specific profile.

'It was brilliant,' he insisted, anxious to make the point for which the conference had virtually been staged. 'Both the amnesty and the Internet Web were profiling suggestions.'

Claudine tensed for the questions the profiling revelation might bring, but almost at once Sanglier picked up an amnesty query, producing the explanation Poulard should have given but had forgotten: that as any legal dispensation would apply only to victims' families it was not a sudden opening of borders to illegal immigrants.

Claudine was actually deciding, admiringly, that it was a remarkable performance when the question she thought had been overlooked was posed. It came from the men whom Scott Burrows had identified as *Newsweek* correspondents and was, inevitably, how much an FBI profiler seconded from Washington had helped create the murder profiles.

Sanglier concentrated upon the questioner, looking at neither Burrows nor Claudine, when he said that for operational reasons he did not want to disclose such details. And with the impotent anger burning through her Claudine realized everyone in the room would take the absence of a denial as confirmation that the psychological guidance had come from an unnamed American, not anyone else.

From the look Burrows directed at her from across the room it was obvious he thought so, too.

At the other end of the hall Henri Sanglier was gripped by a new and greater fury than all the others at recognizing, too late, what he had done.

Needing physical action to vent her anger Claudine thrust out of the hall before the conference ended. Her initial thought was to quit the building altogether but just as quickly she recognized the petulance and was embarrassed by it. Instead, to calm down, she took the longer route around the building to get to the incident room. Yvette said nothing had come in during the afternoon and Rosetti and Volker had both left for the evening. Claudine waited almost an hour, long after she knew the press briefing was over, but neither Poulard nor Siemen returned.

It was dark by the time she got home. The message light was blinking and when she played the answering machine back she heard Bickerstone protesting that she hadn't called and saying that he was probably making the Paris trip in the next two or three days, so could she get back to him.

The replay ended as the telephone rang again.

'Claudine!' said a voice she knew at once. 'Henri wants you to come to dinner. So do I, very much! Let's make plans!'

Chapter Twenty-Five

So successfully did things appear to be going in his favour that, once again, Henri Sanglier suspected the mediation of divine intervention.

Within just five hours of the digitalized photographs and descriptions being put into the Web the white victim in Brussels was named as Inka Obenski and the girl in Amsterdam identified as Anna Zockowski. Both had extensive police records for prostitution and theft in their native Warsaw, where the computer enthusiast superintendent in charge of vice had accessed the Europol appeal site the moment it came on line and — initially for his own interest — run a manual comparison through their uncomputerized criminal records. And got a perfect match. His excited response came directly on to Volker's screen. Claudine, Poulard and Siemen crowded behind him, watching the information materialize in front of them with the barely controlled excitement of prospectors seeing the first dull glint in a washing sieve.

To Poulard it really was gold. He broke away as soon as he assessed its significance — his escape from any censure — to make the first contact with Henri Sanglier.

It prompted an entirely different thought from Claudine, although she showed no immediate reaction. She needed to think it through thoroughly to find any flaws for herself before discussing it with Kurt Volker.

Poulard's call reached Sanglier an hour before the commissioners' meeting convened overnight to review the complete video of the previous day's conference. Sanglier had already watched it privately himself before turning on the television news and reading a wide selection of European newspapers that morning.

The coverage was far beyond his expectations. Nowhere in anything he saw, heard or read was there any serious criticism or condemnation of Europol. Instead, national police forces and even governments were pilloried for obstructing the investigation: three German newspapers took up Sanglier's demand that the Cologne police produce, in full, Europol's profile describing ahead of their arrest who the murderers of Sulva Atilla were most likely to be.

Most satisfying of all — wiping away the very last residue of regret at coming forward as he had been forced to do — were several newspaper and television comparisons, some even with archival photographs, between Sanglier and his father. *La Monde* carried the phrase he liked best, the lion son of a lion father.

Sanglier decided the unintended episode marked the beginning of his political career.

The only smudge on an otherwise unclouded horizon was the suggestion of American involvement — intrusion, a Belgian newspaper called it — in the preparation of the profiles, but so overwhelmingly favourable was the coverage that it did not concern Sanglier as much as it might otherwise have done. More worrying — although something momentarily to be put aside — was Françoise's account of her strained telephone conversation with Claudine Carter the previous night. And Scott Burrows' written request, which lay before him, for a meeting. Buoyed as he was by everything else, Sanglier was sure both were setbacks that could be overcome. Considering how bad it could have been — and almost was — the escape had been miraculous.

He scheduled separate meetings with the American and Claudine for the afternoon, leaving the morning clear for the emergency gathering of commissioners. He intentionally arrived last to avoid prior contact with any of them. They were, in fact, all seated when he entered the room. They looked expectantly at him, waiting for his lead, and Sanglier decided their automatic deference gave the revolving chairmanship little purpose beyond political necessity. He was in charge whoever occupied the position. He proved it, to his own satisfaction, by at once demanding they watch the video without any prior discussion. No one objected.

At its end Villiers said: 'I think we should congratulate our colleague on a masterly performance.'

There were mutterings of agreement from around the table. Quickly, Sanglier announced the Internet identification of the Dutch and Belgian victims. And then sat savouring the realization settling among the group.

'But that means —' started Villiers, only to be cut off by Sanglier.

'— that in less than thirty-six hours we've got the promised breakthrough. And the announcement can be made by Europol. It does, of course, totally justify the Web site and vindicate, if indeed any further vindication is necessary after yesterday, linking an amnesty to the continuing identification appeal for the other victims.' Sanglier was quite relaxed, moving his attention from one commissioner to another as he talked: if he ordered it, most of them would jump backwards through a blazing hoop, he thought. He went on: 'In our announcement we shall, of course, acknowledge the vigilance of the Polish authorities. Name the officer even.'

'What about Brussels and Amsterdam?' demanded Villiers, with a personal as well as professional interest.

Sanglier looked unnecessarily at his watch. 'Both were fully advised an hour ago. By which I mean not just told of the identification but faxed copies of the crime sheets we received from Warsaw on both women. Poulard and Siemen are already on their way to Amsterdam, to work with the vice division there. I'm expecting the invitation from Brussels before the day is out. Depending upon what Poulard tells me I shall decide whether it's necessary to draft more of our people into either city. Quite clearly the profile was right: these two killings were quite separate from the other five, so my feeling is that extra manpower from here will be unnecessary.' He knew he sounded authoritative, on top of the situation, and he was pleased.

'Had there been any contact from Warsaw before yesterday's conference?' asked Holland's Hans Maes, the other personally involved commissioner.

'There is a sex trade from East to West. It was a logical line of inquiry. I understand there has been frequent contact between my officers not just with Poland but Hungary, the Czech Republic, Slovakia and Romania . . .' Sanglier hesitated, considering whether to extend the lie. Unable to foresee any danger, he said: 'I understand the speed with which we were informed today resulted from those earlier contacts.'

'It was still premature to talk of break-throughs, though?' persisted the Dutchman.

Poulard had been a total prick and Sanglier had told him so, in front of Siemen, at the inquest he'd held immediately after the conference. Now it was separation time. 'I have already told Poulard it would have been better to wait, despite the indications he assures me he was getting from those he talked to in the East.'

'I hope he understands that in future,' said Maes.

'He does,' said Sanglier. The bloody man really had been an abysmal choice.

'I think the assumption of American involvement that was allowed during the profiling discussion was most unfortunate, particularly after our earlier recognition of Dr Carter's efforts,' complained David Winslow.

'It was an unfortunate misunderstanding,' said Sanglier, coming as close as he intended to an apology.

'Should we make it clear to her that is how we regard it?'

Sanglier felt a twitch of discomfort at the agreeing head movements, reluctant for yet another acknowledgement to be added to the woman's file. 'I have already arranged a meeting with her later today. Unfortunate as it is, I don't see any purpose in trying to correct it by issuing a formal public statement, particularly in view of the other announcement we have to make. And don't forget Dr Carter specifically sought to avoid any personal publicity.'

'You'll pass on our thinking?' demanded Villiers.

'That's the reason for the meeting,' lied Sanglier.

'Then I think that's sufficient,' said the Belgian.

'I agree there's no point in making a public correction today,' conceded Winslow. 'But I think a note should be made in the record to give her full credit at the end of all this.'

'An excellent idea,' Sanglier agreed, seeing his way out. The end wasn't in sight yet and a lot could go wrong before they reached it. He was going to do his best to ensure it did.

'Then everything appears to have resolved itself very satisfactorily,' said Villiers. It was difficult to believe how different everything was now compared to how it had appeared the previous day.

'Very satisfactorily,' echoed Sanglier. It would still have been better described as a miracle.

'You put me in a hell of a position,' accused Burrows. He was redder than usual, aggressively angry.

'It was totally unintentional.' Sanglier respected the American's ability, proved beyond any doubt by the reputation that had preceded him, but he didn't like the man personally. Burrows had actually called him Henri on several occasions. And the wretched man had never disagreed with any of the opinions put forward by Claudine Carter.

'I had to send Washington a list of every American publication represented yesterday,' the American went on. 'The Director himself is getting on to every publisher, *Newsweek* particularly. They know me by name.'

The concern registered in Sanglier at last. *'What?'*

'And then he's coming on to the European Union Commission and the Council of Justice Ministers in Brussels: each of them individually if necessary.'

'Why should he do that?'

Burrows told him, thinking, Roast, you bastard, like you've skewered me on the spit.

'I didn't know this: none of the commissioners here did.'

'It was a US government to EU Justice Ministers' agreement.'

'We should have been told!' It was a defence of sorts.

'Don't you think now that I wish to Christ you had been?'

'It's ridiculous imagining a problem,' said Sanglier.

'You want me to have the pictures and the reports sent over?'

'Of course I don't doubt you!' This was a

completely unexpected complication that he needed time to consider. On the surface it looked serious, politically. And he was inescapably identified — on film and in front of more than a hundred witnesses — the sole cause. Why the fuck hadn't any of them been warned? It was absurd — unforgivable — that he, that Europol, had been put in this position!

'Neither will the publishers or the Justice Ministers have any doubt after the Director's finished talking with them. He's a forceful guy.'

Sanglier couldn't have cared less about cigar-chomping American publishers but he was very exercised at being the named shuttlecock in every cabinet and chancellery in the European Union. It was those cabinets and chancelleries in which he was planning his future, for Christ's sake! 'We're talking of a distance of three thousand miles!'

'Henri, we're talking sick, murderous minds you can't shift a thought from, once it's embedded there! Fucking madmen I've spent my life protecting people from.'

Henri! Outrage built upon outrage as the overfed slob actually lighted one of his strange-smelling cigars — without asking — and literally did start to chomp on it. 'I don't think there's any reason to panic.'

'What the hell do you think I'm doing here in the first place?'

'Things can easily be corrected by a rectifying statement.' It meant reversing the opposition he'd voiced at that morning's meeting but the circumstances were very different now. Like a distant bell (*sick, murderous minds . . . fucking madmen*) an idea began to ring in his head.

'Yesterday was a live TV newscast. Featured on all three majors, coast to coast. How do you think a flat press statement is going to play by comparison? It won't even get air-time. Or that much newspaper space.' Burrows narrowed his thumb and forefinger until they were practically touching.

'What can be done, then?' asked Sanglier, not liking the note of helplessness.

'Hope you're right and I'm wrong,' said the American. 'It was the Director's idea I tell you. He doesn't want any more snafus.'

'Pity he hadn't thought of that in the first place,' said Sanglier stiffly, refusing to take the entire responsibility.

'You want me to tell him that?'

'I'll tell him myself if he's got the courtesy to call,' said the Frenchman belligerently. 'That's what you can tell him.'

Sanglier had fully regained his frayed temper by the time Claudine arrived, occupying the intervening hour exploring the idea the American's complaint had given him. Burrows' experience was not, of course, a guarantee. In fact, objectively, there was a desperation about it, but it was very much something to keep in mind if it became necessary. Far too much — virtually everything — of whatever else he'd tried had for a variety of reasons not just gone wrong but rebounded in the woman's favour. Even now, to get her with Françoise, he would have to appear the peace-maker.

He adopted that role at once, striding almost the entire length of the office to greet her, leading her away from the officialdom of the desk to the informal area where she'd set out her first profile. He patiently went through the drinks and coffee ritual, which she rejected with less patience, and then announced: 'The profiling discussion yesterday was a mistake.'

'Yes,' she said unhelpfully. 'It was.'

'I did not wish to convey the impression that Burrows was in any way involved in anything that you've done.'

'But you did.' Fuck him, she thought. Before she'd left the incident room Rosetti had cautioned against appearing overly annoyed (*What's done is done*) but she didn't see why she had to show respect to someone she didn't believe deserved it.

'It was unintentional,' he said, the unaccustomed humility sticking in his throat.

'Whites hate blacks, blacks hate whites,' she paraphrased.

Sanglier looked at her blankly.

'Your theme,' she reminded him. 'Burrows' too.'

479

'The American is the acknowledged world expert on criminal profiling,' said Sanglier, understanding. In total honesty he went on: 'I sought his views: it would have been ridiculous for me to let pride — yours, mine, anyone's — stop me using everything available to solve crimes of this horror and magnitude.' The honesty bent. 'Scott Burrows has not monitored any of your assessments. Points have, of course, come up during discussion between us, made by me. He's never once opposed or argued against a view you have taken. At a meeting of commissioners this morning I was asked to make absolutely clear to you how much everyone regrets the misunderstanding that occurred yesterday.'

The only thing missing was sackcloth and ashes, decided Claudine. She had intended challenging him about not outlining for the commissioners the justification for an amnesty, after her conversation with Winslow, but it suddenly seemed a pointless inquest. What's done *was* done. She felt uncomfortable, oddly embarrassed, not immediately able to think of a suitable response. The only thought that did settle was the decision not yet to reveal to the man what she intended asking Volker to attempt the moment she went back to the incident room. If Sanglier was telling the truth, which sometimes she doubted, it was petulant to hold back until she had something more with which to impress the commissioners: according to Sanglier there wasn't the need to impress them further, and anyway, although it was her idea, it would need Volker's expertise to make it work. She would, in fact, be imposing on someone else's credit, the very offense that had caused her so much anger. Nevertheless, she decided to keep it to herself. At last she said: 'Thank you for the explanation. And the assurance.'

'I was afraid it might have influenced your reaction to Françoise last night.'

It hadn't been the only factor, but it had definitely been a major one. Now she felt embarrassed at the petulance of that, too. 'I was reluctant to commit myself. Something might come up at a moment's notice.' It sounded appallingly weak.

'It's hardly likely we wouldn't understand the reason for a last-minute cancellation, is it?' Sanglier was openly mocking.

'I suppose not. It's extremely kind of both of you.'

'And after yesterday's misunderstanding I even think I *owe* you a dinner.'

'I take it the invitation is for two?'

Shit, thought Sanglier, imagining another attempted evasion. 'Of course,' he said.

Poulard and Siemen had already left for Amsterdam by the time Claudine returned to the incident room, but to her relief Rosetti was still there. On her way to Volker's station with the most recent files to arrive from the various forces, she asked if she could see him later.

At the computer area, she set out everything there was about the attempts to trace the outlets for the Dutch-manufactured baling wire with which the Céleste five had been tethered: each dossier was preceded by a protest at the impossibility of the task.

She outlined her thoughts to Volker. 'Britain is an island that's kept its border controls in place. It's still a hell of a task but trying to do it backwards might be a short cut.'

'It might indeed,' agreed the German.

'Could you do it without being detected?' At the pained look the German gave her, she said 'Sorry' and turned away to where Rosetti sat, waiting.

Claudine closed the door behind her, although the room outside was empty apart from Volker, whose concentration was elsewhere, and Yvette, at the far end. Rosetti listened, frowning, as she recounted the reception encounter and Sanglier's persistent dinner invitation.

'You sure about her?' he asked.

'I'm not interested in finding out.' Half smiling, she said: 'So I'm asking for help again.'

Rosetti didn't smile back. 'All right,' he agreed.

The doubt was very obvious in his voice. 'If

it's inconvenient . . .' she said, letting the sentence trail.

'I'll escort you,' he said.

'That sounds very formal.'

'That's how I want it to be,' he said.

'Am I being told something?'

'That I can't let it become anything else, even if I wanted it to.'

Claudine was numbed, half-formed emotions colliding at the rejection. She wasn't sure if it was embarrassment or humiliation: perhaps embarrassment *at* the humiliation. *Even if I wanted it to.* What did he mean? That he would have liked their relationship to go further but was prevented from letting it happen because of his permanently damaged wife? Or that he wasn't interested? It didn't matter. He'd rebuffed her and now she felt a fool. With difficulty she said: 'Thank you.'

'I'm not sure you've anything to thank me for.'

Neither was Claudine. 'You're going to come with me. Which is what I asked you to do.' But she wanted much more.

Chapter Twenty-Six

Claudine sought labels and couldn't find the right one. There was outrage and offense and bewilderment and then — *know thyself* — she abandoned the pretence. She wasn't at all outraged or offended or bewildered by what Hugo Rosetti had said. Wrong. There was a little of each of those reactions at *what* he'd said: the refusal. But not at what that refusal meant.

The labels better attached to herself than to Hugo. To be hung around her neck like an accusation. Shouldn't there be bewildered, offended outrage — still at herself — that she could be excited by an emotion she shouldn't feel just seven months after finding her husband dead? Of course there should. But there wasn't. Shame perhaps, although not enough. Embarrassment, although again not for the right reasons: because he'd blurted the words out in his glassed cubicle, making her glance startled towards the incident room as if the two people there might have heard, which of course they hadn't, leaving her to seem stupid in front of him. Which she'd never wanted to seem. Or to be.

She had hurried from the tiny office but then not known what to do in the larger room, staring unseeingly at the electronic hat out of which Volker was trying to pull a cyberspace rabbit before starting a conversation about the detectives' Amsterdam trip with Yvette of which she now couldn't remember a single word.

All she could recall with any clarity was Hugo's quiet-voiced promise — too quiet, she was sure, for even Yvette to hear — to collect her that night as arranged.

She had difficulty even in concentrating upon that: certainly upon what to wear and what sort of evening it was going to be with Henri and Françoise Sanglier. She chose black, for the first time conscious that it was the predominant colour in her wardrobe, unadorned with any costume jewellery. Apart from diamond earstuds, she wore only her wedding ring.

Her entry bell sounded precisely on time and she announced she was coming down at once, which she did because she'd been standing in the vestibule, waiting. Rosetti was wearing black too, with only a faint stripe in the suit, and Claudine decided they looked very funereal. Rosetti even seemed to drive more slowly than usual and as the Italian picked up the Delft road Claudine realized she was unconsciously aping his habit of twisting her wedding ring around her finger. It symbolized, she supposed, the barrier behind which each was held. She was relieved she was still breathing easily.

The Polish breakthrough was their neutral ground. When Claudine admitted not having seen or heard any newscasts — she'd been too disorientated — Rosetti recounted the television appearance of the Warsaw police chief, whose insistence on close cooperation with the Dutch and Belgian forces had been confirmed by a television appearance by the head of the Amsterdam vice squad. Poulard and Siemen had appeared with the latter, who had publicly acknowledged Europol.

'So Sanglier should be very happy,' said Claudine.

The French commissioner certainly appeared so when they arrived, the hesitation when he realized who Claudine's escort was only momentary. The Sanglier home was what the French called a *manoir*, a solid three-storey country house cresting a hill from which Claudine guessed the original squire could survey in every direction all the land he owned. She wondered how much now belonged to Sanglier. Dark and presumably old wood panelling dominated the interior, particularly in the expansive entrance hall where Sanglier greeted them. It was not, however, what attracted Claudine's immediate attention. That was caught, as was obviously the intention, by the large, spotlight-illuminated photograph of Sanglier senior standing stiffly to attention to receive the Légion d'Honneur from Charles de Gaulle. It was flanked by two smaller photographs of the man at other ceremonies with the late French president.

Only Sanglier greeted them in the hall. Françoise was statuesquely waiting in the drawing room, the vermilion of the ankle-length gown shimmering into lighter and darker hues in the folds in which it fell from her shoulders. Claudine guessed it was Versace again. The short, side-parted hair shone where gel kept it immaculately in place: the pale, matt make-up heightened its blackness. Like Claudine, Françoise had been sparing with her jewellery, with just a three-strand gold choker at her throat. There was no wedding ring. The red paper of the cocktail cigarette in a black malacca holder came close to matching the colour of the dress and Claudine acknowledged the entire, brilliant effect was very *belle époque*. Or was it art deco? Whatever the correct definition, she liked it, staged and obvious though it all was.

The handshake was overlong and caressing, as it had been at the reception. The contact with Rosetti was far quicker, although the interest grew when he was identified as the pathologist involved in the investigation. From her attitude and the way Françoise treated her Claudine decided the obediently eye-lowered uniformed girl offering drinks was a house servant, not someone brought in specially for the evening. When Claudine took mineral water Françoise, who was drinking the same, said: 'I remembered, from the reception. I wonder how many other preferences we share.'

'That was considerate,' said Claudine, ignoring the heavy double entendre.

Rosetti and Sanglier chose Scotch. Attentive to everything — still unsure why she was there — Claudine was aware that Rosetti was according the other man the politeness befitting his seniority but stopping far short of Poulard or Siemen's obsequiousness. She noticed, too, how positively a divide had been immediately created, Sanglier guiding the Italian to the far side of the room to another photograph she guessed to be of his father while Françoise remained where they were.

'It's the Sanglier hall-of-fame tour,' said Françoise contemptuously. 'I'll show you later. It's an obligatory part of the visit.'

Claudine gestured to a large photograph in an ornate silver frame on a side table. It was of Françoise, maybe ten years earlier, giving a backwards-looking professional smile at the end of a catwalk pirouette. 'You were professional?'

'I am, in a lot of things.'

'Where were you, there?' asked Claudine. After the verbal juggling she'd had to perform in the last few weeks, she was unworried by this pressure, although intrigued by the other woman's tenacity.

'Dior. I was there for eight years.'

'Do you miss it?'

'Not at all. I've kept all my special friends. And made a lot more. I go back to Paris all the time. Virtually every week.'

'It's conveniently close.'

Françoise savoured a head to toe appraisal. 'Chanel?'

'That's right.'

'You'd have made a good model.'

'Hardly.'

'You've got a beautiful body. The bust is perfect.'

'Too late now,' said Claudine briskly.

'For some things.'

When Claudine refused any response Françoise said: 'What about you? How often do you get to Paris?'

'Not often. My family — my mother — is in Lyon.' She wondered if she would get back to the apartment in time to telephone. She'd missed the previous evening.

'Why don't you come with me?' demanded Françoise, with new-idea enthusiasm. 'I've a lot of friends you'd find fascinating . . .' She glanced briefly down at the shimmering dress. 'And I pay only about half the price for things like this.'

'Shopping trips hardly fit in with what I'm doing at the moment,' said Claudine easily.

Françoise held her eyes. 'It isn't all shopping.'

'Still no time.' That hadn't been a particularly good reply, Claudine realized: it hinted time could be found.

'When this investigation is over, maybe.'

'Maybe.' Still not good.

Now Françoise indicated the photograph. 'Do you think I am still just as attractive?'

The directness momentarily robbed Claudine of a reply. 'Unquestionably,' she managed.

'Or perhaps more so now?'

The earlier replies *hadn't* been good. It was time to improve. 'Are you trying to discomfort me?' She smiled, to take rudeness from the question.

Françoise smiled back. '*Am* I discomfiting you?'

'No.'

'Good. I wouldn't want to do that.' The stare was practically unblinking. 'Not unless you wanted it to happen.'

'I don't think we have the same preferences, Françoise.'

The woman moved to speak but stopped at the return of the two men. They accepted fresh drinks but both women declined. It was Françoise who initiated the conversation about the murders, hurrying the talk towards the dismemberment and autopsies. Rosetti refused to indulge the woman, avoiding the details upon which she was determined, and Claudine did the same when Françoise switched the demands to her.

'Who can watch autopsies?'

'People with professional reason,' said Rosetti. His voice was stiffening with irritation.

'Could I watch?'

'No,' said Sanglier quickly.

The woman looked fixedly at her husband for several moments. 'You could arrange it for me.'

'No,' Sanglier repeated. He was flushed, refusing to meet the eyes of either Claudine or Rosetti. Claudine was fascinated and realized she was using Françoise's word.

'What about you?' said the woman, transferring her attention to Rosetti.

'I won't have anyone in my examination room who does not have an authorized reason to be there,' said the pathologist formally.

Françoise sniggered, looking around the three of them. 'You all thought I was serious!'

'You were very convincing,' said Claudine, allowing the woman the retreat.

The dinner, served by a subservient girl older than the one who had offered drinks, was as magnificent as the *manoir* and the hostess. There was genuine *foie gras* and sole slivers in coulis before wild duck. There were separate French wines — a Chablis, Poulignay Montrachet and a claret — with each course. The dining hall was large and panelled in ornate carved wood, like every other room in the house. The huge dining table matched the panelling, but was unlaid. They ate at a separate circular table small enough for their legs occasionally to touch. Françoise's did often against Claudine's. Urged on by their dominating hostess, Rosetti and Claudine talked as generally as possible about cases in which they had been involved before joining Europol. Towards the end Sanglier took over the encouragement, pressing Claudine to explain her profile of the current investigation by putting the indicators against the conclusions she drew from them. Françoise said 'fascinating' a lot of times.

A fresh separation, for brandy and cigars, was not suggested, for which Claudine was grateful, but immediately they rose from the table Françoise said she'd take Claudine to freshen up. Undeterred when Claudine said she didn't need a bathroom Françoise insisted on 'the obligatory visit to Henri's special place'.

It was special and briefly Claudine was so overwhelmed she was distracted enough to allow Françoise to hold her arm in such a way as to be able frequently to brush her left breast, occasionally even the nipple. Claudine wished it hadn't hardened under the pressure before she managed to disentangle herself.

The study was next to the room in which they'd had drinks and was a virtual shrine to

the man who had become Sanglier. The man's
birth certificate was actually there, in a glass
case along with his marriage certificate and the
wartime ration book and identity documents
that had been issued in Berlin. In an adjoining case there were photocopies from Gestapo records referring to the unknown
Sanglier, complete with a copy of the death
warrant in that name 'on the personal orders
of the Führer'. The walls were festooned with
photographs. Sanglier with de Gaulle and Sanglier with Churchill and Sanglier with Schu-
man and Sanglier restored in his office in St
Cloud and visiting the new headquarters in
Lyon, accompanied by the Director General.
In every picture he was smaller in stature than
the men around him but made bigger by the
Légion d'Honneur ribbon in his lapel. On a
table were all the books that had been written about him, along with the bound accolade that accompanied his entry in the
French archive of heroes. Claudine presumed the boxed video cassettes were the
films and documentaries that had been made
about the man.

From across the display case of Gestapo
memorabilia that Claudine had intruded between herself and the other woman Françoise
said: 'Incredible, isn't it?'

'Totally,' said Claudine, meaning it.

'I think it's ridiculous but it occupies his
time. He's fanatical about it.'

493

It certainly explained the curious references to her own father, Claudine accepted. Judged professionally it most definitely indicated a fanaticism, as Françoise's sexual persistence betrayed a fanaticism of a different sort. She succeeded in rejoining the men with only the minimum of fondling and reached a single chair ahead of Françoise's efforts to guide her to a larger sofa.

'Was your father in any of the pictures?' asked Sanglier. 'There's a lot from Interpol.'

'They weren't contemporaries,' said Claudine. It hadn't occurred to her to look anyway.

'My father made several visits to Lyon after he officially left the organization. Your father would have been there, I should have thought.'

'I didn't see him in any of the photographs.'

'It would have been quite a coincidence, considering the association now,' offered Rosetti.

The remark succeeded in gaining Claudine's attention and from his look she realized Rosetti was as anxious to leave as she was. Sanglier pressed one further brandy on the Italian before they were able to begin their excuses, which Claudine did against renewed insistences from Françoise of an expedition to Paris together, when the investigation was over. Before then she promised to keep in close touch. She brushed her lips lightly against

Claudine's cheek at the door.

As he started the engine, Rosetti made an exaggerated blowing sound and said: 'That was one of the most unusual evenings I've ever endured!'

'Me, too,' agreed Claudine. Homosexuality in every direction, she thought.

'Did she frighten you?'

'No,' said Claudine. With hindsight she added: 'But it was probably a mistake for me not to have appeared so.'

'She might misconstrue it as interest, you think?'

'It's possible.'

'He's as strange as she is, with that monument to his father.'

'But not quite so dangerous.'

'You worried about the autopsy fixation?'

'I think she's probably a very strange bed partner. But I suppose they're consenting adults.'

'Do you imagine she uses the two girls in the house?'

'Almost inevitably. She's very predatory.' Claudine saw the outskirts of The Hague forming shapes in the darkness ahead.

'I'm surprised Sanglier lets her behave as blatantly as that, even in their own home: certainly among people who know him professionally, aware as he must be that Europol is just one great big revolving rumour and gossip mill.'

'He didn't appear to have a lot of control over her.'

'Isn't he lucky we don't gossip.'

'We've got more to talk about than the Sangliers,' Claudine said abruptly.

'Yes.'

'And I think we should.'

'So do I.'

The one message on her answering machine was from her mother, who said she was fine and hoped everything was all right because Claudine hadn't telephoned for two days and that she would expect a call from her tomorrow. Claudine suggested Rosetti choose some music while she prepared coffee and he tried to lessen the tension by saying his physics degree was inadequate to operate the equipment and she smiled, dutifully. Each waited for the other to begin when she came back from the kitchen.

It was Rosetti who blurted: 'I'm very sorry. I should not have said what I did. I'm embarrassed and I know I embarrassed you and I'm . . . sorry.'

'I wasn't embarrassed. I'm not embarrassed.'

He didn't seem to hear her. 'It was offensive. Arrogant of me to think . . .' He let the sentence slide away, unfinished.

Determined to reach him, she said: 'I was flattered.'

'What?'

'Flattered,' she repeated.

'That's difficult to believe.'

'Why should it be? Professionally I seem to be getting on all right but personally life's been pretty shitty for a long time. Too long. And could get much worse. It was a surprise, a shock, to have something nice to think about for a change. To remember I was a woman. I think I'd actually forgotten that.'

'I meant to say —'

'I know what you meant to say,' Claudine interrupted, but Rosetti went on.

'— I'm attracted to you, which isn't the way I want to say it but is probably the safest. It *was* arrogant, talking as I did so soon after what happened to Warwick. I really do apologize for that, because it was as offensive as imagining that your interest could extend beyond work. And to use our word, none of it was fair. Because there's Flavia. Because I love her. I accept, although I told you I didn't, that she'll never get better. That she'd never know: never be hurt more than she already has been . . .' He swallowed. 'Did you understand any of that?'

'All of it,' said Claudine.

'I don't know how that leaves us.'

'I'm not sure I do, either.'

'Platonic relationships seem to be unknown here: even supposing you'd consider that.'

Plato, thought Claudine: know thyself. 'I think I'd find it very easy to consider.'

Rosetti smiled doubtfully. 'People say there's no such thing.'

'We could prove them wrong.'

His smile went. 'Or we could keep everything professional: confine everything to work.'

'I don't want that,' said Claudine. 'And I was the one to take things beyond work, remember?'

'Not like this.'

'It's a semantic argument.'

The smile returned, more strongly. 'The coffee will have been ready a long time ago.'

As Claudine returned with the tray Rosetti said: 'Can you imagine how people — Françoise Sanglier, for instance — would have laughed if they'd heard the conversation we've just had?'

'I'm not laughing.'

Rosetti took the remark seriously. 'We don't, do we? Laugh, I mean. There's not a lot of cause to, in what we do. But we haven't laughed a lot outside work either.'

'There hasn't been a lot of reason to, so far. Now perhaps we will.'

'You were outrageous,' Sanglier protested.

'I'm always outrageous.'

'With your own people, maybe. Not with those I work with.'

'You asked me to test her out, for fuck's sake!'

'You practically raped her!'

'That would have been fun.'

'Well?'

'It wouldn't be easy. But she might. Just might. It would be a hell of a challenge. Is Rosetti a lover?'

'I don't know. It didn't look as if he is. He didn't do much to rescue her from you. Or appear offended.'

'Perhaps he enjoyed it.'

Sanglier sighed. 'What about Father's room?'

'She agreed it was incredible.'

'That all?'

'Yes.'

'Nothing about her own father?'

'Not a thing. I don't think she looked for him in any of the pictures, either.'

'Nothing about the Gestapo photocopies?' He'd intentionally left them at an incomplete section, where there was an obvious omission.

'Not a thing.'

All he'd done was risk the one thing he wanted most to avoid with Françoise, embarrassing gossip. 'It was a wasted evening.'

'Henri?'

'What?'

'I *was* outrageous, wasn't I?'

'Probably made me a laughing stock within the organization.'

'Just imagine what I could do if I really tried.'

'What's that mean?'

'I don't like these conversations you've been starting lately. It's almost as if you want to divorce me. Don't try to do anything silly like that, will you?'

The following morning Claudine received the official notification that the cervical smear and mammogram were entirely satisfactory.

Kurt Volker was waiting for her when she entered the incident room, his face split by his even-toothed grin. 'Come and see what I've got!' he invited triumphantly.

Chapter Twenty-Seven

Volker actually giggled in his excitement, dancing his fingers across the keyboards as he pulled up his discoveries on his various screens. 'You were right. Doing it backwards was the way. And it wasn't even difficult!'

The key that unlocked everything had been Claudine's suggested use of the United Kingdom's refusal to open its borders within the European Union. Which means that British Customs have to maintain entry and exit records of imported and exported goods, together with cargo manifests for lorries covered by the European *Transports Internationaux Routiers* system under which vehicles are Customs sealed at points of loading and exempt from border checks.

He had, Volker explained, chosen Harwich, Dover and Newhaven as the three most convenient ferry ports into England from Holland, the country in which they knew the wire that bound the Céleste five had been manufactured. He'd only had to hack into one Customs computer system — at Harwich — to access the other two because they were all linked. If necessary he could have penetrated every Customs terminal and database in the country. Without any intended irony, he said: 'The security is virtually non-existent. It's criminal.'

He'd concentrated upon the month prior to the finding of the English victim, obviously targeting refrigerated delivery lorries because they knew the body had been frozen. During that month a total of nine hundred and thirty such pantechnicons had entered England through the three ports, between them owned by forty companies spread throughout the European Union. He'd accessed the databases of each and eliminated thirty-one because their purchasing records proved they did not buy Dutch manufactured wire. Of the remaining eight food packaging and delivery companies that did, three were French, two based in Paris and one in Bordeaux. A further three were Dutch-domiciled, in Amsterdam, Haarlem and The Hague itself. There was one trading from Munich and the eighth had its offices and factory in Linz. All eight factories had extensive refrigeration facilities and all bought their binding wire from the same Dutch company, Alfred Koonig, in Rotterdam.

'This is unbelievable,' said Claudine, openly astonished as figures and facts and addresses materialized in front of her.

'I haven't finished yet,' said Volker briskly, filling each of his screens with comparison programs. 'Delivery sheets,' he identified. 'Of the eight only three trade in France, England and Austria, where the Céleste bodies have been found.' There was a sideways grin as all but one of the screens went blank. 'But only this one, Wo Lim Ltd, of 32–40, Van Diemen Straat, Amsterdam, shows deliveries within a week of each of the five killings, along the routes where the parts were discovered.' One of the blank screens abruptly filled with addresses. 'It seems to be one of the biggest delivery companies supplying Chinese shops and restaurants in Europe: it's got these subsidiary offices and factories in London and Marseille, which again fits the pattern. The Dutch company itself is owned by another registered in Hong Kong, the Lo Ling Corporation . . .' the words and figures scrolled up '. . . the parent company of which, Ho Yat Ltd, is listed in Macao but without any disclosure of directors, which is permissible under their law . . .'

'It's all there,' began Claudine, as euphoric as Volker. 'We've got everything we —' She stopped as quickly as she'd begun. 'No,' she corrected. 'We haven't got everything we need. We know who and where to target, which is incredible. But we got it illegally, so none of it can be produced in any court: it has to be obtained legally. And even then it could be judged circumstantial. There's no fucking proof!'

She was conscious of Yvette staring in surprise at the outburst, from the other end of the room, and Rosetti, of whose arrival she'd only been vaguely aware, came to the door of his office and said: 'What is it?'

Claudine shook her head, not replying.

Volker said: 'But we do know where to look.'

Quickly Claudine said: 'I'm not dismissing what you've done. You're a genius.'

'I know,' said the German.

Claudine couldn't decide whether he was accepting her apology or agreeing with her assessment.

Claudine was unsure whether Volker should accompany her to the meeting with Sanglier, anxious for the computer expert to be given every credit for what he'd achieved but apprehensive of Sanglier's reaction when he learned how the information had been obtained. In the end she offered Volker the choice. The German said he thought he should come to avoid her being criticized.

She handwrote three drafts of her account, trying to gloss over how Volker had made the sensational breakthrough, before she finally dictated it to Yvette, Rosetti listening at her shoulder. She attached supporting, annotated print-outs of all Volker's computer programs, but in Sanglier's office she had Volker verbally explain it all, as he had to her, believing that it would be more quickly understandable than subjecting the French commissioner to initially incomprehensible charts.

Sanglier listened throughout without expression or interruption. He was still expressionless when he said, at the end: 'Absolutely and totally brilliant!'

'It is,' agreed Claudine hopefully.

'But all obtained quite illegally?' At last! There was no urgency — he could take all the time he wanted — but after all the false starts and wrong turns he finally had the lever to prise her out. And with the most satisfying irony of all by using the very material with which he could, eventually, bring the whole investigation to a conclusion to his maximum personal benefit!

'Yes,' she admitted.

'Did you condone it?'

'I encouraged it: the intrusion into the Customs records particularly.' There was a bitter paradox that in trying to draw condemnation away from Volker she risked drawing credit away from the man as well.

'So it's completely unusable.'

'Legally.' Irritated, Claudine fought back. 'But not practically. We know where to concentrate, absolutely: all of this becomes legal when it's seized in a police investigation. The way we've got it need never become public.'

'Any means justifying an end,' sneered Sanglier.

Claudine knew damned well there wasn't a

policeman from Outer Mongolia to Patagonia who hadn't bent the law to solve a crime, and found Sanglier's professional moral outrage preposterous. 'If it stops kids being raped, mutilated and dismembered I can live with it.'

The undisguised contempt, which an hour earlier would have concerned him by its implied confidence, brought Sanglier up short but didn't worry him now: she was more his victim than he was hers. There was nothing to be gained by taking it any further at this point. Careless even of the contradiction he said: 'From this moment it becomes entirely a police inquiry.'

Momentarily Claudine could not comprehend the remark, and from his facial reaction beside her she knew Volker didn't either. Then she thought she did, although it didn't help her to understand the reason for it. 'The inquiry is still far from complete.'

'A profile is to tell us where to look. We know that now. And it didn't directly come from a profile.'

What the fuck was this man trying to prove? 'Are you disbanding the task force?'

Sanglier was brought up short again. 'Of course not!'

'Removing me from it?'

'Not at this moment.'

'Then I don't understand what you've just said.'

Sanglier realized the moment he briefed the

Amsterdam police he would be condoning the very computer illegality he intended to condemn the woman for condoning in the first place. 'I mean that for the moment *how* this information was obtained remains a separate, internal matter.' Which, so total was his control within the Commission, he could manipulate in whichever direction he chose.

Claudine didn't think that was what he'd meant at all: it made no more sense than so much else of what Sanglier did or said. Could she have been wrong in believing there was latent ability beyond the advantage of a special name qualifying the man for the position he occupied? Or was he, like so many others within the organization, someone of limited capability his own country didn't know what to do with and had shunted into an organization European law enforcement considered an elephants' graveyard? 'Is there anything else we can help you with?'

'I don't think so,' said Sanglier, in a tone of what Claudine thought to be self-satisfaction. 'I will personally handle things from now on.'

Claudine's hesitation was not second thoughts about having accepted Rosetti's invitation before leaving Europol, nor because of the answering machine's 'please call me' message from Françoise Sanglier she'd expected to be waiting — and was — when she returned home. It held her, though, directly in front of the telephone for several moments while she reached the final decision before picking up the instrument. Her first call was much briefer than those that followed. The longest was with her mother, who insisted she couldn't remember a time when she'd felt so well. She'd put on half a kilo and was being fitted the following day for the suit she was having made for the wedding. The appointment had been confirmed with the *notaire* but he'd been warned Claudine might have to rearrange or even cancel, at short notice. Claudine said she wouldn't have to do either.

There were a lot of photographs throughout Hugo Rosetti's immaculate bachelor apartment, which was very close to the Kloosterkerk church, but in no way did Claudine think of it as a shrine as she had the Sanglier house. Her immediate reflection was Rosetti's remark about their not laughing: in virtually every photograph of Hugo and Flavia they were, several times where they hadn't been aware a picture was being taken. In a great many they were holding each other: he lifting her, hair flying, or grasping her hand or touching her face. In one taken from behind they were walking into the light, each with an arm tightly around the other, so that it was impossible to see any separation between them. There were also two studio portraits, the poses different but from the same dress obviously taken during one sitting. Flavia was very beautiful. The hair — tightly coiled in a chignon in one shot, long enough to reach her shoulders in the other — was deeply black, like the eyes that gazed directly at the lens. She was wearing a high-necked dark dress, a sweater maybe, so the slight but full-busted figure was more obvious in the unposed shots, which showed her just a little taller than Rosetti. Sophia was in three. In one she was being swung between the two of them, in another laughingly astride Rosetti's shoulders with her hands covering his eyes, he play-acting with his arms outstretched to grope forward. She was crying in the third, with Flavia and Hugo kneeling either side to comfort her. The child had been with Flavia at the studio session, best-dressed in frills and bows and trying hard to be grown up, serious-faced and doe-eyed — blackhaired and dark-eyed like her mother — only betraying a smile that never developed in one shot.

'I almost put some of them away.'

'Why?' She didn't have any photographs of herself and Warwick showing the joy that was evident in the pictures all around her.

He shrugged. 'That's what I thought. So I didn't.'

'I'm glad.' She held back from the aren't-they-beautiful cliché. He didn't need to be told that.

'It's spaghetti,' Rosetti announced enthusiastically, hurrying the conversation on. 'The

509

trick is in the Bolognese sauce: minced pork as well as beef and left to marinate overnight. You're going to miss the final piquancy without the Argiano Brunello di Montalcino: I prefer it to Chianti.'

'Maybe a glass.'

He stopped with the bottle briefly suspended over his own goblet, which he then filled and handed to her across the table without comment.

'Surprised?'

'Yes.'

'The reason for not doing so was pretentious.'

'I know. As it would have been if I'd put the photographs away.'

'Why didn't you tell me?'

There was a slight shoulder movement. 'It was your pretension. Your business.'

'Non-interference?'

'I'd probably try to stop you jumping off a cliff.'

'But not try to stop me drinking wine?'

'No one should be stopped drinking wine.'

The spaghetti was sensational, the sauce unlike anything she'd ever tasted. She told him so without making too much of it, not wanting to remind him he'd cared for himself for so long.

After that day's encounter with Sanglier their major conversation was more predictable than ever. Rosetti initiated it. 'What I can't believe is how quickly — and easily — it's all been solved. From virtually nowhere to a conclusion, in one mighty leap.'

'It hasn't been solved, not yet,' Claudine pointed out. 'And Volker just made it seem easy. Which is a bloody sight more than Sanglier is doing.'

'He's certainly odd.'

'Odd? The bastard just doesn't make sense. He hasn't done from the very beginning.' She was enjoying the wine and decided to accept more.

'You're the mind-reader,' Rosetti reminded her lightly.

'I can't read his. I don't think he knows it himself. It was an open threat, for Christ's sake!'

'Officially he had to say what he did,' insisted Rosetti. 'He won't actually *do* anything. That would be ridiculous.'

'He is ridiculous. Nothing should happen to Kurt.'

'What did Kurt say afterwards?'

'That a lot of people did what he does before Europol became operational, because it was the only way. And everyone knows it. So he couldn't understand the fuss Sanglier was making.'

'Sanglier is right though, in a way,' Rosetti pointed out. 'It becomes a straight police investigation now. Your job's over.'

'It's too soon to say that, too,' she warned.

'Volker's use certainly isn't over.' She didn't want it to end: to go back into meaningless limbo, attending meaningless seminars and having meaningless arguments about theory with Scott Burrows for no other reason than to fill the time.

'I hope you're wrong: that nothing stops it being wrapped up.' He gestured with the wine bottle and she nodded.

'At the moment there's absolutely no provable evidence,' Claudine reminded him unnecessarily. Was she being totally objective or was she being influenced by her reluctance to see the task force, with Rosetti a part of it, disbanded.

'But without any bodies it's a respite for both of us.'

Claudine looked towards the biggest photograph of Flavia, immediately hoping he hadn't seen her switch of attention. 'You going to use it to go to Rome?'

He nodded but said nothing.

'I'm going to Lyon, for my mother's wedding.' She paused. 'But there's something else I have to do first.'

He frowned at her across the table. 'What?'

'I called Paul Bickerstone before coming here tonight.'

'You bloody idiot!' said Rosetti.

Three and a half thousand miles away, on the outskirts of Baltimore, Maryland, two specially trained, body-armoured FBI assault teams surrounded an isolated farmhouse as the third, wearing breathing apparatus, coordinated the jack-hammering of the door with firing tear-gas grenades into the ground-floor windows.

The owner, his wife and two daughters were all in the basement. The autopsy estimated they had been dead for more than three weeks and that it would have taken them several days before that finally to die from the torture that had been inflicted.

From the evidence upstairs they guessed they'd only missed the killer by hours. He'd quit leaving behind a lot of what he would have regarded as his personal belongings.

The full details of the failed raid were immediately cabled to the Bureau station at the US embassy in Holland.

Chapter Twenty-Eight

Henri Sanglier decided he had every reason to feel as he did, all-powerful, all-important, in total command of everything. Every law enforcement officer in Holland was on standby to be at his instant disposal. The only unit uninvolved was that investigating the separate killing of Anna Zockowski.

He held back from taking over the Amsterdam office of the Dutch police chief, Willi van der Kolk, satisfied that the man automatically accepted the secondary role in whatever was to happen. Poulard and Siemen just as automatically became his personal assistants, liaising with his personal secretariat which he had brought with him from The Hague. Convinced it was now the moment to put himself into the forefront and anxious to be associated with every success, he insisted that Poulard and Siemen also keep in daily contact with the Zockowski inquiry as well as that of the other Polish girl in Brussels to take instant advantage of a development in either.

Sanglier would naturally have delegated to ensure his self-protection against personal error. But it was essential anyway, because no briefing could be given outside the security of a police building and there wasn't a room large enough at any in the city to accommodate at one time the sheer size of the combined forces. And because of the problem of gossiping leaks from such numbers there was additional security in dividing into tightly controlled and supervised units an investigation that Sanglier was determined, at its successful conclusion, would be recognized throughout Europe — and beyond if possible — as a copy-book formula for anything like it ever again.

He allocated the largest concentration of manpower to twenty-four-hour surveillance upon 32–40, Van Diemen Straat. Sanglier decreed it should go beyond identifying every employee and user of the premises to creating dossiers on their wives, partners and friends. Each one had to be photographed and those photographs compared with criminal records first in the city itself, then in Holland as a whole and finally in Europol. The ownership of every private vehicle driven by any employee or user had to be established through licensing records and each car assigned a permanent, round-the-clock watch squad to follow it when it was driven not just by the owner, but by his wife, partner or acquaintance.

A second unit had to discover through Dutch company records the named directors and managers resident in Holland and through liaison with the first group identify them photographically. Once that had been done those photographs had to be compared against whatever international records Interpol held of known Asian criminals, and if that check drew a blank Interpol was to be asked to extend the check to every one of its Asian member countries.

Sanglier devoted an entirely separate division to maintaining a minute-by-minute vigil on every truck, lorry or commercial vehicle — refrigerated or otherwise — owned by Wo Lim Ltd. A fleet of unmarked cars was allocated so that each could be followed wherever it went throughout the European Union. This division was composed entirely of officers from Europol, whose establishing Convention permitted cross-border pursuit among every one of the fifteen EU countries. Every stopping place, business, restaurant and outlet had to be logged and every contact photographed if possible. Only if the following detectives became convinced the lorry they were following contained something suspicious were the local police to become involved. All local force liaison was to be through Sanglier, who had decided to be personally present at any body part seizure. To make that possible he had Europol's plane on permanent standby at Amsterdam airport.

There was an obvious flaw in that part of his planning but Sanglier was prepared when the challenge came from van der Kolk. The Dutchman pointed out that with the major highway checks throughout the Céleste killing countries already in place they could coordinate a concerted, Europe-wide interception of every Wo Lim lorry.

'And throw away whatever chance we might have?' Sanglier snapped back aggressively. 'How long do you think it would take them to realize their vehicles were being specifically targeted? Minutes. The random road checks, which *might* find something in a Wo Lim lorry, can be nothing more than back-up at this stage, concealed as a drugs search.'

'There could be more dismemberment killings,' protested van der Kolk, an avuncularly broad-bellied, white-haired Santa Claus of a man.

'In a war platoons are sacrificed to save brigades,' said Sanglier, enjoying the analogy and unembarrassed by its doubtful hyperbole. He actually reflected, as he spoke, that it was not something he would have said in front of Claudine Carter. But then she was no longer a problem, if indeed she'd ever been one. That had never been the consideration. She'd been an uncertainty that had to be removed. And was now going to be.

'I'm not sure what you're saying,' complained the Dutchman, who thought the remark had been absurd.

'I want to get a lot of other things in place — take the investigation a long way beyond where it is at the moment — before we make

517

a positive move against their vehicle fleet. We can only do that once. If we found nothing incriminating we would have lost everything.'

'I don't like gambling with kids' lives,' persisted van der Kolk.

Sanglier became irritated at the unexpected opposition. 'I don't like *losing* kids' lives: lots of kids. Which we'll go on doing if we make the slightest miscalculation. So I'm not going to do anything prematurely.'

'Everything is going to be kept constantly under review?' insisted van der Kolk.

'Minute by minute.'

He assigned another group to obtain from Amsterdam's public planning department all the building, development and conversion plans for 32–40, Van Diemen Straat. It turned out to be a former dockside warehouse bordering the main North Sea canal into the city. All the architectural details were supplemented by ground and aerial photographs and combined into a specifically drawn survey of the building itemizing all entrances and exits either by road or sea. Marked on these special drawings was every fire and burglar alarm detail available from the city's safety departments. Additionally Sanglier had van der Kolk arrange a court order to obtain from the company that installed it the code to immobilize the alarm system. At the same legal hearing the judge issued an open-ended search warrant for the premises, although Sanglier announced he didn't intend using it immediately.

He limited the promised minute-by-minute control group to himself, van der Kolk, Poulard, Siemen and the senior control officer from each ascribed unit. There was a conference room adjoining van der Kolk's office large enough to accommodate the group and conveniently the computer and communication centre was on that level.

The final unit, whose job was to assemble and index all the documentary and photographic information, was housed next to the computer centre. Sanglier moved two computer specialists from Europol to help handle the huge volume of material that began to come in almost at once. Although it greatly added to their workload he had everything duplicated to the original incident room at The Hague, knowing it would overwhelm Kurt Volker whom he ordered — directly, not through Claudine — to remain there. He knew, too, that it would satisfy any Europol curiosity as to why Volker, someone involved in the inquiry from the beginning, had not been transferred to Amsterdam.

At the end of the first control body review Poulard said, sycophantically: 'It *is* a war plan, isn't it?'

'Why don't we use the search warrant now?' demanded van der Kolk, still not totally convinced by Sanglier's argument against isolating the Wo Lim transport at the established road blocks.

'We don't need to invoke it until we have to,' smiled Sanglier, prepared for that demand as he had been for the Dutchman's previous one. 'It's a food preparation and storage facility, to which inspectors can make unannounced visits to enforce health and hygiene regulations.' The smile widened. 'We're going to make ours very early tomorrow.'

Sanglier reluctantly accepted that the enormous picture coverage of the Europol press conference precluded his personal participation in the factory visit, as it did Poulard and Siemen's, quite apart from any language difficulty. To the two authentic hygiene officers necessary for the inspection to appear genuine to Wo Lim staff familiar with the procedure Sanglier attached two Dutch-speaking Europol detectives — one, Hans Claus, from the management identifying team later to study the photographic selection — and a female photoanalyst from the Dutch force.

The waterfront factory operated twenty-four hours a day but the squad timed their arrival for just after 8 A.M. because bone fide inspections were rarely made at night and they wanted all the senior staff to be in the building long before their supposed tour ended.

There was no obvious surprise or consternation at their unannounced appearance, although the uniformed guards refused to allow them beyond the gatehouse while their documentation was checked and the duty manager summoned from the main building. From where they waited they saw that the building was surrounded by a metal fence topped with razor wire and counted three dogs, with their handlers, patrolling the inner perimeter. Later, in a seemingly casual conversation inside the building, their attentive escort assured Claus such high security was necessary against widespread pilfering and robbery.

He introduced himself as Mr Woon and was a wide smiling bespectacled Chinese in a spotless white coat whose Dutch was impeccable. During the tour he engaged in conversation with each of the five in the squad.

The factory was immaculate.

Every worker they encountered wore a coat or overalls as spotless as Mr Woon's and the hair of men as well as women was completely covered by the required white hats. The huge building was divided throughout its entire length and width into separate sections from the point of delivery of unprepared food, meat and vegetables through various stages of washing, trimming, butchering and packaging to dispatch areas on the far side. Every preparation table and slab was scrupulously clean, every floor area gleaming, every oven and stove shining from constant attention. Each section was quite separate from its neighbour and at each were men introduced as quality control and cleanliness officers. It could obviously have been staged for their benefit but the frequent hand-washing and surface-mopping appeared a well-established habit to the real hygiene officials.

By prearrangement the inspectors lingered in the butchery area, which was further subdivided between meat and fowl. Here the floors were tiled and glittered in the centre of every work alley to dispose of any blood flow, and there were permanent cleaners disposing of the waste. Birds were plucked beneath loudly sucking vacuum devices and again there were cleaners stationed to collect feathers not immediately removed.

The cold stores were vast caverns each preserving specifically separated foods, animal carcases in one, offal in another, birds in a third, vegetables and eggs in the fourth. Each was sealed by a huge metal door, operated by a central pronged wheel. Again by prearrangement they entered each one and in the carcase store both Europol detectives were able to study the method of hanging.

The final dispatch area was entirely covered but open at one side to admit the huge lorries into their individual bays. Each bay was served by a conveyor belt delivering consignments controlled by a series of dispatchers at a central, airport-style carousel.

There were twenty Wo Lim lorries being

loaded while the squad were there. They examined the interior of three, two of them refrigerated. Hans Claus pretended to misunderstand the loading procedure briefly to get beyond the covered area out on to the service road that encircled the factory.

It had been agreed that the proper inspectors should insist upon examining previously issued health certificates to get the squad on to the first-floor management level. There were five partitioned and glass-doored offices, each occupied by Chinese who looked up in apparent surprise at their presence on the central corridor. At the end, beyond another glass door, were two rows of head-bent men. In front of the individual computers at which they sat were the traditional Chinese calculating abacuses.

The Dutch inspectors dutifully examined the previous certificates and announced they were giving the Wo Lim factory the highest possible health grading. The beaming Mr Woon offered tea or Dutch beer and while they were drinking two unidentified Chinese entered, smiling as broadly as Mr Woon, and profusely thanked the group as a whole for the pass category.

As they drove away from the factory, one of the genuine inspectors said: 'In twenty years I've never examined a cleaner food processing and packing plant.'

'It had to be, didn't it?' said Hans Claus,

unimpressed. It was the opinion he maintained throughout his account an hour later to Sanglier and the rest of the control group back at Amsterdam police headquarters.

'It's suspicious because there's absolutely nothing to be suspicious about,' said Claus, who'd tried to evolve telling phrases on the return journey. 'The health inspectors couldn't have given it anything but their highest classification. We weren't denied access to anything or anyone. Not that we'd have gained much trying to talk to anyone. Every last employee — every person — in the place is Chinese: I didn't see a single European face. I'm sure I'll be able to recognize Mr Woon and the two who weren't introduced to us when we get the photographs.'

'I've got the features of everyone on the top floor well established,' promised the photoanalyst, Berta Snaap. 'And you're right. Everyone was Chinese.'

'Woon was described as the duty manager,' resumed Claus. 'But I'd put him much higher. He was certainly clever. We were held at the gate for exactly twenty-three minutes, more than enough time for anything they didn't want us to see to be got rid of, not that I think today there was anything they didn't want us to see —'

'Got rid of how?' broke in Sanglier.

'I got outside for a few minutes before Woon

524

brought me back. A vehicle could be driven through any one of the three subsidiary exits we've got marked on the plans without anyone inside the factory or at the main gate knowing a thing about it. And the sea comes right up to the edge of the dispatch area at one end, which I don't think we've properly allowed for. We'll need seaborne surveillance. Boats can come and go without anyone knowing about it from the shore.'

'There's something else that struck me,' offered the second detective, Albert van Kleiper. 'Woon made a point of talking to each of us. I think he was checking we were all Dutch.'

'You think he suspected it was a phoney check?' demanded Sanglier, alarmed.

'No,' said van Kleiper. 'I don't think he or anyone else in that factory leaves the slightest thing to chance.'

'Which is why the fence is topped with razor wire and the inner perimeter patrolled by dogs,' said the woman. 'It's an incredible amount of security against petty pilferers.'

'What about the butchery section?' asked Siemen.

'Very big. I counted thirty butchers, actually handling and disjointing meat. Very expertly, with fine-toothed saws. And there's something important in the deep freeze storage facilities. The hooks from which the carcases are hung are double-pronged. I had to estimate, obviously, but I'd say the tips of the prongs were about forty-five centimetres apart.'

'So would I,' agreed van Kleiper.

'The distance between the outside abdominal or anal lacerations on each of the five,' remembered Sanglier.

'We managed to get inside two of the refrigerated lorries,' continued Claus. 'Even part-loaded, it would be totally impossible to see from a road check — remember, anyone would be looking in with his head virtually level with the floor of the vehicle — what was at the far end. Fully loaded it's not even worth trying.'

'And *all* the refrigerated vehicles we saw carried the *Transports Internationaux Routiers* protection,' added van Kleiper.

'What are our chances of a surprise entry?' asked Sanglier.

'Nil,' said Claus simply.

'So what have we got?'

'A lot more circumstantial suspicion to go with the circumstantial suspicion we had in the first place,' said Claus, who thought it was the best phrase he'd managed to think up.

Scott Burrows examined without speaking all the material recovered from the unsuccessful Baltimore raid and Joe Hardy sat silently opposite him in the FBI office of the American embassy.

'Five cuttings from the press conference reports referring to American profiling assistance,' said Burrows at last, unnecessarily.

'All with your name inked in on the margins,' said Hardy, equally unnecessarily. Offering a sealed envelope he added: 'I'm to give you this. To save you opening it it's an offer personally signed by the Director. You can move to wherever you want. Your choice.'

'Fuck it,' said Burrows. 'I'm not going anywhere.'

'There's a port and airport watch, stateside.'

Burrows snorted a laugh. 'Don't hold your breath.'

'You think he'll try?'

'I wish to Christ I knew,' said Burrows. 'That's been my problem from the beginning. Not being sure.'

Chapter Twenty-Nine

Claudine was frightened, although her breathing was still easy.

She couldn't remember such a positive feeling before — not even during the near collapse — and like too many others in recent weeks it disorientated her and she already felt too disorientated. It was a long time — too long — since she'd been fully in control of herself and things around her.

Tonight she intended putting some of that right, despite the most recent and persistent apprehensions, because tonight a lot — more than she knew or could anticipate — depended on it. And very quickly after tonight she had to resolve a lot of the other doubts.

Seeking patterns, as always, she tried to package the uncertainties, no longer caring if personal considerations encroached into her sacrosanct professionalism or her sacrosanct professionalism intruded into her personal life. It wasn't possible any longer — perhaps it never had been — to separate one from the other.

It had been pretentious to try. The conversation with Rosetti echoed in her mind, which was hardly surprising as she stood wine glass in hand in front of the drinks selection she'd had delivered that day, in preparation for the evening to come and for the Italian's visits she hoped would come frequently in the future. With it echoed her tattered axiom, seemingly more a taunt than the anchoring reassurance she'd once regarded it to be.

Had she ever known herself? Properly, honestly, sensibly known herself? Or had all of it been pretension upon pretension, act upon act for an audience of one: not drinking because she despised her father for doing so; and swearing — more mentally than verbally — because people she worked with swore; dominating the marriage because she'd accepted her mother's judgement of Warwick's weakness; and imagining there was no encounter she couldn't manipulate and orchestrate?

No, she decided, refilling her glass as if in defiance of herself. Not all of it: not everything. But too much. She'd cheated everyone — cheated Warwick and cheated her mother and perhaps, even, cheated her father — by building a pretension for every situation into a wall behind which to hide who she really was and what she really felt. And most of all cheated herself, her always applauding audience of one.

So who was she, this new person she didn't know? And what did she feel? She was Claudine Carter, who had every reason to believe herself a first-class criminal psychologist but no right to arrogance and conceit because of that awareness. But she used it as a shield, going too far beyond justifiable confidence to disguise the vulnerability she'd always secretly suffered from but never admitted, the fear that she might not be as good as she thought she was and that one day — with one profile — she might be caught out.

She hadn't been caught out with the mass killings. She'd got those assessments right, every time. Proved herself to herself. And to Europol's ruling body, not just to Henri Sanglier. He remained an enigma, as his sexually predatory wife with her daily unanswered telephone messages remained an irritant. Claudine was confident — confident, not arrogant — that she could handle both. She'd officially appeal against any censure, if Rosetti was wrong about Sanglier's motive: appear in front of the full Commission if necessary and simply set out the facts, concede the illegality and challenge them seriously to censure either her or Volker.

And she would continue to ignore Françoise Sanglier's calls.

How much longer was she going to continue ignoring her biggest personal pretension: her refusal to consider the situation between herself and Hugo Rosetti? No longer. She thought she loved him. And if she did then she'd never loved Warwick because what she felt now was quite different from any emotion she'd known before. When she'd worked in London — travelled all over England at the ring of a telephone — she'd never had Warwick constantly in the corner of her mind, as she had Hugo wherever she was and whatever she did; never imagined or hoped that the ring of that telephone would be Warwick, for her, and felt the sink of disappointment when it wasn't. Never . . . Claudine stopped the reflection, refusing it. It wasn't right — cruel, if only to herself — to try to discover how she felt about Hugo by comparing her feelings for him with those for Warwick. And if she hadn't loved Warwick and he'd realized it, it put into perfect context — made totally understandable — everything he'd written in his tortured suicide note.

Which brought her to that night, about which for the first time she'd recognized how frightened she was, just as she recognized it was too late now to do anything about it, and that Hugo had been right when he called her a bloody idiot for agreeing to meet Paul Bickerstone.

Claudine was making towards the telephone to call Rosetti, just wanting to hear his voice and hopefully some reassurance, when the entry bell sounded in the lobby.

'It's Paul. I'm early,' said the voice.

Claudine would never have recognized Paul Bickerstone, with or without his gorilla outfit.

He was a sleek man, polished hair tight against his head, rounded by business lunches and tanned by luxury yacht cruises: switching her mammal imagery, Claudine's impression was of a seal. Maybe, in view of what he was supposed to have done, a shark would have been even more appropriate.

In the momentary hesitation in the apartment entrance she thought he was going to kiss her — he actually leaned forward — but then he drew back to offer his one free hand. She was surprised he had sufficient strength in the other to carry a bouquet she genuinely had to enfold in both arms to accept. Struggling with it to the kitchen she decided it would have needed a Kew Gardens botanist to identify all the blooms. He followed with champagne she hadn't seen him carrying and she was glad she'd included it in her selection, because she was able to serve hers chilled, even though it was Moët and not the superior Roederer Crystal he'd brought. Bickerstone solicitously carried the bottle, in its cooler, and glasses back into the lounge, opened it and poured.

He began his examination of the room, in readiness for the dutiful admiration, but stopped at the wall-spanning music assembly. 'What the hell is that?'

'It was Warwick's.'

'Warwick's?'

'Surely you remember jazz was his hobby?'

'Yes. Of course,' said Bickerstone quickly. He went closer, as if to study the dials and adjustments and levels. 'There are lights on.'

'They're on all the time,' said Claudine easily. 'I only just understand enough to play music. I had an expert install it.'

'I've never seen anything like it,' said Bickerstone, abruptly reaching out to twist dials and flick switches up and down.

'What are you doing?' demanded Claudine, not moving from where she stood in the centre of the room. 'I told you I don't turn it off.'

'Can you record on this?'

Not any more, thought Claudine: two of the operating lights had gone out. She said: 'Probably. I don't know.'

He turned, smiling. 'I couldn't work it either. I didn't get any music.'

'Do you want music?' If it hadn't been so serious — and if he hadn't been so blatantly obvious — it would have been farcical.

The smile widened and Claudine thought that was sleek, too. He said: 'No. Silly thing to have done. I just wanted to play with it.' He came closer, studying her fully. 'Claudine. Claudine!' he said, as if he were making a discovery. 'It's so good to see you again . . . so very, very good. You look wonderful . . . beautiful . . .'

'It has been a long time,' she said.

'I'll never forgive myself. Ever.'

'Water under the bridge.' She gestured him

533

towards an easy chair close to the window and sat down opposite, with the champagne on the table between them.

'I should have asked you to choose,' he announced, confusing her momentarily. 'As it is I took a guide book recommendation and had a table booked at the Royal.'

'It's very good.'

'There's no hurry, though. Hours yet.'

Will I be equal to you, Paul Bickerstone? she wondered. Then she realized she had to be more than equal. She had to be better. 'Business finished in Paris?'

'End of a deal. Just signing papers.'

'Is that why you were early?'

Briefly he appeared not to understand. 'Oh, yes. I got away sooner than I expected.'

'Flying back tonight?' She hoped it didn't sound like an invitation.

'I might. The plane's in Amsterdam. If I change my mind I've taken rooms at somewhere called the Hotel des Indes.'

'All the diplomats use it,' said Claudine. She'd bat the small talk back and forth as long as he wanted: as he'd said, they had hours yet. And she wasn't going to risk anything until she was surer of herself than she felt at that moment.

'You involved in this murder thing? Europol's got a lot of press in the UK.'

'A lot of people are, one way and the other,' Claudine said, curious at the question but unwilling to let the conversation drift too far, no matter how much time they had.

'Not missing London, then?'

Here we come, she thought hopefully. 'Too many bad memories.'

Bickerstone shook his head: not a hair moved. 'I just can't stop putting my foot in it, can I?'

'That's all right.' Snatching the chance, she said: 'I was shocked about Gerald.'

'I still haven't got over it.'

'Were you very close?' It was his lead, so why shouldn't she follow it?

'Very.' The man looked down into his drink, as if in reverie.

'Warwick always thought of him as a good friend . . . his best friend,' Claudine ventured.

'I know. That's what Gerald told me. That's how I thought of him, too.'

'Warwick? Or Gerald?'

'Gerald.' Bickerstone raised his hands in a halting gesture. 'Of course Warwick was my friend, too; always was. But after your marriage I spent more time with Gerald.'

'We did seem to drift apart, didn't we? I don't think we saw him more than twice, afterwards. Like we didn't see you.'

Bickerstone gave an apologetic shrug, leaning forward to offer more champagne. There was hardly room in her glass but Bickerstone refilled his own. 'These things happen. Sad.' He smiled. 'I'm embarrassed to ask but do you mind if I use the bathroom?'

'Not at all. It's at the end of the corridor.' She stood to direct him and called out 'That's a bedroom' at his first mistake and 'That's the other' when he opened the second wrong door. Then she said: 'Try the one on the right. The door to the left leads out to the fire escape.'

Bickerstone returned very quickly.

'You were telling me about Gerald,' prompted Claudine. As clumsy as playing with the music system but just as effective, she thought.

'Not a lot to tell, really. We were both at King's with Warwick. Both enjoyed rugby. Regulars at Twickenham. I've got a country place in Sussex. He used to come down for weekends. Didn't I invite you and Warwick down a couple of times?'

'I don't remember it. Gerald wasn't married, was he?'

'No. He envied Warwick, being with you. Often said so.'

'To Warwick?'

Bickerstone frowned. 'I'm sorry?'

'I must have misunderstood something you said on the telephone,' said Claudine, hoping she hadn't tried to steer the conversation too obviously. 'I travelled a great deal when I was in London. I thought the three of you met?'

Bickerstone's reaction was quite different from anything Claudine expected. He thrust forward in his chair and said: 'Did Warwick tell you that?'

What was the right answer? wondered Claudine desperately. 'I don't really remember. I know he got together with Gerald from time to time.'

'Warwick told you about that?'

Bickerstone was taking a direction she couldn't follow. 'Told me what?' she said, needing to become the questioner.

Bickerstone covered the hesitation by offering more wine. There was still very little room in Claudine's glass. 'What he and Gerald talked about?'

'Not in any detail,' floundered Claudine. She was close although she didn't know to what and if she didn't get it right in the next few minutes — the next few seconds — she was going to end up the bloody idiot that Hugo had accused her of being.

'What did he say?' persisted Bickerstone, his refilled glass forgotten. Claudine was conscious for the first time of the hardness the man had to possess to have achieved all he apparently had.

Claudine could think of only one way to keep the conversation on this uncertain, blind course. She was reluctant to take it although she thought — hoped — that psychologically it might work. But on an ordinary person, she qualified. With private yachts and private planes Bickerstone was hardly an ordinary person. Certainly not one accustomed — or willing — to surrender control. She wasn't working from just one agenda, she reminded herself: she knew more than he suspected. Strengthening her voice, Claudine said: 'I'm very good, at what I do.'

It confused him, as she wanted it to. He blinked and said: 'I'm sure you are.'

'So you don't think I'm a fool?'

'Of course I don't think you're a fool.'

'So why, when I haven't seen you or heard from you for more than two years, have you suddenly emerged from nowhere and flown all the way from London with champagne and flowers? What is it you want me to tell you, Paul?'

Bickerstone's face mirrored a variety of emotions. Anger was the most obvious, at being spoken to in a manner to which he wasn't accustomed, but she thought she detected uncertainty as well as a lot of other attitudes she couldn't identify. 'I want you to tell me what you know.'

She'd done it! thought Claudine. She was still fumbling but he didn't know that because he was in her territory — territory in which he wasn't trained and didn't know how to operate — not in a boardroom or a finance house or a trading pen, where words were figures without nuance or inflexion. She shook her head, outwardly more positive than she inwardly felt, and said: 'I'm waiting.'

The head went down again over the champagne glass and for several moments — several lifetimes — Bickerstone remained silent. Claudine steeled herself against speaking, either, knowing it would be wrong. At last the man said: 'He didn't have to do it. He didn't have to kill himself.'

Surely not? thought Claudine, in no doubt about whom the man was talking. Surely it wasn't so simple? She even had facts to support the possibility confronting her, facts that Toomey had possessed but misread, as he'd misread Gerald Lorimer's note and she, in turn, had doubted Warwick. She said: 'Gerald didn't envy Warwick being married, did he?'

'No.'

'Are you married?'

'Yes.'

'Happily?'

'Enough.'

'I'm still waiting for you to tell me, Paul.'

'Letters. Some photographs.'

'Why should Warwick have had them? Why wouldn't Gerald have kept them himself? They were his: special to both of you.'

Bickerstone gulped at his champagne, the brash ruler-of-the-world ebullience totally gone. 'There wasn't anything among his things. I had my people check with the police. Warwick's the only person I can think of. Was there anything?'

Claudine had her own questions to be answered first. 'Did Warwick know about you and Gerald?'

'Yes. He never told you?'

Claudine shook her head instead of replying, not wanting the roles to change. 'How did Warwick feel about it?'

'He never criticized, if that's what you mean. It was our business, Gerald's and mine.'

'No,' said Claudine. 'That wasn't what I meant but it doesn't matter, only to me. But there's nothing, Paul. I obviously went through all Warwick's things. There was nothing involving you or Gerald. No letters. No photographs.'

'There must be something,' pleaded the man. 'I'm not ashamed . . . no reason to be . . . but I'm frightened of blackmail . . . of Juliet finding out . . . the children . . . isn't there anywhere you haven't looked? Might have *over*looked?'

'Nowhere.' Claudine took a proper drink for the first time, not totally satisfied but believing there was no more to be gained at this stage: unsure if there were any further stages in which she needed to be involved.

'Do you despise me?'

Claudine came forward in her own chair. 'What a ridiculous question! Why should I despise you?'

'I despise myself.'

'That's equally ridiculous. And self-pitying;

I despise self-pity. It doesn't suit you.'

'I'm very frightened.'

'Haven't you done your own investigation?'

'Of course.'

'If there were going to be threats from anyone they would have come by now, wouldn't
they?'

'Did Warwick have a lawyer? Someone with
whom he might have deposited some papers?'

'Paul! You're talking about love letters, from
you to Gerald. Intimate photographs. Why
would Warwick deposit things like that with a
lawyer? Why would Gerald have even shown
them to Warwick? They were yours and Gerald's, no one else's.'

'I'm desperate, Claudine!'

'Too desperate. Warwick and I only had one
lawyer. I've been through the will . . . everything . . . with him. That's all there was. The
will and some insurance policies.'

The man pulled the champagne bottle from
the cooler but it was empty.

Claudine said: 'You don't want to take me
out to dinner, do you?'

'I invited you.'

'For a reason. Which we've gone through.
The flowers were lovely. The champagne,
too.'

'I'm sorry.'

'What for?'

Bickerstone made a listless shoulder movement. 'I don't know. Just sorry. You wouldn't

bother to contact me when you came to London, if I asked you to, would you?'

'Probably not.'

'You've got the number if you change your mind?'

'Yes.'

'You sure about dinner?'

'Go home to Juliet and the children.'

'You do understand, don't you?'

'I think so.'

'Thank you.'

He did come forward to kiss her as he left and Claudine offered her cheek. Bickerstone remained momentarily on the threshold, his mouth working but forming no words, and then abruptly he turned and went towards the elevators without saying anything. Claudine closed the door while he was still waiting for a lift to arrive.

Hugo Rosetti answered on the second ring. 'I didn't expect you for hours.'

'Dinner was cancelled.' She was warmed by his voice.

'Well?'

'Come and hear for yourself.'

She offered him, unasked, a glass of the Chardonnay she'd been drinking before Bickerstone arrived, which Rosetti accepted without comment. Claudine said: 'It was impressive, like all the James Bond movies you've ever seen. He pretended to be interested in the music system and played with all the dials and knobs and switches sufficiently to bugger any recording. Then he pretended he wanted to pee so he could check every room in the place. And never once looked embarrassed.'

'So the great plan didn't work,' accused an unamused Rosetti. 'You didn't get any admissions on tape?'

'Oh, I did,' smiled Claudine. 'I got it all.' She gestured sideways. 'All that nonsense against the wall is too obvious, isn't it? It was a great distraction, though, from the recorder I had running behind the window curtain. It was the one I had at the Sorbonne, to take down my lectures.'

'You cunning bitch!'

'I become a witch at full moon.'

The bottle of Chardonnay was empty by the time the tape ended but Claudine didn't feel any effect, despite her comparative newness to alcohol. Adrenalin must compensate, she decided.

Well aware of what was most important to her, Rosetti said: 'So Warwick wasn't gay?'

'Not according to that.'

Rosetti stopped with the glass he was about to empty raised halfway to his mouth. 'What?'

'I think Paul Bickerstone is the best actor I've ever encountered in my entire life. And I love the theatre.'

'Don't you believe him?'

'I think I believe him about Warwick. But

then I want to, don't I? And I think he and Lorimer were lovers. But it's more than just letters and photographs.'

'What?'

She shrugged lightly. 'I've no idea. And couldn't care less. It's not my problem. I don't have to worry about Peter Toomey any more.'

There was little discussion and certainly no argument about who cooked what Claudine had available. Rosetti flared the garlic-scattered steaks in the newly installed brandy and opened another bottle of wine, a Gevrey Chambertin, although they didn't finish it. Even so, towards the end of the meal, Rosetti lifted his glass and said: 'You seem to be making up for all the years of abstinence.'

'Getting rid of a lot of pretensions.'

'That's good.'

A response occurred at once but Claudine didn't say it: their relationship wasn't that strong, not yet.

Almost immediately after the meal he said: 'It's late and we've both got planes to catch early tomorrow.'

Claudine didn't speak then, either.

'Goodnight.'

Claudine remained silent.

Although the *notaire* had been the family lawyer for as long as Claudine could remember he still treated both her and her mother as strangers. His name was Pierre Forge and he was as dry and desiccated as the legal tomes among which he sat, like a black-suited spider: his fingers were extraordinarily long and thin and the way he frequently flexed them actually reminded Claudine of spiders' legs. She didn't like spiders.

Claudine was concerned the arrangement — completing the new will in the morning before the afternoon's wedding — would be too tiring for her mother but the older woman insisted Claudine never knew when she might be summoned back to The Hague, which was more important than anything involving her. Claudine didn't bother to argue: the schedule was already fixed anyway. Certainly her mother showed no sign of strain. She'd definitely put on weight and her natural colouring, far healthier than she'd looked for a long time, made rouge unnecessary. She wore formal black for the encounter with the lawyer but had shown Claudine her wedding outfit, a pale cream suit with contrasting beige hat, gloves and handbag, before they'd left the rue Grenette. She'd done so with a young girl's excitement and Claudine couldn't recall her mother ever being so obviously happy, not even at the Sorbonne graduation.

She was conscious of her mother's chair-grating impatience, beside her in Forge's office, half expecting an outspoken protest at the painstaking formality. Forge insisted upon going pedantically through every available document, starting with her mother's certificate of marriage to William Carter and proceeding through Claudine's birth certificate — taking a statement witnessed by his chief clerk that there had been no other offspring, either inside or outside the union — before recording by hand the details of William Carter's death certificate and even the plot number of his grave. The property and effects — predominantly the restaurant, the apartment above and an adjoining block of four apartments which Claudine was unaware her mother owned — were already listed in the will that was being superseded. Forge nevertheless went through them, item by item, to Monique's visible impatience. Everything took three hours to complete, concluding with a mass signing of papers which Monique said she didn't have time to read.

As he shook her hand Forge said to Claudine: 'You are a very rich young lady.'

Outside, her mother said: 'Whether you're rich or not is none of the old bastard's business. And he doesn't know about the cash.'

'Do I need to?'

'Of course you do! I'll explain it all when the time comes.'

Her mother's spirits lifted back at the rue Grenette. She giggled while Claudine dressed her hair and insisted she wasn't concerned about the treatment — chemotherapy, not radiotherapy — that was to start the next week.

Claudine understood the hesitation when Monique was ready to change from the dressing gown she'd put on in the privacy of the bathroom into the blouse and the laid-out suit, and left the bedroom so she would not see her mother undressed.

The restaurant was closed to the public for the meal that preceded the wedding, and Claudine was surprised at the array of guests, which included an impressive array of Lyon's leading citizens. The tricoloured mayor, necessary for the later ceremony, headed the dignitaries. At the champagne reception before they sat down Claudine was introduced to the police chief. Her mother whispered that she hadn't told the man of Claudine's role at Europol or of her involvement in the Céleste investigation, although she'd wanted to.

Despite having surrendered the kitchen to his two underchefs for his wedding day Gérard Lanvin supervised the preparation. There was Périgueux *foie gras* broken by sharp lemon sorbet before the Strasbourg goose and crêpes Suzette flared in a flat-bottomed cauldron, with separate wines with each course and more champagne for the toasts, which the mayor led, followed by a banker. Throughout Monique sat bright-eyed and flushed, laughing at every remark, modestly dipping her head to every compliment.

The actual ceremony seemed almost an anticlimax, although in front of so many of the city's leaders the registrar performed the ceremony with as much flourish and pomp as possible.

Claudine returned to the restaurant with Gérard and her mother to collect her overnight case: disregarding their protests that it was stupid and unnecessary, she had booked into a hotel for the night. By the time they returned to the rue Grenette all traces of the wedding party had been cleared away and the restaurant prepared for the evening. Gérard insisted on more champagne, although almost at once he disappeared into the kitchen.

'How long have you been drinking?' demanded Monique.

'Not long. Not doing so was a silly act.'

Her mother pulled a face. 'Have you got a new man?' she asked.

'A friend.'

'Are you sleeping with him?'

'No.'

'Why not?'

'He doesn't want to.'

'*He* doesn't want to?'

'It's complicated.'

'Being married isn't usually an obstacle,' said the older woman, still intuitive.

'It is in this case.'

'Do you want to get married again?'

'It's not that sort of situation. It can't be.'

'Someone you work with?'

'Yes. An Italian.'

'Don't like Italians. You can't trust them.'

Before she'd decided he was weak her mother hadn't liked Warwick because he was English, Claudine remembered. 'Hugo's different.'

'Hugo doesn't sound like an Italian name.'

Claudine shrugged. 'It's the one he's got.'

'Will I meet him?'

'I don't know. I don't think so. He goes back to Italy a lot at weekends.'

'To see his wife.'

'She's ill. An invalid.'

Some of the challenge went out of the older woman. 'You don't have much luck with men, do you?'

'I'm happy enough.'

'I am,' declared Monique, fervently. 'I don't think I've ever been so happy in my life. And I'm going to live to be a hundred because there's so much to enjoy.'

Chapter Thirty

The tidal wave of information was so engulfing Sanglier had to call upon the promised additional manpower and by the end of the third day had more than doubled his record-keeping staff. It was still insufficient to deal with the backlog and Sanglier introduced a twenty-four-hour shift system to catch up.

The fresh breakthrough emerged on the fourth day and came close to causing the internal sensation Kurt Volker's initial location of the Wo Lim factory had done. As well as Mr Woon, three other Chinese — Zhu Peiyuan, Li Jian and Chen Jinhu — were positively identified as members of K-14, China's largest and most violent Triad, by computer comparisons against surveillance photographs taken in Van Diemen Straat.

Sanglier quickly detached a three-man unit to build up detailed fact-files on the four men and the Triad societies to which they belonged, as well as intensifying the surveillance upon each of them.

Every available criminal record was accessed in Hong Kong, Macao, Interpol and Europol, and Sanglier, nervous of the offence he'd caused by the press conference gaffe, nevertheless personally invoked Scott Burrows' presence at Europol to persuade America's FBI to search their index. The names and photographs were also run against Dutch immigration archives. The visas and residency permission for all four were valid and legal but Washington responded within a day that a man whose photograph matched that of Li Jian had been expelled from San Francisco five years earlier under the name of Luo Qi after serving four years of a ten-year sentence for extortion in the city's Chinatown. In Hong Kong there were open files on the man under both names involving loan sharking and running illegal brothels. Chen Jinhu had been jointly accused on two occasions but acquitted on the prostitution charges, as had Li Jian, because witnesses had failed to appear. The loan charges had also been dismissed because of the refusal of witnesses to testify.

The parallel progress in the investigations into the Polish prostitute killings came about initially by accident, as it so often does in criminal inquiries. In an unconnected swoop on a window-sex house in Amsterdam's Bethamien Straat where a tourist client complained of being robbed, a Polish whore without a passport or residency permit was arrested.

Because of her admitted nationality she was questioned about Anna Zockowski and admitted knowing the woman, who had been smuggled into the country a week before her own illegal entry: for a further week, before being put to work by the pimp to whom they had been virtually sold, they had both shared a house in Roomen Straat and they stayed friends afterwards. But she'd begun to distance herself from Zockowski about three months before she was killed, because Anna was a troublemaker, dangerous to be around. From the start, when they'd been together in Roomen Straat, she'd refused to work for the money she was to get until her ponce crushed her thumb in a vice and even then she didn't stop arguing. She'd had a baby in Warsaw, a girl she'd put up for adoption, and she loved kids. That was why she made so much fuss about all the children — boys as well as girls — being brought in from the East for child sex and paedophile pornography.

The whore hadn't been smuggled into Holland by the same man as Anna. The only name she knew for Anna's contact was Karel. He'd run Anna in Warsaw.

Amsterdam liaised with Brussels, whose vice squad had picked up similar rumours about Inka Obenski protesting against child sex: there was even a story that she'd threatened to expose the trade to the police in exchange for legal residency. They hadn't heard anything about a Polish pimp named Karel.

The Warsaw police chief had, though. Karel Kaczmarek had a record stretching back fifteen years for criminal assault, robbery, brothel running and pimping. Within twenty-four hours Amsterdam and Brussels received copies of Kaczmarek's file and a photograph of a bloated, crinkle-haired man with a scar down the left-hand side of his face that narrowed his eye into a squint.

It was issued to every member of each city's vice squad and in Amsterdam the house in Roomen Straat was put under surveillance. The vice squad chief supported the window shop whore's appeal for residency in exchange for the help she'd provided but the immigration department ordered her immediate deportation, reluctant to set a precedent.

With traditional police routine to follow and impose René Poulard and Bruno Siemen emerged as efficient, practical officers. Sanglier was perfectly satisfied, believing he could provide all the necessary initiative. Siemen moved between the various units, short-circuiting the unceasing documentary avalanche by verbally picking up the important developments: Sanglier heard first from the German of the K-14 discovery. Poulard linked the Polish inquiries between Amsterdam, Brussels and Warsaw and by so doing kept the cases officially and very firmly under Europol control, upon which Sanglier insisted.

Despite all of this — and very much aware of the first-day dispute with the Amsterdam police chief — Sanglier remained worried by the potential personal disaster he couldn't devise a way of avoiding now he'd established himself as the responsive head of the inquiry. His first protective move was officially to meet Dutch Justice Ministry lawyers, together with the deputy Justice Minister, all of whom listened attentively to his fear of another murder, agreed its justification but failed to provide an answer, which he knew to be impossible because if there had been one he would have already thought of it himself.

Although the journey between Amsterdam and The Hague was easily commutable daily, Sanglier took a suite at the Amstel Intercontinental. He had no personal wish or need to be with Françoise and professionally it showed total commitment. It also put him that much closer to the waiting Europol aircraft if one of the pursuit squads became sufficiently suspicious of a Wo Lim vehicle to recommend its being stopped.

He did, however, go personally to The Hague to deliver a report at the Commission's weekly conference, relishing his obvious supremacy among the other fourteen commissioners as much as he enjoyed being in charge of his multi-force detective army. That was not, however, the reason for the return, which was to reinforce the self-protection he'd begun to put in place by meeting the Dutch officials. He was listened to at the Europol headquarters with the respectful silence of the Dutch meeting, and when he finished the current chairman, Belgium's Jan Villiers, said: 'I think we should congratulate our colleague on a brilliant summary of an extraordinarily well planned and already productive investigation.'

There were assenting nods and gestures around the table until Holland's Hans Maes, who believed himself the most closely involved commissioner, said: 'How is it to go forward? Overwhelmingly convincing though it is to us, as professional policemen, there is nothing whatsoever positively to connect the Wo Lim factory or anyone employed in it with the Céleste murders. And I don't see how that evidence is going to come unless we intercept a lorry or raid the premises and find a body. Both of which seem impractical: you've even told us today a surprise assault upon the premises is virtually impossible.'

Everything going precisely to plan as usual, thought Sanglier, contentedly. He said: 'The Wo Lim factory is unquestionably a criminal enterprise, established for criminal purposes. The extent and completeness of our surveillance virtually guarantees detection the moment a crime is committed.'

'Are you saying you're waiting for another murder?' demanded David Winslow.

'Of course not,' said Sanglier. 'Triad societies are not illegal under Dutch law. And there is no legal proof of membership of K-14 against the four we've named: it's police intelligence never substantiated in any court of law. And their visas and residency permits are legal and valid. We have a search warrant, sworn out on probable cause, but at this moment we have no legal reason to move against Wo Lim Ltd or their factory.'

'You mean we've just got to sit and wait?' demanded Franz Sobell.

'I'm not any happier about it than any of you are or the Dutch Justice Ministry is, but we don't have any alternative,' insisted Sanglier. 'The moment we get an arrest — which we will — we can exercise the warrant. The factory can be stripped, forensically. Everyone can be interrogated and then the connection with K-14 can become a threat to enforce cooperation.'

The statement was not greeted with the unquestioned acceptance of Sanglier's earlier report.

Anxious to show his knowledge, Hans Maes said: 'Holland is no stranger to Triad societies. As well as K-14 our criminal intelligence believe we have operating in the country the Wo Shing Wo, the Won On Lok and the San Yee On. I say "believe" because as far as I am aware we have never gained an admission from an arrested Chinese criminal. And what you seem to be relying upon, once you've made your move, is a confession.' The man shook his head. 'You won't get it.'

'It's absurd!' protested the Italian, Emilio Bellimi. 'There must be something more that we can do.'

'What?' demanded Sanglier, addressing himself more to Maes than to anyone else. 'I've set out the facts and our problem . . . the problem I've discussed with Dutch officials. They couldn't come up with an answer. I'd be delighted if you could.' He was totally safe and beyond reproach. The verbatim records being assembled by unseen note-takers and recordings in the smoked glass eyrie above them would actually show the responsibility had been made that of the Commission.

The discussion, which he knew to be pointless, continued for a further hour before ending as ineffectually as it had begun. Expectantly Jan Villiers said they could talk in more detail about the actual investigation at lunch, but Sanglier said he couldn't spare the time and intended returning immediately to Amsterdam. The refusal was as calculated as leaving the building without bothering to contact Claudine. She learned of Sanglier's visit from Scott Burrows, who'd accidentally encountered Sanglier on his way out. Burrows was heading in the opposite direction, towards Claudine's office.

It didn't amount to a formal meeting, although the American telephoned to ensure it was convenient and Claudine, with her new-person resolve, determined against betraying the irritation she'd felt in the past, which she'd already put on her list of abandoned pretensions. She was also curious at Burrows' changed attitude. He hadn't telephoned in advance before, and this time he'd asked if they could meet in the privacy of her office, not the incident room. He arrived without a perfume-billowing cigar, which was another departure from normal. Instead he carried a sagging briefcase.

'Sanglier didn't make any contact?' said Burrows, when Claudine expressed ignorance of the visit.

'It's strictly a police matter now. No need for me or Rosetti. And he's got other computer people in Amsterdam.' From her suspicions in the past she would have imagined Sanglier more likely to have sought out the American but dismissed the thought because it didn't seem important any more.

'Still seems a bit odd. But then he's an odd guy.'

The invitation was there but Claudine didn't take it. Instead she said: 'There was something specific you wanted to talk to me about?'

'I want your advice.'

'*You* want *my* advice?'

Burrows smiled, embarrassed, and Claudine wished her instinctive astonishment hadn't been so obvious. 'You're going to hear something else you'll find difficulty in believing. I think you're the best goddamned profiler I've ever come across.' He said the words hurriedly, the embarrassment becoming a positive facial redness.

Claudine expected him to cover his difficulty with a cigar but he didn't. Trying her hardest, she said: 'You're not coming on to me like all the other dirty old bastards around here, are you?'

The smile remained, grateful now. 'In my dreams. But I'm talking professionally.'

'So talk.'

He didn't do so at once. Instead he took a bundle from the briefcase at his feet and slid it across the desk towards her. It seemed to be equally composed of FBI statement and report forms, newspaper cuttings and photographs: the photographs were all scene-of-crime, of mutilated although not dismembered bodies, apart from a crime file selection of a fresh-faced, blond-haired and moustached man looking clear-eyed at the camera, with the vaguest suggestion of a smile.

'Lance Pickering,' identified Burrows, sparing Claudine the trouble of looking at the print-out beneath.

Before he could continue, Claudine picked up. 'First murder in 1990 or maybe 1991: I can't remember exactly. Evanstown, Illinois. A fourteen-year-old boy, sexually mutilated. Three more within a matter of months, all around the same age, virtually in a line down through the mid-West. The sensation after the arrest was the line-up of psychologists and psychiatrists claiming he had a mental illness that could be cured. You wrote the psychosis was irreversible.'

'So you did read the books,' said the American, clearly flattered.

'Every one of them. And I remember the Pickering case because it was the first time a serial killer was claimed, professionally, to be capable of being cured.' Claudine spoke looking down at the dossier, flicking through it.

'And the bastards were wrong. They only said it because Pickering's old man is loaded and they could charge a hundred thousand dollars a shot. But the cockamamy judge fell for it and sent him to a supposedly secure psychiatric installation instead of a penitentiary.'

'Where you saw him?'

'It was a hot idea at the time. Official policy of the FBI's National Center for the Analysis of Violent Crime to interview as many serial killers who'd agree, to produce the definitive profiling manual. A hell of a lot did, to break the monotony of a lifetime's imprisonment. Pickering was one of them and I was the guy appointed. Saw him three times, at the hospital in Wilmington, North Carolina. I didn't see the fixation coming. No one did. I just knew he was totally insane and always would be and said so, in the official report and then in my own book . . .' He gestured towards the pile in front of her. 'The first letter has the yellow tag. Two and a half years ago.'

'After he escaped?'

'Trussed the laundry delivery man like a mummy after overpowering him and taking his uniform and drove out of the gates with him in the back of the van, so he could amuse himself for as long as he liked afterwards killing the poor fucker. The Bureau got that first letter about me a week later . . .'

Claudine isolated the yellow tag, reading aloud. '*Scott betrayed our friendship, our trust. He'll die now. I'll take his heart. My trophy . . .*'

'That's become the trademark, taking the heart as the souvenir,' said Burrows. 'It was dismissed by everyone except me as a kookie threat at first. Everyone was far too busy showing how the professional mind-doctors had fucked up. Then there was some hype about my going to San Francisco on a case. Two days after I'd left a dispatcher at the local Bureau office was murdered. Her heart was cut out and two rings taken from her fingers. The rings came with the next threat note. It happened again a month later in Salt Lake City, that time only a day after I'd finished. I knew the agent-in-charge there: had a wife and a disabled kid. I got sent his fraternity ring. The note promised he'd get me next time.'

Claudine's mind was working on several levels. She was listening and analysing as best she could what Burrows was telling her while separately realizing the effort it must have cost such an outwardly macho man to come to her and talk like this — to admit fear. Remembering how she'd behaved at their seminars, she felt humbled. 'So your coming here wasn't a simple exchange between two bureaux?'

'There was a lot of diplomatic shit, between Brussels and Washington. Visiting adviser seemed a good idea to the seventh floor. Put your guys here in debt for a favour to the Bureau in the future and conveniently got me quietly out of the way until they got a jacket back on Pickering. I still thought then it was over the top but Miriam was worried to hell so I went with it.'

Claudine picked out the reservation. 'What's happened since?'

'Last case in the bundle.'

The photographs of the Baltimore massacre were uppermost, the bodies obviously decomposing. The cuttings from the American newspapers and from *Newsweek* were next, with Burrows' name scrawled in the margin on every one.

'Now I understand the aversion to personal publicity,' she said.

'It was a hell of a job for the Director to keep them from publishing my name,' said Burrows. 'In the end it wasn't worth the trouble.'

'You think he'll come here?'

'Do *you* think he'll come here?'

He must be around sixty, she guessed, although neglect had aged him. 'You can't expect me to give a definite answer on other people's files and assessment. But I'll try, of course. Think about it, Scott. We're on the other side of the world. As far as he's aware, from what he's read, you could be anywhere in one of half a dozen countries. He'd need money. A passport . . .'

'I told you the family's loaded. Money he's got. Probably passports, too. He's travelled all over and he's cleverer than a monkey on a sharp stick. Bastard's got a 160 IQ.'

'Let me read the file.'

'Washington say I can go where I like. But I don't want to run. I don't want to die but I don't want to run. I just want to go home.'

'Let's talk about it tomorrow.'

'I never contradicted any of your profiles,' declared the American suddenly. 'Sanglier ran them by me, maybe expecting me to, but I never did because I never had to. I talked with him, sure. But I never went against you.'

The devious French bastard! Although it offended her Claudine could understand — although only just — Sanglier's using Burrows as a monitor, considering the American's reputation. But why should Sanglier have expected Burrows to dispute her assessments? It was as if the American was telling her Sanglier had wanted him to challenge the profiles. She accepted the revelation as another warning. She smiled at Burrows and said: 'You think I was a smartass at the seminars?'

'All the time. So did everyone else.'

'Seems I owe you an apology. Lots of apologies.'

Burrows made a movement towards the FBI material. 'This'll call it quits.'

'You think he'll try to find you here, don't you?'

'Yes.'

Claudine refused Rosetti's invitation to lunch and spent the next three hours alone in her office, deeply immersed in the FBI dossier and re-reading Burrows' chapter on Lance Pickering as well as studying three treatises on fixation syndrome in the *Journal of Interpersonal Violence.*

Claudine made sure of returning to the incident room while Rosetti would still be there, hoping he'd suggest dinner to make up for the refused lunch, which he did. Volker was at his computers, upon which material was scrolling up in an apparently uninterrupted stream. Aware of Claudine's approach he said: 'You know what I think? I think Sanglier is having everything copied here because he imagines I'll be buried by the stuff.'

'Aren't you?'

'Of course not. They're doing all the work in Amsterdam. When they transmit it to me I simply put it automatically on to a back-up disk.'

'Is that what you're doing now?'

Volker gave one of his conspiratorial smiles. 'That and a little bit more. It *would* bury us if we tried to read it all. So I've made up this trigger word program. Everything from Amsterdam is filtered through it. The computer automatically recognizes key words or symbols, like Triad and all the Triad society titles and the names, in every variation, of the Chinese Amsterdam have already identified from the photographs. The Polish girls and their ponce are included, too.'

Having spent so much time with the man Claudine thought she knew the answer to her next question but asked it anyway. 'So we aren't bothered by the dross but learn everything at the same time as they do in Amsterdam?'

'It's important for us to keep up to date, here in our lonely backwater.' The smile widened. 'Sanglier has had a master database created. You'll never guess the password he chose?'

'Sanglier,' said Claudine at once. 'You inside it?'

The German's face creased in disappointment. He pointed to two hard-copy dossiers beside him. 'Sanglier's is the one to the right.

The other is all the Triad stuff, with the photographs.'

Yvette called from the other end of the room, holding out the telephone. Claudine listened, asked two quick questions and then turned back into the room.

'There's been a response in Paris to the amnesty appeal. It could be the father of our first victim. Céleste herself.'

'You want me to send Sanglier a message?' asked Volker. 'The line's open.'

'I think the commissioner is far too busy in Amsterdam,' decided Claudine. 'I'll go. You never know what I might learn.'

She was later to remember the remark and decide it was probably the most prophetic thing she'd ever said in her life.

'We're ready to go then?' said John Walker. Now that the moment had arrived the Serious Fraud Office superintendent was nervous. 'I can't think of anything we haven't covered.'

'And you're going officially to inform the British commissioner?'

'It's got to be done by the book. We already decided that,' insisted Toomey.

'I'm looking forward to a trip abroad.'

'So am I. I'm told Dutch food is very good. They do a lot of things with mussels.'

'I can't stand mussels.'

Chapter Thirty-One

At the height of the Raj, when Britain guarded its empire with an enormous army, soldiers rarely told their easily abandoned conquests their real names, to avoid the inconvenience of identifiable parenthood. It became an unwritten custom to call themselves by the jobs they did, creating incongruous lineages of Engineer and Sergeant and Clerk: occasionally, even, Officer.

The cowed and nervous man who shuffled to his feet, hands clasped subserviently in front of him and head bowed against eye contact, was named Shankar Sergeant and Claudine's first thought upon entering the holding cell of Paris's Neuilly district police station was that he was descended from a long line of the much abused and always cheated. He wore a collarless Indian shirt, no longer white, beneath a stained and creased striped Western jacket that didn't match the bagged and grease-shone black trousers that stopped inches above shoes cracked across both insteps. He was extremely thin and his chest sounded hollow when he coughed, which he did frequently. He was shaking.

Instead of replying when she said who she

was the man lifted his hands in front of himself in the Hindu greeting of peace and Claudine was momentarily disconcerted at the identical representation of how the hands — his daughter's hands — had been wired together. He did not sit when she told him, looking apprehensively sideways to the station commander and his deputy who had insisted upon accompanying her, hoping for their moment of glory from involvement in a national sensation.

Claudine repeated it, in English, sitting down herself. Hesitantly he followed on the opposite side of the table, tensed to stop at the first correction. He perched on the very edge of his chair, hands between his knees, head remaining lowered. He still shook, twitching slightly at the grate of their chairs when the two policemen sat.

Claudine pointed to the tape machine and said: 'We are going to make a record of what you say. You understand?'

He nodded, without speaking. Claudine poured water from the carafe intended for her and pushed the glass across towards the man, who looked confused at the kindness. Gently she said: 'Tell me about your daughter.'

Beside her the two Frenchmen shifted and she guessed neither had adequate English, which she'd also guessed and chosen to be Shankar Sergeant's most comfortable language.

'Indira,' he said, his voice little above a whisper, quieter than the persistent cough. There was a long pause. 'After Mrs Gandhi. A wonderful woman.'

Nothing was going to come unprompted, Claudine decided. 'How long have you been in France?'

'A year.'

'Indira came with you? The whole family?'

The man shook his head. 'By myself at first.'

'From where?'

'To begin with?'

'Yes.'

'Calcutta.'

'But there was somewhere else?'

There was another head movement, a nod. 'Bahrain.'

'Was your family with you there?'

Beside her the station chief, whose name she knew to be Leclerc but whose rank she couldn't identify from his uniform, said impatiently: 'I'm finding this difficult to follow. I would like it in French.'

'There's a recording,' said Claudine, curtly and in French. 'English is better for him. I'll explain what you don't understand later.'

Ignoring their increased shifts of irritation — irritated herself at the interruption — she smiled hopefully back at Shankar Sergeant and repeated her question.

'No. I was by myself again,' he replied.

'Why did you go to Bahrain?'

'To work in the oilfields.'

'Did you?'

Another nod. 'As a cleaner.'

'That wasn't what you expected?'

'In Calcutta there were stories of a lot of money, working on rigs. I didn't know until I got there that these are not jobs given to people like me.'

'So there was no money?'

'Not what I had been told. I had to send money home, to keep my family. Live myself.'

'How did you get to Bahrain?'

'Ship.'

Claudine wished she didn't have to drag the pitiful story from the man, sure that she already knew it: knew it all. 'I meant who paid?'

'I saved, for five years. Borrowed the last fifty pounds from a money-lender.' He looked down at himself, holding out his arms slightly in despair. 'I am a tailor. I have a certificate.'

'An Indian money-lender?'

'Yes.'

'Whom you had to repay, as well as sending money to your family and living yourself in Bahrain?'

'Yes.'

'Could you do it?'

'I tried to gamble. It's illegal but all the migrant workers do it. Sometimes they win but not very often. I came very close. Once I won the whole fifty pounds but then I lost it, before the game ended. Mah-jong. Do you know mah-jong?'

Claudine nodded. 'Chinese run the gambling?'

For the first time the man looked at her properly, not speaking for several moments. 'I lost. Couldn't pay.'

'What did they offer?' persisted Claudine. Much abused and always cheated, she thought.

'A way out,' said the man, coughing in short spasms. His head had sunk down on his shoulders again but he was suddenly animated, not needing any urging. 'Everything solved. A man came to me, the day after I lost. I was frightened. Told him everything and he said he could help me. He said Bahrain was a lie: I shouldn't have believed what I'd heard in Calcutta. Europe was where a lot of money could be earned: more than I'd ever thought possible, actually working in the job I was trained for. There would be enough to have my family with me . . .'

'He'd even fix the permits?'

'After I got here. It was the way the system worked. I would be with friends, all the time. I was to do as they said: I had to give them my passport and they would get me in. Within a month I would get it back, with the legal work visa.'

His account of the story was probably true. He wouldn't totally have believed the visa part of it but Claudine didn't feel like challenging the man. 'You had to sign papers?'

'Of course. It was a very big loan but I could have paid it off. There were ten of us on the boat. We had to take our own food but they gave us water. It was a very old boat, a freighter. There were big boxes on deck, as well as in the hold. I never knew what was inside. My food ran out two days before we got here but one of the other men, from Calcutta like me, shared what he had left. We got off at night, I don't know where but someone said later near Marseille. We had to climb down rope ladders, over the side of the ship, into small boats. We were split up then —'

'Did you come straight to Paris?' broke in Claudine quickly.

'Yes.'

'How?'

'In a lorry.'

'What sort of lorry?'

'It delivered food. We kept stopping and things kept being unloaded. I had to hide when that was done. It was easy. There were many things inside.'

'Was it cold? Refrigerated?'

'No.'

Claudine refused the disappointment. 'Was there a name on the lorry?'

'Yes.'

'Do you remember what it was?'

'Short words. Chinese.'

'Can you tell me what they were?'

The man shook his head, sadly. 'I'm sorry.'

'Would you recognize them, if I showed you?'

'I might.' His shaking had stopped, but everything he said was still punctuated by coughs.

Hurriedly Claudine picked through the photographs of the identified K-14 Chinese. There was only one showing the Wo Lim lettering, in Roman script, on the rear of a refrigerated truck. 'Just look at the words,' she ordered, offering the man the photograph. 'Are those the words that were written on the lorry that brought you up to Paris?'

The man squinted, tilting the print slightly. 'It might be.'

'I want you to be sure.'

'I don't know, not for certain.'

'It doesn't matter,' lied Claudine. 'What happened when you got to Paris?'

'It was just as the man had promised, in Bahrain. There was another Chinese man waiting for me. He took me to a house where he said I could live and gave me a meal and the very next day I started work in a tailor's shop: it wasn't really a shop. It was a warehouse where other people like me worked, doing all sort of jobs. It had been a long time since I'd done any tailoring but they said it didn't matter: I'd soon get better. When I asked about my passport the man said there was a hold-up but that I shouldn't worry.

Everything was all right. For three months it was wonderful. I could send money home and pay off what had been agreed on the loan and keep myself. I couldn't save, though, to bring my family over. It was Mr Cheng who began talking about it —'

'Cheng?' Claudine interrupted.

'That's what he said his name was, Mr Cheng. He said it wasn't right for a family to be broken up, but that he could help me like I'd been helped in Bahrain. He'd lend me the money to bring my whole family to France. Living all together meant there would still be enough money to repay the extra I borrowed.'

'How many were there?'

'Three. My wife, Indira and Ratri.' He began to cry, without any sound. 'We were so happy. It was a dream. We even got an apartment, one room but our own bath, here in Neuilly.'

'How long did it last?'

Shankar Sergeant became embarrassed at his tears and scrubbed his jacketed arm across his face. 'A month. At the warehouse they said my work wasn't good enough and fired me. When I asked for Mr Cheng they said he wasn't here any longer. There was another man now, Mr Tan. He shouted a lot. He said I couldn't work there any more but that I had to go on paying back the money. He was going to keep all our passports until I did and laughed at me when I said I'd go to the police because we were all here illegally and we'd be deported back to India . . .' The man's voice trailed away, head forward again.

'But he offered a way, didn't he?'

There was a nod but no words for several moments. 'Indira was sixteen: they'd given her a job in the factory, too. At a loom. He said she was too beautiful to go on doing that. That men would pay, to go with her. She'd earn a lot of money doing that, enough to go on paying off the loan and to keep the family. And that there would be even more money. There was Ratri. She was just twelve. Men would pay even more for her.'

'What did you say?'

'No. That I would go to the police and be sent back to Calcutta before I allowed that.'

'What happened then?'

'The day I told Mr Tan that, Indira didn't come home from the warehouse. When I went to get her she wasn't there. People even said they didn't know her. That she'd never worked there. But Mr Tan said he was giving me one more chance but that he had to have her and Ratri. When I still said no two other Chinese men hit me and wouldn't let me leave. They locked me in a room. They gave me water and some meat — a sausage — and laughed when I said I couldn't eat meat because my religion wouldn't allow it. It was a week, I think . . .' He began to cry again but louder this time, sobs shuddering from him which made him cough all the more, and when he spoke the words came in short, gasping bursts. 'I counted five days. Then they showed me newspaper . . . read out to me what they'd done to Indira and Mr Tan said they had Ratri anyway and that they'd do the same to her if I made trouble. Then they let me go . . .'

'Do you know where Ratri is?'

'No.'

For once Claudine's professionalism — her ability to suspend herself from feeling or involvement — had deserted her. Her eyes fogged and she had to swallow and cough herself before she could say anything and when she did the only words she could find were: 'You poor, poor man . . .'

The pity brought Shankar Sergeant's head up. He raised his hands, too, in the supplicating gesture and said: 'Please help me. Help me get Ratri back . . . to stop everything . . .'

'I want you to look at more pictures,' Claudine said, forcing herself on. 'I want you to look at the faces now. Tell me if any of the men you see are Mr Cheng or Mr Tan. If there is anyone you know . . . ?'

Carefully, giving him several minutes between each examination, she set the Amsterdam surveillance pictures out on the table. He bent studiously over each, brow furrowed in fervent concentration, his face breaking further when he finally looked up. 'They are Chinese men,' he said, as if that were sufficient

explanation for his difficulty. 'I have a problem . . .'

'None of them are Mr Cheng or Mr Tan?'

'No.' He put his finger to the left side of his
face and drew it down. 'Mr Cheng had a scar,
there. Deep. like the moon, when it is new.'

'You've never seen any of them before. At
the warehouse . . . anywhere . . . ?'

'I don't think so.'

She had the link, the final explanation to
complete their jigsaw, and again it couldn't
form part of any legal prosecution. But there
was more information that could. 'Can you
show us the house where you were taken when
you first arrived in Paris?'

'I think so.'

'And the warehouse, where you all worked?'

'Of course.'

It took her less than five minutes to encap-
sulate the essential things the two French officers needed to be told and before she finished
the deputy commander was issuing telephone
orders. When Claudine translated to Shankar
Sergeant he said: 'Please. Will you be with
me?'

'Yes,' said Claudine, who hadn't intended
to be.

She was about to stand when the man said:
'I will be allowed to stay in France? There was
a promise.'

Claudine sat again, positively, and restarted
the recorder the deputy commander had

switched off. 'Ask me again,' she said.

Frowning, Shankar Sergeant repeated himself. Claudine, in return, recited the question in French, had the mystified Frenchmen identify themselves, and said, still in French, 'I guarantee that the amnesty offered by the government will be totally honoured, that no charges will be proffered against you or your family for your illegal entry and that you will be given permission to reside permanently in this country.'

'You have no authority for giving that undertaking,' protested Leclerc as they crowded into the police car.

Amusing herself by invoking the name, Claudine said: 'But Commissioner Sanglier could make a hell of a row if it wasn't fulfilled, couldn't he? With your names on a legally sealed tape as evidence.'

Shankar Sergeant, cringing in the back of the unmarked car, took them directly to the shuttered warehouse in an alley off the rue Gide but it took him almost an hour to identify the house to which the Chinese immigrant smugglers had taken him, months earlier, and even then Claudine suspected he was unsure. Back at the police station and pointedly in front of the two policemen Claudine gave Shankar Sergeant her card and said: 'This is where you can find me, if anyone says you can't stay in France. Go to the Indian embassy and get them to contact me. Do you understand?'

'I think so,' said the man.

'I will warn them. Tell them that the Neuilly station know all about you.'

'Thank you,' said the man doubtfully. 'You've been very kind to me.'

'I'm surprised you can recognize kindness any more,' said Claudine.

Claudine hadn't anticipated Shankar Sergeant's plea to accompany him and the two French police officers, nor planned her own attempted protection of the man against the ultimate abuse of being denied the promised residency, but she still left the Neuilly station by midday, with the entire afternoon ahead of her. She didn't doubt she could have changed her ticket from her early evening reservation, which might even have enabled her to rearrange the meeting with Scott Burrows, which she'd had to cancel that morning.

Instead, she coupled the emerging prestige of Europol with Sanglier's name, to get within an hour to Manmohan Singh, the head of protocol at the Indian embassy. She had the man listen to her copy of Shankar Sergeant's taped interview, which she'd insisted upon having duplicated while they'd toured the Neuilly streets, and suggested the diplomat contact the Neuilly station to pre-empt any difficulty for a man whose life had already been over-burdened by too many. Singh assured her he would, and Claudine left another contact card in case problems arose.

Still with time to kill she decided to visit the Chanel emporium off the Champs-Élysees. The decision prompted thoughts of the couture bait so hopefully dangled by Françoise Sanglier just as the Algerian taxi driver, chancing that she was a tourist, made a totally unnecessary detour to increase the fare by going over to the Left Bank to drive past the National Assembly. She changed her mind, as well as her destination, and when she got to the national archive building she stood outside for several minutes, unsure why she'd done it. Then she went inside.

The archivist of national heroes was a fussy man with flyaway hair given to quick, bird-like movements, who talked in breathless spurts with pauses in the wrong places. His odd way of talking became even more disjointed with his exasperation at Claudine's innocent enquiry about how long it would take to see the Sanglier material, because of her evening plane, until he saw her name on the identity card which had to accompany the written request. His protest stopped at once. To her total bewilderment he smiled, as if they'd met before, and said: 'Ah, yes, of course. I understand.'

Claudine wished she did. It took her less than half an hour to do so, enclosed in the darkened solitude of a viewing cubicle before the microfiche screen. Had the Sanglier history not been supplemented with an index Claudine might still have missed the reason for the name recognition, because it was an extensive archive. She scrolled through the index first, knowing she couldn't read it all and seeking references to obvious highlights.

And saw, under an appendix listing, 'Carter, William: Inquiry and Findings.'

Initially everything rushed in upon her, a jumble of impressions and awarenesses. She comprehended at last the seeming absurdity of the conversation about her father initiated by Sanglier. Much later in the reading she understood why the man had not been more direct — and why her father had been prematurely retired, although not why he hadn't appealed against the demand, which he'd had the right to do.

She consciously stopped her mind butterflying from point to point, forcing the logic and the analysis in which she'd been trained, reading the account of the tribunal as she would have studied a scene-of-crime dossier.

She quickly realized that the tribunal hearing provided as complete an account as possible of the wartime heroism of Marcel Temoine who became Sanglier, the wildly uncatchable boar. So analytical was Claudine's fact-retentive mind — and so practised the habit — that she found herself constructing a pattern from the accusations made against her father. And for once a pattern didn't make sense because it couldn't make sense. But it was there.

The true Interpol records that Sanglier had risked his life secretly to maintain and preserve, which had later been accepted as genuine by the organization — with the phoney Nazi attempts at rewriting also kept, for comparison — were matched and corroborated by captured Nazi and Gestapo records. But the material known from captured Nazi files to have existed which her father had been accused of mislaying — as he'd also mislaid what should have matched it from Sanglier's secret Interpol notes — created in almost every case a break in the chronology impossible to fill from German records that had survived in Berlin. Specifically, the trial records of the Ruhr cell, of which Sanglier had been the only one to escape capture and execution.

Momentarily her eyes fogged, blurring the screen, at the abrupt realization that had obviously stunned her father as much as it stunned her. Sanglier hadn't *been* part of the Ruhr cell. He had invented his participation, intruding his code-name into the records to make himself appear even more heroic than he had provably been by re-routing the deportation trains in the concluding chaos of the war.

It was obvious that the majority of the tribunal had accepted the disparities as faulty or careless fact-keeping in the final hysterical months of the collapsing Third Reich. That explained why her father's censure had been so comparatively light, sufficiently so for him to have appealed. But to have appealed would have risked a more detailed inquiry and the exposure of Sanglier which her father had sacrificed himself to prevent.

Her father's evidence had been transcribed verbatim. Despite the flatness of the words, without inflexion or stress, Claudine was caught by the strength and feeling of nearly everything he'd said. There was spirited and coherent praise of Interpol — more coherent than she could ever remember him being in real life, even before the daily intake of pastis — as an international police organization to which he was dedicated and would do nothing to bring into disrepute. He also lauded Sanglier, pleading that a lot of what he was accused of mishandling had never been available in the first place but only assumed to have survived and insisting that the omissions did nothing to detract from Sanglier's acknowledged heroism or reputation.

Claudine did not try to access anything more. She stared sightlessly at the flickering screen, confronting another upheaval in an already overturned life.

She had been away at school during the hearing but been regaled with every detail by her mother, during weekends and vacations. Except there hadn't been any details. Her father's total refusal to tell Monique even why he had been summoned before an inquiry had done more to infuriate the woman than any of his other much criticized failings.

So her mother had speculated. She'd come closest, Claudine now knew, by guessing that he'd made some disastrous mistake and lost an enormous amount of Interpol records. Another suggestion, which upon objective reflection would have been impossible for a man with no association whatsoever with any finance division, was that he'd been caught embezzling and was being tried quietly to avoid a scandal. Excessive drunkenness had been a further theory, although he hadn't started to drink to any extent until after leaving the organization. The only accusation Claudine could not remember her mother levelling was sexual impropriety, although she'd thought about it. 'He's not capable,' had been the dismissive judgement.

Knowing her mother's reverence for the Sanglier legend and the breadth of her contempt for the man she always called William Carter, Claudine did not consider telling her the true facts. Instead, she contemplated her own position, now that she knew what her father was supposed to have done. She'd already dismissed the abstinence from alcohol as a pretension, and thought now that her attitude towards the man had been one, too. Quite apart from whatever had happened at Interpol her father had been unduly weak and her mother was unduly strong. Claudine had allowed Monique's attitude to be imposed upon her: to be brainwashed, in fact. *Know thyself* could never again be anything but a mocking taunt.

She arrived at Charles de Gaulle airport with time to spare before her flight so she called the direct line into the incident room, half expecting to get the answering machine. Instead she reached Yvette, who sounded agitated and at once went off the line.

'You on your way back?' demanded Rosetti, Yvette's replacement.

'Yes. Why?'

'All hell's broken loose. Toomey and a policeman are on their way from London. Winslow thinks they've got a warrant for your arrest. There's a Commission meeting going on at the moment. Sanglier came back from Amsterdam for it. You're to return directly here.'

'I think I can handle that, don't you?' said Claudine, unworried.

'I hope so. I'm not sure. And there's something else. Foulan, the oncologist, came through here when there wasn't any reply from your apartment. He wants to talk to you.'

Claudine tried immediately but the message on Foulan's office answering machine was that

585

he would not be available until the following morning. She didn't bother with a message of her own but tried his home number. There was no reply.

Her mother said she felt fine and that she and Gérard were very happy. The chemotherapy sessions were going well and so far there had been no ill effects.

Claudine had to run to catch her plane, and was the last to board.

Back in Paris the bird-like custodian of the archive of heroes, who had reached an arrangement with the man who was becoming practically as famous as his father from his involvement in all these horrific killings, sealed the envelope with the photocopy of Claudine's access request and put it in the collection basket to be posted to Henri Sanglier.

Chapter Thirty-Two

Claudine tried André Foulan's home again from her office but there was still no reply. She was at the safe when Yvette Fey hurried in, eyes wide behind her heavy spectacles, and said Sanglier was demanding she go at once to his office: there had been orders at the reception desk for him to be told the moment she entered the building and he and others were waiting. Yvette added that Rosetti was at home expecting her call the moment the interview finished.

'Is there anything I can do?' asked the French girl, her face creased with concern.

'Go home and stop worrying,' said Claudine. Although there had been nothing he could have done by waiting, she had expected Hugo still to be there when she got back. But what, she asked herself, would have been the point?

There were two men among the six in Sanglier's office whom Claudine did not know, although she thought one looked familiar. They were assembled and waiting around an oval conference table that had replaced the normal couch and easy chairs at the side of the room and she wondered why it had been so important for furniture to be moved about to keep everything in Sanglier's territory: the building was honeycombed with suitable conference chambers. The French commissioner was at the head of the table, flanked on either side by David Winslow and Jan Villiers, the chairman. The man whom Claudine thought she recognized was beside Winslow. Peter Toomey and the other unknown man were on Villiers' side of the table. There was one empty chair, towards which Sanglier gestured her. As she sat Toomey looked directly at her without attempting to hold back the smirk. His companion remained expressionless. Claudine felt a flicker of impatience at the pointlessness of it all but told herself none of them knew that yet. They would, soon enough. Then she could get back to the apartment to keep telephoning Foulan until she finally got him.

Sanglier was rigidly straight-faced but it was difficult. He'd heard it all and was euphoric: he'd come dangerously close at one stage to laughing aloud and thought he probably would, later. First he wanted to enjoy what was to come and it was going to come at his pace and at his orchestration. He wanted to share with someone the pleasure he would get from every second of it. He supposed he could tell Françoise, within limitations. She'd be titillated by the idea of two male lovers dying in a suicide pact: probably become even more sexually interested in Claudine Carter.

Adamant upon every formal propriety — he'd hurried the furniture change to create a tribunal atmosphere — Sanglier indicated the stranger beside Toomey and said: 'This is Detective Superintendent John Walker, from the United Kingdom Serious Fraud Office. He and Mr Toomey have told us of the serious allegations of which you are a subject. We understand you have several times ignored advice to consult a lawyer.' He gestured to the familiar man. 'In view of what we have heard I have asked Michael Harper, the English member of our legal department, to be present at this interview.'

'That's extremely considerate of you, but I don't believe I need legal representation,' said Claudine.

'We don't think that decision entirely rests with you,' said Villiers, desperate to avoid any scandal during his period of office. 'There is the position of Europol to consider.'

'Indeed there is,' agreed Claudine. 'And I want at once to state that I have done nothing, nor will do anything, to embarrass this organization.' She looked towards Toomey. 'I have already made it clear during two separate interviews that I know nothing about, nor am I in any way connected with, the inquiries being made in England into financial irregularities involving a man named Paul Bickerstone.' She was unsure why she'd felt the need to be so formal.

'Please,' interrupted the lawyer, raising his hands. 'I don't wish you to say anything more until certain things have been established.' Turning to Walker, he said: 'Do you intend to proceed under formal caution?'

'If you so wish,' offered Walker. He was a square-bodied, burly man.

'Just a moment,' said Claudine, bringing from her handbag the two tapes she'd earlier retrieved from her office safe. 'Before this gets on to any formal footing I want you all to listen to these. They are of conversations I have had with Paul Bickerstone, once by telephone and once personally, in my apartment here at The Hague.'

'What?' said Toomey. The smirk developed into a full smile. 'You're admitting collusion!'

Claudine looked contemptuously at the man. 'They prove my total innocence of any involvement in what you are investigating. I want you to hear them and I want all this nonsense ended. Now.'

'I don't think anything will be gained by losing our temper,' said Sanglier. What the hell did the tapes contain?

Claudine was irritated by the childish rebuke. 'This is all totally unnecessary.'

'I'll need to take advice on their legality but I am not sure we want to introduce anything at this stage that might form part of any defence,' said Harper. He was a thin, precise man wearing a waistcoated suit like Toomey.

Harper's waistcoat was looped by a gold watchchain. Like Toomey at their previous meetings the lawyer was making notes with a slim metal pencil. Claudine knew the writing would be cramped and neat.

'I've nothing to defend myself against,' she said, her exasperation growing at their refusal to listen to the recordings and get it over with. 'I'm trying to save everybody a lot of trouble and time, myself most of all.' She immediately regretted adding the last four words.

Sanglier felt a stir of unease at her confidence, but reassured himself there was no way she could escape from what Toomey and Walker had already outlined. They were being very clever, letting her do all the talking, digging her own grave. He wondered, with a sudden different concern, if he shouldn't have had the encounter officially recorded. 'I think we have to follow the legal advice.'

'You're all wasting your time,' protested Claudine.

'If these tapes show Dr Carter to be uninvolved in any criminality then we would be wasting time, wouldn't we?' said Winslow, as hopeful as Villiers of avoiding a scandal involving the British representation, of which he saw himself the nominal head. 'Europol would not have a problem.' And neither, he thought, would I.

'It would be unfortunate if a charge were made prematurely or on ill-founded information,' added Villiers.

'I would have hoped that after what we have already discussed you would have accepted our inquiries are neither premature nor ill founded,' said Walker stiffly.

'They're both,' insisted Claudine. Talking directly to Michael Harper she said: 'I did not retain you and you are not representing me. You are representing the interests of Europol. I wish these tapes to be heard now.'

'I think that is extremely ill advised,' said Harper.

'If it is the wish of Dr Carter for the tapes to be played then so be it,' said Toomey, sure of himself.

Dismissing any further delay, Claudine said to Sanglier: 'Do you have a machine upon which I can play these?' regretting that she'd been so preoccupied by trying to reach the cancer specialist that she'd forgotten to bring one herself.

He did. It was the one upon which he'd hoped, at the beginning, to record something he could manipulate against her. To get it now would mean fetching and carrying for her, he realized furiously. He hesitated, unsure whether to deny its existence, but eventually got up and took it from a desk drawer. The longer he delayed the longer he postponed her final humiliation and he didn't want that put back a moment longer than necessary.

Claudine played the telephone call first,

then the much longer conversation in her apartment, alert to the expressions around the table. Sanglier was frowning. So was the lawyer, head bent over his legal pad. Villiers smiled and nodded to Winslow, who smiled and nodded back, suddenly as confident as Claudine. Toomey wasn't smirking any more but there wasn't the concern she expected as his case collapsed around him. Walker remained enigmatic. Everything sounded very convincing to her.

'Well?' she demanded, snapping off the machine.

Inwardly Sanglier was in turmoil, a hollowness gouged from him by the words, unable to speak. She couldn't escape! It wasn't possible!

Villiers said: 'I think that very satisfactorily exonerates Dr Carter.'

'I agree,' said Winslow, with hurried relief.

'It would seem so,' added Harper, looking at Toomey and Walker.

'Or it could be seen as the complete opposite,' said Toomey, smiling again.

'What?' exclaimed Claudine, astonished.

'It could be a very clever exchange between two accomplices.'

'Don't be ridiculous,' she said, contemptuous again. 'You've heard for yourself we scarcely know each other!'

The detective looked at Toomey, who nodded. Walker took a notebook from his pocket and said: 'Did you and your husband have an account at Harrods, when you lived in London?'

'Yes.'

'Numbered 656392 00 510 9844?'

'I've no idea what the account number was. I closed it when I moved here.'

'But you didn't close your late husband's account, did you?'

'What account?'

'The account numbered 564391 00 314 7881.'

'Warwick didn't have a separate account.'

'He did, Dr Carter. He also had a safe deposit box there. Could you help us by telling us what is in that box?'

'I have no knowledge of any account in my husband's name. Nor of a safe deposit box.'

'We don't believe you,' said Toomey.

'Dr Carter,' said the other man. 'You do not have to say anything. But if you do not mention now something which you later use in your defence the court may decide that your failure to mention it now strengthens the case against you. A record will be made of anything you say and it may be given in evidence if you are brought to trial.'

'I want that box to be opened,' declared Claudine, aware that she had just been formally cautioned.

'That's what we want,' said Toomey. 'We've got a court order empowering us to do that. But we want you to be there, fully within British legal jurisdiction, when we do.'

Sanglier felt like laughing again.

Claudine remained bewildered by a safe deposit box about which she knew nothing, all the doubts she thought she had allayed stirred up again in a fog of uncertainty. But the sleeplessness was the result of finally reaching the oncologist, close to midnight. She'd spoken to Rosetti by then but called him back after her conversation with the French specialist, wanting to be told something different although she'd known she wouldn't be: wanting, even, a platitude about experts sometimes being wrong which she'd known Rosetti wouldn't give either. He didn't try. It wasn't his field, but he understood what Foulan said to be medically factual, that the cancer Foulan suspected to have reached her mother's liver was painless but that it wouldn't be if it had also reached the pancreas, which Foulan further suspected. It was Foulan, in fact, who'd offered the straw at which to clutch, that the biopsies hadn't yet proved positive. By dawn Claudine had stopped holding on to that fragile hope, forcing the acceptance upon herself: confronting it.

She was going to have to face the coming day, too. She wondered briefly if there would be time to contact the Neuilly police for news of the intended raid on the warehouse off the rue Gide, but decided that would have to wait. Sanglier remained the self-appointed ringmaster, declaring the potential difficulties for Europol justified the use of the organization's plane, which Claudine considered an overreaction, like insisting all three commissioners accompany her and Harper to London with the two investigators.

With the exception of Harper there appeared to be a positive attempt to ostracize her in the comparatively small executive aircraft. The lawyer hurried back to her after takeoff to insist it was both pointless and dangerous for her to continue to refuse his representation. He further insisted, soft-voiced, that anything she could tell him before they got to the department store vault would be covered by client confidentiality and could greatly help his response to whatever was discovered when the safety deposit box was opened. Claudine repeated there was no need for her to have a lawyer and that she had no idea what was in the box. To escape the lawyer's halitosis and refuse the commissioners' puerile attempt to distance themselves, Claudine went instead to them. Winslow visibly pulled back in his seat at her approach and Villiers looked nervously beyond her, to the lawyer, as if seeking legal permission for them to talk. Claudine ignored the reaction of both, but included them in her account of the Paris meeting with Shankar Sergeant.

'So now we know the reason,' said Winslow, when she finished.

'The message that I suggested,' reminded Claudine, angry at their obvious belief in her guilt and wanting to irritate them in return by forcing them to acknowledge her success.

'Yes,' conceded Villiers.

'K-14 — probably other Triads as well — are running a vast illegal immigration trade into Europe and using it to stock a brothel and prostitution business,' continued Claudine, not bothering to conceal the satisfaction from her voice. 'And we're powerless to prove it or stop it.' She hadn't intended the final sentence to sound like a criticism of Sanglier's investigation but realized, too late, that it did. She realized, too, from the man's face-tightening reaction that was how he'd taken it. To try to qualify the remark would only worsen the misunderstanding.

Let her have her tiny, imagined victories, thought Sanglier. He'd have his, soon enough. The embarrassment to Europol of a public, sensational trial — which this would undoubtedly be — would actually be minimal, although Villiers and Winslow and all the other pusillanimous idiots hadn't yet understood that. Whatever scheme she'd been involved in with the financier and God knows who else had been before she had officially been appointed to the organization, which could be made clear either during or directly after the court appearances. With fitting and appropriate irony the embarrassment would be that of the United Kingdom, the country that had done most to obstruct and prevent the creation of a European FBI. None of the other commissioners appeared to have realized that, either. It was a point he'd make when he gave an account of whatever happened today to the full and unscheduled meeting of the Commission he'd insisted Villiers convene before they'd left The Hague. He became aware of the woman promising to provide a written account of her Paris meeting and Sanglier contented himself saying that in view of what might transpire after today it would probably be better if she did so as soon as possible.

Claudine met Sanglier's look as he made the remark, and stopped regretting the misunderstanding about the stalled inquiry.

Toomey had risen to the luxury of executive jet travel and had two official Home Office cars waiting. He also invoked Home Office authority to bypass all entry procedures and they arrived at the Knightsbridge store early for the scheduled rendezvous with officials of the Harrods bank and its security division. There were three of them, one a woman, and they were waiting anyway with two other men who, from the deference, belonged to Walker's Serious Fraud Office squad. There were no introductions. Claudine was conscious of a lot of curiosity from customers as they marched to an elevator closed to the public. Sanglier was aware of it, too, and thought it unfortunate there wasn't a press photographer or television camera to record Claudine Carter's moment of ignominy.

There was a Harrods lawyer waiting at the safe deposit vaults. Toomey produced the court order and Michael Harper officially consulted it with the man, although he'd already gone through it on the flight from Amsterdam. Both lawyers pushed into the barred examination room, together with everyone from Europol and two of the Harrods officials. It was very crowded and quickly became extremely hot. Claudine would have liked to use her inhaler but thought she could manage without it. Briefly, for no more than a few seconds, no one appeared sure what to do next and then Sanglier, exceeding any authority but impatient for the *dénouement*, said: 'Let's get on with it, shall we?'

The bank official who'd greeted them on the ground floor turned the two keys and extracted the long, rectangular container from its recess. There was another moment of uncertainty, broken by John Walker, who announced: 'The court order authorizes me to take possession,' and reached forward to receive it.

There was insufficient room for everyone to get around the table and Claudine was almost jostled aside by one of the unnamed policemen. Toomey was next to Walker as the detective began to extract documents and the Home Office man said: 'Bearer bonds!' and looked at Claudine.

Methodically, Walker placed the bonds carefully one on top of the other beside the box, like a croupier dealing cards. 'Six,' he counted. 'Each in the sum of twenty thousand dollars, payable to bearer upon presentation.'

'Unnamed,' said Toomey, at the other man's elbow. To Claudine he said: 'That's very discreet, isn't it, Dr Carter? All you have to do is present them, as the bearer, and receive twenty thousand dollars each time. A grown-up game of Monopoly: twenty thousand dollars for passing Go.'

Walker was sifting slowly through a stapled document upon whose fronting page red waxed seals were visible to everyone. To read it he'd had to break another waxed seal on a heavy manila envelope and untie the sort of pink ribbon Claudine had frequently seen in courts. Everyone was sweating in the confined heat of the room. Claudine felt the tightness increasing around her chest. There was a lot of foot shuffling and coughing.

Walker at last looked up and said: 'It's a legally signed and witnessed affidavit. Sworn by Gerald Lorimer.'

There was nothing else in the box and they'd escaped to the larger office of the bank director, who'd ordered coffee and mineral water which everyone had needed. A solemn-faced Toomey had been the first person to read the document after Walker and when Michael Harper reached forward to be next in line Claudine said: 'I think I've every right to know what it says. I'd like you to read it aloud,' not knowing if she'd like all of what she might hear but not in any doubt about the confusion of both the Home Office man and the detective.

Harper hesitated, looking from face to face for any objection. When there wasn't any he said: 'There is the formal beginning, with the necessary legal entitlement and proof of the deponent. The affidavit itself reads: *Before setting out the facts of this testimony, which I am swearing under oath, I wish to state that a dear and trusted friend whom I have asked to help me has no knowledge of the acts I have committed. He has no knowledge of the contents of this testimony, which is being sealed in the presence of those whose signatures appear both on this document and upon its envelope.*

For a number of years, beginning at Cambridge where we were both students, I was a consenting homosexual partner of Paul Bickerstone. In more recent years I have regularly supplied Paul Bickerstone with confidential financial information, in breach of the undertakings I understood and signed in the Official Secrets Act. I did this because of the personal relationship to which I have already referred. Paul Bickerstone used this knowledge in business dealings and has rewarded me, financially, although I did not do it for monetary gain.

At the beginning of this year I told Paul Bickerstone I wanted our relationship to end. I also told him I would no longer supply him with the classified financial material as I had in the past.

Since that time I have been subjected to a number of threats and suffered physical assault. The threats have been to supply photographs of myself, in certain situations, to my employers. I was also so badly beaten after agreeing to go to his flat by someone I met at a club that two of my ribs were broken. On another occasion my car was deliberately rammed by a hit and run driver in a vehicle later discovered to have been stolen. The attempt was to force me off a road on a high embankment, at the bottom of which there was a river.

I believe that unless I agree to supply classified information again I shall be more seriously injured. Maybe even killed. I am making this statement and depositing with it bearer bonds given to me by Paul Bickerstone with instructions to my friend, Warwick Jameson, to give the package to the police if I die violently or suffer serious injury.

I have been advised by the lawyers to whom I have made this statement and who are prevented by client confidentiality from divulging its contents to go to the police. This I have declined to do.'

There was brief but total silence in the room. Michael Harper said to Walker: 'You're going to need a lot of advice about where to take your investigation now but one thing is quite obvious. There is no way in which Dr Carter is connected.'

'And I want a formal apology and withdrawal of the caution under which I came here,' said Claudine.

'I'm sorry,' said Walker. 'Of course the caution is withdrawn.'

'Mr Toomey?' persisted Claudine.

'I apologize,' said the man tightly, face blazing.

It was a fleeting impression, because Sanglier had already turned to leave the room, but Claudine thought the look on the man's face was one of unrestrained fury.

On the return flight Claudine endured the hypocritical assurances from Villiers and Winslow that they had never doubted her, respecting Sanglier for not joining in the recitation. Michael Harper thought client confidentiality might prevent the lawyers who'd acted for Lorimer supporting any prosecution of Paul Bickerstone and doubted the unsupported statement of a dead man was admissible by itself, unless Lorimer had been murdered, for which there seemed no evidence.

Back at The Hague she told Volker and Yvette there had been a huge misunderstanding over something that had occurred before she'd joined Europol which had been thoroughly resolved. She recounted the entire episode in detail to Rosetti as he walked with her to her office for her twice postponed meeting with Scott Burrows.

'So you won?'

'Hands down.'

'I still think you were lucky: that you should have got a lawyer from the beginning.'

'Winning is all that counts.'

'Not every time.'

'This time.'

They parted at the door, through which the American entered minutes later clouded in aromatic smoke.

'You know I'm not going to consider this a proper profile, not able to do or see anything myself first hand,' Claudine cautioned at once.

Burrows sat but hitched a leg over the arm of the chair in what to Claudine looked an awkward position. 'I know. I just want to talk it through with someone who knows the business.'

'Pickering doesn't fit a mould,' judged Claudine. 'He doesn't need familiar territory, in which he feels comfortable, like most serial killers.'

Burrows nodded at her recognition of the most salient factor. 'So that means he could come?'

'*Could.* But not that he will. I think, though, we've got to take seriously the family history.

According to the background material he was brought to Europe as a kid. And I don't have any doubt about the fixation. It could be wish fulfilment to have scored your name alongside the print references to American participation here, but you're certainly a target.'

'So he wouldn't expect me to be back in America?'

Claudine had wondered how long it would take to emerge. 'That's what you've decided to do?'

The overweight American smiled, admiringly, at her understanding. 'Cheat the bastard if we passed each other going in the opposite directions, wouldn't it?'

'Providing he *was* going in the opposite direction.'

'I'm not going to run,' reminded Burrows. 'If I go anywhere I'm going home, back to America.'

'What sort of protection can the Bureau guarantee?' He'd already made his mind up, she knew. He simply wanted someone else to confirm it as the right decision.

'As much as they can guarantee anyone anything. We even get presidents blown away, remember.'

'I know it's Pickering's too, but you'll be better — safer — in your own territory, somewhere you know where you can better see things that are out of the normal than you would in a foreign place or city, where everything's out of the normal because it's strange to you. If you've got to move you should go back, not try to find somewhere different to hide.'

He smiled broadly, stubbing out the cigar. 'You sure about that?'

'I told you I couldn't be positive. I think it's for the best. But it's a personal decision I wouldn't like to make.'

'That'll do.'

'You told Miriam?'

'Tonight. She'll want to catch the morning plane.'

'Why don't we have a drink before you go?'

'Drink? We're going to have the biggest fucking party this place has ever seen!'

He fumed at Rosetti's arrival, which co-incided with the ringing of her internal telephone. The pathologist had reached her desk by the time Claudine had finished listening to Walter Jones, the media director.

'All the Paris evening newspapers are full of the father responding to the amnesty appeal,' she told them dully, as she replaced the receiver. 'There's pictures of us getting into the car to identify the warehouse. And one of me by myself, apparently. The Neuilly police commander set the whole fucking thing up to get his fifteen minutes of fame!'

'Bastard,' said Burrows.

Momentarily Rosetti looked between Claudine and the American. Then he said:

'There's been another killing. A young girl. They've only found the head and the arms, so far. But they're all in Paris.'

Claudine pressed her eyes tightly shut, wishing the bad things would go away. 'This body won't be widely distributed. Her name's Ratri.'

In his seventh-floor suite above, Sanglier was staring down at the advice from the Paris archivist that Claudine Carter had accessed his father's wartime records.

Chapter Thirty-Three

It was Ratri.

Before Claudine, Rosetti and René Poulard arrived in Paris the torso had been found, discarded by the side of the Seine, where the horrors had begun but far upstream from the *bateau mouche* terminal, close to the Austerlitz bridge. It had not been removed and they needed the police escort that ferried them from the airport to force their way through the media frenzy, which was far greater than it had been in Rome. Claudine was instantly recognized from the earlier newspaper pictures and literally blinded by the explosion of television and camera lights. Her name became a chant from photographers trying to attract her direct attention and the shouted questions blurred into an inaudible cacophony.

'This is absurd. Bloody ridiculous,' complained Claudine, after they'd shouldered their way through the cordon.

'It's something we've got to become used to,' said Poulard, not trying to shield himself from the attention.

'I don't want to become used to it.' She acknowledged that she was using the murder as a focus for a lot of unconnected anger and depression, which was professionally wrong as well as being pointless, but for the moment she didn't give a damn, needing something, anything.

The Neuilly police commanders were with officers from the local *arrondissement*. In the very centre of the group Claudine recognized the Paris police commissioner, Jean Sampire. Both Neuilly officers smiled at their arrival, particularly towards Claudine. She ignored them, going straight to the examination tent. It was larger than the one in Rome, giving more room for her and Rosetti to work inside with the French pathologist. The weather was cooler, too, so it was less uncomfortable in their forensically protective clothing, but she was in the second day of her period and the cramp was as bad as it had been in Italy.

Poulard came no further than the canopy entrance, looking in briefly before announcing that he was going to join the waiting policemen. Claudine ignored him, too.

The naked body lay where it had been tossed, on the very edge of the Quai de la Rapée. Only one leg was missing. It had obviously been dumped from a passing vehicle and before they entered the tent Claudine had seen a forensic team going over the area just inside the cordon for tyre and vehicle traces. She doubted the search would produce anything but thought the effort was better than it had been in Italy.

The ankle on the remaining leg was banded with a thick bruise and the foot was slightly at an angle, where it had broken. Rosetti said: 'An agony fracture. They tied her down but kept her alive when they started.'

There was a lot of vaginal mutilation, although the girl's stomach was not marked with the two downward cuts from cold store meat hooks and Rosetti didn't think they'd find any ice residue in the blood. The only stiffness in the body was the dissipating rigor. He said: 'There's no residual temperature, but considering the state of the rigor I'd say a day and a half. Two days, maybe.'

'It will be two days,' said Claudine, calculating not from the newspaper and television sensation but from the warehouse raid that would have preceded it by several hours. Probably, even, while she had still been at the Indian embassy. She said: 'I want a lot of vaginal swabs, for DNA traces.'

'You're not coming to the autopsy yourself?'

'I don't need to. Not this time.'

Knowing why she wanted the tests Rosetti said: 'The semen could be from clients.'

'I still want it done. They'd have amused themselves.' She was silent for several moments. 'She was twelve years old. Her father asked me to help him get her back.'

Rosetti frowned up from his examination. 'You're letting yourself become personally involved.'

'How the hell can I avoid it?'

The French pathologist turned away from the body, too, but said nothing.

'The Chinese already had her,' said Rosetti. 'How could you have got her back?'

He was right but Claudine refused to admit it. 'It might have been possible, without all the publicity. Someone might have talked; told us where she was.'

'Let it go, Claudine. There's nothing you could have done to have prevented this. You didn't cheat anyone or fail anyone.'

As she had in Rome Claudine put the canopy between herself and the cameras when she emerged, ahead of Rosetti. The police group saw her come out and moved en masse to where she stood, stripping off the outer protective garments.

'What have you found?' demanded Leclerc.

'The body of a twelve-year-old child who's been raped, murdered and dismembered,' said Claudine flatly.

The man's smile faltered. 'I meant something that we weren't already aware of.'

'I know what you meant. Your own pathologist is making an examination and will be at the autopsy. Ask him.' She turned away to pack the overalls.

Behind her Poulard said: 'This is a joint investigation and I am Europol's police representative upon it. I want to be told now of anything you've learned from that examination that will take this inquiry forward and help us when we meet the press.'

Claudine wheeled furiously towards the group. 'Help *me* for a moment! What is more important to all of you? Is it solving a series of horrific crimes? Or is it getting your photographs in newspapers and on television? That's something I really would like to know!' She found herself confronting a tableau of fixed-faced men. The Paris police commissioner was extremely red and a vein pumped in his forehead.

Leclerc said: 'It was our intention to ask you to take part in the conference.'

'I'd like that,' said Claudine. 'I'd like to explain in detail how much I regret being tricked by senior police officers into being photographed and named, turning a potentially important break into nothing more than a publicity stunt. And how I think that the life of a child I've just seen inside that tent, headless and slit apart, might just have been saved if instead of seeking headlines the police of this city had worried more about arresting everyone at premises that were identified to them: people who could have led to the arrest of the killers of another five kids.'

'This is outrageous!' protested Sampire.

'It is the truth,' said Claudine. 'And you should be ashamed of it.' She knew she'd gone too far: lost control, discarded political correctness and committed the most cardinal error of all, against which Rosetti had only minutes before warned her: become personally affected by a professional situation. All the time she was conscious of the unreal brightness in which they stood, the glare of the lights and flashes of a media circus totally unaware of the confrontation unfolding in front of them. Claudine judged the whiteness appropriate for the suspended-in-ice way they were all standing.

Rosetti, who'd heard everything, broke the impasse. He emerged from the tent ahead of the French pathologist and announced: 'The murder is unquestionably linked to the previous ones in France. We'll need to conduct an autopsy but we think she bled to death from her injuries, which were similar to all the others . . .' He hesitated but did not actually look at Claudine when he said: 'The fact that the recovery of the body is concentrated in Paris and not throughout the country as in the other cases indicates that the killers were panicked.'

For the benefit of the Paris police chief, before he hurried with his entourage out of hearing, Poulard said to Claudine: 'Commissioner Sanglier will hear of this.'

'I intend that he should,' retorted Claudine. 'And I'm going to be the one to tell him.' More loudly and more generally she said: 'I take it I'm not required at the press conference?'

No one bothered to reply or even turn.

'That was totally stupid!' said Rosetti.

'I know,' said Claudine.

'Why did you do it?'

'I lost my temper.'

'That isn't a good enough reason: excuse even.'

'It's the only one I've got.'

She commandeered the police escort car to take her to Shankar Sergeant and his wife, a frail, white-haired woman whose back, high at her shoulders, was permanently bent with age and a lifetime's drudgery. They were being held at an immigrant detention centre, which offended Claudine although she accepted it was the most suitable place: they did, at least, have rooms to themselves and were not being kept in the usual dormitories, although the institutionalized smell of ineffective disinfectant, bad cooking and urine permeated everywhere.

The couple were beyond grief, people to whom nothing worse could ever happen. Shankar only just managed the hand-linked peace greeting. His wife remained hunched in her chair, blank-eyed.

'I am so very, very sorry.'

'There was nothing you could have done. She can't be hurt any more, can she? Neither of them can.'

'I've seen Mr Singh, at the embassy.'

'He's been here.'

'Nothing can stop your being allowed to stay.'

'It doesn't matter any more.'

'We'll get them, the people who killed Indira and Ratri.'

'No,' said the man, not rudely or angrily but as a quiet-voiced statement of fact. 'People like them aren't caught. They are too important. They can do what they like.'

'No, they're not. And they can't,' insisted Claudine, in a denial of her own. 'I promise you we will get them. They'll be punished.'

He wasn't interested in arguing. 'You were kind to come. And thank you, for arranging things with Mr Singh.'

'He'll tell me if there's a problem. But there won't be.'

'Yes.'

'Is there anything else I can do?'

'No.' As an afterthought he added: 'Thank you.'

He stood again when Claudine left, his hands held before him as Indira's had been found: found, Claudine thought, in the cathedral, in Lyon where her mother was dying.

Rosetti had completed the autopsy by the time Claudine reached the police mortuary. The only significant discovery was three separate DNA strings in the semen deposits, which Rosetti again warned need not necessarily have come from the child's killers.

'You going to apologize to Sampire and Leclerc?'

'No.'

'You should.'

'Why? It's true.'

'Not completely. The Chinese would have known the moment the warehouse was raided. It would have been a miracle if the French had got a lead to where she was before she was killed.'

'Without the newspaper photographs they might not have known so quickly who'd led the police to the warehouse,' argued Claudine, though without much conviction. 'There might have been a chance.'

Because she was now recognized Claudine wasn't able to go into the room where the press conference was held. She watched instead on a closed-circuit television monitor in another part of the police building. Poulard was on the dais but wasn't included in the speakers until someone asked why Dr Carter was not taking part. Poulard replied dismissively that she was engaged in other inquiries: he couldn't say what they were. Sampire declared the detention of fifteen Chinese, three Bangladeshi and five Indian illegal immigrants in the warehouse raid. That number went up to seventy when all their dependents, who had also been detained, were added. Five legally resident Chinese on the warehouse premises at the time of the raid were being questioned about the illegal immigrants, as well as about the murder of two Indian girls, Indira and Ratri Sergeant, whose father had led police to the unregistered Asian workshop off the rue Gide. Under the terms of the agreed amnesty, he and his wife were being allowed to remain in the country.

As Claudine visibly relaxed Rosetti, beside her, said: 'That's one of your concerns resolved.'

'We'll see,' said Claudine, unconvinced.

'Don't you trust anyone or anything?'

'I'm learning not to.'

'Thanks!'

'With exceptions,' Claudine added heavily.

'Thanks again!' The man began to move and for a moment Claudine thought he was about to feel out for her hand. Abruptly Rosetti halted the gesture, half formed.

When Poulard joined them minutes later the Frenchman said: 'Have you spoken to Sanglier?'

'Not yet.'

'I thought he should be warned.'

'I knew you would,' grimaced Claudine. 'That's why I didn't bother.' Then she said: 'Tell Leclerc to do DNA tests on the Chinese running the warehouse. Three different men have been with Ratri.'

It was time for yet another re-evaluation, which Sanglier didn't at first want to make because it involved re-examination of all the personal failures and there'd been too many of those. At least professionally he was still at the pinnacle, which was the most important consideration. And briefly after the London episode he had imagined his fears of Claudine Carter groundless, a combination of the co-incidence of her appointment — which had, after all, been his first assessment — and the visit from London of Peter Toomey.

But why had she studied his father's official archive when she was supposed to have been in Paris responding to the amnesty offer in the Céleste inquiry?

It put him back virtually where he'd started and as uncertain as when he'd started. So there had to be a new approach. No more false starts and too easily reached misunderstandings this time. No positive moves against her at all, in fact. Frustrating though it would be to do nothing but wait that was precisely what he intended to do. Wait and watch but not try to anticipate because all the mistakes had occurred because he'd too quickly tried to anticipate.

The Céleste investigation with which he was now so publicly linked and upon which so much depended in the future was far more important. Until its conclusion it had to have his total attention. That was why he hadn't presented more positively at that afternoon's Commission meeting Poulard's breathless complaint from Paris, contenting himself with using it as an argument against adopting Winslow's vote of confidence in the woman.

Although she'd clearly ignored behavioural and operational instructions — and could be censured for it whenever he chose — her criticism had been justified. So he'd been wise to remain in The Hague and not go to Paris as well, which he'd been initially tempted to do. He couldn't be linked to any media accusations if the press started thinking like Claudine Carter.

An hour later came the report that the severed head of an Asian girl had been found on the memorial statue to Queen Victoria outside Buckingham Palace. It took Sanglier a long time — more than thirty minutes — to assimilate every significance, the most important of which was that everything he'd done in Amsterdam had failed to prevent another Céleste murder. And everyone would know it.

It was virtually an automatic gesture to telephone Paris, to re-route Poulard to London. So blank was his mind that he wasn't even thinking of Claudine, who was fortunately with all the officers in the police chief's suite and instantly understood what had happened from Poulard's close-to-panic responses.

'Give me the phone!' she demanded and the disorientated detective was so startled that he did so without argument. To an equally surprised Sanglier she said: 'Just the head?'

'Yes.'

'Where?'

'London.'

'Transfer me to Volker! We've got them!'

The humiliated but publicity conscious Auguste Leclerc was among the officers in the room and heard everything Claudine said over the next half-hour.

Chapter Thirty-Four

It was a totally logical pattern, literally needing only one more line to be drawn to make it perfect. Kurt Volker understood it as quickly as Claudine and told her it would be easy. Sanglier understood, too, after a slightly longer explanation, and agreed because he had no alternative, even though it would be condoning the computer illegality for which he'd sidetracked Claudine and the German.

Sanglier remained confused, unsure which path was the safest to take. The instant glory was in England, if Claudine Carter was right: the place he should be when the seizures were made to cover the accusation that everything he'd done in Amsterdam had failed to stop another killing. But there was an 'if'. More than one. If Claudine was wrong and there wasn't a pattern after all, he'd be exposed to even more humiliation by being there. And if the woman was right, Amsterdam remained the focal point where everything would come to a triumphant end: where, in fact, the greater glory would be.

He'd stay. He'd stay because it was safest and because initially all the organization had to be done from here, which kept him at the top, in charge of everything. He stopped Winslow just as the man was about to go sailing and told him to get back to the Europol building immediately, and occupied the time it took the British commissioner to do so with briefing by telephone first Willi van der Kolk and then Bruno Siemen. He specifically instructed both to make no move until he personally arrived back in Amsterdam to order and supervise it. He'd be there in two hours.

The worrying response from the Dutch police chief was: 'So someone else had to die, as I warned?'

Siemen said: 'If it works, it'll all be over.'

David Winslow agreed, although reluctantly at first, that for the reputation of Europol and for the authority to ensure Poulard, Claudine and Rosetti got the unified cooperation they might need in a country that did not have a national police force it was necessary for him to go to London. Sanglier added, impatiently, that he'd already diverted the Europol plane en route from Paris and that Winslow had an hour to get to Amsterdam to join the others. Claudine Carter would fill him in on anything he wasn't sure about on the way: London would be alerted to their arrival while they were in the air.

Sanglier was pleased with the sense of drama he detected in his telephone conversations with London, but it seemingly failed to communicate itself to Kurt Volker. When Sanglier got to the incident room, empty apart from the German, Volker was relaxed in front of his screens, the central one of which was already filled with a digitalized map. Sanglier had to come directly behind the crumpled man before he could see that it was England.

Adrenalin-charged by the speed at which everything was suddenly moving, Sanglier said urgently: 'What's the problem?'

'There isn't one,' said Volker, remaining at ease. 'We're all set up.'

'Show me,' ordered Sanglier, more calmly.

Volker refused to be hurried. 'I've had to hack into databases. The British Customs again.'

'I know,' said Sanglier, his lips a tight line.

'That's all right, then?'

'Show me,' repeated Sanglier.

Volker smiled up, satisfied, looking forward to telling Claudine. He said: 'It doesn't appear to be a Dutch lorry. I've gone back through the British Customs entries at Harwich, Dover and Newhaven again and there's nothing showing from the Wo Lim factory. So . . .'

'The British factory.'

'It looks like it.'

He'd got away with it! There couldn't be any serious accusation. The British could — and doubtless would — try to wriggle out of any responsibility by accusing him of failing to warn them about the Wo Lim Company, but he wasn't worried about arguing the operational need to concentrate everything in Amsterdam. Far more important was that the killing hadn't taken place in the factory he'd had under total surveillance. It couldn't be shown to be his fault!

'Have you got into their system in England?' Sanglier asked, openly accepting the hacking he'd ostracized Claudine and the German for practicing.

Volker indicated the screen to his left. 'That's their dispatch records over the past week. Seven trucks, three in the last twenty-four hours, which are the most likely.'

'What are you waiting for now?'

'Our people to set themselves up with some computers in England, so I can download all this to them. And the next find which will tell us which way to go.'

Like the isolating of the Wo Lim factory in Amsterdam it all appeared so simple, thought Sanglier. 'Providing they stick to pattern.'

'Claudine is sure they will,' said Volker, as if reciting a commandment written in stone.

Sanglier had initiated a lot and Winslow had supplemented it from the plane's communication system while they were still crossing the Channel, so by the time they arrived at the Thameside headquarters of the National Criminal Intelligence Service — the intended British FBI as hostilely opposed by the country's police forces as Europol was within the

624

European Union — they were well on their way towards a smaller copy of the type of operation Sanglier had established in Holland.

As in Amsterdam, there was an accommodation problem, the central control room the only one large enough even when attendance was restricted to division heads. The NCIS commander, Edward Pritchard, and the Metropolitan Police Commissioner, Sir Herbert Brooke, were already waiting. So was Patrick Lacey, the junior government minister at the Home Office. Claudine went through the introduction formalities alert to everything around her, glad that computer terminals were a standard part of the office equipment. She was excited, fuelled like Sanglier by adrenalin but at the same time very calm, her chest quite free. Even the stomach cramps had gone.

'Are you sure about this?' demanded Lacey doubtfully, the moment the courtesies were over.

Winslow at once deferred to Claudine, who said: 'I wouldn't have started it all if I hadn't been,' too late realizing it sounded like a personal boast, which she hadn't intended. Hurriedly she went on: 'For a reason I don't understand — and don't need to, at the moment — the pattern for the Céleste killings is always the same. The victims are always Asian teenagers: we've just learned they're from illegal immigrant families who refused to put them into prostitution. They're always deep frozen. They're always dismembered . . .' she hesitated, to establish her point '. . . and their bodies are always distributed, over the course of a single week, along a food chain delivery route, in the same order: head, hands, torso, arms and legs. And so far, here in England, only the head has been recovered.'

Claudine was disappointed at the lack of instant awareness. When it came it was from the Metropolitan police chief. 'So the hands will be next?'

'Wired together in a mockery of the Asian peace gesture of greeting,' confirmed Claudine.

'What will that show us?' frowned Lacey.

'The route of the delivery truck that can be intercepted and stopped before it has time to distribute the torso and the arms and the legs,' declared Claudine simply. She added: 'Which a colleague of mine will already have gone a long way towards plotting and will send here as soon as we establish a computer link.'

Claudine made no effort to conceal that London had been kept in ignorance of the Wo Lim Company. Nor did she try to defend it, halting her explanation while Winslow confronted the furious interruption not just from the government minister but from Sir Herbert Brooke and the NCIS commander as well.

'You knew, long before alerting us today, of the location here in London where a murder — a horrific murder — was likely to be committed? And didn't warn us?' demanded Lacey, aghast.

'We believed the killings were being carried out in their Amsterdam warehouse,' said Winslow lamely.

'It's incredible!' said Brooke. 'Totally and utterly incredible.'

It was, conceded Claudine: an incredible example of chest-hugging territory-guarding and the very last thing to be arguing about in view of what had to be achieved in the coming three or four days. Not three or four, she corrected herself. They had precisely four days and eight hours until the midnight end of the current week. 'I understand the Wo Lim factory in London is now under total surveillance. There are other things that still have to be put in place, in readiness for what we have to do. If they're not, we risk failing.'

After a moment's silence Patrick Lacey, the professional politician, said to Winslow: 'I agree. But I am officially telling you, as the senior representative here of your organization, that this will be raised at the next ministerial meeting. Is that understood?'

'Completely,' said Winslow, his immediate embarrassment comforted by knowing the ultimate rebuke would be to Henri Sanglier.

'Let's establish the computer link,' demanded Brooke, still angry, ignoring Winslow. Doing so temporarily broke the formality of the meeting. Volker gave one of his conspiratorial giggles when Claudine dictated the NCIS access code identifying where they were working from, saying for her ears only that he already had it ready to dial.

For the first time Claudine was disappointed by a gap in what Volker transmitted, assuming at once what she expected had not existed. She was ready with an explanation for Volker's having what transportation details there were from the London factory — that they'd been obtained through the Amsterdam parent company — if fresh anger erupted at withheld information, but no one picked up on it. Fortunately Volker included the plotted maps showing how the bodies of the previous Céleste victims had been distributed to support their theory and Claudine bustled the illustrations on to display boards to elaborate her earlier explanation. There was very little further discussion about the interception and certainly no challenge.

Diplomatically they deferred to the British police chiefs for the logistical planning. It was agreed it would be wrong to alert every Chief Constable in every one of England's forty-three autonomous police authorities but that army helicopters should be called in to supplement police machines to transport them to wherever the hands were found. Claudine noted, pleased, that her recovery sequence had been automatically accepted. There was the suggestion of the previous animosity towards

Winslow when Brooke insisted the lorry interception be coordinated to the minute with the seizure and total occupation not just of the factory in London but that of the parent company in Amsterdam as well as its other subsidiary in Marseille.

'Have we overlooked anything?' he finished.

'I don't think so,' said Poulard quickly, eager to make a contribution.

'What do we do now?' asked Pritchard.

'The only thing we can do,' said Claudine. 'We wait. It won't be long. It has to be within the next twenty-four hours, according to the pattern.' She paused, before adding: 'That is, according to my profile.'

But when the next development came it wasn't what any of them expected.

They had to cross the river for a convenient hotel and chose one in St James's because it was nearest. They were all too adrenalin-charged to think of sleep and it was still comparatively early anyway, so after settling into their rooms they accepted Poulard's invitation to join him in the lounge. Claudine chose French wine, which was better than she expected, although not as good as it would have been in France. The restaurant was already closed and no one felt like trying to find one still open outside. They didn't feel like lounge-service sandwiches, either. At Claudine's urging they talked through all the decisions that had been made at the NCIS building, to ensure nothing had been overlooked, which prompted Rosetti to admit he'd forgotten to find out about any initial post-mortem examination.

Claudine sat listening but at the same time allowing the conversation to swirl around her, wondering if she'd be able to get to Lyon at the weekend. Foulan didn't expect the biopsy results until Friday at the earliest but visiting her mother didn't depend on that. The oncologist's suspicion was enough to make her going essential: for her to make the trip as often as possible now. She felt quite calm about it at last. She accepted it. She hoped there would be time — proper time — for her mother and Gérard to be together. She also hoped that her mother could go on sitting at her commanding table, in the restaurant that had been her life, for just a little while longer. And she hoped most of all that in the end the pain could be kept away. Would Foulan help: help in a way that could be understood without having to be asked for, directly? Or would he be prevented by his religion? It was something she had to explore, as soon as possible. If he wouldn't do it with his own hand, perhaps he'd make it possible for her to do it when the time came. She was conscious of Hugo's eyes upon her and looked at him. He smiled and she smiled back and saw Poulard intercept the look and smirk and hoped the oversexed

French groper had misunderstood, although not as much as she wished it didn't need to be a misunderstanding.

'What do we do if nothing happens tomorrow?' asked Winslow.

Rejoining their conversation, Claudine said: 'It will.'

'You really think you can read minds?' demanded Poulard. One of the wine bottles was empty and his voice was slightly slurred.

'Of course not,' said Claudine. 'But what people do tells me how they think and from that I can anticipate what else they might do.'

'OK,' challenged Poulard. 'Tell me what I'm thinking.'

'A psychologist couldn't possibly do that,' said Claudine. 'It would need a sewage inspector.'

The affront began to register until the guffaws from Winslow and Rosetti, so Poulard had to laugh too. At that moment there was a public address request for Winslow to pick up a house phone. There was one immediately outside the lounge door. The three of them watched, unspeaking, as Winslow spoke: towards the end he began gesticulating.

His already flushed face was beetroot red when he returned. 'That was Pritchard. The front pages of virtually every first edition British newspaper carry stories of our coming here.' He looked at Claudine. 'You're the lead, using the Paris photographs. Described as

Europol's supersleuth.'

'Jesus!' erupted Claudine. 'How the —'

'All the stories are datelined Paris. Sampire is quoted extensively. So is Leclerc. He talks about a secret plan to catch the killer.'

'All the French were in the room when you talked to Sanglier,' Poulard remembered.

'Fuck!' said Claudine, loud enough for other people in the lounge to look towards her, surprised. Some frowned in distaste. Winslow looked the most shocked of all.

By dawn NCIS was under media siege, made easy by the virtual cul-de-sac in which the building was situated. So was New Scotland Yard and the nearby Home Office. They moved out of the St James's hotel, central to all three, but once she saw the size in which her photograph had been reproduced — in two tabloids it occupied the entire front page — Claudine accepted she would not remain undiscovered for long. Her greater concern was how much might have been published about their plans. She knew she'd initially had to be quite specific to convince Sanglier. She scoured every publication and watched every early morning newscast. Nowhere did the stories go beyond generalization.

'At least there was some integrity,' said Rosetti.

'Which doesn't solve our problem,' Poulard pointed out. 'We can't go to NCIS because we'd become hare to the hounds: *really* endanger everything. And NCIS is where we've established the communication link into which the next discovery will be relayed, the moment it's made. After the way they felt last night about not being informed where's our guarantee of being told when it happens?'

'Volker,' said Rosetti, at once. 'They've got to coordinate the move against the Amsterdam factory through him. That was their decision, last night.'

'But we don't need to be there when the lorry is halted and searched,' Claudine said.

'We *don't* need to be there,' echoed Winslow, turning Claudine's remark. 'It would only ever have been an act of courtesy for us to be included in what, to satisfy jurisdiction, has to be an English arrest.'

'I *want* to be there,' said Claudine vehemently, and because she was talking more to herself than to the others she only just stopped short of adding that it was *her* case.

'I don't think that's our priority,' said Winslow. 'Our concern is whether the driver is frightened into breaking the pattern. Just dumps the rest of the body.'

'Wherever he did that would guide us to him,' said Poulard. 'And there'd be forensic evidence he wouldn't be able to get rid of.'

'Brooke wasn't available when I tried to call him before we left the other hotel,' reminded Winslow ominously. 'Neither was Pritchard.'

He stirred, getting up from his chair. 'So it's time I tried again.'

Would Sampire and Leclerc have done it if she hadn't so publicly humiliated them? wondered Claudine. Perhaps. But then again, perhaps not. Maybe she was having to learn the hard way a hard lesson in her new life, that sometimes there was a reason for the political correctness of which until now she'd been so contemptuous.

Winslow returned smiling. 'Sir Herbert Brooke has invited us to lunch. Not at the Yard. At his club. In a private room.'

'And he'll have to be told about an interception before it takes place, for the move against the factory here in London.'

'Precisely,' agreed Winslow.

Their fear of exclusion was resolved even more simply than that. On their way in the car the Metropolitan Police Commissioner sent for them, a message came in on the radio and the driver instantly detoured to the Battersea heliport. The NCIS commander, Edward Pritchard, stood with Patrick Lacey beside the already engine-whining militarily camouflaged machine.

'The hands were found in a church in Bromsgrove, Birmingham, after matins this morning,' reported Lacey.

'The body will go on being distributed in the north,' said Claudine.

'Your man Volker has plotted us a suggested

route,' said Pritchard, offering Claudine the print-out. 'We don't want to move until you've agreed it's the one we should take.'

Suggested, thought Claudine curiously. And then she remembered her disappointment at the gap in what Volker had transmitted the previous night — the absence of food delivery addresses that would have been in the London factory computer — and realized it hadn't been a gap at all. Volker had held them back until he got the location of the hands. She pretended to study the route, drawn from Birmingham to Stoke-on-Trent before going east to Derby, then Nottingham, directly north to Sheffield and finally west, to Manchester. 'A city for each part of the body that remains to be left,' she said.

'This will be the truck we want?' Lacey demanded.

'This will be the truck we want,' Claudine agreed. As they belted themselves in in the helicopter, she said: 'You needed my confirmation?'

'Yes.'

'If you hadn't, would you have included us in the interception?'

'No,' admitted the man truthfully.

For the first twenty minutes after lift-off Lacey and Pritchard, helmeted and linked not just to the pilot but to ground control through which they could be patched by landline to wherever they wanted, were in constant radio

conversation with Chief Constables throughout the Midland constabularies. The first time
they seemed aware of others in the helicopter
was when a large industrial conurbation appeared ahead and to their left. Lacey turned
briefly and said: 'Birmingham.'

Almost at once Pritchard, in the seat behind
the Home Office minister, announced 'A Wo
Lim refrigerated lorry has been identified by
an M6 motorway patrol, approaching Stafford. It's to be a Staffordshire interception.
Army and police units have been mobilized.'

Lacey was on a separate link-up. He said:
'The London factory is completely sealed.
Telephone lines are going to be jammed at the
moment of intercept against a mobile unit
warning. The factory plans do not show a
radio link facility.'

'There!' said Pritchard, pointing ahead.

The M6 motorway loop around Stafford
could distinctly be seen from the air, with the
town to the right, and literally as they watched
police vehicles began to join from feeder roads,
sealing off the northbound lanes. Others —
unmarked lorries as well as cars — came in
behind to give the impression of normal northbound traffic, ready to block the road from
the rear when the signal came.

'There he is,' said Pritchard.

The Wo Lim lorry was huge, the size of
those using the Amsterdam factory. It was in
the inside lane, the nearest private car at least

twenty yards away and already indicating the intention to overtake.

'It's to be junction 14, just after the loop,' said Pritchard, keeping up the commentary.

As he spoke the helicopter began to descend. Just before they lost elevation Claudine saw police cars streaming the wrong way down the junction's slip road to block the lorry's path from the front and the pursuit vehicles forming up in a solid side-by-side line to the rear. She was abruptly aware of other helicopters below them, on both sides of the motorway. Armed, flak-jacketed special police units were pouring out from some. Soldiers in tiger suit camouflage were disgorging from military machines like their own.

By the time they reached the lorry the rear seal had already been broken and the doors yanked open, emitting a ghostlike cloud of condensation against the outside warmth. Two Chinese were sitting on the bank, hands on their heads. Despite the fact that they looked very small and helpless there was an eight-strong armed guard of police and soldiers. The rosy-cheeked, rotund Chief Constable was already there. He smiled at the approach of the Home Office minister, thrust out his hand and said: 'Baker, Barry Baker. It all seems to have gone rather well. No one's gone in yet. Need to do it properly, I suppose?'

Claudine saw that nowhere among the light-blazing vehicles was there an ambulance and said: 'There's a forensic pathologist here.'

Everyone's attention switched to the Europol group. Lacey said: 'I suppose you're the people to have the first look.'

Claudine fell into step behind Rosetti. No one tried to stop her. The lorry was bisected by a narrow central walkway barely wide enough for one person. The produce was packed on either side, in metal drawers recessed into chest-high metal racks, throughout the entire length of the lorry. Into the open space above, from the same double-pronged hooks as those in the refrigerated store, hung the larger pieces of meat, which she guessed to be mostly pork and none of it of carcase size but jointed down into legs and sides of spare ribs. That stopped at the middle of the lorry. Here, on the slabs formed by the tops of the chests, were hundreds of fowl, mostly ducks she thought. This continued for about ten feet before the space was again filled by hung jointed carcases. It was breath-snatchingly cold, burning Claudine's throat and lungs. Everything was frozen rock hard and was white-encrusted. To Claudine all the carcase joints looked the same.

'Will you be able to tell?' It hurt her to talk.

'Yes.' He went immediately to the far end of the lorry, the most obvious place for concealment, and began slowly to come back towards her, checking every piece. He did the left-hand side first, stopping where the fowls intervened, and went back to where he'd started to begin the right side. He found the torso almost at once, suspended from a hook in the third line. One leg was still attached. The other, as well as the two arms, was in the drawer immediately below.

'You were right, Claudine,' he said, the words groaning from him in the cold. 'It's over now.'

They both needed police car blankets and even then it was some time before they could talk properly. Their clothes became damp where the ice that had formed on them melted in the outside air. Lacey and Pritchard were in separate police cars, using the radio and telephone. Lacey emerged first. 'Went like clockwork, everywhere. There was another body, intact, in the London factory. And at least fifteen Chinese without any papers. And another body in Marseille. No word yet on illegals. There were no bodies in Amsterdam but they're still counting illegals. Fifty at the last count: could be they're the entire work-force.' He paused. 'And there were no police injuries anywhere.'

'Wonderful!' said Winslow.

'I think we've got every reason for a party,' said Lacey.

'I wouldn't think the parents of that kid in there or any of the others will think they've got anything to celebrate, do you?' said Claudine.

'I didn't intend to be disrespectful,' apologized Lacey. 'I meant everyone should be very pleased — you particularly — that all these bastards are under lock and key.'

They weren't, of course. Enough were still free to plan Claudine Carter's murder.

Chapter Thirty-Five

Hugo Rosetti remained in England to take part in the autopsy on the unknown victim but Claudine, Poulard and Winslow returned to Holland for Henri Sanglier's triumphant press conference, slightly muted for the man by the obvious concentration upon Claudine. Under media pressure even before the conference Walter Jones compiled a background release upon her and the coverage was heavily personalized: over subsequent days the British press discovered Warwick's suicide but she refused requests for separate sympathy interviews before and during the main conference and later complained to both Sanglier and Jan Villiers at the intrusion into her privacy the media division had made possible.

Sanglier's name was, however, sufficient to guarantee the man almost matching attention and the personalized concentration was equally divided that first day in Amsterdam and afterwards, in The Hague. The outcome was to relegate the coverage in England and France, despite the actual finding of more bodies in both factories and the dramatic interception of the refrigerated truck in England.

At the conference Claudine specifically re-newed the amnesty appeal to the victims' fami-lies, anxious that nothing would be overlooked or dismissed in the euphoria of the moment.

She stressed that danger as strongly as she could at the following day's official review of the entire investigation, at the end of which fresh commendations were voted for all of them, Sanglier included. Claudine's strongest argument was that against the arrested Am-sterdam Chinese — the obvious ringleaders — the most serious charge was organizing illegal immigration. She persisted until it was for-mally agreed that Europol pressure the police in each country in which arrests had been made — but in Amsterdam particularly — to make DNA comparisons from every detained man with samples taken from the victims.

David Winslow's warning of the intended British protest at ministerial level ruined the self-congratulation for Jan Villiers. Sanglier, refusing to surrender his elation, replied easily that Villiers could argue that security against a leak had been essential to destroy the biggest and most evil criminal enterprise uncovered in the European Union, and Claudine guessed the man had been rehearsing sound-bite phrases for every eventuality.

Sanglier pointed out that the task force had officially to remain in existence until the vari-ous trials at which they were likely to be wit-nesses, and as its now very publicly identified head undertook personally to stress the need for DNA comparison.

Claudine's proposal had even more purpose when she learned in a later telephone conversation with Rosetti that he'd recovered DNA evidence from both English victims. She was disappointed he wasn't going to get back in time for Scott Burrows' farewell party and realized he was not going to be able to make his customary weekend journey to Rome, either, when he said he intended going direct from London to Marseille to examine the body found in the Wo Lim factory there.

'You going to Lyon?'

'Yes,' she said. She hadn't yet told him about the oncologist's fears but decided against doing it now, on the telephone.

'I could come up from Marseille on the Sunday. It's on the way by train.'

Her disappointment vanished. 'That would be wonderful!'

'I wouldn't be intruding?'

So he anticipated meeting her mother. 'Not at all. You could eat the best food in France.'

Scott Burrows had been allowed the executive bar and it was already crowded when Claudine arrived. His wife was a petite, bottle-blonde woman whom Claudine guessed to be at least fifteen years younger than her husband. From the patterned voile suit Claudine decided that while the woman might not have liked Europe she'd visibly benefited from its fashion influence. As the thought came to her Claudine became aware of Françoise Sanglier bearing down. She wore a suit, too, in black silk with billowing trousers, complete with white shirt and a man-length tie.

'Where's Hugo?' the woman greeted her.

'Still in England.'

'So you're by yourself?'

For all her sophistication Françoise Sanglier had the subtlety of a drunken marine, Claudine thought. 'For the moment.'

'And you're drinking?' said the woman, indicating the champagne glass in Claudine's hand.

'I've changed some habits,' said Claudine, regretting the words as she spoke.

There was a quick smile. 'That sounds interesting?'

'Drinking habits,' qualified Claudine.

'You've been avoiding me. I called seven times: I've kept count.'

'I've been very busy.'

'But now you're not. We can make plans for Paris.'

'I don't think so, Françoise.'

For the briefest moment Françoise's face darkened, someone unused to rejection. 'I've made up my mind.'

'So have I. I prefer to shop alone.'

'What can I do to make you change your mind?'

'Nothing. I'm not interested.'

'Not in half-price couture?'

'Nor anything that goes with it.'

'Nothing need go with it.'

Claudine's patience snapped. 'I fuck men, Françoise. I prefer that, too.'

'You ever tried the alternative, to find out?'

'I don't intend to. Don't call me any more, Françoise. You're wasting your time. Mine too.' Claudine looked around for escape, sufficiently grateful for Burrows' approach to forgive the cigar.

Françoise became aware of the anticipation. The anger settled more heavily in her face. 'Am I being dismissed?'

'Judge for yourself.'

'I might do just that,' snapped the woman, in a confused threat.

'Give up, Françoise,' said Claudine, exasperated. 'You're making yourself look ridiculous.'

There was a moment of wide-eyed outrage before the woman turned, model-like, to walk away slowly, the disdain appearing hers. She had, accepted Claudine, made a devout enemy instead of a lover and was quite happy at the choice.

Burrows arrived smiling broadly with a half-filled tumbler of whisky in the hand not occupied with the cigar. 'Miriam wants to meet you.'

'I want to meet her,' said Claudine. 'All ready to go?'

'Packed and parcelled,' said the man.

Claudine didn't answer the smile. Before being led across the room she said: 'Anything from America?'

Burrows became serious, too. 'Not a thing, since Baltimore.'

'You be careful.'

The man's smile came back. 'I will. Let's go and meet Miriam.'

Burrows' wife had a deep Southern drawl not helped by a tendency to lisp and Claudine had to concentrate very hard. The American with her, Joe Hardy from the embassy, had a similar accent but it was easier to understand without the speech impairment. The man said: 'We're getting rid of him.'

'At last!' said Miriam, with feeling. She didn't try to disguise her eagerness to get home by reciting the usual clichés about her sadness at leaving Europe, although there was the traditional insistence for Claudine to look them up if she was ever in Washington. Claudine, just as traditionally, promised that she would.

'Scott says you did a hell of a job on these killings,' said Miriam, to her husband's frown. 'Said it would have taken him much longer.'

Claudine saw Burrows visibly colour. 'I don't think it would, given all the evidence I had to work with.'

'It needed a European mind,' said Burrows, conceding their most protracted disagreement during all the seminars.

Now it was Claudine who felt embarrassed. 'If we keep up this mutual admiration you'll have to divorce Miriam and marry me.'

'You wouldn't like it,' said Miriam. 'He snores.'

'That I could stand,' said Claudine. 'It's the cigars I'd have difficulty with.'

'He's not allowed to smoke them at home,' smiled Miriam.

'I cut down with you, too,' Burrows reminded Claudine.

'I didn't notice,' she said.

Jan Villiers gave a speech and made the presentations, a Europol plaque and a framed photograph of Burrows seated in the middle of the entire Commission, each of whom had signed the memento. There was a bouquet for Miriam which reminded Claudine of the one Paul Bickerstone had brought to her apartment. She was annoyed it hadn't occurred to her to bring a personal gift for the American.

She was one of the first to leave and Burrows walked with her to the door.

'You would come to see us if you ever came over, wouldn't you?'

'Of course I would.'

'I meant what I said about your being careful.'

'Likewise.'

'You thought about asking for some protective security for a while?'

'Of course not!' said Claudine, bemused at the question.

'It might be an idea.'

'You're being paranoid, for Christ's sake. It's a recognized police risk from every arrest.'

The American made a motion with his hand, moving the whisky around his glass. 'Too much of this. Keep safe, you hear.'

'You too. And sorry.'

'For what?'

'Behaving like a bitch, at all those early sessions.'

'You're the only one among them with any balls. It would have been dull if you hadn't.'

The car park had already been crowded when Claudine arrived that morning and she had to pick her way through the vehicles that were still there to get to her car. The sensation of being watched came to her when she was halfway across, so strongly that there was a skin tingle along her shoulders and she stopped, swinging around. She saw nothing and was annoyed at herself. The feeling had been so real that she mentioned it to Rosetti when he telephoned that night to ask about the party. He dismissed it as part of the anticlimax, after the tension of the previous days, combined with the conversation with Burrows, about which she also told him. She laughed awkwardly, sorry that she'd admitted it, and said that of course he was right.

She still stared out into the apartment block

car park and the street beyond when she pulled the lounge curtains but she didn't see the man with the half-moon scar on his face, patiently staring up in the hope of identifying her apartment, which he did the moment he saw her.

Claudine was prepared for a bad day and it became one from the beginning. She overslept, which she rarely did, and could actually see the nail that had punctured her front offside tyre. She decided against delaying herself further by changing it but it took longer than she expected to get a taxi and she missed her intended airport train. The next one only just got her there in time. She didn't have to use her inhaler but it took several minutes for her breathing to settle after belting herself in.

André Foulan was waiting as arranged when she arrived at the oncologist's office and the gravity of his expression told her before she heard the words.

'Beyond the pancreas, even. There's a tumour in the small intestine, as well. I can control the pain for the moment.'

'Does Gérard know?'

'I have asked your mother to tell him.'

'How long?'

'A month. Two. Or it could be next week.'

'Is there any point in going on with the treatment?'

'I never believe in giving up until the very

649

end. There's always hope. And God. Miracles sometimes occur.'

Claudine didn't welcome the religious reference. 'But the liver cancer will be painless?'

'Yes.'

'Is there a chance she'll die from that, before the other things get worse?'

Foulan gave an uncertain shoulder movement. 'No one can say.'

'I don't want my mother in agony,' declared Claudine flatly.

'I understand. I promise you I'll make her as comfortable as I can.'

'My mother is a very proud woman. I don't want her eaten away into a shell, so that she doesn't have any dignity left, either.'

The man looked steadily at Claudine for several moments. 'I understand that, too.'

'How well do you understand what I am saying?' Claudine asked, as directly as she felt able.

'I promise I'll make her as comfortable as I can,' Foulan repeated.

'And enable her to maintain her dignity? Not to become hollowed out?'

Foulan straightened in his chair. 'I don't think I can give you any stronger assurances than I have.'

Claudine wanted more. 'Despite everything you can do, she'll suffer?'

'If the abdominal or pancreatic growths become dominant.'

'I'm asking for positive help, doctor.'

'I know what you are asking for.'

Claudine waited. The silence lasted a very long time. Finally Foulan broke the gaze and said: 'As a doctor I took an oath to preserve and maintain life for as long as possible. Out of my respect for your mother I have already gone beyond what could be considered ethical in meeting you like this, without her knowledge. I think now that might have been a mistake.'

Claudine later regretted leaving the surgery without thanking the man, at the time not believing she had anything to thank him for.

Claudine was shocked when she got to the rue Grenette, for totally opposite reasons from those she'd prepared herself for. Her mother looked healthier than she had on her wedding day, frequently getting up from what was now her permanent table to bustle among the tables and bully the waiters: several times she briefly took up her old station, greeting arriving customers. From the finger-touching, shoulder-caressing way things were between the older woman and Gérard, Claudine knew at once her mother had not told the man of the new cancers.

Monique maintained the pretence in the upstairs apartment during the afternoon break between lunch and dinner, insisting she'd never felt better and was blissfully happy with Gérard and didn't expect to need much more chemotherapy. Her excitement at Rosetti's visit quickly became irritation at Claudine's inability to answer all her questions about the man. Finally she erupted: 'How can you have a relationship with a man you know so little about?'

'I told you we're not having a relationship,' Claudine reminded her.

Rosetti telephoned with his time of arrival and Claudine went to the station to meet the TGV, abandoning the intention to spend every possible moment with her mother to relieve the strain on the older woman of having to maintain the constant artificial ebullience.

She was early and again, briefly, felt the skin prickle of being looked at. She imagined she actually saw a Chinese on the furthest platform, but didn't admit it to Rosetti when he arrived. He insisted upon detouring to the Sunday flower market which gave her the opportunity to tell him of the cancer spread. He didn't search for words. He put his arms around her shoulders and held her very tight and momentarily, curious at how much she needed the comfort, Claudine thought she was going to break down. She didn't and was glad. Rosetti helped by talking briskly of the Marseille murder, announcing that yet again he'd recovered three different DNA strings from what had evidently been a gang rape.

Claudine was nervous her mother would

pepper Rosetti with the questions about himself she hadn't been able to answer, but instead Monique adopted the role of grande dame and Rosetti played up to the performance, paying respectful homage. Claudine discerned the immediate approval. Her mother had never behaved like this with Warwick: had barely accepted him, even.

Gérard personally prepared the meal of quail in a sharp berry sauce and then joined them to eat it at Monique's special table. What the woman wanted to know emerged naturally in conversation. There was instant rapport with Gérard when Rosetti said that his father had been a chef, and from the conversation that ensued Claudine understood how the Italian had learned to cook so well. There was a family villa in Tuscany that his brother occupied and a family legend that a grandfather had been a Mafia don, which he didn't believe because tradition would have demanded his father be one too and initiate him into the society. In the feudal region of Tuscany it did no harm, however, to keep the legend alive when dealing with officialdom. Claudine was reminded of how long she had lived away from home when her mother talked of enjoying opera, which Claudine had forgotten, and conducted an appreciative conversation with Rosetti, who was manifestly even more knowledgeable.

'Her husband liked jazz: made her like it

too,' protested Monique, as if the hobby equated with bare-breasted mud wrestling.

'I promise to educate her,' laughed Rosetti.

The open acknowledgement of a relationship came quite naturally and embarrassed no one, but Claudine wondered if her mother believed she and Rosetti were lovers. She wasn't any more worried about the misunderstanding than she had been in front of the smirking Poulard in London.

As they were leaving for the airport Monique invited him to come again soon and stay longer and Rosetti said it would be difficult because he returned most weekends to Rome. In the taxi Claudine said: 'Would you have talked about Flavia, if she'd asked?'

'Of course,' he frowned. 'You've told her I'm married, haven't you?'

'Yes. I told her we weren't lovers, too.'

'Do you think she believes you?'

'I'm not sure, after today. Thank you for being as kind as you were.'

As they settled themselves on board the plane, Claudine said: 'It's difficult to believe she's as ill as she is, isn't it?'

'I'm told that's the way it is.'

'It won't last, though, will it?' She turned, so she could look at him.

'No,' he said, looking back.

'I don't want her to suffer. To be reduced to a freak by everything they do to keep her alive.'

'There's morphine. Heroin. We talked about it before.'

Claudine paused, refusing to speak over the engine sound as the aircraft lifted off. When the shuttle began to level out she said: 'Foulan says there'll still be pain. But it won't just be the pain. Worse, for her, will be what she becomes.'

'Did you discuss it with Foulan?'

'Yes.'

'What did he say?'

'That his oath was to preserve life.'

'It is.'

'Did you take the Hippocratic oath?'

Rosetti held her eyes, not replying. Eventually he said: 'I qualified as a doctor.'

'I thought you would have done.'

'I don't like this conversation, Claudine.'

'I'm not asking you to do anything. Just help *me* to do it. All I need is something in the hypnotic drug range. And then some potassium. There would not be a post-mortem, upon someone as ill as she is: someone expected to die.'

'Stop it.'

'Please!'

'I can't.'

'I'm begging you, Hugo.'

'Don't.'

'Think about it! Do you imagine that's how she'll want to be, for me and for Gérard?'

'Don't you imagine I haven't thought like

655

this about Flavia?'

'It's not a comparison and you know it. Flavia could recover. Still damaged, possibly. But she could recover. My mother can't.'

'I don't believe you could do it, when the moment came.'

'I could,' said Claudine. 'I love her enough to do it.'

Rosetti turned positively away. 'I'm sorry you asked me.'

'So am I.'

'Let's not make it worse by fighting about it.'

'I don't intend to.'

Nevertheless, she pulled away, looking unseeing through the aircraft window, and he in turn drew himself towards the aisle, so there was a physical space between them. She walked slightly ahead when they disembarked at Schiphol and stayed ahead on the escalator taking them down to the rail platform level for the train link to The Hague. He allowed her the space, needing it himself. It wasn't, in fact, easily achieved. The platform was crowded, people jostling into them at the end of a weekend, and he was glad of the echoing announcement of the train's arrival.

So was Claudine. She'd apologize on the train. She'd been wrong — taken too much for granted — asking him as bluntly as she had: stupidly expected him not to have a moral problem when she'd known too well of another far less understandable morality holding back their relationship.

She became conscious of the approaching train at the same moment as she heard Rosetti shout 'Claudine!' but then everything happened too fast to distinguish. She felt herself shoved sideways and turned at Rosetti's yell of pain and saw a spray of blood and then, terrified, a huge outstretched knife and a lurching Chinese trying to change direction towards her.

She instinctively put her arm up and felt the burn as the blade cut completely along her arm, from wrist to shoulder. Rosetti hit out, not a proper punch but in a warding-off gesture. It caught the stumbling man on the shoulder, pushing him further off balance towards the platform edge. He turned and seemed to reach out with his free hand, as if expecting someone to pull him back, but instead he continued to fall backwards, mouth opening in a shout Claudine didn't hear, directly beneath the wheels of the train.

She only vaguely heard the screams of the people around her beneath the screech of the train brakes, and then the man vanished beneath the train. All three carriages passed completely over him, severing him in two. Incredibly his features were completely unmarked. Claudine stared at the face, down the left-hand side of which was a deep, half-moon scar.

She turned to Rosetti and calmly said: 'The name he used was Cheng. We should check his DNA with what you got from Ratri. Indira, too.'

Then she stared at her blood drenched arm, feeling the pain for the first time, and the shock hit her. She screamed and fainted.

It was an hour later in the very centre of Amsterdam that another door closed, quite literally, in the overlapping investigations.

The Amsterdam vice squad had diligently maintained their surveillance on the house in Roomen Straat identified by the Polish prostitute and an all-unit mobilization went out the moment the Warsaw-registered Mercedes turned into the street: by the time Karel Kaczmarek stopped vehicles were in place at either end to block it. Kaczmarek was filmed urging three girls — one of whom later emerged to be just ten years old — out of the car and into the building. Police did not move until everyone was inside. Then, having had time to prepare, they completely surrounded the house, actually altering the narrow garden at the rear, before the inspector in charge hammered on the front door and identified himself through an amplified loud hailer. Kaczmarek and the three girls ran straight into the rear garden ambush.

Chapter Thirty-Six

Neither wound was life-threatening in itself but both Hugo Rosetti and Claudine Carter almost died. Like any professional assassin the man only ever known as Cheng had treated the bayonet knife he'd wielded to cause infection if the injury he inflicted wasn't fatal: forensic tests on Cheng's knife showed the blade had been smeared with his own excreta.

Claudine's poisoning was made more severe by the allergy link with her asthma. For more than a week she slipped in and out of consciousness, breathing by ventilator, fed by drip and drained by catheter. Her blood was completely changed.

Her first unsteady visitor in the second week, after she'd come off the ventilator, was Rosetti, still a patient on the next floor: his left arm was strapped across his chest and her first horrified thought at seeing the limp dressing gown sleeve was that it had been amputated.

'It almost was,' grinned Rosetti. From police interviews with witnesses he'd been the unintended victim. There were accounts of Cheng suddenly emerging from the rear of the platform crowd with the knife extended like a lance, which was Rosetti's first recollection. If he hadn't pushed her aside she would have been impaled in the very centre of her back. Instead the knife had gone into his arm, deeply cutting the muscle. But it didn't embed itself, which was why Cheng had still been able to slash Claudine as badly as he had. Rosetti's wound, although deep, only needed ten stitches. Claudine's required forty, finishing with skin edges taped together where the cut only penetrated just beneath the surface. He warned her the infection would have widened her wound, still tightly bound, as it had his but said plastic surgery could virtually eradicate any trace.

'I'm going to keep mine like a war wound,' he said.

'So you saved my life?'

'The papers called me a hero. Makes a change from you getting all the publicity! But don't get jealous. You still got your share.' He made a vague gesture beyond the door. 'We're so famous we've got police guards.'

'Thank you for saving me.'

Although he was sitting, Rosetti gave a mock bow. 'You're very welcome.'

She recognized the forced humour. 'What is it?'

'I spoke to Gérard yesterday. Your mother didn't feel well enough to go down to the restaurant.'

'I'll go today,' said Claudine. She actually tried to push herself up in the bed, to swing her legs out, forgetting the drip and the catheter. Dizziness engulfed her and she couldn't stop herself falling back on to the pillows.

'You know you can't. It's not necessary yet, anyway. According to Gérard, Foulan thinks it's temporary. It happens. There's definitely no pain.'

The oncologist confirmed it when Claudine immediately spoke to him from the bedside telephone upon which Rosetti had to dial the number. Her mother had already improved since the previous day's conversation with Gérard. She was to recover fully herself before even contemplating a trip to Lyon. He didn't think it was necessary but of course she could call daily if she wished. He'd always be available.

Outside visitors were not permitted until the third week. Sanglier was the first, with David Winslow and Jorge Ortega: the Commission chairmanship had switched to Spain. The police guard would remain while she was in hospital, Ortega promised. She could have permanent protection when she was discharged. Europol would also install security cameras and an alarm system in her apartment. And she could also, of course, carry a weapon.

'It all seems rather dramatic.'

'Someone tried to kill you. Almost succeeded,' said Ortega.

'An instant revenge attempt. I don't think

661

I'm under permanent threat.'

'You can't be sure of that,' said Sanglier, feeling it necessary to join in the concern. 'We did destroy a major criminal enterprise run by the biggest Triad organization in Asia. And you're publicly associated with having done it.'

'You're just as publicly associated,' Claudine pointed out. 'Do you have all this protection?'

Instead of answering the man opened his jacket to show the Beretta in its shoulder holster beneath his left arm. Claudine thought the gesture and the gun ridiculous.

'We don't think you should disregard the danger,' said Winslow.

'We'll discuss it when I get out,' she said. 'I'd rather talk about what's happened since I've been in here.'

'A lot,' said Winslow quickly, anxious to be the storyteller. 'We've got fifteen positive DNA traces, including Woon and Li Jian and Zhu Peiyuan here in Amsterdam. And Cheng matched the samples taken from Ratri: Li was positive with her sister.'

'So we've got murder charges?' said Claudine.

'Unchallengeable,' assured Ortega.

Into Claudine's mind came the memory of a cowed, nervously shaking Indian in the Neuilly police station. She'd kept her promise, she thought: the men who'd killed his daughters — been part of it, at least — were going to be punished. She said: 'What about the amnesty?'

'The families in England and Austria have come forward,' said Winslow. 'And another in France.'

'There've been votes of appreciation in eight parliaments in the EU,' said Ortega, as if he personally deserved the praise. 'Europol's established.'

'There's something else you might — or might not — like to know,' offered Winslow. 'There isn't going to be a prosecution against Paul Bickerstone. The Crown Prosecution Service didn't think Lorimer's statement was sufficient by itself. Some problem about establishing legal proof, apparently.'

'So the bastard got away with it?'

'Seems like it.'

Claudine did not at first recognize the man who came that afternoon and Joe Hardy had to remind her of their brief meeting at Scott Burrows' farewell party.

'He said I had to come personally and give you this.'

The message said: *If you're going to get in on the act you'll need this. It calms the nerves.* The box contained one of the perfumed cigars the man always smoked. Claudine laughed. 'How is he?'

'OK. Back at work. But he's not making any public appearance lectures at police academies. It used to be his thing.'

'What about Pickering?'

'Still free.'

With that morning's visit still fresh in her mind Claudine said: 'Have the Bureau allocated any protection?'

'I don't know. I guess Scott can look after himself.'

'I hope so.'

'He called me when he heard what had happened to you. Was as worried as hell.'

'Tell him thanks. For the cigar, too. I'll call him when I get out.'

During that third week Claudine's mother recovered sufficiently to start going down into the restaurant again. They spoke daily by telephone. Always the woman insisted she felt fine. Claudine made daily calls to André Foulan, too, and it was during that third week that the man told her he thought the cancer might actually be in remission.

'How long will it last?'

'There's no way of telling. Sometimes weeks, sometimes months. I might even suspend the chemotherapy. It's a difficult balance. If it is genuine remission I don't want to trigger it again with unnecessary treatment.'

Rosetti was discharged before Claudine but visited her daily. On the second occasion he said: 'Why didn't you tell me about your conversation with the commissioners?'

'I did.'

'Not about the protection suggestions.'

'Who did tell you?'

'There was a meeting today, to decide if I needed it.'

'And?'

'I said I didn't think it was necessary. My being hurt was an accident. I wasn't the one being attacked.'

'I think you're probably right.'

'What are you going to do?'

'Think about it. Talk to you about it.'

'You've had two weeks to think. And now we are talking about it.'

'It was an instant revenge attack.'

'Sanglier told me what you said.'

'He's wearing a gun!'

Rosetti didn't smile back. 'I think he's sensible.'

'You think I should carry one?'

'Yes. And I think you should agree to all the other suggestions they made. He told me about those, too. And why Burrows was here.'

'I'm not going to spend the rest of my life with a minder at my side! It would be absurd. I'd go mad.'

'You could leave Europol.'

She looked at him evenly for several moments. 'That would mean leaving The Hague. Do you want me to do that?'

'Of course I do if it means keeping you safe.'

'You're over-reacting. Everyone is.'

Rosetti held up his hand, his forefinger narrowed against his thumb. 'Just that much of a huge mafia has been put out of business. The rest is still operating out there. And you hurt them.'

'Why don't . . .' began Claudine and then stopped.

'What?'

'Why don't I think more seriously about it?' she said. She'd intended to say 'Why don't you look after me?' but changed her mind halfway through.

'I want you to,' Rosetti insisted.

That evening Joe Hardy came again and made her think very seriously indeed.

She knew at once it was a different visit from before and that there could only be one reason.

'When?' she asked.

'Last night. Bastard was waiting for him, when he got home to Alexandria. Son of a bitch jumped him with a knife.'

'That wasn't the pattern in the stuff Scott showed me. Pickering was a torturer. Played with his victims for a long time before killing them.'

Hardy nodded. 'That's what he intended to do. The Bureau did cover Scott but the stupid bastards didn't put it on the house as well, just wherever Scott went. He was ahead of the protection detail: out of the car. Pickering was inside the garage. First thing Scott would have seen when he lifted the door. Had the knife to Scott's throat before the detail, two of them, had time to get out of their car. They had him nailed, of course. Told him to drop the knife. He laughed at them instead and damned near cut Scott's head right off. They shot him down. Five bullets. They're on suspension now for not bringing him in.'

'What about Miriam?'

'He'd got to her first. Roughed her up a little but that was all. Had her tied up ready to start and for Scott to watch while he did it. He'd got Scott's chair ready, too. Had the ropes and the gags all set. Miriam's going to be all right . . .' Hardy hesitated, seeming to think about what he'd said. 'I mean she isn't going to die.'

The following day Claudine telephoned Sanglier and said she wanted the television and alarm system in her apartment and that she'd carry a gun. She didn't want a guard, even for a short time.

'I'll do the anticipation for myself.'

Chapter Thirty-Seven

Monique Carter died a month to the day from Claudine's leaving hospital. The security precautions had already been installed in her apartment and she felt self-conscious signing for the Beretta, which fitted surprisingly easily into her handbag, although it was heavy. Rosetti offered to go with her to Lyon but it was a weekend: she said she was quite able to make the journey alone, so why didn't he go to Rome as he normally did. He didn't argue.

When Claudine queried it with André Foulan the oncologist said the apparent pink-cheeked healthiness in her mother's face was actually caused by the disease and that sometimes it confused patients into thinking they were being cheated. Claudine did have a feeling of being cheated but she didn't say so.

On the Thursday of that first week Monique announced she didn't think she would go down to the restaurant that evening and she never did again. Until the second week, she and Claudine took short, slow walks together in the mornings but on the second Saturday she said she didn't feel like it and she never went out again, either. She demanded to hear over and again of the knife attack, on each occasion insisting upon examining the arm: the wound had healed to leave a wide scar and Claudine promised to have the recommended plastic surgery. She thought Claudine should have accepted an armed guard and was unimpressed by the Beretta, which she also frequently examined, doubting it was powerful enough to stop a determined assassin.

It had been arranged before she left The Hague that Claudine should start learning to use the gun at the Lyon police firing range and she chose to do so in the afternoons. She always delayed her return, too, taking tea at a café overlooking the Rhône so that Gérard and her mother could be alone.

At no time was there any pain. André Foulan came twice every day, morning and evening.

Claudine went down to the restaurant when it closed every night to carry the takings and the pencil-noted reservations ledger upstairs. Into the official reservations book her mother transferred, in ink, the names and amounts paid by customers who settled their bills by cheque or credit card. She then added, again in ink, approximately half those who paid by cash.

'And the rest is mine,' she said, every night. In the second week she changed the announcement and declared the rest was Claudine's. And then her mother led a slow ascent up a narrow flight of stairs to a dust-laden loft that Claudine had never entered, which was dominated by a safe at least four times as large as the one in the apartment below. It contained only money, stacked from bottom to top in elastic-secured bundles.

'Half a million,' declared her mother. 'With my love and blessing.'

Claudine was speechless. Finally she managed: 'But I can't . . . it's —'

Monique brusquely cut her off. 'Who else is to have it, then? No one has been cheated except the tax and they're unimportant. This is mine. What I've worked for for forty years. I can do with it what I like. And that's the end of it.'

She took the telephone during one of Claudine's conversations with Rosetti and said she would like to see him again and he came on the third weekend. Gérard cooked in the apartment and she played the grande dame again and Rosetti dutifully played up to her. They laughed a lot. Claudine tensed for some remark when Rosetti prepared to leave for his hotel but her mother said nothing. After he'd left and before Claudine made her nightly descent for the takings, Monique said: 'Will his wife ever get better?'

'She could.'

'Do you love him?'

'Yes.'

'It's not a good situation.'

'No.'

'What are you going to do?'

'I don't know.'

Monique died three days later. She did so in her own bed, pink-cheeked and clear-skinned, with Claudine and Gérard either side, each holding her hand. She said she'd been a very lucky woman and that she was sorry if she'd hurt either of them with her tongue. She loved them both. She liked Rosetti. He would be a good man, however they managed it. Gérard shouldn't close the restaurant out of respect when she died. That would be stupid. Gérard cried but Claudine didn't, although she wanted to and felt she should have done.

Over two hundred people, including the mayor and all the dignitaries who had attended the wedding, came to Monique Carter's funeral. Rosetti flew down from The Hague. Monique's plot was three rows away from William Carter's grave, in which Monique's will had stipulated she should not be buried. Afterwards they all ate at the restaurant and Gérard made a stumbling speech in which he said keeping it open and serving them all was his mark of respect for a woman he had loved very much. It was then that Claudine cried.

As he was leaving Claudine remarked to André Foulan it had been fortunate the cancer had remained painlessly in her mother's liver. He gazed at her for several moments and said that during the previous two weeks it had become active again in the pancreas and would soon have become unbearable.

'You have to return to The Hague soon, don't you?'

'Yes.'

'So she died peacefully, before that had to happen.'

Then it was Claudine who looked steadily for several moments. She said: 'Thank you. So very much.'

Gérard protested and said if it had been Monique's wish she wouldn't have made the will so shortly before her death, and Claudine demanded if instead the man preferred her to sell the restaurant to a stranger. The same pedantic Pierre Forge didn't know of a precedent for such a valuable property's being made over to a new owner as a gift and Claudine became as irritated as her mother had during their visit and on the spur of the moment insisted instead that the lawyer draw up a bill of sale for ten francs. On their way back to the rue Grenette Gérard insisted the gesture was an even better memorial to her mother than the funeral feast had been. He went directly to the kitchen, to prepare that day's lunch. Claudine climbed the narrow stairs to the loft.

She did not know what to do with the money. She'd carried up with her the largest case she could find in her mother's bedroom, with no clear intention even of what to do when it was packed, and she only managed to fit in about a quarter of what was in the safe. She had to use two hands to lift it, so she unpacked it all again and put it back. There was no reason to take it anywhere, she supposed. It must be how Latin American drug barons felt, with more money than they knew what to do with. She was glad when the door was closed and she couldn't see it any more.

She'd only looked at the safe and what was inside when her mother had brought her up. Now she stared around, realizing how vast the loft was, spanning not just the entire length and width of the restaurant building but the adjoining apartment block that she remembered, belatedly, she also owned. There were three oval fanlight windows, cobwebbed and dust-streaked but still with a breathtaking view of the city. From the central one she had the impression of almost being level with the Notre-Dame de Fourvière. At the end she judged to be over the apartment block there was a jumble of matching furniture, which she guessed to have been discarded years ago from the restaurant. There were several wardrobes. The first two contained dresses which must have belonged to her mother, far more elegant than any Claudine could remember her wearing, cut in a long-ago style but from superb material, mostly silk. The next two closets astonished her even more. They contained men's clothes, suits and sports jackets and even laundered shirts, neatly hung on hangers. All, she supposed, would have belonged to her father. She was incredulous that her mother had so carefully preserved everything that had belonged to a man she so vehemently despised.

At last Claudine moved away, towards the other end. It was much more jumbled than where she'd first looked, dust-jewelled cobwebs hanging from rafters like curtains and more abandoned furniture. She felt the dust in her throat, tightening her breathing.

The hidden desk was beneath a fourth fanlight she hadn't seen, with a round button-backed chair pushed into the knee recess as it would have been in an office. Claudine waded the trailing cobwebs with the arm-spreading motion of a swimmer breasting water, realizing the overhead light could have made it an office and then deciding that was exactly what it must have been and that there was only one man who could have used it as such.

There was even a pen pedestal, empty, and a long-dried-up ink bottle beside it. The biggest drawer, at the top, slid easily open. Inside there was an unmarked leather blotter and several pens and some blank Interpol letter-headed paper. There was still ink in the bottle here. There were photographs to the left, unmounted. The top one was of her mother and father, on a beach somewhere, arms around each other's shoulders. They were both in bathing costumes and laughing. Each succeeding print was of the couple together and they were laughing or smiling in all of them. The last three were of their wedding, her mother demure and beautiful in a layered lace dress with a tight cowled headdress holding a bouquet of trailing lilies. Her father was in army uniform, an officer resplendent in Sam Browne webbing, his lieutenant's hat clamped beneath his arm. There were decoration ribbons on his left breast. Claudine blinked against the wetness fogging her eyes, first bewildered and then angry at never having known that at some time — certainly, obviously, on their wedding day — her father had actually been a serving soldier. Not just a serving soldier: a soldier who had done something brave enough to earn him a military decoration.

The drawer below was locked. She searched through the one she had opened for keys but couldn't find any. She looked around but couldn't see anything to force the drawers. She half turned, to go back to the other end of the loft, and her foot jarred against a box which rattled metallically. It contained a rusted collection of every type of cutlery. The first knife snapped, stinging her fingers, when she tried to lever open the locked drawer. With a thicker carving knife she created a gap between the drawer top and its surround into which she slid the thick sharpening steel. The wood split, loudly, around the lock when she thrust down and the drawer almost fell out completely.

There were several ledgers and thick-backed notebooks at the top, with loose document paper beneath. The year of the diary at the very top registered instantly. She scrambled through to the month and felt her eyes mist again at her father's neatly scripted entries for the tribunal hearing. All the entries were brief. The three words on the opening day — *Hostile. Unimpressed. Chairman unresponsive* — were frequently repeated. There were other entries: sometimes almost sentences. *Disliked by chairman. Not a cheat. Managing to confuse.* The last entry was the fullest, on the day of the tribunal findings. Her father had written *I am surprised at the verdict. Lighter than expected. Achieved everything.*

What did it mean? Having gone so quickly through she returned to the beginning, isolating for the first time not just the words but numerals — 6, 43, 106, 303–4–91 — against some of the days. The last — 391 — provided the answer. Before it was scribbled p. Page numbers then. But page numbers to what? Official documents was the obvious guess. But what sort of official documents? Obviously those that were the subject of the inquiry. Or which featured in it. The dust was troubling her again but there was an excitement, too.

She began to hear herself breathing, wheezily. Putting the diary face down to preserve the opening at the tribunal dates Claudine went to the other contents. Next was a scribble-filled ledger which Claudine again didn't understand until she isolated names and then read *Day One* and decided it was the notebook in which her father had made his own notes of the inquiry. At once, because she had read the printed copy in the Paris archives and had perfect recall, Claudine was able to decipher most of what was written, quickly dismissing it as his own record, with nothing additional.

The third book yielded something new, although not completely and certainly not quickly. The numerals from the diary were in it, with notes attached, and initially she was totally bewildered. There seemed no correlation between numbers and words: what was written, in fact, appeared to be philosophical musing and abruptly Claudine decided that's precisely what it was: her father's commentary about whatever the numerals referred to.

Most confusing of all was that the tract that began the entries, longer than those that followed, was not against an accompanying number. *Has it been brave? Why was it necessary? It was not my duty, as a soldier, when medals came for the valour of others. No one should have known. Wouldn't have known. A hero should not become a coward. A confession would have destroyed a brave man who wanted* to be braver. *For what purpose? None. A test for myself. A silly game, a pointless gesture. But it is done. My fate would be the same. So let them keep their hero.* Against it, inexplicably, her father had signed his name, as if it were a testimony.

Against 6 was written: *A truly brave man makes a secret of his bravery, which is the greatest bravery of all.*

The note for 43 was: *How easy it is, once the lie has begun, to believe rather than remember, because every man is a hero in his own heart.*

The third entry, against 106, was more intriguing than philosophical. *Why Sanglier? Too much, too much.*

Claudine reached into the drawer for the next book and in doing so jogged the pile, exposing the papers beneath. She didn't bother with the books any further.

The document was a German original, a transcript of the Ruhr spy trial like the ones she'd seen in Paris. It was the prosecution's opening of the case, she identified, recognizing the page number, 106. She'd read it, she thought. But she hadn't. The version in Paris was the accusation against Sanglier, the positive link between the Ruhr group and the Pimpernel spy. But nowhere in the version before her was the name Sanglier. Careless of how her clothes would be soiled, Claudine lowered herself, gently to lessen the dust cloud, into the chair in which her father would have sat.

It was her job, her vocation, to solve puzzles. So what was the solution to this one? Her father hadn't mislaid any documents. He'd stolen them: removed them from an official record. But they couldn't be official. The official ones, retrieved from Germany long after the end of the war, were in Paris. She'd seen and read them. She remembered the inconsistencies. Dates that were missing. Carefully, methodically, she set out all the wartime originals on the table before her, in date sequence, looking for the pattern that was always so necessary. It was *in* the inconsistency. There were gaps she hadn't been able to understand in Paris and what was set out before her was disjointed and meaningless by itself. But together they wouldn't have been. If these German originals were put in date order with those she'd looked at in the French archive the picture would have been complete. But a picture of what?

Claudine read everything through again, with a path to follow now, signposted by dates and events, and then she read the statement that her father had signed but which wasn't inexplicable any more.

No one should have known. No one would have done, if the decision had not been made to honour Marcel Temoine as Sanglier in the national archive. Before then — before her father had been entrusted with assembling all the uncollated material — the facts had been those Temoine had himself provided, on the understanding that the omissions came from the chaos of the war's end and the confusion of the false material the Nazis had created.

But the dates didn't correspond, she saw abruptly. Particularly with the trial that established the legend of the hero whom the Gestapo could not catch. *A brave man who wanted to be braver.* Marcel Temoine *had* been brave, in diverting transportation trains in those final, chaotic months. That he had done so was unarguably supported by the genuine German files. But it hadn't been enough. *Why Sanglier? Too much, too much.* Marcel Temoine had invented himself, given himself a code-name — a French code-name, not a German one such as the Gestapo would have accorded — and changed the trial documents to intrude an uncaught spy who had never been part of the Ruhr operation. When the questions were asked he explained it away as wartime confusion, never imagining that the true records would survive to prove him a liar. *No one should have known.* They still didn't. Her father had isolated the discrepancies going through the German material and had filleted out what would have incriminated the man, leaving gaps that couldn't be explained but saved him from exposure. *It was not my duty, as a soldier, when medals came for the valour of others . . . A test for myself.* What medals had William Carter been awarded he felt he hadn't deserved? So he decided to let a deserved legend survive. *A silly game, a pointless gesture.*

Claudine cried again. Sitting in the chair in which her father sat, at the desk at which he'd worked, probably while she and her mother ignored him far below, she confronted her final ignorance. It was not just herself she hadn't known. She hadn't known her parents either. She didn't know that her father had been a soldier or why the love had turned to contempt or why her mother had so carefully preserved all his clothes or why he hadn't told them.

A truly brave man makes a secret of his bravery, which is the greatest bravery of all.

She hadn't had a weak man for a father, Claudine realized. She'd had a hero.

The full reflection came on the homeward flight, after the farewells to Gérard and the promises to come often, which she would because she'd left the loft intact, which he'd assured her she could: after, finally, the renewed self-consciousness at producing her Europol accreditation to satisfy the startled security official at Lyon airport that she could carry the Beretta aboard an aircraft.

Homeward, she thought. To a fortress apartment and a man she loved to whom she couldn't physically prove it and another man with one of the most famous names in France and a lesbian wife. Did Henri Sanglier know the truth about his father? Guess, at least? It would account for so much that remained a mystery: the strange approaches, the fluctuating friendliness and the hostilities. Something else she'd never know. To know she'd have to ask him and she couldn't risk that. She'd keep her father's secret because it wasn't his alone. Unwittingly he'd shared it with her.

Back in her apartment Claudine experimented with the security system, as self-conscious with it as she was with the weapon, before picking up the telephone. She stood with it ringing emptily in her ear for several moments until she remembered what day it was.

Hugo would still be in Rome, beside the bed of a wife who never knew he was there.

She jumped, startled, when it rang fifteen minutes later. Sanglier said: 'I wanted to know if you're fully recovered. Fit enough to come back?'

'Completely, thank you.'

'You're quite happy about your safety?'

'It's very good,' said Claudine.

It wouldn't be, if the answer to his unasked question wasn't what he wanted it to be. And Scott Burrows' killing and the attack upon the woman herself had shown him how easily it could be manipulated. She was the proven choice for subsequent investigations. All he had to do was ensure she was assigned to the right one, where the danger of another personal attack was the greatest: after letting a

little time elapse, for her to become compla-
cent and grow careless about carrying the gun.

It would, he supposed, be the perfect murder. That's how he wanted things. Perfect.